Praise for Radclyffe's Fiction

"…well-plotted…lovely romance…I couldn't turn the pages fast enough!" – Ann Bannon, author of *The Beebo Brinker Chronicles*.

"…well-honed storytelling skills…solid prose and sure-handedness of the narrative…" – Elizabeth Flynn, *Lambda Book Report*

"…a thoughtful and thought-provoking tale…deftly handled in nuanced and textured prose that is both intelligent and deeply personal. The sex is exciting, the story is daring, the characters are well-developed and interesting – in short, Radclyffe has once again pulled together all the ingredients of a genuine page-turner…" – Cameron Abbott, author of *To the Edge* and *An Inexpressible State of Grace*

"With ample angst, realistic and exciting medical emergencies, winsome secondary characters, and a sprinkling of humor…a terrific romance…one of the best I have read in the last three years. Highly recommended." – Author Lori L. Lake, Book Reviewer for the *Independent Gay Writer*

"Radclyffe employs…a lean, trim, and tight writing style…rich with meticulously developed characterizations and realistic dialogue…" – Arlene Germain, *Lambda Book Report*

"…one writer who creates believably great characters that are just as strong as mainstream publishing's Kay Scarpetta or Kinsey Milhone…If you're looking for a great romance, read anything by Radclyffe." – Sherry Stinson, editor, *Outlook Press*

Fated LOVE

by

RADCLY*f*FE

2004

FATED LOVE

ISBN 1-933110-05-8

This Trade Paperback Original Is Published By
Bold Strokes Books, Inc.,
Philadelphia, PA, USA

First Edition: May 2004
Second Printing: September, 2004 Bold Strokes Books, Inc.
Third Printing: December, 2004 Bold Strokes Books, Inc.

Credits
Executive Editor: Stacia Seaman
Editor: Laney Roberts
Cover Photos: Lee Ligon
Production Design: J. Barre Greystone
Cover Design By Sheri (GRAPHICARTIST2020@HOTMAIL.COM)

By the Author

Romances

Safe Harbor

Beyond the Breakwater

Innocent Hearts

Love's Melody Lost

Love's Tender Warriors

Tomorrow's Promise

Passion's Bright Fury

Love's Masquerade

shadowland

Fated Love

Honor Series

Above All, Honor

Honor Bound

Love & Honor

Honor Guards

Justice Series

A Matter of Trust (prequel)

Shield of Justice

In Pursuit of Justice

Justice in the Shadows

Change Of Pace: *Erotic Interludes*
(A Short Story Collection)

Acknowledgments

This book represented a significant challenge to me because I had never before written a book in which children figured so prominently. Children mystify me on many levels, and I wasn't at all certain that I could write one believably. I'm very fortunate that one of my beta readers and her partner have two children who served as consultants for this work. Emma, their daughter, provided inside information on the pivotal role of soccer for many families (as well as invaluable information on the general nature of life as viewed by a teenager). Wally, their son, is slightly closer to Arly's age, and by the time I finished writing this book, I was convinced that my character was channeling him. Thank you, Eva, Jenny, Wally, and Emma, for providing a wonderful model of today's family, and for answering my endless questions regarding "how do children think?"

As always, I wish to thank my other beta readers, Athos, Denise, Diane, JB, Paula, and Tomboy, for taking time out of their busy lives to read, comment upon, and encourage my work. Laney Roberts and Stacia Seaman once again provided expert editorial assistance and guidance, making this a better book as a result.

The cover is a compilation of several photographs that once again Sheri, with her unique artistry and skill, has crafted into a seamless whole that speaks eloquently to the heart of the story.

This cover is also special in that the wedding rings are mine and Lee's. *Amo te.*

Dedication

For Lee,
Fate's Gift

CHAPTER ONE

Quinn Maguire stopped just inside the sliding double glass doors of the emergency room. It was only the second time she'd been there, but it already felt like home. Hospitals everywhere were very much the same—the same drab tiled floors, the same muted color schemes in bland institutional shades, the same stark undercurrent of loss and despair, perceptible beneath the thin veneer of hospitality and welcome. With a brief glance, she swept the admissions area to her left, noting the solitary clerk with her head bent over a computer screen and two patients, both of whom looked to be half asleep, waiting in the unadorned area beyond. A television, perched high in one corner with the volume turned down low, was tuned to CNN.

Hitching up her leather backpack and mentally squaring her shoulders, Quinn walked down a corridor that was just wide enough for two stretchers to pass. She nodded to a lone man in khaki work clothes who was buffing the floor with an electric polisher and turned into the nurses' station that occupied the center of the emergency room proper. Despite the fact that PMC, the Philadelphia Medical College, was one of five major university hospitals in the metropolitan area and the only one in the Germantown-Mount Airy section, the emergency room had an abandoned air at just after six on that Monday morning.

The few hours on the cusp between the end of the weekend and the beginning of the workweek tended to be the quietest time of all in the ER. The night nurses were finishing their paperwork and getting ready for the change of shift, the residents were running down lab and x-ray results before turning over their patients to the incoming teams, and the attending physicians were catching a couple hours' sleep in their on-call rooms.

Quinn scanned the area to orient herself in the unfamiliar space. The patient cubicles were arranged in a U-formation around three sides of the central workstation, a large open area enclosed by waist-high counters. Inside were computers, fax machines, racks of patient charts, drawers containing all manner of forms, and nooks for the staff to complete paperwork. At the moment, the curtains were closed on several of the adjacent examining rooms, suggesting that there were patients inside awaiting final treatment determinations, and the faint beep of an EKG monitor marked time somewhere in the background. A lone resident—or possibly an older-than-average medical student—sat behind the counter making notes in a chart.

Quinn approached and leaned her hip against the edge of the long narrow countertop. The woman looked up, a question in her eyes.

"Yes?"

For just an instant, Quinn hesitated. The nearly ubiquitous emergency room uniform of scrub shirt and pants tended to reduce everyone to gender-neutrality, but not this woman. Nothing could diminish her singular presence. Her almost carelessly layered collar-length hair, a lustrous mixture of golds and browns and a whisper of red, framed a face remarkable for sun-kissed skin, deep brown eyes, and perfectly balanced features. Despite the attractive picture of delicately arched brows, finely etched cheekbones, and full, ripe lips, it was the sharp intelligence in the inquisitive gaze that captured Quinn's attention and drew her in.

"Can I help you?" Honor Blake asked again, her eyes quickly scanning the woman's open-collared pale blue cotton shirt and jeans as she attempted to place her. Not a patient—she would have remembered. Certainly the chiseled features, blazing blue eyes, and jet-black hair formed a visage not easily forgotten, but Honor drew a blank. She suddenly found herself being boldly appraised, and that not only surprised but annoyed her. "I'm sorry. This is a restri—"

"I'm Quinn Maguire," Quinn said quickly, extending her hand with a grin. "A new ER attending. Maybe you can show me the locker—"

Before she could finish her sentence, a shout from the hall caught the attention of both women. They turned as two EMTs careened into the ER pushing a gurney.

"GSW to the chest, pressure's 40 palp," the first EMT yelled.

Rising quickly, Honor pointed. "Put him in trauma one."

"Where's your attending?" Quinn demanded sharply as they sprinted behind the stretcher.

"I—"

"He just lost his pulse," the second EMT announced breathlessly. "Shit. He's flatline."

"Never mind," Quinn snapped to the resident as she grabbed sterile gloves and a mask from a cart just inside the procedure room. She tied on the mask, ripped open the package of gloves, and pulled them on. "Just find me a thoracotomy set and open it."

Two nurses and a wild-eyed medical student ran into the room, pulling on gloves, and instantly began the choreographed trauma routine without need of instruction. One nurse immediately cut off the patient's clothing, the other hung a fresh bag of normal saline and ran it wide open, and the student collected blood specimens in multicolor, rubber-topped vials.

"Can you handle tubing this guy?" Quinn asked, sparing the other doctor a quick glance as she poured Betadine directly from the bottle onto the patient's chest. "Or do you want me to? You need to be quick."

"I've got it," Honor replied evenly. She picked up the curved laryngoscope, which resembled a thin flashlight with a right-angle extension, from a cart beside the stretcher, slid it deftly into the unconscious man's throat, and followed with a plastic endotracheal tube that she passed between the vocal cords and into the trachea. It took her less than ten seconds to complete the maneuver and attach the breathing tube to a ventilator.

"Nice," Quinn grunted.

"Linda," Honor said to the nurse beside her, "get me some morphine and succinylcholine, will you?"

"Sure." The nurse, a small trim blond, cast a curious look in Quinn's direction and raised an eyebrow.

Honor muttered, "New attending."

"Ah," was all the nurse said as she drew up the drugs and passed the syringes to Honor, who then injected them into the IV line.

"Pressure?" Quinn asked as she reached for the number-ten scalpel.

"Nothing," one of the other nurses replied.

"Okay, then. Somebody call and get some blood down here stat." As she spoke, Quinn placed her left hand on the chest with her fingers palpating the fourth and fifth ribs just below the man's nipple and cut a long incision in the space between them directly into the chest cavity. She was about to ask for the rib spreaders when they appeared in her field of vision. "Thanks." *Smart resident.*

"No problem," Honor murmured as she peered over Quinn's shoulder. "Linda, hand me the suction, please."

Honor cleared the clots from around the heart and watched as Quinn used scissors to open the pericardium, the dense fibrous covering around the heart. She'd seen a lot of surgeons do the same maneuver and had done it herself, but she couldn't remember ever seeing anyone's hands move so quickly or so well. "Tamponade?"

Cardiac tamponade was a condition in which the heart was unable to pump effectively because it was being compressed by a collection of blood or fluid inside its own containing cover.

"Looks like it," Quinn replied, gratified to see the heart start to beat. She slid her fingers underneath the left ventricle and carefully turned the heart. "And a big mother of a hole back here, too."

"Pressure's coming up," a voice announced.

"Not for long, not unless we get this bullet hole closed up." Quinn never took her eyes off the beating organ in her hand. She never looked away from the field when she was operating, because it broke her concentration and cost her several seconds of precious time to refocus on the wound. She held out her right hand and hoped to hell that someone there knew something about surgery. "I need a three-0 silk on a taper needle. That's a—"

Miraculously, it appeared in her hand. *Very smart resident.* As she placed a purse-string suture in the muscle around the hole in the left ventricle, she heard the mellifluous alto voice behind her tell the nurses to call the OR and alert the chest surgeons that there was a patient coming up who might need bypass.

"Did it hit the hilum?" Honor asked, referring to the vessels behind the heart that supplied blood to the lungs. She noted the perfect placement of the sutures and the slick, economical way that Quinn handled the instruments. *She's an incredible surgeon.*

"Don't think so." Carefully, Quinn tied down the suture, hoping as she always did at this point that the muscle would hold and not shred as the knot was tightened. "Can you get a chest tube in and hooked up to suction?"

"It's ready to go as soon as you get that bleeding stopped."

Quinn straightened and met the appraising brown eyes. Behind her mask, she grinned, flushed with success. "My part's all taken care of, Doctor. Now let's see how you do."

Honor chose a spot one interspace above and just lateral to Quinn's incision and made a one-inch incision of her own. She guided a blunt hemostat between the ribs and into the chest cavity, then pushed a thick, rigid tube through the opening she had made. The chest tube would create suction inside the thoracic cavity, allowing the lung to re-expand. While Honor worked, Linda hung the first unit of blood.

"He's ready to transport," Honor said as she connected the tube to the Pleur-evac, a canister designed to collect blood and fluid while removing unwanted air from around the lung.

The entire resuscitation had taken fifteen minutes. Quinn and Honor pulled off their gloves, lowered their masks, and walked out into the hall, while the nurses and the medical student prepared the patient and his various monitoring devices, lines, and intravenous bags for the trip up to the operating room.

"Well, now I really feel right at home," Quinn said, rolling her shoulders to ease some of the tension. *Just like old times. Almost.*

But it wasn't—not really—and might never be again.

She glanced down with a grimace, realizing that her jeans were soaked with blood. "I need to shower and change. Can you get me some scrubs?"

"Come this way." Honor strode toward a connecting corridor. "I'll show you where the locker room is. There are plenty in there."

"Thanks."

As they walked, Honor took the opportunity to study the newcomer. She'd already seen her work, and the new attending was exactly as she had been advertised. Quinn Maguire, aged twenty-eight, was a fully trained general surgeon who had just completed a trauma fellowship in New York City. Her résumé had been impressive, and her performance just now matched her reputation. But of course, there hadn't been anything in her academic profile to suggest that she was, in addition to being an accomplished surgeon, a strikingly attractive woman—jet black hair, sapphire blue eyes, slightly above average height, lean and tight and boldly handsome. Cocky, too, as Honor had anticipated. Begrudgingly, she admitted that Maguire just might have reason to be. *She has magic hands.*

"Here it is," Honor announced, pushing open a door marked Staff. "Take any open locker, and check with Marty, the ward clerk, when you're ready. He'll give you a key."

"Thanks again." Quinn leaned her shoulder against the door frame and regarded Honor appreciatively. Beautiful, smart, and skilled. *Things are looking up.* "What year are you? You did a really nice job in there just now."

"So did you, Dr. Maguire." Honor extended her hand. "We haven't been properly introduced. I'm Honor Blake, the chief of emergency services."

"Oops." One dark eyebrow lifted and the corner of Quinn's mouth quirked into a grin again even as she realized that she'd just spent her first half-hour on the job treating her new boss like an underling. "Not a great way to start, I guess."

She shook Honor's hand, instantly struck by the warm strength in the long tapered fingers. The contact felt good, and she wondered if she was the only one to feel the slight spark of attraction. When she searched the brown eyes flecked with gold, she saw nothing but a polite greeting, and, reluctantly, she released Honor's hand. "I didn't recognize you. Sorry."

"No need to be," Honor said neutrally, ignoring the speculative look in Quinn's deep blue eyes. "What better way to get acquainted?"

I could think of any number of ways. Quinn tried hard not to stare at the soft swell of breasts beneath the dark blue scrub shirt or at any other part of Honor Blake's very attractive physique. She did take note, however, of the thin gold band on Honor's left hand with a brief twinge of disappointment. *Well, that takes care of that.*

"Trial by fire, I guess. At least now I understand why you're so good...for a resident." Quinn tried for a bit of humor, but the ER chief merely nodded faintly, her expression impossible to decipher.

"Come find me when you're settled, and I'll give you a brief rundown of our operation." Honor turned and walked away. She had been opposed to hiring Quinn Maguire, but it had been a fait accompli before she'd even had a chance to cast a vote. She had not wanted a surgeon on her staff, especially one she didn't know anything about. Now she'd just have to make the best of it.

Quinn watched Honor stride purposefully down the hall, wondering at the hint of animosity she'd felt from the other woman. *Usually it takes me more than half an hour to piss someone off.*

Quinn sighed. This was not where she'd imagined herself being a year ago. But then, nothing in her life had turned out the way she'd expected. She was lucky to have gotten this position, and now she'd just have to make the best of it.

❖

"So what's the story?" Linda O'Malley asked as she settled onto a stool next to Honor in the nurses' station.

"Huh?" Honor looked up blankly from the paperwork that she was completing on the GSW victim, presently known as UMV— unidentified male victim. "Story...?"

"Dr. Tall, Dark, and Gorgeous."

Honor stifled a sharp retort, uncertain as to why the question aggravated her. She'd known Linda for almost eight years, ever since they'd met when Honor was a medical student and could barely figure out how to start an intravenous line. She'd lost count of the number of times that Linda had bailed her out of difficult situations, and in the course of their professional association, they'd become close personal friends as well.

"I told you that we were getting a new attending," Honor replied, tapping her pen restlessly on the countertop in a completely uncharacteristic fashion. *Why am I so bothered? God, I hate feeling off balance.*

"Yeah, but she's not the usual ER doc, now, is she?"

"No," Honor admitted pensively, thinking about those talented hands, "she's not."

"How could you hire someone for my department while I was on vacation?" Honor was so incensed she could barely stay in her seat. *"I never even had a chance to interview her."*

Mary Ann Jones looked honestly contrite. *"It came up unexpectedly, and I knew that you had a position open. I had to make the decision quickly to get the salary approved for the upcoming fiscal year."*

"You could have called me to discuss it. Linda O'Malley knew where we were."

"You know how these things go, Honor." The chief of medicine shrugged. *"The chief of surgery contacted me and asked me to interview Dr. Maguire that very day. Her credentials were impeccable, and...I owed Fillmore a favor."*

"Great. Politics," Honor said in disgust. *"I need a full-time ER doc, not a prima donna surgeon who probably can't tell a heart attack from heartburn."*

"It won't hurt to have a surgeon permanently on staff in the emergency room," Mary Ann pointed out. *"It will be very good for the residency program, and it will cut down on the number of surgery consults you'll need to request. That will make the HMOs happy."*

"Did it ever occur to you to wonder why a surgeon would want to be an emergency room physician?" Honor shook her head. *"What's wrong with her?"*

"Nothing that I could see. Undergraduate at Duke, med school and general surgery at NYU, and one of the premier trauma fellowships in the country at St. Michael's."

"I ask again, what's wrong with her? A substance abuse problem, mental instability?" Honor leaned forward, her displeasure evident. *"Come on, Mary Ann. No surgeon would take this position if there weren't some kind of problem in their background. It doesn't offer either the status or the salary of surgery."*

The chief of medicine lifted her shoulders helplessly. "I honestly can't shed any light on why she wanted this job. She comes highly recommended with absolutely nothing in her files to besmirch a stellar record. I was delighted to get her, and since she's officially a joint surgery and medicine hire, their *department has to do all the work of credentialing her."*

"More politics. I'm telling you, someone's hiding something." Honor stood, still furious. "As far as I'm concerned, she's on probation in my *department. If she makes one mistake or steps out of line, she's gone."*

"Of course," Mary Ann said. "I won't stand in your way if you have cause for dismissal. Just give her a fair chance."

That had been three weeks ago. In the interim, Honor had reviewed Quinn's CV and made a few discreet calls to friends from medical school and residency who had contacts at St. Michael's where Quinn had trained. Unfortunately, she didn't know much more about Quinn now than when she'd first been told to expect a surgeon as the newest member of her department. All anyone could tell her was that Quinn was rumored to be a rising young star, and if her star had burned out, no one knew why.

"If there *is* a story, I haven't heard it," Honor said with a sigh.

"She was slick this morning in that trauma," Linda pointed out mildly.

"Yes."

"And she's so hot the air around her sizzles."

"God, Linda, Robin shouldn't let you out of the house without a chaperone."

The small blond laughed. "After twelve years and two kids, Robin knows she doesn't have to worry. I was just *remarking*."

"You have drool in the corner of your mouth."

Linda started to raise a hand to her lips, then snorted. "Ha ha. And I suppose *you* didn't notice?"

Honor grew very still, disconcerted when Quinn's intense blue eyes and easy grin came instantly to mind. "No."

"Honor, come on," Linda said gently, resting her fingers on her friend's forearm. "Sooner or later—"

Abruptly, Honor stood. "Let's not go there again, okay? Please."

"I'm sorry." Linda rose and gave Honor a quick hug. "You know me, just can't mind my own business."

"It's okay." Honor forced a smile. "Now, which room did you put the guy with the chest pain in?"

"Number four. The EKG is by the bedside. The T-waves are peaked, but they're not flipped, so I think it's just angina."

"Did he respond to that nitroglycerin?"

"Yep. Felt better in thirty seconds."

"Good," Honor said absently, glancing down the hall toward the locker room. "I'll be in with him for a while. Keep your eye on Dr. Maguire. She might have good hands, but she probably doesn't know anything about medicine. Don't let her go killing anyone."

"Yes, boss," Linda murmured softly, wondering as she watched her friend disappear into one of the curtained rooms just what it was about Quinn Maguire that bothered Honor quite so much. She doubted that in the small world of the hospital and the intimate environment in which they spent much of their day that it would take very long for the answer to become apparent.

CHAPTER TWO

Quinn stuffed her street clothes into an empty locker, pulled on a pair of navy blue scrubs and Nikes, and, hoping to get on better footing with her new chief, went in search of Honor. She found her reading through a stack of papers in the staff lounge, a small, windowless room tucked into a rear corner of the emergency room. The space was unadorned and starkly functional—the only decorations were a bulletin board with the obligatory rules and regulations covering everything from waste disposal to bomb threats, and a large erasable 12-month calendar showing the staff's shift assignments. The furnishings consisted of a single grouping of end tables and chairs along one wall and a central table that looked as if it had been pilfered from the hospital cafeteria.

"You said you wanted to go over some things," Quinn said as she helped herself to coffee from the warmer on the counter. It was her first and only cup of the day, and she fervently prayed it would be decent. She took a cautious sip. *Not bad at all. Maybe that's a good sign.* She and Honor were alone, and Quinn waited for an invitation before sitting down. "Is this a good time to talk?"

"Any time that it's quiet for five minutes in a row is a good time," Honor said with a soft sigh, pushing the messages aside. Most of the time, she enjoyed the administrative aspects of her position, but the paperwork was never-ending. She gestured to the chair opposite her at the stained gray Formica-topped table. "I'm sorry that I didn't get to meet with you when you were here to interview in June."

"So am I." Quinn kept her voice neutral and her face expressionless, wondering if they *had* met if Honor would have hired her. At the moment, the ER chief didn't seem too happy to have her on board. She'd been lucky that her previous chief had been able to pull some strings and get her an interview at one of the few university hospitals that still had an ER handling trauma. Most hospitals, like St. Michael's, had both a trauma unit to handle acute injuries *and* a separate emergency room for the treatment of medical illness. At PMC, however, the ER docs evaluated and stabilized even the level one traumas, only calling upon the surgeons for consultation or when the patient was ready to go up to the OR. It was as close as Quinn was going to get to an operating room for a while. *Face it. Maybe forever.* She pushed away that thought as well as the faint nausea that accompanied it. "It was kind of a rush deal."

"Yes, the way you were hired *was* a bit unusual." Honor studied Quinn's deep blue eyes, searching for some suggestion of evasion or discomfort. The surgeon's gaze was direct and surprisingly serene. The tranquility was not something Honor would have expected of *any* surgeon, but particularly not of this one, especially not after having witnessed Quinn's aggressive handling of the trauma alert earlier. *What an interesting mix of contradictions she is. Or else she's a great poker player.*

Annoyed to discover that she had lost her focus, Honor spoke more sharply than she intended. "I'm not sure what you were led to believe, but it's not going to be possible for you to see only surgical problems down here. We're—"

"I wasn't led to believe *anything* except that I had a job." Quinn tilted her head with the barest flicker of a grin. "Is that still true?"

Despite herself, Honor laughed. "Well, considering that you passed your *practical exam* this morning with high marks, I'd have to say yes."

"Good, because I've already put down first and last months' rent on an apartment."

Honor caught herself as she was about to ask where Quinn was living. For some reason, she couldn't seem to keep her mind from wandering from professional into personal areas, which was distinctly unusual for her. She was friendly with all of her colleagues, but, for the most part, her time was spent on administrative responsibilities or patient care. She didn't socialize very much with any of her colleagues other than Linda, and she almost never saw her fellow attendings outside of work except at departmental functions. *I'm probably curious because she just appeared out of nowhere. It's not like there's really any great mystery about her. So, I'll just get this little introductory talk out of the way, and we can all get back to routine.*

"The Monday morning rush is going to start very soon," Honor began, "so let's go over the ground rules before that happens. We try to see patients on a first come, first served basis as much as possible. Obviously, if there's an acute case, that takes priority."

Quinn nodded, watching Honor unconsciously turn the wedding ring on her left hand as she spoke. The ER chief had beautiful hands—narrow, supple, and long fingered. Those hands appeared very much like the woman herself—graceful and lithe and strong. With a start, Quinn realized that she had missed the last thing that Honor had said. "I'm sorry? What?"

Honor regarded her quizzically. "I said that I don't have a problem with you selecting out the patients with complaints that seem to be surgical in origin, because that just makes sense. But if there's a patient with a critical condition or someone who has been waiting a long time, you'll need to see them even if their complaint is a medical problem."

"I expected to do that," Quinn said evenly. "I've been boning up on my emergency medicine the last few weeks." She lifted a shoulder and shrugged. "I'm not that far out of medical school that I don't remember how to handle medical problems. I'm a little behind on the latest drug treatments, but I'll catch up."

"I'm sure you will." Honor stood. "Don't be afraid to check with one of us if you're not sure about something—just until you're a little more comfortable with the kinds of conditions you'll be seeing down here. I'm sure it will be very different from what you were used to at St. Michael's."

For the first time, Quinn averted her gaze, and a faint flush rose up her neck. Until four months ago, she had expected to be the newest trauma attending at St. Michael's right about now, not a green ER doc at the bottom of the totem pole. "Yes, I expect it will be."

As they walked back toward the main work area, Honor concluded by saying, "There will be at least four attendings scheduled to work during each twelve-hour shift. I put you on days the first few weeks so you can get your bearings. For the time being, you'll basically be on two days and off one, with some variation to accommodate personal days and the like." *The same shifts I work, at least until I can trust you alone.*

"Fine." Since Quinn had no close friends in the city and had nothing planned, she didn't really care when she worked. She just wanted to be busy, because alone time meant too much time to think.

"Okay then. I'll be around if you have any questions."

"Thanks." Quinn took a deep breath, walked to the counter, and picked up the first patient chart. Chief complaint: abdominal pain.

That sounds like something I can handle.

Twenty-five minutes later, Quinn found Linda recording the vital signs on an elderly woman whose chief complaint was low back pain present for five years. As was so often the case in inner-city hospitals, the emergency room frequently served as a primary care clinic for neighborhood people who either had no health insurance or were without a family doctor.

Linda looked up at Quinn and smiled. "How's it going?"

"Okay. Thanks. Uh...how do I get a pediatric surgeon?"

Linda patted the elderly woman's arm. "Somebody will be by to see you in just a few minutes, okay?" Then she motioned for Quinn to follow her back to the nurses' station. Once there, she pointed to a series of lists that were tacked to a corkboard behind the counter. "Here you go—these are the names and beeper numbers for the on-call docs in the various specialties this month. Some change every day, some every week, and some cover for the entire month. What do you have?"

"Acute appendix."

"The nine-year-old with the bellyache?"

"Yep. Peri-umbilical pain localizing to the right lower quadrant, elevated white count, low-grade temp, and guarding on physical exam."

"That was a fast diagnosis."

Quinn shrugged. "Like I said. Classic."

"Does it bother you, that you won't be the one operating on her?" Linda still couldn't figure out why someone who could do what she had seen Quinn Maguire do that morning would want to give that up. And her motto had always been "If you want to know something, ask."

Quinn absently rubbed an annoying itch on the left side of her chest above her shirt pocket, her expression remote as she thought about how much fun it was to do an appendectomy. "Yeah. It does." She blinked and dropped her hand, suddenly self-conscious, and studied the posted lists. "So it's...Baker, right?"

"Yes. I'll page him for you and give you a call when he answers. Or, if you want, I can just read him the vital statistics and tell him what you think."

"Sure, do that. If he has any questions, just come find me. And thanks." Quinn was about to reach for the next chart when she turned back and held out her hand. "By the way, I'm Quinn Maguire."

"Linda O'Malley."

Quinn nodded in acknowledgment of the greeting and pulled the next chart from the rack. She winced when she read the presenting problem: headache. She contemplated sliding it back and looking for something a little more exciting, and then she remembered the first come, first served rule. *I can probably manage to figure this out.*

With a sigh, she tucked the chart under her arm and headed off to cubicle eight.

❖

At 6:45 that evening, Honor finished signing off on her last chart and glanced around the emergency room. There were three new patients waiting to be seen, none of whom had a critical problem. Two patients were waiting for beds to become available upstairs and would be admitted as soon as their rooms were ready. Four were in the process of being evaluated with x-rays and laboratory tests, but they would be nearly ready for discharge when the new shift came on duty. All in all, her ship was tidy. Except for the fact that Quinn Maguire was leaning against the wall outside one of the patient cubicles, staring at her PDA with a frown on her face. With a tired sigh, Honor got up and walked over to her.

"Problem?"

Quinn looked up, surprised. "No, not really. I can just never remember the dosage of Augmentin in kids."

"Sore throat?"

"Earache."

"Ah." Honor told her the dosage of the antibiotic. "That's one you'll be getting very familiar with very quickly around here."

"I'm sure." Quinn rubbed her forehead, suddenly realizing that she was beat. She'd been on her feet the entire day, which in the past hadn't been all that unusual. Nevertheless, it was a different kind of work than she was used to doing in the intensely focused operating room, and it had been quite a while since she'd worked a full shift. And even more than that, she wasn't used to feeling just a little bit behind all the time.

"How did it go today?" Honor found herself feeling slightly sorry for the young surgeon. She'd kept an eye on Quinn throughout the day and noticed that she had worked steadily, barely even stopping to eat. She didn't slack off, and to her credit, she'd also seen her fair share of routine medical complaints. She might be a surgeon, but she wasn't flaunting it or expecting special treatment.

"Fine, I guess. I only had to holler for help a couple of times." Quinn smiled wryly, remembering a time when *she* had been the one making all the calls. The one in charge. "I haven't felt quite so ineffectual in a long time."

Honor couldn't help but hear the frustration and, surprisingly, the hint of sadness in Quinn's voice. It was on the tip of her tongue to ask the surgeon why she had chosen to take this job, but it was none of her business. It *would* have been within her province to ask for an explanation, had she had the opportunity to interview Quinn before she'd been hired. But not now. Now it was done. "You're allowed a lunch hour, you know."

"I'm not used to a formal schedule. I'd rather just work." *At least then maybe I'll feel useful. Like maybe the last ten years haven't been for nothing.*

"Your call. See you tomorrow."

"Right. Tomorrow."

Quinn gave the child's mother the prescription for antibiotics along with instructions to follow up with her pediatrician in two days. After filling out the paperwork, she dropped the chart into the Completed bin and headed back to the locker room. She packed up her gear, stowed the bloodied jeans in her backpack, and headed out.

She ran into Honor and Linda as the two women were leaving together.

"Need a ride somewhere?" Linda asked as the three of them converged on the outer doors.

Quinn couldn't help but notice that Honor looked slightly perturbed by her friend's offer. She shook her head. "No, thanks. I've got my bike."

"Ooh." Linda made an excited sound. "You've got a motorcycle?"

Laughing, Quinn replied, "No. A Fuji road bike."

"A bicycle?" Honor questioned, surprised once again. Thus far, Quinn Maguire had managed to dispel almost every preconception she'd had about her. She'd even been forced to make allowances for her arrogance.

"I'm only a couple of miles from here on Morris," Quinn supplied.

"Hey! We're all practically neighbors." Linda beamed. "Honor and I are a couple of houses apart right around the corner from you on Schoolhouse Lane."

"That's...nice. Well," Quinn put her hands in her pockets, aware that Honor Blake was slowly edging away toward the adjoining parking lot. "Good night, then."

Quinn watched the two women walk quickly away and then turned in the opposite direction toward the bike rack. Clearly she hadn't been wrong in her impression that morning that the chief of emergency services was less than thrilled to have her. Ordinarily, she didn't care what anyone thought of her—except for her previous chief, Saxon Sinclair. But she had cared about what Sinclair thought because she had wanted to be like Sinclair. *Every* trauma fellow to pass through St. Michael's wanted to be like Sinclair. She was a surgeon's surgeon—the best hands, the quickest mind, the ultimate in cool command.

The reasons that Quinn wanted Honor Blake to think well of her were a little more complicated than simply desiring professional respect. Sure, she wouldn't mind if the chief of emergency services was impressed with her skills or thought well of her clinical acumen. But Honor wasn't just her chief, she was also an attractive and intriguing woman. During moments when Honor hadn't been aware of her scrutiny, Quinn had noticed how Honor's eyes softened when she smiled and the way her lips curved upward when she laughed. Those events seemed rare, but worth the wait. She wouldn't mind being the one to make Honor smile that way.

Yeah, right. Remember your own number one rule. Never ever get involved with a married woman.

Quinn shouldered her backpack, straddled her bike, and headed off into the gathering night. The last thing she needed at this point was an involvement with anyone, especially her boss, and her very obviously *unavailable* boss at that.

❖

"Jeez, could you have been any more rude?" Linda turned her six-year-old Volvo wagon onto Wissahickon Avenue and headed north out of Germantown into Mount Airy. The neighborhood along the way was comprised mostly of large three- and four-story stone homes, many of which dated back over a century. More than a few had been subdivided into apartments over the years, but a fair number of affordable single-family dwellings still remained. The northwestern section of the city had gradually become populated by an eclectic assortment of young professionals, artists, blue-collar workers, and a large percentage of the city's lesbian population.

"What do you mean, rude?" Blushing, Honor realized that she sounded defensive and tried to subdue her tone. "Just because I wasn't falling all over her like some people I know?"

"I most certainly was not falling all over her." Linda harrumphed. "I was simply being polite. And *welcoming.*"

"Oh, sure. If that bicycle had been a motorcycle, I think you would've climbed on behind her and ridden off into the sunset."

Linda looked pensive. "I don't think I could have tonight. Robin and the kids should be getting home from soccer practice right about now, and it's my turn to cook dinner."

Honor laughed. "Honestly, why are you so interested in her?"

"Aren't you?" Linda pulled to the curb and parked. "You have to admit that she's really good looking, she seems pretty smart, and she's nice. And there's no good reason that I can think of that she ought to be working in our emergency room. So I'm curious."

"My point exactly. There is no reason for her to be here. No *good* reason." Honor grabbed her briefcase and opened the car door. "So I'm reserving judgment."

Linda made an exasperated sound as she climbed out, too. "About what? The good-looking part?"

"All right, I'll give you that much." Honor had to admit even to herself that no one would argue *that* point. Quinn Maguire was disturbingly good looking in an intense, Black Irish way. "As to how smart she is or exactly how well she's going to work out in this position, we'll see."

"Okay, fine." Linda could tell when she'd run into a stone wall. It was the kind of immovable object that could only be altered by chipping away one tiny flake at a time. "You want to round up your clan and come over for dinner?"

"Did you say you were cooking?" Honor asked dubiously.

"Ha ha. You bring the wine."

"All right." Honor realized that an evening with friends sounded like just what she needed to keep her mind off the disquieting arrival of Quinn Maguire into her carefully ordered world.

CHAPTER THREE

Quinn pushed her bike down the alley next to the three-story building and secured it to the drainpipe with her lock. Her apartment comprised one-half of the second floor and had both a front and back entrance. A wooden staircase with deck landings at each level extended from the rear of the house, and she climbed to the second floor, fit her key into the back door, and let herself into her new home. The door opened onto the kitchen, a long narrow room now nearly filled with boxes. Threading her way around the obstacles, she proceeded into the hallway that ran the length of the apartment. A bedroom and bath opened off one side, a small second bedroom that she intended to use as an office adjoined the kitchen on the other, and a large rectangular living room occupied the entire space at the front.

Every room was filled with unopened boxes, scattered pieces of furniture, and a few suitcases. The movers had finished unloading everything late the previous evening, and Quinn had had no energy to open anything other than the trunk containing her sleeping bag, critical items of clothing, and bathroom gear. Her sleeping bag was still spread out in the middle of the living room on her mattress, and she had a feeling that she would be sleeping in it again that night. She turned once in a small circle, surveying the strange apartment.

What am I doing here? How in hell did I end up like this?

In retrospect, the chain of events that had changed her life had been set in motion a little over four months before, but the particulars of the proceedings seemed to have kaleidoscoped into one endless nightmare that defied logic or reason. When she tried to make sense of them, Quinn found that she could not. She didn't believe in luck or karma or fate. Sometimes bad things just *happened.* But that philosophy gave her very little comfort at the moment.

Wearily, she sat down on her sleeping bag, leaned her back against a pile of boxes, and closed her eyes. She knew she should eat, but strangely, she was not hungry. She knew she should sleep, but felt too restless inside for that. Her phone rested on the floor nearby. Briefly, she considered calling the woman she had dated on and off during the year of her fellowship in New York, but she found that the idea of talking with Beth left her feeling empty. They had gone to the occasional party, taken in a few Broadway shows, and shared a physical relationship that had been satisfying if not earth shattering. They weren't lovers; in fact, they were little more than casual acquaintances.

Quinn hadn't confided in Beth as her world had precipitously tilted and then simply crumbled, mostly because she wasn't used to discussing her problems with anyone. And especially not with someone she didn't completely trust to understand. *Odd that we've slept together, and I don't know her well enough to confide in her.*

She hadn't had much time to think about such things when she'd been working eighteen hours a day as a trauma fellow. Now that she found herself in a professional position to which she had never aspired, alone in a life she had never anticipated, she had far too much time to think. Groaning softly, she rubbed her face, stared at the ceiling, and tried to put the past aside. But the future was almost as difficult to contemplate, particularly considering her uncertain welcome in the ER that morning.

Fleetingly, she wondered if Honor Blake and Linda O'Malley were lovers. They had that easy energy between them, and she'd caught Linda eyeing her speculatively a few times during the day. The nurse hadn't exactly been cruising her, but Quinn had felt the interest. Perhaps *she* was the person who had given Honor that wedding ring.

And just that quickly, Quinn found herself faced with yet another thought she did not want to contemplate. Surrendering to exhaustion as much emotional as physical, she stretched out on the sleeping bag and wearily closed her eyes again.

❖

"Honor," a soft, deep voice murmured.

Instantly awake, Honor jolted upright on the couch and stared into the pale blue eyes mere inches from hers. "Oh my God, did I fall asleep?"

Robin Henderson, a solidly built redhead with a killer smile, grinned faintly. "About halfway through *Wheel of Fortune*."

"Where's Arly?" Honor rubbed her face, trying to clear the mists of vague dreams from her consciousness. She couldn't clearly recall what she had been dreaming, but she was left with a feeling of uneasiness and...peril? *No, that can't be right. What in my life could possibly be dangerous?* For no reason that she could imagine, Quinn Maguire's face flashed through her mind. *That's ridiculous. You* must *be tired.*

"She's in the den. There's some kind of serious Lord of the Rings video game battle going on. Want some dinner?"

"Yes, please," Honor replied gratefully, standing and stretching. "Did the kids eat?"

"All done. We fed them first and then banished them so that we could have some adult time." Robin led the way into the dining room, where Linda was pouring an enormous pot of spaghetti sauce over enough pasta to feed a regiment.

"Yum. Looks great." Honor slid into the seat that she always occupied at Robin and Linda's.

Linda cocked her head and studied the serving bowl filled to the brim with steaming vegetables, sauce, and pasta. "You're going to have to take some of this home. There's only so much in the way of leftovers we can handle. I wish you had been able to talk Phyllis into staying for dinner."

"You know that Monday's her poker night," Honor replied, referring to her mother-in-law's love of gambling. "Nothing in the world would keep her from that."

Robin heaped a generous portion onto her plate and passed the platter to Honor. "Lindy tells me that you've got a new doc at work."

Honor paused with the serving fork in the air and cast a wary glance in Linda's direction. She knew without doubt that Robin's remark was completely guileless, but she also knew that the redhead was naïve enough to be set up by her less than scrupulous lover. And Linda, who refused to give up her self-appointed duty as Honor's social secretary, looked suspiciously innocent as she cut chunks of garlic bread off a long loaf.

"That's right." Honor intentionally kept her voice casual.

"A surgeon, huh?"

"That's right."

Linda interjected brightly, "A really talented, good-looking one."

"Is she gay?"

"If she's not, then neither am I," Linda stated emphatically.

"That's good, then, right?" Robin looked questioningly from one woman to the other.

"Which part?" Honor grumbled. *I know which part Linda thinks is good. If I didn't also know that she loves me and thinks she's helping, I'd be seriously pissed off at her.*

"Uh..." Robin hesitated, sensing a faint chill in the air. "Did I put my foot in something?"

Shaking her head, Honor couldn't help but smile. Robin, a computer software consultant who worked from home and cared for the couple's six- and nine-year-olds, was one of the sweetest people she'd ever met. Honor could never remember being angry with her. "No, but your spouse just can't keep from putting her *nose* in everything."

"Oh." Robin chuckled, tossed her lover a fond look, and went back to her dinner. "So what else is new?"

"Ha ha," Linda retorted. But she leaned close and kissed Robin's ear, murmuring softly.

"Jeez, give it a rest, will you?" Honor complained, but her tone was playful. She loved the way they cared for one another, and rather than making her sad over what she didn't have, their happiness made her feel less alone.

"So are you gonna invite her to the barbecuc next week?" Robin asked.

"No," Honor said immediately.

"Sure," Linda overrode her.

"Linda..." Honor's tone was threatening.

"Oh, come on! She's a new member of the department, and she's new to the city. It's only polite."

Honor sighed, knowing Linda was right. She didn't even know why she felt uncomfortable with the idea. Quinn Maguire had done absolutely nothing wrong, and she seemed personable enough. It wasn't Quinn's fault that she'd been hired without Honor's input. It wasn't her fault that she was a surgeon, and that Honor had no great love for her generally self-centered, egotistical, and often insensitive medical counterparts. It *certainly* wasn't Quinn Maguire's fault that she had the deepest blue eyes of any woman Honor had ever seen, or that for some reason, Honor couldn't seem to stop seeing the way Quinn's hands moved with such surety and grace.

"All right. Fine."

Linda smiled and passed the spaghetti.

❖

"Have you seen Dr. Maguire?" Honor asked Tom Finley, one of the registered nurses who worked in the ER. "I've got a guy in six with a mandible fracture I want her to look at."

"I think she's in ten doing a tendon repair."

Honor raised an eyebrow. "Down here?"

Generally, any hand injury more serious than a simple laceration or straightforward fracture was referred to orthopedics or plastic surgery for treatment in the operating room. But Honor had noticed that since Quinn had started working in the ER, more of those problems were being handled on site. It was only Quinn's second week in the ER, and already the other physicians were triaging anything that looked surgical to her. She was rapidly becoming one of the busiest physicians in the emergency room.

Finley, a thin, sharp-eyed African American, shrugged. "Anything that gets them taken care of and off our board works for me. You know how long it takes for ortho or plastics to get down here for a consult."

Honor couldn't argue. She'd much prefer that patients be evaluated, treated, and discharged rather than have them waiting for hours for a specialist to evaluate them. The long delays clogged up her emergency room and irritated the patients. Still, at this rate, Quinn was in danger of being seriously overworked. Already, Honor had noticed that the new attending was arriving early and leaving late.

"Thanks. Room ten, did you say?"

"Last I saw."

Honor parted the curtain slowly and peeked inside. Quinn and one of the emergency room residents were seated on either side of a narrow arm board. A young Hispanic male lay on a stretcher with his arm extended on the support, palm up. A laceration extended across the width of his forearm, approximately three inches above the wrist crease. From where she was standing, Honor could see exposed muscle bellies, several pencil-sized white bands of severed tendon ends, and a blood clot in the region of the radial artery just above the thumb. "Can you talk?"

Quinn glanced up from the wound and smiled in greeting. "Sure. Come on in."

With an inquiring expression, Honor tilted her chin in the direction of the patient, who appeared to be unresponsive.

"Anesthesia by ethanol," Quinn explained. The patient was intoxicated and, after the resident had injected the lidocaine to numb the wound, had promptly gone to sleep.

"Nerve injury?" Honor leaned over the seated resident's shoulder for a better look into the depths of the wound. Quinn held the edges open with two small stainless steel right-angle retractors that looked like miniature rakes so that the resident could work.

"Got the sensory branch of the radial nerve, but missed the median. Lucky for hi—yo, Zebrowski, don't grab the end of the tendon with your forceps. You'll fray it, and then it won't hold your sutures."

"Sorry," the resident mumbled, his hands shaking as he struggled to place the fine blue Prolene sutures through the ends of the lacerated tendons.

"Get it right down the center of the tendon."

"Okay?" Zebrowski asked tentatively as he edged the needle into the tissue.

"That's better," Quinn commented as she watched him place his first stitch. "Now tag it with the hemostat and put in another one just like it." She looked up to find Honor watching her with a serious expression in her golden brown eyes. Quinn quirked a brow. "What?"

"Nothing." What Honor had been thinking was that Quinn was not only a fine surgeon, but also a good teacher. She appeared on the surface to be precisely as she had been advertised—an excellent addition to the ER. Except that Honor couldn't make sense of the picture. Why should someone with Quinn's skills be working there? All that she could imagine was that there had been some breach in ethics that had cost Quinn her surgical career. That thought bothered her more than a little, because it was difficult not to like the dynamic surgeon.

Quinn divided her attention between watching the resident complete the tendon repair and trying to figure out what she had just seen in Honor's eyes. Curiosity, confusion, and, oddly, compassion. The mix of emotions was powerful and compelling. She caught her breath, feeling her heart trip unexpectedly. In the next instant, it was steady again, and she ignored the slight flutter of uneasiness. "Do you need me?"

"When you get a chance, I want you to take a look at some films on a twenty-year-old who took a header off his bicycle. I think he's got a fracture of the mandibular body, but I'm not sure. The x-ray isn't diagnostic and his exam is equivocal."

"Okay. As soon as we get a cast on Mr. Garcia, I'll be right there."

Honor noticed that Quinn had dark circles under her eyes, and for the first time, she realized that the young surgeon looked exhausted. She knew that Quinn had been working hard—they all worked pretty much nonstop for twelve to fourteen hours—but it hardly seemed likely that the demands of the ER would be that much different than what Quinn had experienced as a surgeon. Once again sensing something amiss, Honor felt a surge of concern. "Take your time."

Ten minutes later, Quinn leaned with a palm against the wall and studied the film, which had been hung on the light box, of the young man with the possible jaw fracture.

"What do you think?" Honor asked as she walked up beside her.

"He doesn't seem to be very tender on physical exam, and his bite looks okay. His teeth come together perfectly," Quinn observed.

"I know. That's what bothers me. The mechanism of injury is right for a jaw fracture, but his physical findings are unimpressive, to say the least. But then, the x-ray *is* suggestive." Honor leaned forward as well, her shoulder brushing Quinn's as she stared at the x-ray. She reached out to trace a faint line between two of the lower teeth. "Looks like a fracture right there. Maybe it's an old inj—"

"Honor, I'm sorry to interrupt," Linda said with an uncharacteristic hint of urgency in her voice. "Robin just called from the car. It doesn't sound serious, but there's been an accident."

"Oh my God." Honor's face lost all its color, and for an instant, she swayed. *There's been an accident. We're sorry to have to tell you...*

Quinn felt Honor tremble, saw the panic in her eyes, and without thinking, rested her hand against Honor's back, supporting her gently. She made small circles with her fingertips, unconsciously hoping to soothe her. She wasn't entirely certain what was happening, but Honor's terror was clear. And seeing her suffer made Quinn ache.

"Honor," Linda said sharply, placing both hands on her friend's shoulders. "She's okay. Robin says she's *okay*. They'll be here in just a minute."

Without even realizing it, Honor leaned into the warmth of Quinn's body, needing something solid to anchor her while she fought the memories and struggled to stay in the present. Heart pounding, her voice tight with fear, she asked, "What happened?"

"I'm not sure. Something about one ball and two heads."

"Is she conscious? Is she talking?" Honor tried to think clearly, but she knew her words were rushing together as fear threatened to overwhelm her. *There's been an accident...*

"I don't have the details. I just got a thirty-second phone call." Linda shook her head in frustration. "But the most important thing is that Robin said it—"

Honor jerked away from Linda's grasp and ran toward the emergency room entrance. Quinn looked after her and saw a muscular woman in a bloodstained T-shirt and gym shorts carrying a softly crying blond child in her arms. The child's face and neck were streaked with blood, and a white gauze pad was taped over part of her forehead and left eye.

"Who is that?" Quinn asked, walking rapidly to keep up with Linda.

"Honor's daughter."

CHAPTER FOUR

The instant Honor saw the blond head turn toward her and the tremulous smile of recognition on her daughter's face, her panic began to ebb. *She's awake and alert, no head injury. Oh, thank God.* Despite the fact that her stomach still churned with anxiety laced with the aftermath of old terrors, she smiled and kept her voice level and steady as she reached for her child. "Hi, sweetie. Come here and let me hold you a while. Aunt Robin probably needs a rest."

"I can walk," the blond child said fretfully, but she extended her arms to Honor nonetheless.

"I know you can, but I want to give you a hug first."

Carefully, Robin passed the child to Honor, who hitched her daughter onto her hip as if she were two instead of nearly eight. Even as she did so, she searched the one eye she could see for any signs of altered consciousness. "I guess you bumped your head, huh?"

"*Jeannie* bumped it," Arly grumbled with a mixture of residual tears and emerging indignation.

Honor glanced at Robin in concern. "Is Jeannie okay?"

"She's got a goose egg on her forehead, but no other damage." She reached out and stroked Arly's hair and looked over at Linda, who stood nearby. "I've got to run. The kids are out front in the car, and the security guard is baby-sitting."

Linda gave Robin a quick hug. "Go ahead, honey. I'll call you later."

As Honor walked back to the nearest open examining room, she explained to Arly, "We're going to have to take that bandage off and see what's underneath, okay?"

"Will it hurt?"

"Does it hurt now?"

Arly seemed to give this some consideration. "A little. It feels kinda like my knee did when I fell off my skateboard."

"Well, it might hurt a tiny bit more for a few minutes while we put some medicine on it to clean it up. But not a lot."

"Will *you* do it?"

Honor hesitated. She still felt the effects of the swift surge of panic accompanied by the unexpected resurrection of past fears, and she wasn't certain how steady her hands would be. Before she could answer, Linda spoke up.

"You know what, Arly? I think Mom ought to hold your hand while one of the *other* doctors fixes you up. What do you say?"

"Who?"

Honor looked past Linda to Quinn walking quietly along beside them, the memory of the reassuring hand against her back comforting still. Deep blue eyes, kind with compassion, met hers. Without a second thought, Honor extended her free hand and Quinn took it, stepping closer. "This is Quinn, Arly. She's a surgeon, and she'll take really good care of you, okay?"

"Okay."

Linda held the curtain to exam room one open, and Honor gently deposited her daughter on the stretcher. Then she pulled a stool close and sat down as Quinn walked to the other side.

"I'm going to take this big Band-Aid off your forehead," Quinn explained. "There's some tape that will pull a little bit when I do. You ready?"

Arly held her mother's hand and nodded.

"So," Quinn said conversationally, surveying the four-centimeter laceration just above the child's eyebrow, "baseball, basketball, or soccer?"

"Soccer," Arly proclaimed as if anyone should know the answer.

"Neat." Quinn glanced at Honor, whose eyes were fixed on the wound on her daughter's forehead. She waited for Honor to look up at her, and then she smiled reassuringly. Honor rewarded her with a swift, if slightly shaky, smile in return. "I'm going to shine a light in your eyes. It'll be really bright."

Quinn pulled a small penlight from her chest pocket and checked Arly's pupils, both of which were equal and briskly reactive to the light stimulus. Then she held her index finger up about twelve inches from Arly's face. "I'm going to move my finger around, and I want you to watch it. Okay?"

"Why?"

"So I can be sure that your bump on the head isn't going to make it hard for you to see the ball during the next game."

Intently, Arly nodded and followed Quinn's moving hand.

"Does your neck hurt anywhere at all?"

"No."

"I'm going to poke around a bit, and you tell me if it's sore." As she spoke, Quinn slipped her fingers behind Arly's head and palpated each of her cervical vertebrae, one after the other. She elicited no tenderness. Then she felt the bones around her eyes, cheeks, nose, and jaws. All fine. Looking in Honor's direction, she murmured, "I don't see any need for x-rays."

"All right." Honor's throat was dry, and her voice came out husky. With each passing moment, she felt better and, unexpectedly, found herself soothed by Quinn's calm voice and gentle compassion.

"Okay, Arly, here's the deal." Quinn leaned over so that the child could see her face. "You've got a cut on your forehead, and it's going to need some stitches. Do you know what stitches are?"

"They're little tiny threads to help the cut get better faster." Arly looked in her mother's direction uncertainly. "Do I have to?" For the first time since she had arrived, the child looked as if she might cry.

"That's what we use when Band-Aids aren't strong enough, honey." Honor smiled reassuringly.

"Yeah, but they don't work on magical cuts, so maybe they won't work on me either." The child's tone was dubious.

Quinn raised an eyebrow. "Magical?"

"Mr. Weasley," Honor stated, as if that would explain things.

"Huh?"

"In Harry Potter!" Arly clarified. "Ron's father is a wizard and he needed stitches, but Muggle medicine doesn't work on wizards."

"Ah. I see." Quinn nodded thoughtfully. "That makes sense. I'm sure they'll work on you though—unless you're a wizard, too?"

"I don't think so." Arly shook her head seriously. "Are you going to put them in?"

"Yep. But first, I'm going to make it so you don't feel it when I do." As she spoke, Quinn pulled on gloves and Linda opened an instrument tray. Turning her back slightly so that the child would not see her draw up the lidocaine into the syringe from the bottle that Linda held out to her, she said, "Soccer, huh? So what position do you play?"

"Wing."

"Midfielder? You must be a really good passer."

"Most of the time." Stitches forgotten, Arly asked excitedly, "Do you play soccer?"

"I used to, when I was in college." Quinn gently wiped Betadine around the edges of the laceration.

"What position did *you* play?"

"Offense."

"Were you good?"

Quinn laughed and glanced at Honor, who merely shook her head and grinned.

"Uh—well, not bad."

Quinn stepped slightly out of Arly's line of vision and leaned down with the syringe. "I'm going to put in some medicine now that will feel a little bit like a big mosquito bite. You ready?"

"Okay."

Softly stroking her daughter's arm, Honor watched as Quinn slowly and carefully injected the local anesthetic. The secret, she knew, to minimizing the pain of the injection was to do it extraordinarily slowly, but most surgeons lacked the patience. Quinn, however, couldn't have been gentler. Her hands were steady and sure, and Honor realized as she watched her child lying quietly during the procedure how truly gifted Quinn was. *Who are you, really, Quinn Maguire?*

When the injection was completed, Quinn glanced at Honor. She'd seen parents, even seasoned medical people, faint when their children were injured. Parents could handle anything, apparently, except their own child's suffering. Gently, she asked, "You okay?"

This time Honor's smile was sure and strong. "Fine. You're very good."

Quinn blushed, her heart racing. "Arly's the star."

In ten minutes, the wound was cleaned, irrigated, and sutured. Throughout the process, Arly and Quinn kept up a running conversation regarding the virtues of various soccer positions and strategies as if nothing were happening. By the time Quinn had applied Steri-Strips in lieu of a bandage, the girl seemed to have forgotten completely about her injury.

"So, can you come to one of my games?" Arly asked eagerly as she sat up, her eyes fixed attentively on Quinn's face.

For the second time, Honor's daughter caught Quinn off guard, and she found herself at a loss for words. Helplessly, she looked at Honor. "Uh..."

"Quinn just moved here, honey," Honor said gently. "She's awfully busy right now."

"Maybe someday, though, right?"

"Maybe," Quinn said awkwardly.

"Thanks," Honor said softly as she lifted Arly down from the stretcher.

Quinn smiled into Honor's eyes, warmed by the tenderness in her voice. "Sure."

"I'm going to need to take off early today so I can get her home. I'll see you tomorrow."

Nodding, Quinn watched mother and daughter disappear with Linda, leaving her in the empty room with the discarded dressings and used instruments. She suddenly felt as abandoned as the space around her. That was often the case after the intense high of dealing with an emergency, but this time she missed more than the adrenaline rush. She missed the heat of Honor's gaze upon her face.

She was checking the tray to be sure that all the needl had been deposited in the sharps bin for disposal when Lin returned.

"Nice job, Doc."

"Great kid," Quinn observed. "How old is she? Eight?"

Linda had to stop and think, putting her two kids and Arly in order. "Almost. She was born right at the end of Honor's fourth year in medical school."

"She looks like she was cloned. She's got Honor's eyes and just about everything else, too."

"She does," Linda agreed, intrigued by Quinn's pensive expression.

Quinn cleared her throat. "Uh, what does Honor's husband do?"

"Honor doesn't have a husband." Linda delivered the statement calmly as she wrapped up the instruments, sneaking a quick peek in Quinn's direction to judge its effect. She smiled when she saw the quick look of pleasure followed by consternation cross the attractive surgeon's face. *Uh-huh, yes, she's interested.*

"Oh." Quinn leaned her shoulder against the door frame, considering the possibilities. *Separated? That would explain the wedding ring still. Divorced? No, she wouldn't still be wearing his ring, would she? Gay? Maybe, because Linda sure is, considering the hug she gave the redhead in the ER earlier.* Quinn gave herself a mental shake. Regardless of the answer, it didn't concern her, because that ring spelled unavailable. "I'd better get back out there. Are the charts piling up?"

"The usual. Listen, we're having a barbecue at my place on Saturday afternoon. Most of the ER staff and some people from the neighborhood will be there. One o'clock."

Quinn's immediate reaction was to make an excuse and beg off. She didn't particularly like social situations in which she didn't know anyone. On the other hand, Honor would be there. *Yeah, like that makes any difference.* To her surprise, she found herself saying, "Sure. Thanks. Can I bring something?"

"How about wine? We never think to buy any."

"No problem."

"Excellent. It'll be fun."

"Thanks again."

Linda stared after Quinn as she disappeared through the curtain, thinking of the way Honor had looked at Quinn as she had taken care of Arly. Appreciatively, which was understandable. But there had been more than gratitude in Honor's face; there had been something that she hadn't seen in her good friend's face in years. Something that looked a lot like attraction. That brought up the image of Quinn's expression as she had asked about Honor's husband. Curious and hopeful. *Oh yes, plenty of interest all the way around.*

❖

At a little before 7:00 p.m., Quinn looked up from the nurses' station where she was completing the follow-up instructions for a seventeen-year-old with a badly sprained right ankle to see Honor, in blue jeans and a faded red polo shirt, coming down the hall. The red of the shirt echoed the highlights in her hair, and her dark eyes shimmered with warmth and the promise of laughter. For an instant, Quinn allowed herself to simply enjoy the sight of her. Then she realized that Honor was regarding her quizzically and that she had been staring at the emergency room chief, very possibly with her mouth hanging open. For the second time in the same day, Quinn blushed.

"Everything okay?" Quinn asked, trying to sound nonchalant, but feeling her heart race.

Honor nodded, aware of Quinn's gaze and, despite her misgivings, enjoying it. "I left in such a hurry earlier, I forgot to finish some paperwork that's already late."

"How's our patient?"

"At the moment, she's ensconced in front of the television with an enormous ice pack on her eye and her grandmother fussing over her." Honor smiled softly. "She's fine. She's actually very tough, and she's already asking me if she's going to be able to go to soccer practice tomorrow afternoon."

"Good." Quinn sat on one of the rolling stools a foot away from Honor, her face at about the level of the other woman's breasts. She tried very hard to cast her gaze elsewhere, but nothing could prevent her from sensing the heat of Honor's body so near. She could smell her sweet fragrance, a lush earthy scent. Never in her memory could she recall being so affected by the mere presence of a woman.

Honor leaned her hip against the counter. "I want to thank you for how good you were with her earlier."

"You're welcome, but thanks are not necessary. I'm glad it wasn't too bad for her."

"It's her first big sports injury." Honor grinned ruefully. "Since she's quite the up-and-coming jock, I'm sure there will be more."

"Well, hopefully you won't require my services too often."

"No," Honor replied softly, thinking how gentle Quinn had been. "Hopefully not."

Quinn was surprised when Honor reached out and lightly touched her shoulder, but before she could respond, Honor turned and walked away. Quinn was left staring after her, her skin tingling beneath the cotton of her scrub shirt. Forcefully, she reminded herself that the gesture had been innocent and that the events of the day had made it very clear that Honor was not available for casual flirtations. *Not only married, but married with children. Get a grip.*

And casual flirtations were the only thing that interested Quinn currently. Her life was much too unsettled to contemplate anything else, even had she desired it. Which she didn't.

She put her mind to the task of completing the paperwork on her remaining patients, and forty-five minutes later, she stepped out through the emergency room doors into a vicious summer storm. The sky was gray-black with rolling thunderclouds, lightning slashed sporadically, striking fiery fingers into the very treetops nearby, and a fierce wind whipped icy bullets of rain into her face. Quinn dug her denim jacket out of her backpack, shrugged it on, and pulled the collar high around her neck in an unsuccessful attempt to keep the rain from running down her back while she unlocked her bicycle.

"You can't ride in this storm!" Honor called from nearby.

Turning her head, Quinn blinked at the rivulets of water streaming into her eyes. She had to shout to be heard above the wind and rain. "It's not far! I'll be fine."

"That's insane!" Honor grabbed Quinn's arm and tugged. "Come on—we'll put your bike in my car, and I'll drive you home."

Quinn saw no point in arguing while they both got drenched to the skin. She merely grabbed her bike and followed as Honor ran to the parking lot opposite the emergency room entrance. Before they had even reached the Subaru station wagon, Honor had keyed the remote to unlock the doors. After Quinn hefted the bike into the back, they both piled into the front seats in a breathless rush.

"God, that's brutal," Honor gasped. Soaked to the skin and freezing, she started the car and prayed that the heater would warm up quickly. She glanced at Quinn, who was running her hands through her sopping hair. "Has it occurred to you that riding a bicycle in this is inviting lightning to strike?"

"One in a million chance." Quinn grinned.

"Well, I'd prefer not to have to defibrillate you, all the same." To Honor's surprise, Quinn actually paled. It was the first time Honor had ever seen Quinn appear even slightly off balance, and—even more than that—there was a fleeting shadow of pain in her expression. Without thinking, she rested her hand on Quinn's thigh, feeling the muscles beneath her fingers tighten in response. "You okay?"

Quinn glanced down, unable to understand what Honor's hand was doing on her leg. The graceful fingers curling gently over the arch of her midthigh looked completely natural there. She had to resist the urge to put her own fingers over Honor's. The touch was electric, and her stomach clenched with the swift rush of arousal. She sat very still as she struggled to answer.

"Yes." Quinn's voice was low and husky. "Fine."

Beneath her fingertips, Honor was aware of Quinn trembling faintly. She was also aware of the fact that she liked the way the lean, tight thigh felt. As casually as she could, she withdrew her hand.

"We're both soaked. We'd better get going."

"Yes."

Even with traffic crawling because of the poor visibility and occasional tree branch blowing into the road, it took less than fifteen minutes to reach their neighborhood.

"My house is just up the block," Honor remarked, the first words either of them had spoken since leaving the hospital. "Where are you?"

"Just around the corner there on Morris. I can walk—"

"Of course not," Honor said emphatically. "I'll just circle the block and drop you off. It's no problem."

"Thanks. I appreciate it."

Two minutes later, Honor pulled to the curb in front of the house that Quinn indicated. "Well, I'll see you tomorrow, then."

"Will do." Quinn pushed the door open, stepped out into the downpour, and looked back into the car. "Thanks again, Honor."

Honor just nodded, waited while Quinn pulled her bike from the back, and continued to watch as Quinn made a run for the front porch. For just an instant, she had contemplated inviting Quinn home with her for dinner. She had no idea why, because it was completely out of character for her to be spontaneous in any kind of social situation. All she knew was that she hadn't wanted to say good night to Quinn. And *that* thought was enough to spur her into action. With a quick glance into her mirrors, she pulled away from the curb and headed toward the comfortable security of home.

CHAPTER FIVE

Honor parked in the narrow drive beside her half of a three-story Victorian twin and entered through the back door into the kitchen. Her mother-in-law, Phyllis Murphy, was doing dishes in the sink that faced a window overlooking their shared backyard. Phyllis lived in the other half of the twin, the mirror image of Honor's.

At the sound of Honor's arrival, Phyllis turned to survey her with a mild frown on her smooth, heart-shaped face. Although close to sixty, Phyllis could easily be taken for fifteen years younger, with her still-shapely form and her wavy chestnut hair that showed not a trace of gray. Her blue eyes were piercing and bright, and at the moment, sparkling with fond exasperation. "Well, you're a fine spectacle. You're soaking wet. Get out of your shoes right there, and then go directly upstairs and take a warm shower."

Wordlessly, Honor kicked off her shoes. She'd known the woman since she'd been a teenager, and Phyllis was as close to a mother as Honor's own. Now that her parents had retired to the Southwest to escape the cold winters, she saw them only at major holidays. Phyllis, on the other hand, was a central part of her and Arly's daily life. Phyllis not only provided essential child care, she was one of Honor's best friends.

"Where's the munchkin?"

"In the living room. Did you eat?"

"Not yet." Honor pulled a hand towel from a rack above the counter by the sink and gave her head a brisk rubdown, soaking up most of the water from her hair. "I'll fix something—"

"I put a plate for you in the oven. As soon as you've changed, *and* showered, come down and have your dinner."

Honor knew better than to argue. As she passed the older woman, she gave her a fond hug. "Is she okay?"

"Seems to be. Most of the time she forgets about it, and then when she remembers, I think she's rather proud of herself."

"Proud of herself?" Honor raised an eyebrow.

"I think she's looking forward to showing her stitches to all of her friends tomorrow."

Honor laughed. "Sounds like she's going to survive, then. I'll be back in a minute, then you can go home if you want."

"I'm in no hurry," Phyllis replied as she began loading the dishwasher.

On the way down the hall to the main staircase at the opposite end, Honor peeked into the living room with its brick fireplace, walnut hardwood floors, and bay windows. Her daughter sat curled up on the sofa, the television tuned to a nature program, and a dark, curly haired form sprawled in her lap. At Honor's approach, the shapeless black mass metamorphosed into a tail-wagging standard poodle.

"Hi, sweetheart." Honor leaned down to kiss the top of Arly's head and simultaneously scratched behind the dog's ears. "Hiya, Pooch."

"Hi, Mom." Arly gave her mother a smile and then turned her attention back to a caravan of wildebeest trekking across the African savanna.

Honor settled a hip on the arm of the sofa and rested her fingers against the back of her daughter's neck, stroking her softly. "How's your head feel?"

"It hurts a little, but most of the time it's okay."

"Good." Honor tipped Arly's chin up and studied her face. "Hmm. You have a shiner."

"What's that?"

"A black-and-blue mark like when you bang your knee—"

"Or get bumped in the game."

"Yep. Except this time it's around your eye."

"Why's it called a shiner?"

Honor considered that. "Beats me."

"It's cool though, huh?"

"Very. I'm going to change my clothes, and then it's time for you to go to bed." Honor leaned down and kissed her again. "Come upstairs when I call you, okay?"

"Uh-huh. Can you read me the part about Muggle medicine again?"

"You don't want to do the reading out loud tonight?"

Arly shook her head. "Will you?"

"You bet."

Five minutes later, Honor stepped into the steaming shower, leaned against the slick tiles with a weary sigh, and closed her eyes. The warm water felt wonderful after the chill of the cold rain and her damp clothes. She was emotionally exhausted from the stress and brief panic surrounding Arly's injury. As tired as she was, however, she was aware of an unexpected undercurrent of exhilaration, a sense of anticipation, although she had absolutely no idea of what. Or why. *Odd,* she mused. *There's nothing new going on in my life that I can think of.*

Out of nowhere, the image of Quinn, her blue eyes intense and her expression kind, bending over Arly in the ER that afternoon flashed through Honor's mind. In the next instant, she felt the taut muscles of that long, lean thigh under her fingers and saw again Quinn shake the rainwater from her hair. *She looked so wild, so... sexy, just then.* A shiver passed down Honor's spine and a stirring in her stomach, so long forgotten that she barely recognized it, caused her to catch her breath in surprise.

Oh no, I must really *be tired. It's just that she was so wonderful with Arly. That's all it is. Gratitude.*

Ignoring the faint pulse of excitement that accompanied the unbidden memory, Honor quickly finished her shower, pulled on sweatpants and an oversized T-shirt emblazoned with the PMC logo, and called for Arly to come to bed. Her daughter was apparently more tired out by the afternoon's events than Honor had realized, because she had barely begun reading when Arly dropped off. Carefully, Honor closed the book, turned off the bedside light, and crept quietly from the room.

Downstairs, she found Phyllis at the kitchen table with a cup of coffee and Pooch beneath her feet, watching her with a hopeful expression.

"You're not feeding him from the table, are you?" Honor helped herself to a cup of coffee and sat down opposite her mother-in-law at the rectangular oak peasant table.

"He only gets sushi, because he likes to eat off the chopsticks."

Honor nodded as if that made perfect sense. "Thanks for leaving school early so I could go back to the hospital."

Phyllis was an administrator at Green Street Friends School, where Robin and Linda's two children, Dennis and Kim, and Arly were students. Usually, Robin picked all three children up when their after-school activities were over and kept them at her house until Phyllis came by for Arly at the end of her workday. Since Robin was one of the soccer coaches and all three children played, it made that simple. During the summer, all the kids were at day camp, so the same arrangement worked well.

In the evening, Phyllis usually made dinner at Honor's. When an emergency came up that kept Honor in the ER longer than usual, or when she was on night duty, Phyllis stayed with Arly or took her granddaughter to the other half of the house, where Arly had her own room as well.

"No need for thanks," Phyllis said quietly. "I'm just grateful she's got a hard head."

Honor imagined that Phyllis had been as shaken as she herself had been initially, even though when she had called the older woman at work to tell her about Arly's injury, her first words had been that it was only a *minor* accident and that Arly was fine. Nevertheless, she knew that neither of them would ever be able to hear the word *accident* without an involuntary surge of dread. Honor slid her fingers over Phyllis's hand and squeezed.

"She's going to be just fine."

"I know." Phyllis smiled. "Actually, she couldn't stop talking about it. Seems like she made a friend at the hospital."

Honor looked inquisitively at her mother-in-law.

"Someone named Quinn?"

"Ah," Honor sighed, "that would be the new ER attending, Quinn Maguire. She's the one who put in the sutures."

"Sounds like she's a cross between a savior and a soccer star."

"Hardly. But she *was* great with Arly."

Phyllis heard the note of reservation in Honor's voice. "You don't like her?"

"No," Honor said quickly, blushing. "No, it's not that. It's... complicated."

"Complicated how?"

"I don't know *what* it is, really." Honor ran a hand distractedly through her hair, frowning at her own jumbled thoughts. It was hard to recall just what exactly about Quinn bothered her, especially when she remembered sitting with her in the car while the rain beat down around them, enclosing them in a thundering gray cocoon, and seeing that sliver of pain flash across Quinn's expressive face. "She was hired without my input, so that annoyed me at first. Her qualifications don't really fit the job description, so that makes me suspicious of a problem in her background."

"Don't fit how?"

"She's not trained in emergency medicine; she's trained in surgery. There's no reason she should want this position."

"Is she doing a good job?" Phyllis continued her gentle probing because she and Honor often talked over Honor's frustrations and triumphs at work. More than that, she sensed that her daughter-in-law was troubled.

"Yes. Fine. Considering her training wasn't in emergency medicine, better than I had hoped at this point." Honor sipped her coffee, finally feeling warm. "She works hard, never complains, and is reasonably good natured about what has to be a difficult adjustment for her."

"Sounds like she's a great new addition to your staff, then."

"I suppose you're right." Honor aimlessly turned her coffee mug on the tabletop, staring at the swirling liquid. "I just can't help feeling that there's something she's hiding."

"We all have things we'd rather not talk about, Honor," Phyllis reminded her gently. "Those things aren't necessarily bad, only painful sometimes."

Honor raised her eyes to Phyllis, and, as was so often the case, they shared a moment of mutual sadness and understanding.

Quinn blinked the sweat from her eyes, and despite the ominous shaking in her arms, pushed the barbell straight up in the air one more time and slowly lowered it until it almost touched her chest. She held it to the count of two, then laboriously raised it and levered it back onto the cleats. With a gasp of relief, she closed her eyes and let her arms hang down by her sides as she waited for her breathing to return to normal. She hadn't had a full workout in months, and despite the fact that she had been advised to start slowly, she'd been pushing herself hard for the last hour. Now her entire body was so tired, she wasn't certain she could sit up. Absently, she reached up with her right hand and rubbed the annoying itch above her left breast.

"I wasn't certain you were going to make that last one," a soft voice with a sensuous drawl said from beside her.

Quinn turned her head, opened her eyes, and looked into the emerald green eyes inches from her own. Those striking eyes, shadowed by long honey-colored lashes, were set in a Meryl Streep face that was framed by thick blond hair. Quinn blinked. "Hello?"

The wide, full mouth stretched into a lazy smile. "Hello yourself. I'm Mandy."

"Quinn."

Mandy, who crouched beside Quinn, wore a black jog bra and spandex workout shorts that left her toned midriff bare and showed off the rest of her body to perfection. She rested her fingertips lightly on Quinn's left upper arm. "I know this sounds like a line, but are you new in town?"

"I've been here a few weeks." Quinn laughed and pushed herself upright on the workout bench, then swung around until she faced the kneeling woman. "First time *here,* though."

"I'm one of the personal trainers. I was going to ask you if you needed any help, but I can see that you don't." As she spoke, Mandy's eyes drifted slowly down Quinn's body.

Quinn wore gray Champion shorts and a T-shirt that had been cut off above the waist and at the shoulders. Her skin shone lightly with perspiration. She was warm, and it wasn't entirely from the workout. Mandy's gaze was openly appreciative, and it didn't escape Quinn's notice either that Mandy's hand now rested ever so gently against Quinn's knee. Unexpectedly, Quinn felt her heart race.

Mandy gave a startled laugh and pulled her hand back. "God, I believe I felt sparks!"

Quinn blushed, quickly suppressing a gasp. "I think that's what you call static electricity."

"Really," Mandy said disbelievingly, tilting her head and giving Quinn another lazy smile. "Whatever you call it, it was nice."

Abruptly, Quinn stood, anticipating the dizziness and waiting for it to pass. "I've got to run. It was nice meeting you, Mandy."

Mandy rose to her feet, momentarily barring Quinn's path. "It was nice meeting you, too, Quinn. I hope I'll be seeing you again soon."

"I'm sure I'll run into you here. Night."

It was after ten, and, deciding to shower at home, Quinn hurriedly packed her gear. Outside, the storm had abated, leaving behind only a thick clinging mist that shimmered in the air and felt heavy on her skin. The health club that she had discovered in the neighborhood guide and had joined just that evening was in Alden Park, a collection of ornate red stone buildings clustered on a hill overlooking Lincoln Drive and the wild, northern extension of Fairmont Park. It was a brisk ten-minute walk from her apartment, and she decided to take the "long" way home by circling a small corner park that bordered her street to the south.

It was a residential neighborhood and, late on a weeknight, the streets were deserted. Moisture floating in the air cast halos around the streetlights, and as Quinn walked through the dark from one circle of light to the next, she felt isolated and eerily alone. That was a new feeling, that sense of being alone. Or to be accurate, she thought, her *awareness* of being alone.

She'd either been too busy or too focused to notice before. She'd been on the fast track since she was fifteen years old, skipping a year of high school and then entering an accelerated combined college and medical school program. At about the time others her age were finishing college and contemplating the benefits of taking a year off before entering graduate school, she had begun her internship. Nothing had stood in her way, nothing had ever slowed her down, until everything had come to a screeching halt just when she thought she had accomplished her goal.

Quinn was so immersed in her reminiscences that when a shape materialized out of the shadows, she gasped in surprise and stumbled to a halt. Realizing almost immediately that it was just another late-night stroller, she moved forward again, feeling foolish. As the figure neared, she stared, thinking at first that she merely imagined the familiar stride and unmistakable form.

"Honor?" Quinn asked when it became apparent that she had not been mistaken.

Honor halted within touching distance of Quinn, and Pooch obediently sat at her side. She brushed her hair back with one hand, taking a moment to hide her discomfort. She had been thinking about Quinn, remembering the events of the afternoon again, and to see her suddenly appear was disorienting. "Hi. I...uh..." She motioned to Pooch with her chin. "Walking the dog."

"I see that." Quinn extended her fingers toward the dog and got a warm lick as a reward. "Hi, pooch."

"Yes." Honor laughed. "That's him. Pooch."

Quinn raised a brow.

"His name. Pooch."

"Ah!" Quinn laughed. "He's very well behaved."

"That's an anomaly, I can assure you." Honor smiled, feeling foolish for her previous discomfort. "What about you? Kind of late for a stroll."

Quinn lifted her gym bag. "Working out."

Honor shook her head. "Don't you ever relax?"

"It was either that or unpack boxes." Quinn shrugged. "Seemed like a no-brainer to me."

By silent agreement, Honor turned around, and together they walked in the direction of their homes, making intermittent stops so that Pooch could smell a particularly delightful morsel of trash or leave his mark on top of one left by some interloper into his territory.

"I take it you didn't have much time to move," Honor said conversationally.

Quinn hesitated, then said, "I wasn't certain I would get this job, and then when I did, I only had a couple of weeks to find a place to live. I was lucky to get one so close to work."

"Do you intend to bike all winter?"

"As long as I can. I can always walk if the weather gets too bad."

Honor laughed. "I think you'll change your mind round about January. I'll see what I can do about getting you a parking space in the doctors' lot. They're rare as hen's teeth, but I'll cash in on some favors."

"Don't bother," Quinn said without thinking. "I can't drive."

"What? You don't know how to drive?"

"No, I...uh...*don't* drive," Quinn amended quickly. "No car."

Honor cocked her head and gave Quinn a curious stare. *She's lying.* She knew it as surely as she had ever known anything. *But why?*

"Well, then. I'll hold on to those favors."

"Thanks anyways," Quinn said awkwardly. Being around Honor made her forget her usual caution, which was not only disconcerting, but dangerous.

"This is my house," Honor said, indicating a dwelling set back from the street behind a white picket fence.

"Good night, Honor," Quinn said softly.

"See you tomorrow." Honor turned quickly into the driveway, pulling Pooch along while ignoring the insistent urge to watch until Quinn disappeared from sight. But as much as she would have liked to, it was hard to deny that she was already looking forward to seeing Quinn in the morning.

CHAPTER SIX

Honor leaned over the bed, her stethoscope against the chest of a ten-year-old asthmatic, listening to the air flow in and out with each cycle of respiration. A few scattered wheezes still remained, but she was satisfied that the inhalation therapy she had prescribed to ease the constriction in the little boy's bronchial passages had begun to work. She looked up as Linda poked her head around the edge of the curtain. The expression on Linda's face brought Honor hurrying toward her.

"What is it?" From the alarm on her friend's face, she expected to hear that there'd been a multivehicular crash on the Schuylkill Expressway and that they were expecting six major traumas.

"Rodney just called from the job site. There's been an accident."

"Accident? What kind of accident?"

"I don't know. Something about Terry being in an accident. Then the ambulance arrived and he had to go."

"Ambulance? For Terry?*" Honor's heart began to race. "Terry's been in an accident? What happened?"*

"That's all he said, honey. That's all I know."

Honor looked around the emergency room as if seeing it for the first time. Everything was so white, so sterile, so incredibly impersonal. Terry. They're bringing Terry here. *Honor was a second-year resident, and until two minutes ago, she had thought she could handle anything.* Terry. *She took a breath, reminded herself that this was her domain, her kingdom. She* could *handle what was coming. That's what she did. She'd take care of Terry.*

"Did they say how bad?" Her voice came out hoarse, but steady.

"Nothing." Linda's eyes were round, the pupils dilated. "Rodney...wasn't making a lot of sense. I'm sorry."

Honor's chest was tight, every breath an effort, and when she started toward trauma one, she found that her feet would barely move. Surely it's nothing serious. Contractors are always getting banged up. Twisted knees, jammed shoulders, bumps on the head. God, I hope she wasn't fooling around with the carpenters again. She knows how much I hate her doing anything with those damn power tools. She's supposed to be the job foreman—keeping the crews organized—not spending her time actually rebuilding the damn houses!

"Can you get the ambulance on the radio?" Honor finally managed to start moving. "Get an update on her condition?"

"Sure." Linda nodded vigorously. "Right away."

Before Linda had a chance to make that call, the ambulance bay doors burst open and three EMTs pushing a stretcher came crashing through. One look at the still form strapped to a backboard with sandbags on either side of the pale face turned Honor's legs to jelly, and her stomach heaved. Not just a minor accident. Oh my God.

When she tried to speak, no words came out. When she tried to raise her hand, her arm felt leaden. As if in a dream, she watched, nearly paralyzed, as Linda directed the EMTs into the procedure room. Two ER attendings, another resident, and as many nurses rushed after them. Finally, Honor followed.

At the threshold, Honor halted, staring at the flurry of activity surrounding her lover. She recognized the routine, but it seemed so out of place with Terry lying there so still. After only a moment, the activity abruptly halted, and Linda materialized from the crowd, a strange look in her eyes. She walked to Honor and took her arm.

"Come over here, honey."

Honor protested when Linda started to draw her away from the room. "No. I have to help. I have to take care of her."

"Honor...Honor, sweetheart, her neck is broken. It must have been instantaneous." Linda's face was white. "There's nothing they can do. She's dead, sweetheart."

"Of course she isn't. That's ridiculous." Honor turned and started back toward trauma one. This time, it was as if she were

swimming against a tidal wave. As hard as she tried, she couldn't seem to make any progress. It was difficult to see, there was so much water in her eyes. She kept wiping them, but the moisture covered her cheeks, blurring her vision. Beneath the roar of the rushing water, she could hear Linda's voice, soothing and gentle.

"Honor. She's gone."

By the time Honor forced her way through the crowd, she could see through her tears. That's when she knew they were wrong. Terry was just asleep. There wasn't a mark on her face or her body. Her eyes were closed, her expression peaceful, and she was warm when Honor rested her fingers against her cheek. Her lover looked just exactly as she had that morning, still bundled under the covers of their bed, when Honor had kissed her goodbye. Of course she wasn't gone.

"Terry, honey?" Honor leaned down, her lips close to her lover's ear. She could smell the distinct scent of her shampoo. "It's Honor, love. Can you please just wake up for a few minutes? I only want to hear your voice, and then you can go right back to sleep. I promise."

Linda, tears streaming down her cheeks, wrapped her arm around Honor's waist. "Sweetheart, she can't hear you. She's gone, baby."

Honor straightened, furious. "Will you stop saying that! Can't you see she's just asleep?"

Over Linda's shoulder, Honor could see the expressions on the faces of her friends and colleagues. Pity, sadness, compassion. She reached out and picked up Terry's left hand, running her thumb over the gold band on her ring finger that matched her own. With her other hand, she brushed the hair from her lover's forehead, then leaned down again and softly kissed her lips. "I love you. You know that, right? Forever and always."

With a start, Honor jerked awake, gasping. The room was dark, and when she turned her head, she saw that there were still fifteen minutes until her alarm was due to go off. Heart pounding, she lay in the damp sheets, waiting for the faint nausea to pass.

God, I haven't dreamt of that in so long.

For the first year after Terry's death, she had revisited the scene countless times, in her dreams and in her waking moments. Sometimes it had been with the absolute clarity of perfect recall, as this dream had been, other times merely a jumble of distorted images as she searched frantically through dark mists and frightening shadows, knowing that Terry was waiting for her just at the edge of awakening. But each time she awakened, she had been alone.

As the years had passed, the dreams had become less frequent and eventually had stopped.

Six years, and I still miss you so much.

With a sigh, Honor rolled over and turned off the alarm. She slipped from bed and reached for the robe thrown over the nearby ancient upholstered reading chair. Pulling it on as she walked, she padded quietly down the hall to Arly's room. She peeked inside and saw with relief that her daughter was sleeping soundly. There had been a time when Honor's nightmares had been accompanied by screams. Thankfully, that had stopped.

Arly had been just over a year old when Terry had died and had no memory of her. Honor had never been sure whether that was a good or bad thing. She was happy that their daughter had not consciously suffered the loss of a mother, but she would be eternally saddened that Arly would never know Terry, who had dreamed along with Honor of conceiving her and raising her together as a family.

Sighing, pushing the memories aside, Honor headed downstairs to start the coffee. Phyllis would arrive soon to get Arly off to day camp after Honor left for work. She had just finished pouring her first cup when Phyllis came in through the back door.

"Rough night?" Phyllis asked as she helped herself to coffee.

"How do you do that?"

"Do what?" Phyllis brushed the tousled bangs off Honor's forehead.

"Always know."

Phyllis shrugged. "You have incredibly expressive eyes. And this morning, they're sad."

"Just bad dreams." Honor smiled wanly, knowing she didn't have to explain. Phyllis had moved in with Honor and Arly after Terry's death and had stayed for six months before "moving" back to the other half of the twin. She'd been there for the nightmares and the screams and the agony of loss, bearing up under her own pain to help her daughter's lover cope.

"Something happen to get you stirred up?"

"No, why?" Honor knew she sounded defensive and had no idea why. Thankfully, Phyllis didn't seem offended.

"It's been a long time since you've been bothered. When things come up again like that, it's usually because something has changed."

"Nothing has changed." Abruptly, Honor took her coffee cup and headed toward the winding rear stairs that led from the kitchen to the floor above. "I've got to get moving or else I'll be late."

Wordlessly, Phyllis watched her go. She loved Honor every bit as much as she had loved Terry, and watching Honor's devastation had pained her almost as much as the agony of losing her child. The sadness of that loss was eternal, and she would always miss Terry, but with time, she had let go of the pain. She had always hoped that someday Honor would as well.

Everyone comes to their own truth in their own time, she reminded herself. *Honor will do the same.*

❖

Quinn rolled over in her sleeping bag with a groan and grabbed her right shoulder. A cramp so severe she wanted to scream out loud gripped her trapezius muscle, and it took her a full thirty seconds of massaging it before the charley horse eased. She flopped onto her back and stared at the ceiling.

"That's it. Tomorrow I'm getting the bedroom together."

The next day she was off. She could spend the entire morning getting her apartment organized. Then she remembered Linda's barbecue in the afternoon and briefly contemplated canceling, but feared that if she did, Linda might show up on her doorstep demanding to know where she was. The woman was persistent.

And, Quinn had to admit, she was looking forward to seeing Honor away from the emergency room. Although why, she couldn't imagine. Honor showed not the slightest interest in her, and she was clearly involved in a relationship.

"That's probably just what I need. As soon as I see her with her partner, I'll stop thinking about her smile."

As she heaved herself to her feet and rummaged around in a nearby carton for clean jeans and a shirt, Quinn tried to pretend that she wasn't lying to herself.

❖

"There's our intrepid new attending," Linda commented as she pulled the car wide around Quinn on her bicycle. It had stopped raining, but the streets were still slick.

Honor glanced out the window from the passenger seat as they passed Quinn. "God, you'd think she'd at least have the good sense to wear a helmet."

"There's hardly much traffic at this time, or on *this* street at any time of day," Linda pointed out, surprised at the vehemence in Honor's voice.

"All it takes is one car to hit her."

"You okay?"

"Yes, of course."

Linda spared her friend a quick glance, noting the dark circles beneath her eyes. "You don't look okay. Is Arly all right?"

"She's doing fine. The first thing she did when she woke up this morning was run into the bathroom to look at her eye. Now she can't wait to show everyone at school."

Both women laughed.

"So what's going on?"

"Absolutely nothing," Honor insisted. "I just didn't sleep well last night."

"Okay. I'll stop nudging."

"Promises, promises."

After gathering their lunches and briefcases from the car, they walked toward the ER. Quinn cycled to a halt nearby and dismounted.

"Hi," Quinn called, shrugging out of her backpack as she looked in their direction.

"Hi." Linda smiled brightly and gave a little wave.

"You ought to get a helmet," Honor noted sharply as she passed.

Quinn stared after her. *Good morning to you, too.*

❖

"I need your opinion," Quinn said quietly, folding her arms on the counter and looking down at Honor, who was seated on the opposite side. When gold-flecked brown eyes met hers, Quinn's pulse gave a little jump. She cleared her throat. "If you've got a minute."

"Of course." Honor initialed the lab report she was reviewing, clipped it to her current patient's chart, and regarded Quinn neutrally. They'd barely said one word to each other for the entire ten hours of the shift. It had been a busy day, but even with that, she had the feeling they were *both* intentionally avoiding one another. Still, seeing her brought a whisper of warmth to Honor's depths. Carefully keeping her voice steady, she asked, "What have you got?"

"A seventeen-year-old girl with severe abdominal pain, nausea, and vomiting."

"Pelvic inflammatory disease?" One of the common causes of abdominal pain in young women was infection in the uterus or fallopian tubes from sexually transmitted diseases, most often gonorrhea. Honor was surprised that Quinn was asking *her* opinion about someone with abdominal pain, because that was one of the classic symptom complexes surgeons were taught to evaluate and diagnose.

"Nope." Quinn turned to face Honor as she came around the counter. They were close enough to touch, but the distance between them was palpable. "She denies recent sexual activity, and I believe her. Her pelvic exam is completely unremarkable."

"You don't think it's surgical, I take it."

"No, I don't. At first I thought it was a simple case of viral gastroenteritis," Quinn said, frowning. "But the symptoms seem too marked for that."

"Food poisoning?"

"That's my working diagnosis, but it just doesn't feel right." Quinn ran a hand through her hair, frustrated. "*She* says she thinks it's from bad seafood that she had last night at a friend's house."

Honor nodded, watching Quinn's eyes darken to nearly purple. *She's so intense. So focused. So...* Abruptly, Honor reached for the chart that Quinn held in her right hand, dragging her eyes from Quinn's face and forcing herself to concentrate. "Does she have a fever or a headache?"

"No. And she says the pain only started two hours ago."

"Where is she? There's something off about this."

Quinn led Honor to the patient's cubicle. When they entered, she said, "Karen, this is Dr. Blake. I've asked her to take a look at you."

The girl, pale and shaking, looked frightened. "Why? What's wrong?"

"We're just trying to figure that out," Honor said kindly. She took the young woman's wrist and felt her pulse, which was weak and racing. The skin beneath her fingers was clammy and damp. As she watched, a tear slid from beneath the girl's lashes. Then another. The girl seemed unaware of the steady trickle.

"We can't take care of you properly if we don't have all the information," Honor said, her eyes fixed on the girl's face. Another tear slid down the pale cheek. "Did you *eat* anything strange, besides the...*seafood?*"

Quinn stood across the bed from Honor, watching. Honor's eyes were compassionate, but she exuded a sense of strength and command that was compelling. She had an air of certainty that made you believe you could lean on her. *Jesus, where did that come from?*

"What do you mean?" The girl's voice was tremulous now.

"Are any of your friends sick, too?"

Friends? Quinn couldn't figure out what was going on, but it was clear that Honor was after something.

"I don't know. I left..." The young woman looked away.

"...the party?" Honor finished.

The girl nodded miserably.

"When was this?"

"This afternoon. A pool party this afternoon."

"And you *all* took the mushrooms?"

Mushrooms? What the hell? Quinn shook her head. *I sure missed the boat on this one.*

At the girl's pitiful expression of assent, Honor turned to Quinn. "*A. muscaria* poisoning...excessive tearing, nausea, vomiting, acute abdominal pain, excess salivation, and a host of other symptoms. Kids take the mushrooms thinking they're going to be hallucinogenic, but most of the time they're just poison."

"Treatment?" Quinn asked sharply.

"She'll need an IV, a gastric washout with activated charcoal to bind whatever toxin hasn't been absorbed from her stomach already, and some medication to counteract what *has* gotten into her system. I'll go over the meds with you in a minute." She turned back to the young patient. "I'll need the address where the party is, and we're going to have to call your parents."

"They're in Martha's Vineyard."

"I guess they'll need to come back, then."

It took close to three hours for Honor and Quinn to stabilize the young woman and the two friends whom the police found in a comparable state of toxicity at the home of one of the teenagers. By that time, it was close to nine p.m.

"Man, am I glad I asked you to take a look at her." Quinn arched her back and groaned. "If I'd sent her home, who knows what would have happened. Christ."

Honor heard the self-recrimination in Quinn's voice. "Listen, Quinn, the important thing is that you sensed that something unusual was going on, and that's what counts down here. No one expects you to know everything."

"*You* seem to know it all."

"Yes, but that's because I'm the boss."

Their eyes held for a second, and then they both laughed.

"So, can I buy you a late dinner?" Quinn asked impulsively. When she saw Honor flush, she realized that the invitation was inappropriate. *What the hell is wrong with me?*

"Uh, thanks. But I should get home. My mother-in-law is with Arly, and—"

"That's okay. I understand," Quinn said quickly. "Thanks for your help, Honor. I appreciate it."

"No problem." For a second, Honor hesitated, thinking that she could call Phyllis and ask her to stay with Arly a little while longer. Then she caught herself. *What am I doing? I can't go out to dinner with her! Mixing business with pleasure is always a bad idea, and Quinn Maguire has trouble written all over her.*

Abruptly, Honor stepped away. "Good night, Quinn."

Quinn just nodded, feeling supremely foolish and inexplicably disappointed.

CHAPTER SEVEN

"So what happened with the mushroom kids?" Linda asked as she arranged carrot and celery sticks on a serving platter. "Sorry I couldn't work overtime and help out. Robin had bowling."

"No problem. Quinn stayed. We finally got them all washed out and stabilized around nine." Honor stirred the sour cream and chives dip and scooped it into a small bowl. "I haven't seen anything like that since I was in college. Thank God I was smart enough then not to try it."

"I'm amazed you recognized it yesterday."

"Classic presentation." Honor shrugged. "It's right there in the ER manual."

"Sure, and so are about a thousand other things."

"I'm lucky. I have a memory for esoteric facts."

"Uh-huh." Linda knew that there was a reason that Honor was the ER chief at such a young age. Honor had been a star, even as a med student. She just had that uncanny sixth sense that made some people true physicians. Honor had the art as well as the skill for healing. "But we both know it takes more than memorizing what's in the book to recognize it when you see it."

Embarrassed by the praise, Honor kept her eyes down, busying herself with peeling potatoes for the salad. "Besides, Quinn was the one to pick up that something was off. I was just the cleanup batter."

"Right." Linda snorted, separating chicken pieces into separate bowls. "I agree with you about Quinn, though. She not only has good hands, she's got good instincts."

Honor thought about Quinn's hands, about how they were a microcosm of the woman herself. Certain and sure in the midst of a crisis, moving with a surgeon's self-assured touch. Then, surprisingly, so gentle and tender when she had cared for Arly. A heady mixture, especially in a woman so confident and attractive and—

"Honor? Hello?"

"Huh?" Honor jumped, startled. "Sorry. I was...wandering."

"I noticed." Linda cocked her head and gave Honor a long stare. "What's up?"

Honor shook her head and reached for the onions. "Absolutely nothing."

❖

Quinn stood in the middle of her living room and turned slowly, surveying her progress. "Not bad."

She'd jockeyed the two bookcàses against the wall opposite the windows and unpacked most of her books. The sofa and the television were situated so she could sit on one and see the other. She needed a coffee table, she realized. She had nowhere to put her feet *or* her dinner while watching the news. She hadn't acquired much furniture while in Manhattan, because she had subleased a furnished apartment during her year of trauma training. She had planned to buy a place once she had settled into her new position as an attending at St. Michael's. Now, she wasn't sure what she would be doing in another year.

No point going there. Time to start on the bedroom. She tried to remember where she had seen the box marked Sheets and, on her way down the hall, glanced at the plain, round clock she had hung from a hook in the kitchen. *Almost noon.* She skittered to a stop.

"Hell. I still have to shower, get dressed, and figure out where to buy wine." A surge of happiness caused her to smile. "Guess I can't do any more unpacking."

Thirty minutes later, she was clean and dressed in faded jeans, Nike running shoes, and a navy blue polo shirt. She spread out the plastic city street map on the kitchen counter and opened the neighborhood guide next to it. She found an ad for a wine and liquor store in her zip code and traced the street names on the map until she knew how to get there. She slid her wallet into her rear pocket, her keys into her right front one, and set out for the barbecue.

Once in the liquor store, she took a few minutes to choose both a bottle of red and a bottle of white wine. Then it occurred to her that she should bring something for the hostess.

"Where's Jude when I *really* need advice?" she muttered to herself. Saxon Sinclair had been more than just Quinn's former boss. The chief of trauma at St. Michael's, and her partner, Jude Castle, a documentary filmmaker, had been good friends. The year of her trauma fellowship had been an intense time when she had spent nearly seventy-five percent of her waking hours in Sinclair's company. In addition to their constant physical proximity and similar professional goals, they had discovered a number of other interests in common. Now Quinn owed her present job to Sax and a great deal of her sanity to Jude.

Giving herself a shake, Quinn took the wine to the counter and paid. Then she stepped out onto the sidewalk and looked around for some kind of shop where she could pick up a small thank-you gift for Linda.

❖

"Honor, could you get that?" Linda, up to her wrists in potato salad, asked when the doorbell rang.

"Sure." Honor reached for the dish towel and dried her hands on the way through the house to the front door. She pushed the screen door open and regarded the woman who stood on the other side with her arms laden with packages. She took in the dark blue shirt that matched the gorgeous eyes and the long, clean lines of her, liking the way she looked with that half-shy, half-cocky grin on her handsome face. "Hi, Quinn."

"Hi." Quinn's initial surprise at seeing Honor at the door was quickly eclipsed by the sight of Honor in casual clothes. She wore cargo shorts and a cotton T-shirt that displayed her smoothly toned arms and legs. Her hair was pulled back with some kind of tie at the back and she looked about twenty. For some reason, Quinn always had difficulty not looking at Honor's breasts, and today was no exception. The T-shirt clung to her curves in all the right places, leaving just enough to the imagination to make Quinn's throat go dry and her pulse race.

Both women jumped at the sound of Linda's voice behind them.

"I thought maybe you got lost out here, Honor. Hi, Quinn." Linda looked from her friend to Quinn and back again, noting the simultaneous blushes and shuffling feet. Smiling to herself, she reached out her arms. "I take it those are for me?"

"Yeah," Quinn mumbled as she shifted bags around, handing over the wine. "I got red and white, because I couldn't figure out what else to do."

Both Honor and Linda laughed. Honor finally stepped aside so Quinn could enter.

"And this is for you and your family." Quinn held out a rectangular package about the size of a shoe box.

"Oh, a present!" Linda shamelessly clutched the box to her chest while simultaneously pushing the wine into Honor's arms. "I *love* presents. Let's go into the kitchen so I can open this."

Not waiting for a reply, Linda turned and hurried away, leaving Honor and Quinn to follow.

"How did you know?" Honor asked, laughing gently.

"Know what?"

"That she adores surprises."

"Just lucky."

Honor glanced up at Quinn, aware that Quinn had been watching her intently as they walked through the house. "That was very nice of you."

"It was kind of her to invite me."

Yes, and I didn't want her to. At the moment, Honor couldn't remember why that was. She was inexplicably happy to see her new colleague.

"Will you two hurry up," Linda called from the kitchen.

"Go ahead, open the darn thing," Honor said affectionately as she and Quinn crowded around Linda at the kitchen table.

Linda lifted the lid from the box and carefully folded back the tissue paper, giving a small cry of pleasure. Carefully, she lifted out a small crystal wind chime. The delicate glass rods, suspended from a polished silver disk by clear nylon strands, varied in length from four to ten inches and sparkled with a rainbow of colors. When she gently brushed them with her fingers, the tinkling sounds were high and pure.

"It's beautiful," Linda breathed. She glanced at Quinn in delight. "Thank you so much. That was so kind of you."

Quinn blushed. "My pleasure."

"I think we should put it in the tree in the backyard, don't you, Honor?"

"Sure. You'll be able to hear it inside when the windows are open."

"Could you put it up now?" Linda gave Honor a hopeful glance. "Pleeaase?"

Honor smiled, shaking her head. "Can *anyone* ever say no to you?"

"Not that I can ever recall," Robin said fondly as she came through the back door. She nodded at Quinn and extended her hand. "Hi. I'm Robin, Linda's spouse."

"Quinn Maguire." Quinn took the sturdy hand and shook it firmly. "Nice to meet you."

"Look, honey." Linda held up the wind chime, causing the rods to ring melodiously once again. "Quinn brought it for us. Isn't it great?"

"Beautiful." Robin slid her arm around Linda's waist and kissed her cheek. "*I'd* put it up for you myself, but I just fired up the grill. Aren't I supposed to be cooking something?"

"You go tend to the barbecue," Honor said, reaching for the wind chimes. "I'll put this up. Where's the ladder?"

"In the garage," Robin said. "If you give me a minute, I'll get it for you."

Honor shook her head. "Never mind. I can find it. The tools are in there, too, aren't they?"

"Wait until Robin can help," Linda cautioned. "I don't want you climbing up in that tree by yourself. All we need is for you to fall and break your ne..."

Linda's face paled as her words trailed off. She looked stricken.

Honor blinked, then gave her friend a kind smile. Her voice was gentle when she spoke. "Not to worry."

"I'll give her a hand," Quinn volunteered into the silence that ensued. She glanced at Honor, trying to decipher the expression on her face. Not unhappiness exactly—more like a poignant sadness. Hesitantly, she added, "If that's okay."

"Perfect," Linda said, squeezing Honor's hand and then making shooing motions with her own. "Everybody out so I can get the rest of this organized. Robin, who has kid duty?"

"Phyllis is playing Trivial Pursuit Junior with the older ones, and Bill and Sue are taking a lifeguard shift by the pool."

"Okay, then. All bases are covered. Go. Go."

Obediently, the three trooped out. Quinn and Honor headed for the garage behind the house while Robin returned to the center of activity in the backyard.

"Looks like quite a crowd," Quinn observed, taking in the gathering of men, women, and children of all ages. She had a moment of feeling completely out of place, but when she glanced at Honor, she didn't care. She just liked being around her.

"Linda and Robin's parties are legend. Plus, once they invite all their kids' friends, then they have to invite all the parents. Most everybody knows everybody else because of soccer, anyhow."

"Soccer is big here, I take it," Quinn remarked, standing aside as Honor rolled up the garage door.

"You could say that." Honor laughed. "From the middle of the summer until the snow falls, our lives revolve around soccer. Afternoon practices, Saturday morning games—which, by the way, start next weekend—and all of the events surrounding that. It's a social phenomenon."

"Sounds like fun." Quinn realized that she meant it. She hadn't done much of anything except study and work for over a decade. She had participated in organized sports in college, but once involved in the clinical portion of her medical training, followed quickly by residency, she hadn't done anything except work. It occurred to her as she watched Honor sorting through a toolbox that she'd never had anything approaching a normal life. She wasn't sure she wanted one. Or that she'd know what to do, even if she had one. *That hardly matters, since it's not likely to happen.*

Honor turned abruptly, a hammer in her hand, and caught the contemplative look on Quinn's face. Those piercing blue eyes were fixed on her, but Honor didn't think the other woman was actually seeing her. She appeared lost in thought, and there was a hint of both melancholy and resignation in her expression. It surprised Honor and just as quickly touched a chord in her. For one wild moment, she had the irrational urge to reach out and stroke Quinn's cheek.

"Found it," Honor said softly.

Quinn gave a small start, then smiled sheepishly. "How about the ladder?"

"Over there," Honor indicated with an index finger. "Can you handle it? I'm going to hunt for a hook of some kind."

"No problem." Quinn took the ladder down from the double hooks that held it to the wall and rested it over one shoulder. She carefully maneuvered it out of the garage, taking care not to pivot abruptly and endanger Honor's head. "Ready when you are."

Honor, carrying the tools and the wind chime, led the way around the periphery of the crowd toward a large maple that loomed high above the rear corner of the house. A horizontal limb stretched out above the back deck below and arched over the slanted roof toward the rear bedroom windows. Honor pointed upward. "That's Linda and Robin's bedroom. If we get this up on that branch, they'll be able to hear it in the house."

Quinn craned her neck and estimated the distance. "It's probably twenty feet up to that limb. How are you on heights?"

"Piece of cake." Honor studied Quinn speculatively. "Why?"

"I...uh...I hate being more than two feet above sea level. I have to take Valium to get into an airplane."

"Why, Dr. Maguire," Honor laughed, charmed by the genuine blush that suffused Quinn's face. "I never would have imagined that a stunning butch like you would be afraid of anything."

Quinn's mouth dropped open at precisely the same instant that Honor's eyes grew wide with shock.

Oh my God, I can't believe I just said that.

Did she just say that I was stunning?

"I mean...that is..."

"Ah...I..."

Honor finally recovered her voice, if not her composure. She pointed over her head with the hammer. "Shall we?"

Quinn nodded, then realized that she still held the ladder balanced on her shoulder and quickly moved forward. She found level ground for the foot supports and braced the top against the tree limb. Just looking up made her queasy. As Honor stepped onto the first rung, she murmured, "I'm quite happy to be out-butched in this particular instance, Dr. Blake. As unusual as that may be."

A flush rose up the back of Honor's neck. "Just hold steady."

"Don't worry," Quinn said firmly. "I'm not letting go."

Honor turned and looked down into Quinn's eyes. She found the calm strength in them comforting. "Thanks."

"My pleasure."

As Honor made her way nimbly up the ladder, Arly appeared by Quinn's side. "Hi, Quinn."

"Hi Arly." Quinn spared Arly a glance before looking back up to where Honor now leaned out to one side, screwing a small hook into the horizontal portion of the tree limb. "How you doing?"

"My stitches itch."

"Uh-huh." Quinn couldn't take her eyes off Honor. *Don't stretch out so far. Jesus!*

"What's my mom doing up there?"

"She's hanging a wind chime."

"Is that what's making that noise?"

"Uh-huh." Quinn's throat was dry and her pulse racing. Honor's thighs were braced against the ladder, but she wasn't holding on since she needed both arms to affix the nylon loop over the hook. *Hurry up. Just come down. If you stay up there much longer, I'm going to embarrass myself.*

"Neat." Having satisfied her curiosity, Arly ran off to rejoin her friends.

To Quinn's complete and utter relief, Honor started to back down the ladder. Now that her anxiety was abating, Quinn was able to appreciate the toned thighs and enticing backside coming her way. She stood with her legs spread on either side of the ladder and both arms holding it just above shoulder level to steady it. As Honor descended, she unconsciously slid down between Quinn's arms until her body was between Quinn and the ladder. As Honor's hair brushed Quinn's cheek, Quinn's mouth was millimeters from Honor's neck. Her breasts pressed lightly against Honor's back.

If she moved her hips forward half an inch, her pelvis would rest against the soft swell of Honor's buttocks.

And Quinn very much wanted to do just that. She could smell Honor's sweet scent—spices and fruit and some deeper aroma, like warm fertile earth just turned in the sun. There were tiny beads of sweat collected along the edge of her jaw, and Quinn wanted to lick them off. Her heart pounded wildly, her stomach did one slow roll, and everything from her waist down turned to fire. She gasped sharply, surprised by the hard pulse of desire.

"Quinn." Honor's voice was pitched low, husky.

"Yes?" The word came out on a warm breath that lifted the hair at the base of Honor's neck.

"I can't get to the ground unless you move." Honor turned her head, her lips almost brushing Quinn's ear. Quinn's body was like a furnace, throwing off enough heat to warm her all the way through. To sear her in places that had been untouched for so long that the sensation terrified her. She trembled. "Please."

"I'm sorry," Quinn said quickly, stepping back. *Holy God. What am I* doing? *She's* married! *But why doesn't it feel that way?*

Honor made it down and turned. Her voice was shaking, but she smiled. "No problem. Thanks for the spot."

"Sure."

Quinn lifted a hand toward Honor's face, and Honor's eyes grew round. Carefully, Quinn brushed her fingers through Honor's hair. "You've got a leaf in your hair."

Honor held her breath as gentle fingers extracted the offending object. In her mind's eye, she could see Quinn's hand gently cradling a beating heart. *Such wonderful hands.*

"There you go." Quinn released the leaf and it fluttered away on the breeze. Her eyes bore into Honor's. *You're so beautiful.*

"I should get this stuff back to the garage." Honor indicated the ladder and tools, but she didn't move. *I don't want you to touch me. I don't.*

Quinn shook her head. "I'll do it. I think your presence is required elsewhere."

Honor looked in the direction that Quinn indicated. Arly was waving frantically, trying to get her attention. It looked as if she was ready to go into the pool. "So it seems. I should go."

"Yes."

Motionless, Quinn watched as Honor walked to the edge of the pool and sat down, dangling her legs over the side while Arly joined half a dozen children in the water. The sunlight sparkled on her hair, and Quinn remembered the way those soft strands had felt sliding through her fingers just minutes before. It felt like forever before the trembling in her legs subsided enough for her to move.

CHAPTER EIGHT

Honor watched the eddies swirl and splash around her feet as she circled her legs in the clear blue water. Those churning currents echoed the turmoil in her depths, as if she were poised to break into a million bright, sparkling droplets and fly away on the wind. She clutched the edge of the pool so tightly her knuckles turned white. *What's happening to me?*

"Mom! Watch me, Mom," Arly called.

Dutifully, Honor raised her head and smiled as her daughter cannonballed into the deep end of the pool. Terry had taught Arly to swim as an infant, and she was as comfortable in water as she was in air. Honor nodded encouragingly when Arly broke through the surface and looked expectantly in Honor's direction, but her mind was elsewhere. She turned her head a fraction and glanced back toward the house. Quinn still stood beneath the maple, the ladder upright by her side, one arm hooked over a rung. She was incredibly attractive standing there, looking directly at Honor. *Looking at me like I'm the only one here.*

Quickly, Honor turned away. Her heart pounded, and she still sensed the faint pressure of Quinn's body against her back. As Quinn's chest had brushed fleetingly against her, she had felt the unmistakable impression of nipples hardening beneath soft fabric. Quinn's, and her own. She closed her eyes, shivering. The rush of arousal that had accompanied that brief contact was overwhelming. It was the last thing she had expected to feel. The furthest thing from her desires. She had neither sought nor welcomed the excitement, but her body had embraced it as naturally as the next breath. She was stunned, horrified, and completely undone. *I don't want this. I don't.*

❖

Mechanically, Quinn carried the ladder and tools back to the garage and stowed them away. She pulled down the door and then stood by the corner of the building to look out over the wide rectangular yard. A split-rail fence, nearly obscured by rhododendrons and small shrubs, ran along the opposite side and rear, isolating the property from the view of neighbors. A wooden picnic table sat under the huge maple tree, and lawn chairs were scattered about nearby. A long expanse of grass ran down the gently sloping rear of the property, and a swimming pool occupied a portion of that area. The pool was currently the center of activity, with most of the children in it, and a fair number of their parents sitting nearby and observing.

But only one person captured Quinn's attention.

It was as if no one existed for her except Honor. The pull that drew her to Honor had been present since the first moment they had met, and although she didn't understand it, the feeling was too overpowering to deny. She wanted to be sitting there in the sun beside her, watching the children swim, talking of nothing and everything. She wanted the hand that curled around the damp tiled edge of the pool to be resting on her thigh, the way it had done so briefly in the car. Lightly, casually, confidently—as if she were Honor's own.

Quinn made her way across the yard and settled down at the picnic table, straddling the bench sideways, her right arm stretched out along the slatted tabletop. From where she sat, she could see Honor in profile and imagined the faint perspiration dewed on her skin. She could still smell her, rich and tantalizing. She could still feel her, warm and strong as she gently rested against Quinn's body.

Involuntarily, her nipples tightened as they had done at that first startling contact, and ached. Her fingers trembled as they lay against the rain-grayed wood. Her stomach tightened with urgency and need, and she hungered for something she had never known. Watching Honor lightly stroke the hair from her daughter's forehead, Quinn wanted to rest her head in Honor's lap and feel those tender fingers soothe her sorrows. She wanted to lie with her in the dark, in the aftermath of passion, and confess all her secrets.

This is impossible. For so many reasons. Then why don't I want the feelings to stop?

But she knew why. She watched as Honor lifted her hand again to brush stray strands of hair from her cheek. The unconscious movement was both gentle and sure. Somehow she knew Honor's hands would feel the same on her skin. And she wanted that, and all that would follow.

❖

Phyllis intercepted Linda on her way out of the house with another tray of appetizers. "Quite the party, my dear."

"Having fun?"

"Scads." Phyllis, who was dressed for the occasion in loose tan cotton slacks, a brightly colored embroidered blouse, and an enormous straw farmer's hat, surveyed the crowd. "I notice there's an interesting-looking newcomer, too."

Linda followed Phyllis's gaze and saw Quinn seated at the picnic table, gazing toward the pool where Honor sat with her legs in the water. Quinn's face was a study in desire. "Phew. Hot out, isn't it?"

"Mmm. She seems to be enchanted by Honor."

"Uh..." *Lord, this is Honor's mother-in-law!*

"That wouldn't be...Quinn, would it?"

"How did you know that?" Linda turned surprised eyes to Phyllis.

"Two reasons." Phyllis reached over and snagged a cream cheese–covered celery stick. "Arly hasn't stopped talking about her since the day she got her head cracked, and every time her name is mentioned, Honor gets cranky." *Plus, Honor hasn't been sleeping well, and that young woman over there looks hungry to the bone.*

"Yes, that's Quinn. I guess you know she's a new ER attending."

"Uh-huh. I also gather she and Honor aren't getting along?" Phyllis shaded her eyes, automatically checking for Arly in the pool. Honor, she noticed, looked shell-shocked. *Something has happened, all right. Is it that handsome girl who's turned you inside out, sweetie?*

Linda hesitated, reluctant to discuss Honor without her friend's knowledge.

"Don't mind me, I'm just being nosy." Phyllis patted her arm understandingly. "And you don't have to tell. I just couldn't help noticing that Quinn hasn't looked anywhere except at Honor for the last ten minutes."

Carefully, Linda asked, "Does it...you know, bother you?"

Phyllis was silent a moment, and Linda said quickly, "God, me and my big mouth. I'm so sorry, Phyl. That was inappropr—"

"No, it wasn't. I don't mind you asking." Phyllis patted her arm again. "Most people wouldn't ask because they're afraid that mentioning the dead will bring up memories, as if we don't always carry some part of them with us." She smiled. "Talking about Terry, thinking about her, is not a hardship for me. She was the light of my life, just as Honor and Arly are now."

"Could you be my mom?" Linda asked, meaning it. Her own mother still refused to acknowledge her marriage and her children.

"Don't you know that I think of you and Robin and Kim and Denny as family, too?" Phyllis wrapped an arm around Linda's waist. "Just as much as my two girls."

Linda just nodded, afraid to speak lest she cry.

Phyllis stared across the yard at Quinn, a stranger, who looked at Honor the way Terry once had. She felt many things, protective most of all. Honor carried scars, still bled from them on occasion, and Phyllis would do anything to see that she was not hurt again. *As if I could prevent it. If you live, you risk being hurt. If you never take the risk...* She sighed.

"Does it bother me that someone might be interested in Honor? That *Honor* might be?" Phyllis watched her granddaughter swim over to Honor and look up at her with a brilliant smile. Honor leaned down and brushed the wet hair from Arly's forehead, saying something that made the child grin. "Can you imagine how many times I've wished that Terry could see that child grow and help raise her with Honor?"

"No, I can't," Linda said softly. "But I know how many times *I've* wished for it."

"I suppose I might have fussed, five years ago. Maybe even three years ago." Phyllis shook her head. "Honor is lonely, and she has no idea how deeply."

"Yes."

Phyllis reached up and took the tray from Linda's hands. "So no, it doesn't bother me. Not if it turns out to be the right woman."

Linda watched Phyllis carry the food down to the picnic table and offer the hors d'oeuvres to Quinn. *Quinn Maguire. Who are you?*

❖

"Hello," Phyllis said, sliding the tray onto the table in front of Quinn. "I'm Phyllis Murphy, Arly's grandmother."

Quinn jumped to her feet, extending her hand and hoping that the woman hadn't noticed her staring at Honor. "Quinn Maguire, Ms. Murphy. How do you do?"

Smiling, Phyllis took Quinn's hand, finding her courtly manners charming. "I haven't had anyone stand up for me in a very long time."

Quinn grinned. "The world is being overrun with heathens."

"Indeed." Laughing, Phyllis slid onto the seat, patting the bench next to her. "Please."

Settling back down, Quinn said, "Arly seems to be doing well."

"Yes, famously. Speaking of which, you're her new hero."

Quinn blushed. "She was the hero. Along with Honor."

"Honor?"

"She was great. Sometimes the hardest part of taking care of children is dealing with the parents. Kids take their cues from them, and if you have a hysterical parent, it's almost impossible to keep the child calm." Quinn's face took on a distant expression. "I've had to take children to the operating room and sedate them to close minor wounds that I could've done in the trauma admitting area, except their parents wouldn't even let me try."

"I imagine it helps when the parents are doctors, like Honor."

"Don't you believe it," Quinn pronounced with a laugh. "God save me from medical parents. But Honor was fabulous, calm and steady, and she let me do my job."

"She must trust you, then, if she let you take care of Arly."

Unconsciously, Quinn glanced back to Honor, her gaze intent. "I hope so."

Phyllis smiled and reached for a carrot stick.

"By the way," Quinn asked. "What is Arly short for? I never noticed when I filled out her chart."

"It's short for Arlyn, which is actually her middle name...her full name is Murphy Arlyn Blake."

"What a great name. I'm surprised no one calls her Murph."

Caught off guard, Phyllis gave a small start. Then, her voice soft, she said, "We probably would have, but that's what most people called my daughter."

Quinn turned her attention from Honor and met Phyllis's gaze. "Honor's...spouse?"

"Yes. Terry."

That's what most people called *my daughter.* Quinn didn't need an explanation; she saw it in Phyllis's eyes. *Oh, Honor.* "I'm so terribly sorry."

"Thank you."

Quinn didn't know what else to say. She didn't know what to feel. Tragedy was nothing new to her; in her specialty in particular, it was a common occurrence. Most of the time she kept the heartbreak of human frailty at a distance, doing what she could with the gifts she had been given, accepting that fate or circumstance were things she could not change. Sometimes, however, for reasons she could not discern, someone would reach past the barricades of her defenses and touch her heart. Their pain would become *her* pain, until she was able to put it away again and carry on. But right now, all she felt was pain. Honor's and Phyllis's and Arly's.

Watching her, Phyllis saw the flood of emotions cross her face and swirl in the depths of her incredibly blue eyes. She was comforted by the unspoken understanding, and some of her concern for Honor's well-being abated. She had no idea what life held in store for *herself,* much less for Honor and this intense young stranger—if anything at all. But she could see the extent of Quinn's compassion, and she had seen the way that Quinn had looked at Honor. If anything could draw Honor completely back into life, it would be that combination of love and desire.

Phyllis patted Quinn's arm, as if she were the one who needed solace. Then she smiled. "Robin is the best barbecue chef in the entire neighborhood. When lunch is ready, you must be sure to sit with Honor and Arly and me. Arly will love it."

Surprised, Quinn agreed before she could think to say anything else. "Yes. Thank you."

"Now I'm going to go relieve Honor of lifeguard duty for a little while."

As Phyllis rose, Quinn stood as well. "It was very nice meeting you."

"You too, my dear."

Quinn contemplated following Phyllis down to the pool as a pretense to speak to Honor again. However, a voice at her elbow stopped her.

"Hey, good-lookin'. I didn't expect to see you here."

Surprised, Quinn looked around and found Mandy standing close enough that Quinn's shoulder brushed Mandy's breasts as she turned. One quick glance down revealed another spandex top, this one stopping at her navel, and low-cut skintight shorts. Her body was as buff as Quinn remembered.

"Uh...hello."

"Mandy, remember?" The blond's tone suggested that she doubted anyone could forget.

"Of course." Perplexed, Quinn looked around, searching for a partner or child. There didn't seem to be many unattached people at the party, although she didn't really know anyone well enough to be certain.

As if reading her mind, Mandy laughed and rested her fingertips on Quinn's bare forearm. "I'm the anomaly in this gathering. A single lesbian without children."

Quinn couldn't help but laugh. "Well then, that makes two of us."

"See there? We have something in common already, besides liking to work out and..." Mandy raised an eyebrow. "Other physical pursuits, I'll bet."

"So," Quinn said casually, "I take it that you're a friend of Robin and Linda's?"

"Mmm. Believe it or not, I grew up right here in Germantown and still live just a block away. I ref in the soccer league." Her fingers glided lightly up and down Quinn's arm. "I've known Linda and Robin for ages."

"Small world, I guess." Quinn realized that Mandy had slid even closer as they were speaking and felt the pressure of Mandy's thigh against her own. She backed up as unobtrusively as possible.

"I'm quite a bit *younger* than them, of course," Mandy informed her, her lips parting in a slow smile. "And they're *so* married."

"So...uh...you're into soccer." Quinn wasn't in the mood to flirt. In fact, as attractive as Mandy was, Quinn didn't have the slightest interest in pursuing anything further with her.

"Mmm-hmm." Mandy's fingers trailed feather-light across Quinn's abdomen. Her smile grew heavy at the swift contraction of the firm muscles. "I played quite a bit in high school. Plus, my dad owns the gym, so it's good PR for the business if I'm involved."

"You like it?" The insistent touch was starting to get irritating.

"Sure. There are always so many interesting women around." Mandy stretched and pushed her hand through her hair, a practiced move that thrust her breasts forward. "It's so nice to see someone *extra special* arrive on the scene, however."

As Mandy's hand returned to her waist, Quinn backed up another step. "Uh-huh."

"Let's go find someplace more private so we can have lunch together. I'll even feed you with my fingers."

"Thanks," Quinn said quickly. "But I'm eating with Honor and her family."

Mandy raised an eyebrow. "Really?"

"Honor and I work together."

"How nice."

Her tone, however, suggested that was anything but true.

❖

Honor walked into the kitchen and slammed the screen door. "You're out of Coke. Robin said it was in here somewhere?"

"You're ticked off because we ran out of soda?" Linda, her hands covered with barbecue sauce this time, blew hair off her forehead and gestured with her chin to the pantry behind them. "Remind me again why I like to throw these parties? I haven't been out of this kitchen for more than fifteen minutes at a time."

"There are plenty of people to help you, if you'd only *ask*." Honor yanked open the pantry door. "Where? Never mind, I see it."

Linda rested her butt against the counter and wiped the worst of the sauce off with a paper towel, regarding Honor curiously. "Honor, honey? Who pissed in your Cheerios?"

Honor spun around, two six-packs of Coke in her hands. "Do you really have to invite *her* to every one of these parties?"

"Just a minute while I translate that." Linda stared off into space. "Mandy's here, and she's annoying you already."

"She's practically crawling into Quinn's pants right in the middle of the lawn."

Linda was momentarily speechless, then she rushed to the door. "Where? Let me see."

"I swear to God, someone needs to put her on a leash." Honor slammed the cans down on the table, rattling the bowls of food.

Linda turned back, regarding Honor in amazement. "Are you still burned about something that happened ages ago? She was a child when she came on to Terry."

"She was *not* a child. She was eighteen years old. And she didn't just *come on* to her, she cornered her at a party and kissed her!" Honor flushed at the memory. "If I'd caught her at it, I would've killed her."

"As I remember Terry's version, it was over in a second, *and* she informed Mandy in no uncertain terms that she was off limits." Linda recalled Terry recounting the story of Mandy catching her alone at a party, and Mandy's shock when Terry had told her to go away. It had been funny then, and it was funny now, but she held back a laugh because Honor was clearly upset. She just wasn't entirely certain what Honor was upset about. *She's practically crawling into Quinn's pants...* "Ah..."

"Ah, what?"

"Nothing," Linda said quickly. "So, what's *Quinn* doing?"

"I have no idea, and I couldn't care less."

"Ookaay. So, if you're not going to be busy killing Mandy for a while, you want to help me with the chicken?"

Honor stared at her and then at the piles of chicken parts, contemplating homicide. *I'm losing my mind.* "Sure. Give me a really big knife."

The two friends grinned at one another, then broke into laughter.

CHAPTER NINE

Quinn made her way through the crowd gathered around the barbecue grill to where Honor was arranging the food that Robin passed to her. There were two large platters nearly filled with chicken and burgers.

"I hope you don't mind that your...mother-in-law...invited me to have lunch with you," Quinn said, feeling inexplicably shy. In the hospital, Dr. Quinn Maguire knew instinctively how to interact with Dr. Honor Blake. But this was different. *Honor* was different here; so was she. Outside the ER, Honor seemed unapproachable, remote—as if she didn't want anyone, except Linda and Robin, too close. Quinn was used to maintaining emotional distance, most surgeons were. But all she wanted *now* was to find a way through Honor's invisible shield, to get Honor to look at her with that special smile in her eyes. That longing for connection was new to her, and damn scary.

"Why would I mind?" Honor said without looking up. She was still feeling off balance from the unexpected surge of anger evoked by seeing Quinn with Mandy. She'd almost been... *jealous.* And that was absurd.

"I just didn't want to intrude on your family time." Quinn reached for the full platter of barbecue chicken. "Here, let me help you with that."

In a move that surprised them both, Honor wrapped her fingers around Quinn's forearm, stopping her from moving away. She looked up into Quinn's eyes and smiled. "It's fine. It will be nice. And I'm sure Arly will be thrilled."

"Good, I'm looking forward to it." Quinn's heart beat triple-time, and for once, it was a wholly pleasant experience. "I'll take this up to the table for you."

"Thanks. I think Arly and Phyllis have snagged seats under the tree." Honor's fingers drifted down over the top of Quinn's hand in a light caress. She didn't even realize she'd done it until she felt the faintest of tremors in Quinn's arm and saw the blue of her eyes shade to purple. Honor's voice came out husky and low. "I'll be right there."

"I'll be waiting." Quinn backed up a step, because as long as Honor was touching her, no matter how lightly, she wasn't going to be able to move. "I'll save you a seat."

Honor nodded appreciatively. *You are a charmer, Quinn Maguire.* "I don't care if I sit on the ground. Just save me some food. I'm starving."

"I'll do better than that. I'll fix you a plate." Quinn smiled, slow and easy. "You want a leg...or a breast?"

Startled, Honor's lips quirked and then she laughed out loud. *"Wing."*

Quinn laughed, too, glad that her hands were full, because she desperately wanted to run her thumb over the tiny cleft in Honor's chin. She had to force herself to keep walking away. "See you in a minute."

After Quinn delivered the chicken and fixed a plate for Honor, she found Phyllis and Arly seated around a small glass table under a dark green canvas umbrella. They had paper plates piled with food, drinks in plastic cups, and happy smiles.

"Hi, Quinn," Arly said enthusiastically.

Quinn settled in a lawn chair nearby and balanced her plate on her knee. "Hi, Arly. How's it going?"

"Great. I have a shiner."

"I see that," Quinn agreed seriously, narrowing her eyes and leaning forward to take a quick look at the suture line. *No swelling or redness, incision looks clean.* "It's very impressive."

"Yeah, and cool, too."

"Absolutely."

Honor picked up the plate from the chair next to Quinn and sat down. "Thanks for this." She smiled at Arly. "We took a picture this morning for Arly's scrapbook."

Quinn grinned. "Neat."

"That's what I said, too," Arly stated.

"So, Quinn," Phyllis interjected. "Where are you from?"

"You mean, born?" At Phyllis's nod, Quinn said, "Out near Pittsburgh. My father was a steelworker."

"No other doctors in the family, then?"

"Not by a long shot." Quinn shook her head, smiling. "My brothers are both steelworkers, just like my father and his father before him. My mother was a housewife."

"They must be very proud of you."

"I was a...surprise," Quinn said noncommittally, thinking that her parents had never known quite what to make of her ambition or her accomplishments. "How about you, Ms. Murphy? Let me guess...you're either a psychiatrist or a...private detective."

Phyllis laughed in delight. "First, you must call me Phyllis, and then you must tell me why you think that."

"Easy. You get people to talk about themselves without them realizing it, and you're so charming they don't mind when they do figure it out."

"Grandmom works at my school," Arly informed her seriously as Phyllis laughed again.

"Ah, a teacher?"

"Once upon a time. I'm one of the assistant principals now," Phyllis clarified. "Honor tells me you just started working at the hospital."

"Quinn just finished her training in Manhattan," Honor explained.

"I imagine this neighborhood is a real change after that," Phyllis said.

"Yes, but a very pleasant one." Quinn gestured to the gathering. "This is not the kind of city living I'm used to."

"Mom." Arly rested her hand on Honor's knee. "Can I go back in swimming now?"

"Are you done eating?"

Arly nodded vigorously.

"I think you'll have to wait until everyone is done with lunch, so that we have people to watch the pool."

"Can I go get something out of the house?"

"Ask Linda or Robin, honey," Honor said. "It's their house, and that's polite. Okay?"

"'Kay."

"So you're a surgeon, Quinn," Phyllis said, continuing her gentle questioning as Arly dashed off.

Quinn flushed. "Actually, Ms. Mur—Phyllis, I'm an ER doc. I have surgical training, though."

"That must come in handy all the same."

Quinn glanced at Honor, who was staring at her plate. "Sometimes. I'm still getting the hang of things."

"I'm sure that won't take long," she said kindly.

"I hope—"

"Quinn," Arly said eagerly as she skidded to a stop next to Quinn's chair. "Do you want to play?"

Quinn looked over and grinned when she saw the soccer ball that Arly eagerly extended. She glanced at Honor questioningly.

"Up to you."

"Sure," Quinn said as she stood and placed her hand lightly on the top of Arly's head. She looked around and pointed to the lower part of the yard. "We'd better go down there, though, so we don't end up kicking the ball into somebody's lunch."

"Okay," Arly replied, happily heading off with Quinn in her wake.

"She's very nice," Phyllis observed as she watched the two of them go.

"Should I ask about the third degree?" Honor set her plate aside and leaned back in her chair, observing Phyllis curiously.

"I was just making conversation."

"I thought you were going to ask her whether she was single next."

"No." Phyllis leaned over and picked up an uneaten chicken leg from Honor's plate. "That was going to be my second question. *First,* I was going to ask her where she was living."

"Why are you so interested?"

Phyllis met Honor's gaze. "She seems interested in you."

Honor flushed, and despite the fact that she was used to Phyllis's direct approach, she was disconcerted. "Nothing's going on."

"I didn't think there was, honey." Phyllis looked around and found her iced tea. She picked up the glass and sipped. "Would you like there to be?"

"No," Honor said quickly. "No, not with anyone. But especially not her."

"Has she done something wrong?"

Honor stood, looking across the heads of the people around her who were sitting and having lunch. Quinn and Arly were kicking the soccer ball back and forth to each other at the far end of the lawn. She could see her daughter laughing. "No, but there's more to her than she's telling. I'm not sure I...trust her."

"Ah. That's a problem then."

"Yes, it is." To Honor's relief, she saw Robin headed their way and waved. She did not want to talk any more about Quinn Maguire or why she couldn't help thinking that the surgeon was hiding something. She did not want to think about the way Quinn looked at her, or the way she felt with that steady, intense gaze upon her. She did not want to think about what she wanted, or didn't want, or feared having.

Robin kissed Honor's cheek. "Having a good time?"

"Terrific. Great lunch, Robbie. Thanks."

"Sure thing." Robin gave a satisfied sigh and looked around the yard. Linda was deep in conversation with the father of one of their daughter's classmates, probably coordinating carpooling schedules. Their two kids had joined most of the other children in the far back corner of the yard. "Quinn's drawing quite a crowd."

"I know." For the last few minutes, kids of all sizes had been making their way down to where Quinn and Arly were playing. Now it looked as if there was an impromptu soccer clinic in progress, with Quinn surrounded by the children, all of whom seemed to be watching her intently.

"She's like the Pied Piper," Robin observed. "And she's really good. I think I'm going to try recruiting her."

Before Honor could protest, Robin walked away.

❖

"You've got some good moves there, Quinn."

Quinn turned around and grinned at Robin. In a quiet voice she said, "It's not too hard to look good when your toughest competition is nine years old."

Robin laughed. "Listen, we could use another coach for our team. Right now, we have two, but if one of us gets held up at work, it's a lot for the other one to handle alone. What do you think?"

"Me?" Quinn looked around at the milling, boisterous children. "Jeez, Robin, I don't know. I don't have any experience with kids."

"Looks like you're doing really well to me. Besides, they're at an age when they still do pretty much whatever you tell them. They're really an easy bunch."

"My schedule is kind of crazy at work." Quinn's tone was dubious as she struggled with the decision. She'd never been involved in anything like this before. It would be a significant responsibility, but then, she didn't have anything else to do with her time. And she was having fun. "Okay, sure. If you don't think it'll be a problem if I miss a few practices."

"None at all." Robin clapped her on the back. "Excellent. Before you leave today, make sure I get your telephone numbers, and I'll give you mine. If you've got a fax machine, I can send you the practice times and the game schedules."

"A fax machine?" Quinn laughed. "I've barely got silverware."

"I forgot you're a bachelor." She thought for minute. "I'll give it all to Linda, and she can bring it to you at work."

"That's good."

Arly came up to them and grabbed Quinn's hand. "Can you show us that passing drill again, Quinn?"

"Sure." She grinned at Robin and followed Arly back into the melee.

It happened so fast, there wasn't even time to think about it. One of the older boys with a really strong leg teed off on the ball and kicked a line drive that was worthy of Mia Hamm. Unfortunately, his ball control was not yet equal to his strength, and the kick went well wide of its target. Quinn saw the ball take off and realized it was going to slam into a toddler who was playing not far away.

She took two running steps and launched herself into the air, her body almost parallel to the ground as she stretched out her arms to intercept the projectile. She managed to get her fingers on the ball, but she was so extended that she couldn't control her fall. She came down with all her weight on her left shoulder. The pain was immediate and blinding. Groaning, she curled up around the pain and tried desperately not to vomit.

The instant Honor saw Quinn hit the ground, she started running toward her. She didn't need to hear the sharp cry of pain to know that Quinn was hurt—the angle of contact told her that. She reached Quinn at the same time that Arly and Robin did.

"Quinn!" Arly cried, her voice trembling. She looked from Quinn, moaning on the ground, to Honor, her eyes huge. "Is she hurt, Mommy?"

"Let me see, honey." Honor glanced at Robin. "Take the kids up the hill, Robbie."

"I'm okay," Quinn muttered hoarsely, trying as hard as she could to keep her voice steady. She opened her eyes, her vision swimming with tears. The agony in her shoulder was nearly unbearable. She managed a crooked grin when she saw Arly peering at her from a few inches away. "I'm...okay, kiddo. Just got the...wind knocked out."

Arly nodded solemnly. "I had that happen once when I fell off a swing." She turned to Honor, who knelt beside Quinn. "She'll be okay, right, Mommy?"

"Yes, honey. Go with Robin now," Honor said gently. As soon as the children were out of earshot, Honor leaned close to Quinn, her fingers on the pulse in Quinn's neck. Racing, but strong. "Tell me where you're hurt."

"Shoulder," Quinn gasped. "Dislocated. Oh God, Honor...it hurts."

"Did you injure your ribs? Your back?" Honor blocked out everything except what needed to be done. She blocked out the harsh sounds of pain, the labored breathing, and the wash of sweat that dampened Quinn's pale face. She buried the fear that had lanced through her when she'd seen Quinn fall and lie still. "Any numbness anywhere? Quinn? Is your neck all right?"

"Nothing else. Just the...shoulder."

Honor did a cursory neurologic exam, checking for movement in all four extremities and lifting each lid to check Quinn's pupils. Her blue eyes were dilated and black with pain. *Oh baby. I'm so sorry.*

Linda dropped to her knees on the other side of Quinn. "God, what happened? Should I call an ambulance?"

"Yes," Honor said sharply. Seeing Quinn in pain was making her ill. She gritted her teeth and focused. "I'll stay with her. Go call."

"No," Quinn rasped. She tried to turn onto her back, but that caused another spear of pain to shoot down her arm. She groaned. "Old injury. Honor...you can put it back in."

Honor shook her head. "We still need to go to the ER. I'll need to sedate you for the reduction. Linda, call 91—"

"It'll go...in easy. Please just do it." Quinn groaned again, and her stomach heaved. She didn't want to vomit, but she couldn't stand it much longer. "Please. Please...can't wait. So bad."

Linda looked at her friend across Quinn's prone form. "She's really hurting, Honor. One try?"

For a second, Honor hesitated. Medical treatment in the field was always risky. On the other hand, she trusted Quinn to know her own injuries, and a dislocation was excruciatingly painful until the joint was relocated. Quinn's eyes were shut tightly, her shirt soaked through with sweat, and her every breath was a moan. "*One* try. If we don't get it, that's it."

Linda nodded. "Whatever you say. Just tell me what you need."

Gently, Honor placed her hand on Quinn's right shoulder and murmured, "We're going to turn you over now, Quinn."

"Okay." She clamped her jaws tightly against a scream.

Together, Honor and Linda carefully maneuvered Quinn onto her back. Quinn's left arm hung limply by her side, projecting at an odd angle. The shoulder prominence was depressed, the contour abnormal. An unnatural bulge protruded from just below the normal joint, distorting her upper arm. The end of the upper arm bone had slipped out of the cuplike fossa formed by the collarbone, the shoulder blade, and the surrounding muscles. The unnatural pressure and strain on the ligaments and nerves around the joint caused severe pain. If left unreduced for long, permanent nerve injury could occur.

"Linda," Honor instructed, her expression neutral and her eyes sharply focused on Quinn's face. "Brace your legs against her side. You're going to have to hold her while I reduce this." She waited a moment for Linda to get into position. "Quinn, are you sure?"

Quinn opened her eyes and focused on Honor's face. A smile flickered for a second. "Yes. Don't let...the kids see. They'll be... scared."

For a second, Honor's composure slipped, and she brushed her fingers tenderly through Quinn's hair. Her voice trembled infinitesimally. "They're all up at the house. They can't see. Close your eyes now."

Quinn complied, and Honor situated herself so that she could grasp Quinn's left arm, flex the elbow, and rotate the arm outward until the rounded head of the humerus popped back into the socket. She met Linda's eyes and nodded. "Hold her."

As Honor pulled and twisted, Quinn stiffened and cried out sharply once, then sagged back, gasping. Honor gently placed Quinn's arm across her midsection and held it there with her palm. She was breathing hard and her stomach was in knots.

"Quinn? Okay?"

"Better." Quinn gave a long shuddering sigh and opened her eyes. This time her smile was stronger. "About a thousand times better. Thank you."

"We still need to go into the ER so that I can get an x-ray and do a proper examination. But I'll drive you in—no ambulance."

"It's not necessary. It's happened before."

"This is not negotiable, Dr. Maguire." Honor's face was set. "I have to be sure that you didn't fracture your clavicle *or* your humerus, and I need to do a proper neurologic evaluation."

"I'm telling you—"

"And I'm telling *you,* no exam—you don't come to work tomorrow."

Quinn blew out a breath and tried to sit up. Linda automatically wrapped her arm around Quinn's shoulders and supported her against her side.

"Okay," Quinn said weakly. Her head was spinning. "Can I say goodbye to the kids, please."

"Of course." Honor regarded her tenderly, her quick surge of anger and fear abating. "Can you stand?"

"I think so."

Between them, Linda and Honor got Quinn upright. Honor threaded her arm around Quinn's waist and took most of her weight. "All right?"

"Just don't let go," Quinn muttered, sweat streaking her face and neck as she cradled her injured arm.

"I wouldn't think of it." Honor's voice was thick.

The fiercely tender expression on Honor's face and the comfort of her body pressed close drove the pain from Quinn's mind. "Thanks."

"That was some move, Quinn," Honor murmured as they made their way slowly up toward the group of people who were gathered beneath the maple tree.

"I used to be a lot better at that. Ten years ago."

Honor laughed softly. "It still *looked* good."

"Thank God for that. Because I'm very embarrassed."

"You have no reason to be." Unconsciously, Honor held her more tightly. "You have valiant instincts."

Robin came up to them then, her face creased with worry. "Jeez, Quinn. Are you okay? Man, that looked rough."

"Fine, now. I knocked that shoulder out when I was nineteen, and it's always been hinky. I just landed on it wrong."

"You sure you're okay?" She looked questioningly at Honor and Linda.

"I'm going to check her over, but she seems okay," Honor assured her.

Quinn grinned weakly at Robin. "Is this gonna cost me my new job?"

For a second, Robin looked confused, and then she burst out laughing. "Hell, no. It takes more than a dislocated shoulder for me to fire a coach. Now, if you make the goalie cry, that's a different story."

Quinn grinned. "Not to worry. I'll go easy."

After assuring Arly and the other children that she was fine, Quinn allowed Honor to help her to the car and buckle her into the front seat. As they headed to the emergency room, she wondered what she was going to do when it came time for Honor to examine her.

CHAPTER TEN

Honor glanced over at Quinn as she pulled into the doctors' section of the ER parking lot. Quinn, silent for the entire ride, sat with her head back and her eyes closed. Carefully, Honor brought the car to a stop and shut off the engine. She turned in her seat and rested her fingers on Quinn's leg.

"How are you doing?"

Quinn slowly rolled her head to the side and opened her eyes. "Not too bad. It throbs, but I can handle that. My stomach is in a bit of an uproar, though."

Honor nodded sympathetically. "I can imagine. We'll get you some Compazine once we get inside."

"Will you do me a favor?"

"Of course," Honor replied, her brows furrowing. "What is it?"

Quinn sighed. "Will you try to make sure that no one sees my records or my films?"

"I'll see to it," Honor said kindly. She appreciated how difficult it was for a medical person to be treated at the institution where they worked. Curiosity was a normal human trait, and everyone wanted the details whenever someone who worked in the hospital was ill or injured. She rubbed Quinn's thigh gently. "Let's get you taken care of. I'll come around and help you get out."

"I think I can—"

"Quinn, sit still," Honor instructed sharply when Quinn reached for the door handle.

"No choice," Quinn gasped, feeling weaker than she had anticipated, her stomach roiling as the pain unexpectedly escalated and shot through her chest.

A moment later, Honor opened the car door, released Quinn's seat belt, and bent down to slide her arm behind Quinn's back. "Put your good arm around my shoulder."

"I'm heavier than I look," Quinn warned, as Honor lifted.

"I'm stronger than I look. Now lean on me."

Quinn got her legs under her and pushed upright, gripping Honor's shoulder tightly with her functioning hand. She swayed unsteadily. "Jesus, my legs aren't working quite right."

"Any weakness or paresthesias?" Honor questioned, a slight edge of panic in her voice. *Oh my God, don't tell me I missed a cord injury! I should have called the EMTs. I should have used a backboar—*

"No, nothing like that," Quinn said firmly. Sensing what worried Honor, she rubbed her hand comfortingly over Honor's arm. "Sorry, didn't mean to scare you. My legs just feel a little rubbery."

"You're sure? Because I can get a wheelchair out here in just a second."

"I'm sure. It's just my shoulder, Honor. I'm certain of it."

"Let's just get inside so *I* can be certain of it, too."

As soon as they were through the emergency room doors, Honor grabbed one of the wheelchairs lined up inside and pulled it oward them. "Here, sit down and I'll take you right into one of the examining rooms. Do you happen to have your insurance card?"

Quinn shook her head. "Not the new one from PMC. I didn't get that yet. I can give you my New York insurance information, though."

"Fine. I want to get you squared away first. We can give all that info to the clerk later."

"You're the boss."

As they spoke, Honor guided the chair efficiently through the hallways, maneuvering around equipment and stretchers, and nodded to the charge nurse who looked up in surprise as they passed the nurses' station. In response to the inquisitive glance, Honor said, "Page the x-ray technician for me, will you, Nancy?"

"Okay, Dr. Blake," the nurse called after them. "You need me for anything else?"

"I'll let you know. Thanks."

Honor pulled the curtain aside, slid the chair into the cubicle, set the small hand brake, and walked around to the front to help Quinn stand. She reached down at the same time as Quinn pushed up, and they ended up nearly touching. As if it were the most natural thing in the world to do, Honor threaded her arms around Quinn's waist and moved closer. At the same time, Quinn's right arm went around Honor's shoulders, and Honor felt Quinn's fingers brush through the hair at the base of her neck. Quinn's breasts nestled against hers, and their bodies melted effortlessly together.

They were almost the same height, and Honor's body fit flawlessly against Quinn's. In the brief second before she had time to react, before her rational mind could protest, she had the sensation of perfect *rightness,* as if being in Quinn Maguire's arms was destined. She felt Quinn's heart beat, then her own, and then the two together, point and counterpoint, in perfect harmony. *You feel so good. So right. How can that be?*

She stiffened when Quinn's warm breath fluttered against her neck, and a shiver of heat flickered through her belly. She felt Quinn's thighs tighten against hers, heard Quinn moan softly, and heat became flame. She wanted to press closer, hungered to fuse her flesh and bones to Quinn's, and she knew she could not. Must not. Yet even as she sought escape, her body soared.

Mindful of Quinn's injury, Honor placed her palms on Quinn's hips and pushed gently away until their bodies no longer touched. When she spoke, her throat was dry and her voice rough with unexpected longing. "I need you on the exam table. Can you make it?"

Wordlessly, Quinn nodded, struggling to clear her head and find some semblance of control. What she wanted was for Honor to hold her again. Not because her shoulder hurt, but because she ached in her distant reaches, in places far deeper than flesh. And because she knew that in a few minutes, she would lose any chance of finding solace in Honor's embrace.

But she had already put this confession off far too long.

"Yes, I think I can get up there." On still-trembling legs, Quinn shifted outside the circle of Honor's warmth, braced herself with her good hand on the edge of the vinyl-covered examination table, and levered herself up into a sitting position with her legs dangling over the edge. The movement started a new barrage of pain in her shoulder.

"We're going to need to take your shirt off." Honor met Quinn's gaze steadily, silently acknowledging the intimacy that had just passed between them. "Do you want me to get one of the nurses to help you?"

Slowly, Quinn shook her head. "No. If you help me, I can get it."

"All right." Honor stepped forward as Quinn spread her legs, allowing Honor close enough to assist. "Pull your shirt out of your jeans."

With her right hand, Quinn worked her shirt free of her waistband. "I can't raise my left arm."

"Mmm. I know. We'll take it slow." Honor smiled softly. "Let's get the right one free first, then we'll work on the left."

Nodding, Quinn raised her right arm and shrugged her shoulder down and free of the garment as Honor pulled on the bottom of the sleeve. That left the shirt dangling around Quinn's neck, angling across her chest and over her injured arm. Quinn suggested, "If you just pull up the bottom, I can get my head free."

As the shirt came loose, it became apparent that Quinn wore nothing beneath it. Honor kept her eyes on Quinn's face as they slowly freed her of the restraining garment. Finally, all that remained was to slip it down and off the injured arm.

"Just keep your left hand in your lap so we don't stress the joint, okay?" Honor directed as she worked the polo shirt down Quinn's arm. As she did, she lowered her eyes to the injured shoulder and stopped abruptly when she saw the fresh three-inch surgical scar a few inches below Quinn's left collarbone. A slight swelling distended the tissue from there to the upper edge of her breast.

Honor stared, recognizing but unable to absorb its significance. *That can't be right.* She raised her eyes to Quinn's, whose expression was oddly penitent. "Quinn?"

"ICD."

Implantable cardiac defibrillator. Honor shook her head. "I don't understand." *How can I not know this? What in God's name is wrong? Oh, Quinn. No.*

"I—"

Honor held up a hand and stepped back a pace. "No. I need to do this right."

While Quinn stared, Honor leaned over, opened a drawer in the lower portion of the examination table, and lifted out a faded cotton hospital gown. Efficiently, professionally, she finished removing the polo shirt from Quinn's injured arm and replaced it with the gown. When Quinn was completely covered, Honor regarded her expressionlessly. "I'll get a chart together. I need to take your medical history."

"Honor—"

"Where's your insurance information?" Honor concentrated on the routine that was as ingrained and familiar to her as breathing. That way, she didn't have to think about the device implanted in Quinn's chest. Or what it meant. "I should take that to admissions so they can get you into the system."

"In my wallet." Quinn reached back, removed her wallet, and balanced it on her knee. After a few seconds, she gave up trying to extract the card one-handed. Wordlessly, she held the wallet out to Honor. "It's in there somewhere."

Honor sorted through the cards until she found the proper one. Her hands shook.

"Honor, please. It's not what you think."

"You don't *know* what I think," Honor snapped. Then she drew a long steadying breath, and when she spoke again, her voice was calm. "I'm sorry. I'll be back in just a minute."

Honor stepped outside the cubicle, pulled the curtain closed, and walked several feet down the hall. Then she stopped, leaned her back against the wall, and closed her eyes. A medical problem was the last thing she had imagined. She had thought of drug addiction, alcoholism, sexual misconduct, a breach in ethics. Even though none of those things fit with her experience of Quinn, she had never thought that Quinn might be ill. She couldn't bear to think of it now, and yet she had to.

"Dr. Blake?"

Honor's eyes snapped open and she straightened. Nancy Hickok, the nurse manager, stared at her curiously, a look of concern on her face. Honor forced a smile.

"Nancy, can you put a chart together for me, please? And be sure not to leave it lying around where anyone else can see it."

"Of course. The x-ray tech said to tell you that she's just finishing a facial series. She'll be ready for you in fifteen minutes, if you can wait that long."

"Fine."

Honor walked out to the admitting area and found the senior admitting officer, a man she had known for many years and whose discretion she trusted implicitly. She handed him Quinn's insurance card. "Jim, Dr. Maguire needs to be signed in. I want you to do it yourself and then give all the paperwork directly to Nancy."

"Sure, Doc." He looked as if he was about to ask more, but something in Honor's expression stopped him. "It'll just take me a second."

Five minutes later, Honor stepped back into the examination cubicle with the metal ER chart and all the appropriate paperwork inside. She opened to the history page, uncapped her pen, and looked at Quinn. "You're twenty-eight?"

"Yes."

Honor concentrated on charting. "Drug allergies?"

"None."

"Medications?"

Quinn's voice was steady. "Aspirin. Cordarone. Betapace."

Honor wrote the names of the cardiac medications without pause. "Medical history?"

"I..." Quinn took a breath. This was not the way she had wanted to tell her. At first she hadn't thought she would *need* to tell her. She wasn't under any legal obligation to reveal her medical history, and she didn't want that to be the first thing people learned about her. But it hadn't taken very long for her to realize that she *wanted* to tell Honor everything, not just for professional reasons, but for personal ones. She just hadn't known how. Now it was too late, and it was happening all wrong. "Honor, I wanted to tell—"

"Let's get the information down, Quinn," Honor said calmly. "I want to get your shoulder and chest x-rayed."

Honor's tone of voice was perfectly appropriate. Professional, nonjudgmental, calm and controlled. But there was nothing in her eyes when she looked at Quinn, and that was worse than worry or recrimination or even anger. At least those feelings were personal, and Quinn very much wanted what was between them to be personal. Sighing, she gave Honor the facts. The facts, however, were nowhere near the truth of what she had endured. That she tried not to think about. "Four months ago I developed viral myocarditis. It started out as a respiratory infection, I think, and within a few days the inflammation had spread to my heart."

I almost died before I admitted anything was wrong. I was young and healthy and never sick. I didn't want Sinclair to think I couldn't handle the pace. She never slows down; I don't think she ever sleeps. But then, in the middle of the case...

"Quinn?" Honor's tone was gentle. The color had drained from Quinn's face. "You want to lie down?"

Quinn shook her head. Hoarsely, she said, "No. I...uh... developed some scar tissue, apparently, and it created some arrhythmia problems. My heart rhythm was all over the place there for a while."

"How severe?" Honor was pleased that her voice was steady.

"I had an episode of ventricular tachycardia and arrested in the middle of a surgery."

Honor put the pen down and looked into Quinn's eyes. She couldn't even begin to pretend that thinking of what had happened didn't affect her. The very thought of Quinn nearly dying made her physically ill. Her stomach churned, and every breath burned in her chest. She could only imagine how terrifying it must have been for Quinn to live through that. Now she not only lived with the memory of it, but she had to endure the fear of it happening again. "Oh, Quinn. I'm so sorry."

Quinn smiled wryly. "The good news is that the area of scarring in my heart is very small. My cardiac function is excellent." She ran her right hand through her hair and sighed. "The bad news is, they can't seem to control the arrhythmias."

"So you need to have the implantable defibrillator in case it happens again." Honor knew that certain cardiac arrhythmias, or irregular heartbeats, could be treated by radiofrequency ablation, a technique in which the focus of the irregular heartbeat was actually destroyed so that it no longer acted as an irritant. It was the sporadic electrical discharge from abnormal areas of the heart muscle that caused arrhythmias. When the heart didn't beat regularly, it didn't pump blood normally, and there wasn't enough blood flow to sustain consciousness. Thus, some arrhythmias posed a significant risk for sudden cardiac death. *SCD...sudden cardiac death.* The words sliced through Honor like a knife.

"It's only been a few months," Quinn said. "There's a chance that as time goes on the cardiac irritability will lessen. I might recover enough not to need the defibrillator."

"Of course," Honor said with forced optimism. She picked up the pen again. "When was the defibrillator placed?"

"Two months ago."

"How often has it discharged?"

Quinn was silent long enough that Honor looked up from the chart. Quinn's expression was bleak.

"Four or five times."

Honor's stomach clenched. *God, she's not even stabilized. What are they thinking, letting her work?*

"My cardiologist knows about it, and he thinks it's probably not significant. Sometimes the defibrillators are hypersensitive, depending on the settings. He fiddles with the sensitivity thresholds, but he doesn't seem too worried."

"Are you having any symptoms?"

Quinn shrugged. "Every once in a while I'll have a few palpitations. Very rarely a few seconds of dizziness. I'm not even sure it's related."

"Are they monitoring your rhythm by remote telemetry?"

"I'm supposed to send them random heart rhythm traces every week."

Honor arched her brow. "*Supposed* to send? When was the last time your cardiologist looked at one of your rhythm strips?"

"It's been a...few weeks...the move and the new job and all. I just put it off."

"Jesus, Quinn," Honor said sharply, her emotions breaking through the veneer of control for the first time. "Are you at least taking your meds?"

"I'm not crazy, Honor. *Yes,* I'm taking them."

"Still, I'm admitting you to the telemetry unit for observation."

"Honor, it's not my heart here. My *heart* is fine. It's my goddamn *shoulder*." Quinn tightened her right fist in frustration. "That's what's *killing* me."

Honor's head jerked up, fire flashing in her eyes. Quinn stared back, her blue eyes just as hot.

"Why didn't you tell me?" Honor demanded.

"Because I was *embarrassed*."

Honor blinked. For a second, she was at a loss as to what to say. All of sudden, she wanted to touch Quinn so badly. Not just for Quinn. For her. "It's not your fault."

"Can you honestly say you still think of me the same as you did an hour ago?"

"That has nothing to do with anything."

A muscle in Quinn's jaw jumped and her whole body tensed. *That has everything to do with everything.*

Honor looked away, because she couldn't lie to her, and she knew that Quinn would see the truth in her eyes. Knowing this changed everything. But she would have to deal with that later.

"Is there anything *else* I need to know about your medical history?"

Quinn grimaced, her heart aching. "How much more could there be?"

"I'll take that as a no. How's your stomach?"

"Better. My shoulder feels like someone is hitting it with a sledgehammer, though."

"Can you do without the Compazine?"

"Yeah. But I wouldn't mind a pain pill."

"I'll ask Nancy to bring you something right away, and then we'll get you x-rayed." Honor reached for the curtain, but before she opened it, she asked the one critical question that would determine if even friendship would be possible between them. "Does anyone here at PMC know about your medical condition?"

Quinn stared at her, confused. "Of course."

"Who?"

"The chief of surgery. I presume the chief of medicine, because he talked to her when he got me the interview."

But they didn't tell me. And neither did you, Quinn. How am I ever going to trust you?

CHAPTER ELEVEN

Honor was alone in the small viewing room that was part of the ER's auxiliary x-ray department when Linda opened the door and walked in.

"Hey," Linda greeted her, "how's Quinn?"

Startled, Honor pulled down the film she had been inspecting and turned to face her friend. "What are you doing here?"

"I was worried about Quinn, and I wanted to find out what was going on." Linda joined Honor in front of the light box and regarded Honor quizzically. Her friend looked troubled—more than troubled, distraught. "Honor? What's going on? Is it worse than you thought?"

"I don't think so," Honor said dully, still not able to comprehend just how bad it really was, "but I'm just getting her squared away."

"Whose chest x-ray was that?"

"Uh..." Honor fished around for some excuse and came up short. Her expression must have answered for her.

"Oh my God, was that *Quinn's*?"

Sighing, Honor put the film back up. "Since you've already seen it, there isn't much point in pretending otherwise." She returned her gaze to the x-ray, seeing what she knew she would see, but continuing to stare at it until she believed it.

A miniature battery-powered computer was housed in the small plastic case that rested just above the major muscle of Quinn's chest. From it, electrical leads coated in silicone were threaded into the subclavian vein beneath her collarbone and directed into her heart. Sensors at the end of those leads sent information to the programmable computer inside the defibrillator, allowing an electrical discharge to regulate Quinn's heart rhythm if it became unstable. *That's assuming that the defibrillator is functioning properly and sensing her heart rate appropriately. If it isn't, she could develop a fatal arrhythmia and die within minutes.*

"Is that a pacemaker?" Linda's voice was tight with concern.

Honor shook her head. "Implantable defibrillator."

"Oh, poor Quinn. God, Honor, is she all right?" Linda moved closer, resting a comforting hand on Honor's back. *Are you?*

"Her clavicle and humerus look fine. She's got a tremendous amount of soft tissue swelling around the shoulder area, which is to be expected, but—"

"What about her *heart?*"

Honor extended a finger, pointing to the cardiac shadow on the chest x-ray. "Heart size is normal. Rate's good. Blood pressure's fine. I'm waiting for an EKG trace right now. So far, there's no evidence of any instability."

Linda tilted her head and stared at Honor as she recited the litany of facts in a monotone. "Honor? Are you okay?"

"Fine." Honor continued to stare at the x-ray. Quinn's heart *looked* normal. But it wasn't. She wanted to tear the x-ray down and shred it, as if destroying the evidence would mitigate the truth. She wanted that x-ray to be someone else's, *anyone* else's, as long as it wasn't Quinn's. Her voice was flat, the helpless fury so pervasive it blocked every other emotion. "No one told me, Linda."

"Is she sick?" Linda felt a little sick herself. She liked Quinn. She liked her a lot. And she knew that Honor liked her, too.

"I don't know yet." Finally, Honor managed to drag her eyes away from the x-ray that mocked her, reminding her that despite all her training—all her skill—she couldn't make a difference when it truly mattered. Not with Terry. Not with Quinn. She turned, edging her hip onto the counter that ran below the view boxes, and pushed a hand through her hair. For the first time, she realized she was exhausted. "I haven't had a chance to complete my evaluation. Other than her shoulder, she seems to be all right."

"So this isn't so bad, right?" Linda indicated the x-ray with a tip of her chin.

"I suppose that's a matter of definition." Honor gave a short, mirthless laugh. "She has a potentially lethal condition which is poorly controlled at the moment, and she's twenty-eight fucking years old. God." She closed her eyes, and all she could see was

Quinn. Those brilliant eyes, that mesmerizing grin, those incredible hands. In a whisper, she asked of no one, expecting no answer, "Why is life so unfair?"

Linda heard the anguish in Honor's voice, appreciating that it wasn't just about Quinn. Honor had lost her lover, and whether she knew it or not, wanted it or not, she already cared about Quinn. And right now, Honor was struggling with past pain and present fear all at once, a fight that was too much for anyone. Linda slid her arm around Honor's waist, giving her a little shake even as she hugged her comfortingly. "Honey, you know better than to ask that. Thinking that way around here will make you crazy."

Honor leaned her cheek against Linda's shoulder and laughed shakily. "Yeah, I know. I'm just tired, I guess."

"Understandable. It's been a hell of an afternoon." She kissed Honor's forehead fleetingly. "So, where's Quinn right now?"

"In three. I wanted to admit her, but she's refusing. God, she's stubborn."

Linda grinned, happy to hear the irritation creep into Honor's voice. *Better.* "Gee whiz, a surgeon who's stubborn? How about that. I even know some ER chiefs who are just a little bit obstinate."

Honor glared at Linda, but just having her there was helping. She wasn't entirely certain what it was about Quinn's underlying condition that had thrown her so badly. She didn't seem to be able to sort things out clearly; all she felt was a sense of panic that was clouding her judgment. And that was totally unlike her. "Do you have something constructive to add to this situation, or do you just intend to heckle me for the rest of the day?"

Much better. "Why do you want to admit her?"

"Because she hasn't had proper monitoring for *weeks,* and she told me that the defibrillator has discharged as recently as two days ago!" Honor's voice rose as the fear threatened to re-emerge. "Do you want her to drop dead?"

"Of course not," Linda said softly, not taking offense at Honor's tone. She knew her friend well enough to know that this wasn't Honor. At least not Honor when she wasn't terrified. "You're getting a rhythm trace, right?"

"Yes, it should be done by now."

"Okay. Do you want her to have a sling for the shoulder?"

Honor rubbed her forehead, considering priorities. Her brain still felt sluggish, but the tightness in her chest was easing now that she had something to focus on besides the shock of seeing that scar on Quinn's chest and what lay underneath. "For a day or two. She shouldn't be immobilized any longer than that, because adhesions will develop around the shoulder joint. Motion is actually good for it."

"Right. I'll get her fixed up with the shoulder immobilizer while you review the EKG. If that looks okay, what do you say about her spending the night with Robin and me?"

"At your place?"

"Why not?" Linda shrugged. "If her heart's okay, she really doesn't need to be admitted, right?"

"Not for the shoulder injury, no."

"But she lives by herself, and neither of us would feel very comfortable letting her go home alone. We've got room."

"All right." Honor smiled fondly. "I'm sorry I jumped on you. I don't know what's wrong with me."

Linda squeezed her hand. *I know you don't. So let's get Quinn squared away. That way, when you figure out what's scaring you, you just might be able to handle it.*

❖

Quinn had managed to get her shirt back on and was sitting on the side of the exam table when the curtain parted and Linda and Honor stepped into the small room. She smiled at Linda, but her eyes were on Honor, who was holding her chart and looking at some point over Quinn's head.

"Hi, Quinn," Linda said affectionately. "How's the shoulder?"

"What shoulder?"

Linda laughed. "Uh-huh. Aren't we just all tough."

"Yeah, that's me." *Honor, why are you angry? Why won't you look at me?*

Linda tilted her head, studying Quinn's face. *She looks more worried than sick. She surely doesn't look in danger of dying. If I hadn't seen that x-ray with my own eyes...no wonder Honor is having a hard time. I can't believe it either.* "I'm going to get you a shoulder immobilizer, tough guy. I'll be back in a few minutes."

Alone with Honor, Quinn tried desperately to gauge what the other woman was feeling. She didn't care about her rhythm trace or her chest x-ray or her shoulder; she cared about the distance in Honor's eyes. She sensed disappointment and anger, and beneath that, something she wasn't quite sure she understood. It seemed like fear. "Honor? Everything okay?"

Honor gave a small shake of her head. "I'm not sure where to start with that one." She blew out a breath and stepped over next to Quinn, resting her left hand on the dark red vinyl a few inches from Quinn's hip. She might have touched her, except knowing what she needed to do, she couldn't. "Your chest x-ray is normal. You have an occasional extra beat on your rhythm strip, but nothing that looks problematic to me. Of course, your cardiologist needs to compare it to your previous traces."

"I'll make sure he gets that first thing on Monday," Quinn said quickly. *Please don't look so upset.* "I promise."

"Good." Honor hesitated, then straightened her shoulders. "I want you to take a few days off, Quinn."

Quinn's stomach plummeted. "I can work, Honor. This has happened before, and my shoulder will be stiff for a few days, but—"

"It's not about your shoulder," Honor interrupted quietly. "It's about your medical condition."

"What about it?" Quinn's throat was dry.

"Right now, I'm not certain you should be working in the emergency room." Honor drew a shaky breath. This was harder than she had imagined, because she knew she was going to hurt Quinn. But she had a responsibility as the ER chief to see that the patients as well as the department were protected. "No one informed me of your medical status. If they had, I'm not sure I would've hired you."

The panic hit Quinn hard and fast. She was going to lose everything—again. Only this time it was so much worse. It wasn't just about her job. This time it was about *everything* that mattered in her life.

"Honor, please. I want to work." Her hands were shaking, and she clenched them tightly against her thighs. The only thing that had gotten her through the last few months was Saxon Sinclair's promise that she'd be able to work—the promise to help Quinn find the kind of position that would let her be a little bit of who she was. "I *need* to work."

"And I need the patients *and* you to be *safe*. This isn't an ordinary ER, for God's sake. A few days ago, you were doing an open thoracotomy in the procedure room. What if you'd...arrested then?" Just saying the words made Honor nauseous.

"You were there," Quinn pointed out. "You could've done what I was doing."

"Maybe." Honor saw again the empty heart with the ragged tear, the quick sure movements of Quinn's hands, the skill that went beyond training to some inherent gift that only a few surgeons had. She wasn't certain she could've done what Quinn had done; she wasn't certain anyone could have. "Maybe."

"I've been medically cleared to work, Honor." Quinn struggled to keep her voice steady. "The hospital has approved my hiring."

"Without me being involved!" Honor's frustration broke through. "The hospital administrators don't know what we do down here, and you know it."

"Do you think I'd work if I thought I would compromise patient care?" Quinn's eyes searched Honor's. *Do you really think so little of me? Do you distrust me that much?*

"No." Honor's expression grew tender, and despite her resolve, she moved her hand to Quinn's shoulder and stroked her softly. "I don't think you would. But it's not about what I think, Quinn."

"What then?" Quinn's voice was a whisper of longing and hurt. She was so tired of fighting this battle and of losing, over and over. Unthinkingly, she leaned into the comfort of Honor's touch.

"I need to talk to my chief and the hospital attorneys, Quinn." It was all Honor could do not to thread her fingers into Quinn's thick dark hair and draw Quinn's head to her breast. Quinn's torment was palpable, and Honor's heart ached for what Quinn had suffered and for what she herself now added to that pain. "Medico-legally, if...something...happens to you down here that could even remotely be construed as adversely affecting patient care, it would be a nightmare."

"Do you think I don't know that?" Briefly, Quinn closed her eyes, and when she opened them again, despair swam close to the surface. "Why do you think I'm here and not at St. Michael's?"

"What are you talking about?"

"I can't get malpractice insurance to practice surgery." Quinn rubbed her face with her good hand and took a deep breath. "As a trauma surgeon, I'd be alone in the OR. At night, and sometimes even during the day, there wouldn't be another surgeon available to take over if I...became incapacitated."

"Surgeons aren't interchangeable," Honor said softly, beginning to understand. If Quinn collapsed during a critical part of a procedure, the nurses and anesthesiologists in attendance would not be able to stand in for her. And other readily available surgeons were unlikely to have the training to take her place.

"Right. If I've got the aorta cross-clamped and my heart decides to quit, by the time they find someone else who could do what needed to be done, the patient could be dead." Quinn sighed. "That's why the law requires two heart surgeons for every case, and two general surgeons for a lot of straightforward abdominal cases that are a lot less complicated than trauma surgery. No insurance company will touch me."

"But we always have at least three attendings present in the emergency room," Honor stated. "And *that's* why you could get coverage for this position."

Quinn nodded. "In the ER, I'd always have immediate backup."

"I'm still surprised the hospital hired you."

"So am I, to tell you the truth. I'm qualified—"

Honor gave a short laugh, removing her hand from Quinn's shoulder because she wanted to put her arm around her. "*That* is an understatement."

"Thanks." Smiling weakly, Quinn blew out her breath. "They must have figured it was financially advantageous, and some administrator was probably afraid I'd invoke the Americans with Disabilities Act if my medical condition was used as a reason not to hire me."

"You could, you know," Honor said quietly. "If I contest your hiring."

"God, Honor." Quinn frowned. "You can't believe I'd do that."

"No. No, I don't think you would." Honor sighed. "Quinn, I'm sorry. I still need to look into this whole situation."

"I won't fight you, Honor," Quinn said just as quietly. "This is your ER. I appreciate your concerns." Carefully, Quinn slid down off the table, gritting her teeth as the movement rekindled the pain in her shoulder. "I'll accept whatever you decide."

"Where are you going?" Honor asked sharply as Quinn started slowly toward the curtain and the hallway beyond.

"Home." Her voice was dull with fatigue and resignation.

"Just how do you plan to get there?"

"I'll call a cab." Quinn reached for the curtain. "Thanks for taking care of me."

"Damn it." Quickly, Honor moved to Quinn's side and grasped her right hand. "Wait just a minute, Maguire. Linda needs to get you into the shoulder immobilizer. Then *I'll* take you home."

"That's not necessary."

Gently, Honor turned Quinn to face her. Then, because she had to, had wanted to for hours, she lifted her hand and rested her palm tenderly against Quinn's cheek. "I want to. Please."

"Honor," Quinn whispered in a voice filled with longing and desire.

Silence closed around them as they leaned into one another, their eyes locked. Quinn's lids were heavy, her throat tight, as she watched Honor's lips slowly part. A breath away, then not even that. *Oh God, yes.*

The curtain slid back, and Linda gave a small cry of surprise to find them just on the other side, and just about to kiss. "Uh...hey, hi! I've got that immobilizer."

In a daze, Honor stepped back, her hand dropping to her side. Her heart pounded wildly. *Oh my God. I was going to kiss her. This is crazy.*

"Do you want me to get this on her?" Linda held up the soft padded sling and looked uncertainly from her friend to Quinn.

Honor appeared confused, almost bewildered, and the expression on Quinn's face was enough to make any woman melt.

Huskily, Honor said, "Yes. Go ahead." Carefully, she stepped around Quinn and into the hall. "I'll finish the paperwork, and we can get going."

Quinn stood cooperatively while Linda adjusted the straps on the immobilizer, not even noticing the discomfort as her shoulder was manipulated. Her gaze was fixed on Honor, who leaned against the counter at the nurses' station down the hall, writing in Quinn's chart. At that moment, Quinn wasn't thinking about her medical career, or her heart condition, or anything else in her life except the look in Honor's eyes when their lips had almost touched. There had been tenderness, and compassion, and beneath the caring, desire. She shuddered, remembering.

"You okay, sweetie?" Linda asked as she stepped back, satisfied that Quinn's shoulder was taken care of.

"No, I don't think so."

Linda followed Quinn's gaze, and she laughed softly. "Everything is going to be fine."

Quinn looked at her, uncertainty and disbelief on her face. "I don't see how."

"Just give it a little time." She slid her arm around Quinn's waist and gave her a quick hug. "Now I'm taking you home with me."

"I'm okay," Quinn assured her.

"Oh, I know that. But I'll feel much better if you spend the night with us."

"That's very kind of you, but—"

"If you don't stay with us, Honor is going to insist you be admitted for monitoring. Do you really want to go a round with her on that again?"

Quinn sighed wearily. "I'm not exactly at my fighting best right now. So thank you, I accept."

"All set?" Honor asked as she rejoined them. She studied Quinn intently. *Pale, but she looks steady. I wish she were coming home with me, instead of going with Linda.* That thought startled her so much that her next words came out more sharply than she intended. "We should go."

"Right," Quinn said as Honor turned and walked away. *Everything is going to be fine. Right.*

CHAPTER TWELVE

"Where are you parked?" Linda asked, stopping by the side of her Volvo, which she had parked in the fire lane in the ER turnaround.

Honor stopped walking a few feet away with Quinn by her side. "Just up ahead in my usual spot."

Leaning against her open car door, Linda suggested, "Why don't you come in and have a drink when you drop Quinn off? I think the party is pretty much over, so we can just sit around and unwind."

"Thanks, but I think I'll just pick Arly up and call it a day," Honor said quietly. She was still reeling from the afternoon's events, to say nothing of the near-kiss moments before. *I don't know what I'm doing anymore.*

"Phyllis took Arly home when I was leaving to come over here."

"Then I'll go on home and give Phyllis a break."

"I can ride back with Linda, if you want," Quinn said in a voice too low for Linda to hear. "I've already taken up enough of your time, and I appreciate everything you've already done."

Even though the ER experience had been traumatic for Quinn, emotionally *and* physically, she knew that Honor's intervention had truly made it as painless as possible. She couldn't blame Honor for wanting to look into the legal ramifications of her medical situation, now that Honor was aware of it. And no matter what the eventual result of Honor's inquiries, she was far from angry at her.

"No, I want to drive you," Honor insisted. The afternoon had been an emotional roller coaster for her, first with the stress of handling Quinn's shoulder injury in the field, then the shock of discovering Quinn's much more serious underlying medical condition. Honor feared that if she just turned her back and walked away now, she'd drown in the feelings of helplessness, anxiety, and anger. She desperately wanted just a few moments alone in the car with Quinn when they wouldn't be struggling with professional differences or emergencies. She was stunned to realize that that was the only thing she could think about. "I'm only a few houses away from Linda's, so it's really no trouble. If that's okay?"

"It's more than okay." Quinn smiled, wanting nothing more in the world than to be with Honor—anywhere, for any reason. "I'd like very much to go with you. Thank you."

"You're welcome." Honor smiled softly at Quinn's impeccable manners even in moments of tension. "Your mama sure did a good job of raising you."

"She'd be pleased to hear that," Quinn said seriously. Then she grinned. "There were quite a few times when I was growing up that I'm pretty sure she had her doubts."

"Now why do I find that completely believable?" Laughing, suddenly feeling her spirits lift, Honor waved goodbye to Linda, led the way to her Subaru, and held the passenger-side door open for Quinn. Automatically, she slid her arm around Quinn's waist to steady her while she climbed in, and it was then that she felt a faint tingling in her arm. At the same time, Quinn shivered and gave a small gasp.

The sensation was so fleeting that Honor might have ignored it if she hadn't already been so sensitized to the situation. She recognized immediately that the slight buzz she'd experienced was Quinn's cardiac defibrillator firing. The focal electrical discharge from the internal defibrillator was not painful, but the current was large enough for someone in direct contact with Quinn to feel it.

"Quinn?" Honor consciously kept her tone light, although her own heart had begun racing.

"I'm all right." Quinn blinked, then grimaced faintly. *God, just what I* didn't *need to happen now!*

"Is that the first time it's gone off since the accident this afternoon?" Honor asked intently, studying Quinn's face.

"Yes." Quinn said grimly. "The last time was two days ago, when I was in the gym. Fortunately, Mandy thought it was static electricity, so I didn't need to explain."

Honor's eyes narrowed. "*Mandy* was touching you?"

Surprised by the edge in Honor's tone, Quinn lifted a shoulder and rolled her eyes. "She's got wandering hands."

No kidding. Keeping her arm around Quinn until she was situated in the front seat, Honor bit back a retort and concentrated on what mattered. "Were you symptomatic that time at the gym?"

"I had a little irregularity then, but *not* this time." Quinn brushed her fingers over the top of Honor's hand as Honor withdrew her arm. "Thanks. I'm absolutely okay now."

"Did you have any pain just now?"

"No. Honor, I'm fine."

"Dizziness? Anything at all?"

Quinn shook her head. "No. Nothing. I promise."

"Good. That's good." Honor's pulse continued to pound, but Quinn seemed fine, and that helped quell her anxiety. Nevertheless, it concerned her that the defibrillator had discharged, indicating that Quinn's cardiac rhythm was erratic. "I don't like it triggering this frequently, Quinn."

"About twenty percent of the time it's firing unnecessarily." Quinn sighed. "Dan Caroli, my cardiologist, says it's *inconvenient,* but nothing to worry about. That's probably all it was this time."

"Is it painful, when it happens?" Honor stood with her forearm braced against the top of the car, leaning in slightly so that she could study Quinn's face. She hated to think of her in pain.

"Not really. It surprises me, and gives me a bit of a jolt, but it's over pretty fast." She smiled reassuringly, concerned by the worry in Honor's eyes. "I'm okay. Really."

"Mmm. I know," Honor murmured. She rested her fingers against Quinn's shoulder, rubbing her lightly in small circles. "I want you to stay with me tonight."

Quinn's eyes grew round and her lips parted in surprise. "I'm sorry?"

Honor smiled gently. "I want you to stay at *my* house, not Linda's. I'm sure you're absolutely fine, but I'm a little bit worried that your defibrillator fired so soon after the accident. You hit your left shoulder very hard, and the leads go right through that area."

"It's a pretty sturdy device, Honor," Quinn pointed out. "You know, Dick Cheney has one, and *he* got to *keep* his job."

"He has friends in high places." Honor closed the door, walked to the other side, and slid behind the wheel. "But you're a *lot* more important than Dick Cheney. So, if you start having more irregularity, I want to be close by. Linda's terrific, and supremely competent." She started the engine, looked over her shoulder, and backed out of her parking place. "But I'm the boss, remember?"

"I got that." Quinn leaned back, tired and sore. The truth was, she *wanted* to go home with Honor. She didn't want to be alone, not because she was worried about her heart or because her shoulder hurt like hell. She just wanted to be where Honor was, because she felt things when she was around Honor that she'd never felt around any other woman. She liked to look at her, to listen to her voice, to watch her with her child. She liked the fleeting caresses that Honor wasn't even aware of bestowing, and the precious moments when Honor forgot herself and let her touch linger. And most of all, she liked the way Honor's lips had parted in that instant before they had almost kissed. "Believe me, I know you're the boss." She laughed. "I got that, loud and clear."

"Good. Then no arguing." Honor reached over and patted Quinn's knee. "Thanks, Quinn. It will save me a lot of worrying if you're somewhere I can see you."

"I appreciate your concern, really. Thank you."

Honor stared straight ahead, knowing that it was much more than concern and much more than her sense of professional responsibility. If there was even the remotest chance that Quinn could develop a problem, she wanted to be the one to take care of her. And more than that, she enjoyed the way she felt when Quinn was around. She enjoyed the undercurrent of affection and excitement, and, unexpectedly, the sense of easy companionship.

Almost all of her personal time was spent either with Phyllis and Arly, both of whom she loved more than life, or her good friends Linda and Robin. But she had not had the company of a woman whom she admired and found as intriguing as Quinn for years. She hadn't thought she'd wanted it, or needed it, or missed it. In the last few days, though, she had discovered that she did.

When she turned onto the residential street where she, Linda, and Robin lived, Honor tooted her horn and pulled up alongside

Linda's car. Linda rolled down her window, and Honor motioned for Quinn to do the same.

Leaning across Quinn to see Linda, Honor called out Quinn's window, "I'm taking Quinn to my house."

"Everything okay?"

"Yes—just a slight change in plans."

Linda looked surprised as well as curious, but just nodded. "Okay. If you need anything, call us. We'll be home. Take care of your shoulder, Quinn."

"Will do," Quinn replied. "Thanks for the help earlier."

"No problem, sweetie. I'll talk to you both tomorrow."

With that, Linda drove on and Honor followed her for half a block and then turned into her driveway. She swiveled on the seat after shutting off the engine and once again rested her hand gently on Quinn's thigh. "I'm just going to tell Arly and Phyllis that you're staying with us because of your shoulder. They don't need to know about the other, okay?"

"Thanks." Quinn hesitated, then placed her hand over Honor's. "Are you sure it will be all right with Phyllis if I stay?"

Honor raised an eyebrow in surprise. "Why wouldn't it be?"

"I...uh...wouldn't want her to get the wrong idea."

"And what idea would that be, Quinn?" Honor asked softly, unconsciously turning her hand so that their palms met. When their fingers intertwined, she didn't move hers away.

"You were married to her daughter, weren't you?"

Honor gasped, startled by the question and caught off guard by the thousand images of Terry that instantly flew through her mind. Her hand trembled against Quinn's. "Yes."

"You're still wearing her ring."

"Yes." Honor's voice came out a whisper.

"I wouldn't want Phyllis...or you...to think I don't respect that."

"Oh, Quinn," Honor breathed, touched and grateful. "I know this afternoon has been difficult, but I hope you consider me a friend."

"I do." Even as Quinn said it, meaning it, she also knew that her feelings for Honor were already much more than that. "But—"

"No," Honor said quickly, assaulted by so many conflicting emotions that she felt almost dizzy. "Let's just let that be enough. Please."

Quinn heard the tremor in Honor's voice, and even as disappointment settled like a stone in her depths, she nodded. "Of course."

"Phyllis and Arly will be delighted with your company." Honor squeezed Quinn's hand and gently withdrew her fingers. Then she took a deep breath and smiled tremulously. "So will I."

❖

Quinn followed Honor through the back door into the cozy kitchen and stopped just over the threshold, feeling suddenly awkward. Arly perched on a stool by the kitchen table, deftly manipulating a Game Boy, a glass of milk by her side. Phyllis was in the midst of making a salad, and the counter next to the sink where she stood was covered with vegetables in various stages of preparation. The scene harkened back to a time that Quinn had long forgotten, a time of lazy summer afternoons and family dinners. The last twelve years of her life had been a nonstop climb to professional accomplishment, with almost no time for anything personal. She hadn't even been aware that anything was missing until everything had come to a screeching halt a few months before, and when she had looked around, she'd realized that she was alone in a life that was empty except for her work. If it hadn't been for Sax and Jude's friendship, she wasn't sure she would have made it. *I don't belong here, in Honor's home, in Honor's life. What was I thinking?*

"Quinn!" Arly hopped down and came running, stopping an inch away to stare wide-eyed at Quinn's shoulder and the blue sling with its Velcro straps and buckles. "Wow. What is that? Does it hurt? How long do you have to wear it? Does this mean you won't be able to coach soccer?"

Laughing, Quinn felt her discomfort dissipate a little. "It's called an immobilizer, and I only need it for a couple of days. No, it doesn't hurt much, and it sure isn't going to keep me from coaching."

"That's good!" Arly turned to Honor. "How did you fix Quinn's shoulder, Mom?"

"Find me your *Color Anatomy!* book, and I'll show you."

"Oh, cool. I'll be right back," Arly called to the room in general and ran off.

"Is that her normal speed?" Quinn chuckled.

"She has two speeds," Honor explained affectionately. "Fast and faster."

Phyllis regarded Quinn intently. Her color was ashen, and there were shadows beneath her eyes that hadn't been there only hours before. "How are you feeling, Quinn?"

"Just a little sore," Quinn assured her.

"Uh-huh." Phyllis pointed to a chair. "Sit down. You're staying for dinner, I hope?"

"Actually," Honor interjected, "Quinn is staying with us for a day or so."

A day or so? Quinn's eyebrows rose in surprise.

Honor continued smoothly, "That shoulder immobilizer makes it a little hard for her to manage things alone, and I thought it would be easier for her here."

"That's sensible," Phyllis agreed, aware of something unspoken passing between the two younger women, yet accepting the explanation at face value for the moment. Clearly Quinn *did* need some help; she looked like she was about to fall down. "Dinner won't be for at least an hour or so. Quinn, maybe you'd like to lie down for awhile?"

"I'm not really worth much with just one arm," Quinn said, "but I could still probably help you get dinner ready."

Phyllis laughed. "Thank you, but I enjoy doing it. It makes me feel useful."

Honor gave her a quick hug. "Useful doesn't even come close. You know we couldn't manage without you."

"Take Quinn upstairs, Honor," Phyllis directed. "Something tells me that shoulder is hurting a little bit more than she wants to let on."

Quinn blushed. "I can see that I have no secrets from you."

"I've had some practice over the years with bumps and bruises and tough girls who pretend they don't hurt," Phyllis said, regarding Honor affectionately.

At that moment, Arly skidded back into the kitchen, extending the coloring book with its anatomic images. "Here it is. Show me what you did to Quinn."

"I will, honey, in just a minute. I'm going to take Quinn upstairs first so she can have a nap."

"Maybe she can come up with us and bring the book along?" Quinn asked carefully, mindful of Honor's authority. "*I* want to see this, too."

"You win." Laughing, Honor threw up her hands. "Let's go, you two."

A minute later, Honor opened the door to the guest room on the second floor and motioned Quinn in. "The bathroom is just down the hall to your right. I'll put some fresh towels and sundries out for you. The phone is by the bed over there, in case you want to make a call."

Quinn looked around the warm, comfortably furnished room, feeling instantly at home. It had the kind of personal touches that her apartment lacked—small area rugs on the hardwood floors, bright curtains adorning the windows, and walls and furnishings in soothing earth tones. She was tired and sore and the double bed with the patterned comforter looked enormously appealing. "This is wonderful." She looked at Honor, wishing she could tell her how much it meant to her to be there. Huskily, she said, "Thank you."

"No need," Honor replied, her throat tight. Quinn's eyes were smudged with pain, and Honor had the sudden urge to take Quinn by the hand, lead her to the bed, and lie down with her. She wanted to cradle Quinn close and hold her while she slept. The desire was so powerful, she ached. "Why don't you stretch out for a while, and I'll call you when dinner is ready."

"I think I will, in a minute." Quinn sat down on the edge of the bed and patted the spot next to her. "Come on, Arly. Sit here. Then Mom can show us what she did."

Honor sat down, too, with Arly between them. She reached for the coloring book, found a drawing of the human skeleton, and, while Arly watched with rapt attention, pointed out the various structures around the shoulder. Then, in simple terms, she explained what had happened when Quinn had fallen. "So, in order to fix it, you have to move the bones so they fit back together again."

Arly looked up at Quinn with a serious expression. "Did it hurt?"

"It hurt when I dislocated it," Quinn explained. "But it felt much better as soon as your mom put everything back where it belonged."

"So you'll be all right now, right?"

Quinn nodded. "In a few days, I'll be back to normal." She looked at Honor over Arly's head, smiling ruefully. "Just like nothing happened."

Honor, her eyes tinged with sadness, held Quinn's gaze. Never had she wanted to ease someone's hurt as much as in that moment. Knowing that she had contributed to Quinn's unhappiness made it all the worse. She cleared her throat and said softly, "We should let Quinn rest now, honey. Maybe you can go see if Grandmom needs some help with dinner."

"Can I stay here with Quinn? I could read to her like *you* do when I'm sick."

"Maybe later," Honor said gently. "Now scoot."

"Okay." Arly looked hopefully at Quinn. "I'll see you later, right?"

"You bet."

Quinn smiled as Arly jumped down and hurried away. "She's something."

"Yes." Honor laughed fondly. "You're very good with her."

"I'm winging it," Quinn admitted with a grin. "Not much practice with kids."

"Like I said earlier, you have very good instincts."

Quinn met Honor's eyes. "You think?"

"I do." *You are such a wonderful combination of everything I admire.* Fearful that Quinn could somehow read her thoughts, Honor reached down and lifted Quinn's right foot, pulling off her sneaker. "You're about to cave, Quinn. Let's get you under the covers."

"I can manage."

Honor shook her head and picked up the other foot. "Undoubtedly, but it will be easier if I help. You should take your jeans off, too. You'll be able to sleep more comfortably."

"Those I can get," Quinn stated adamantly.

"Of course." Honor blushed. *God, what am I thinking? I can't undress her. Not when I want to touch her, just...touch her.*

"Do you maybe have some aspirin?" Quinn asked quietly, getting to her feet. *All I need is for you to put your hands on me. I'll come apart if you do.*

"I'll get you another pain pill." Honor averted her gaze as she realized that Quinn was waiting to unzip her jeans and headed hastily for the door. "I'll be back in a couple of minutes."

When Honor returned, a glass of water in one hand and a Tylenol with codeine tablet in the other, Quinn was in bed with the covers drawn up to her waist, fast asleep. She had kept her polo shirt on, since it was impossible for her to remove it alone with the shoulder immobilizer in place. With her vibrant blue eyes closed, she seemed defenseless and young. For one fleeting second, Honor envisioned the mechanical device lodged in Quinn's chest, a silent testament to her vulnerability. Honor hurt, thinking of all that Quinn had lost.

Quietly, she crossed the room and placed the pill and the water on the bedside table. For a long moment, she stood still, watching the slow rise and fall of Quinn's chest and the restless flutter of her eyelids in sleep. Ever so carefully, she rested her fingertips against Quinn's cheek. She touched her out of tenderness and caring, but the subtle heat from Quinn's skin stirred an answering fire that caught her unawares. She had forgotten the wonder of the quick flare of passion when it was least expected. She had never thought to experience that excitement again, and the unmistakable thrum of desire that swelled within her was both exulting and terrifying.

Oh, Quinn. What have you done to me?

CHAPTER THIRTEEN

When Quinn awoke, the room was dark. For a moment, she had no idea where she was, and the quick surge of anxiety produced a flutter in her chest. It was the kind of feeling that ordinarily went unnoticed to most, but that for her—even as she recognized Honor's house and her pulse settled—caused a clenching in the stomach and a ripple of fear. She'd gotten used to the heightened awareness of the beat of her own heart in the weeks since her illness, and for hours at a time, she rarely thought about the defibrillator beneath her skin and the electrical wires implanted in her heart. Were it not for the resurgence of professional problems resulting from Honor learning of her condition, she probably wouldn't be thinking of it now.

Waiting for the shock that didn't come, Quinn wondered if there would ever come a time when she would be able to forget that her life was dependent upon a mechanical device. She didn't even dare imagine a time when the defibrillator might be removed, although in her distant reaches, she hoped.

Needing the defibrillator isn't so much different than what we all live with every day—depending for our survival upon fragile cells and vulnerable organs that can be damaged or destroyed by accident or disease. It just seems unnatural.

That's what she told herself, and that's what she wanted to believe.

She also reminded herself of what her cardiologist and Sax had told her—that there was no reason she couldn't lead a normal life. But it was difficult to accept that when her chosen career had been derailed and the alternative one was about to be. And now, lying in bed in Honor's house, she wondered if she could even *have* a normal relationship. Would it be fair to anyone, but most especially to a woman like Honor who had already lost one lover, to encourage intimacy and attachment when Quinn's medical condition made her existence so tenuous?

And there was no doubt in her mind that that was what she wanted—a relationship with Honor that went beyond friendship. She'd felt the connection to Honor from the instant they'd met, and every moment they'd been together thereafter had strengthened it. She was drawn to Honor's strength and certainty as well as to her tender compassion. And there was no denying the desire that simmered whenever she thought of her, and that burst upon her like an inferno in Honor's presence. The sound of her voice, the touch of her hand, the curve of her smile—everything excited Quinn.

Sighing, frustrated by events she could not control and plagued by a physical urgency she could not quench, Quinn thrashed restlessly beneath the sheets. She heard no sound in the house and had lost her usual intrinsic sense of the time, probably as a result of the earlier pain medication. Although she presumed that everyone had gone to bed, Quinn found herself wide awake. And not just wide awake—thinking about Honor had stirred more than her loneliness. She was aroused in a way that she had not been even *before* her recent illness had overshadowed her sexual urges. In the past, sex had been a pleasant form of recreation and a satisfying outlet for stress. The physical hunger she felt now was an ache that reached to her very soul, and she knew in a place beyond reason that only Honor could assuage the need.

Quinn pushed the sheets aside and swung her legs over the edge of the bed. The immobilizer kept her arm strapped across her midsection, hampering her movements and promising to make undressing a challenge. Nevertheless, at the moment, she desperately needed a shower to divert her from the insistent unrest that beat between her thighs. She could, she supposed, attempt to quiet her physical turmoil by her own hand, but that option held no appeal. Relief that sated her body but not her soul would be empty of pleasure.

She pushed herself upright, searched until she found her jeans folded over a nearby chair, and, with her pants over her free arm, padded barefoot to the door. The hallway beyond, lit dimly by a single sconce at the top of the far stairway, was deserted, and she headed in the direction of the bathroom Honor had pointed out earlier. She'd almost reached it when Honor stepped out of the room directly across the hall.

Silently, they regarded one another in the deep stillness of the sleeping household.

"I thought I heard you," Honor said quietly. In truth, she'd been lying awake for hours, thinking about Quinn in the room down the hall. Remembering the way she'd looked asleep, and how it had felt to touch her. Knowing that she wanted to touch her again—everywhere. Admitting that she wanted to be touched in return. She hadn't wanted that since Terry.

"Sorry," Quinn whispered, trying desperately to read what she saw in Honor's eyes. Their dark depths were hazy, liquid and warm. She recognized desire, and although her mind might question the rightness of it, her body did not. Her belly fluttered. Distantly, it occurred to her that she was naked except for a shirt and briefs. As if in apology, she lifted the jeans in her hand. "I was going to take a shower."

Honor's eyes flickered down Quinn's body. The bare legs were smooth and strong. The navy shirt stopped just at Quinn's hips, and a triangle of white nestled between her thighs. Honor wrenched her gaze upward before she could reach out and rest her palm over that soft pale swelling. Her heart thundered madly in her chest, and her legs trembled. Her desire was a wild thing, not rational, not reasoned, but sharp and clear as summer lightning. Scorching and hot and impossible to hold.

"You'll need some help with that shoulder," Honor said hoarsely.

"Yes."

"I could call Phyllis...or *I* could help you."

"You." Quinn couldn't take her eyes from Honor's. She doubted that Honor had any idea that her eyes spoke of arid plains long thirsting for rain and the promise of blossoms opening to the kiss of moisture upon their petals.

If I touch her, she won't tell me to stop. If I touch her, I won't be able to stop. And if I touch her now, it will be too soon. Because she doesn't know what's in her eyes. Her body might welcome me, but not her heart.

Honor's legs trembled and her hands shook. She didn't recognize herself; she didn't recognize what she was feeling. Or she did, and was stunned by it. *How can I desire her this way? How can I feel that if I don't have her hands on me, I'll die from the wanting?*

Quinn backed up a step, knowing that if she remained within touching distance, no amount of rationalization would keep her from reaching out and tracing her fingers along the delicate edge of collarbone laid bare by the soft cotton robe that came to Honor's midthigh.

"If you give me a hand with the buckles and straps, I can handle the rest of it."

Throat dry, Honor nodded. "Okay. I'll find you some sweats and leave them on the counter. Then, when you're ready to get dressed...I'll give you a hand."

"Good. That sounds good." Quinn found the handle behind her, opened the bathroom door, and slipped inside. Honor followed, and now they were even closer within the confines of the small room.

"How do you feel?" Honor asked as she opened the first strap holding Quinn's arm confined to her chest. Her fingers brushed against the curve of Quinn's breast under the cotton shirt as she carefully lifted the sling.

Quinn bit her lip, unsuccessfully willing her nipple not to tighten. *Apparently, the autonomic nervous system does not respond to mental commands.* In another minute, Honor had released the last buckle and Quinn cradled her injured left arm with her right while Honor worked the strap over her neck and eased the supporting material down her shoulder.

"All right?" Honor's touch was gentle.

"Not bad," Quinn informed her. She suddenly felt exposed in only her polo shirt and underwear.

Honor looked up, catching Quinn's eyes on her and liking the quick rush of pleasure at the appreciation she saw in those blue depths. "Your shirt."

Quinn nodded. "At least we've had some practice with that."

"Mmm. Remind me to bring you something with buttons." Once again, Honor carefully and efficiently worked the shirt off until Quinn stood naked except for her briefs. Honor didn't mean to, or maybe she did—she wasn't certain anymore of *what* she intended—but her gaze dropped to Quinn's breasts. They were beautiful—high and firm and rose tipped, the hard nipples blushed dark with desire. Slowly she lifted a hand, her fingers trembling. *Oh God, this is a mistake. But she's so, so lovely.*

"Quinn, I..." Eyes slightly unfocused, Honor took a step closer

The light danced along the sliver of gold that encircled her ring finger as she reached to touch Quinn's face. She seemed unaware of it, but Quinn wasn't.

"Honor," Quinn breathed, stomach and chest tight as she ached for the offered caress. "I...should get...the shower."

"Yes." Honor's tone was nearly mournful as she let her hand fall. She backed away, a hard knot of need in the pit of her stomach. "I'll get those clothes."

"Thanks." Quinn feared that the next time she stood alone with Honor with nothing between them but desire, she wouldn't be able to say no. Instinctively, she knew that Honor would regret it if anything happened between them, and that regret would at the very least erect a barrier between them. Worse, it might create a chasm that could never be breached. There was a connection between them, and Quinn hoped desperately that Honor felt it, too. But she would not risk losing everything to ease her longing now. "I should lock the bathroom door, I guess, in case Arly wakes up and wanders in. You can just leave the clothes on the hall table."

"Of course." Honor shook her head as if dazed. "Come get me when you're dressed, then, and I'll help you with the sling. My room is the one across the hall."

"All right."

"If you need anything..."

"Thanks," Quinn said softly. "I'm okay for now."

"Right," Honor replied, working to sound casual as she let herself out of the bathroom. "I'll see you in a few minutes."

When Quinn had showered and dressed in the gray PMC sweatpants and soft blue cotton work shirt that she'd found folded on the small telephone table in the hall, she stepped quietly to Honor's door. It was slightly ajar, and as she closed her fingers around the knob, a fist of anticipation curled deep in the pit of her stomach, causing her to hesitate. *I'm not so sure the* bedroom *will be safe ground when even the bathroom wasn't.*

❖

The door opened quietly, admitting a splinter of light that slashed across the bed, backlighting the figure in the doorway for an instant before darkness descended once again.

Lying alone in the night, feeling her heartbeat accelerate in anticipation, she searched the darkness for the soft sounds of movement, so ordinary and yet so exciting. The quiet thud of a shoe, the rasp of a zipper sliding open, the gentle sigh of breath as clothes fell from weary flesh. As she listened, her body awakened to the promise of a familiar touch—exciting still—and her legs twitched beneath the sheets. The slight pressure of a body easing onto the bed beside her brought blood rushing to her belly, and she grew hard with the insistent beat of desire. Welcoming dew anointed her thighs, and her nipples, not yet touched, rose in eager expectation.

"Did I wake you?" came the soft voice as a hand gentled over her cheek and down her neck.

Fingers drifted over her throat, traced her collarbones, and came to rest along the curve of her breast. A thumb flicked knowingly over her nipple, and she whimpered with the swift spear of pleasure that shot deep inside her.

"No, I...was...waiting." She lifted her face to meet warm lips, reaching up with one arm to encircle the strong back. Her breasts brushed against breasts; her nipples glided over muscle and satin-smooth skin and tightened to the point of pain.

A gasp of pleasure, a moan of urgency. She pushed the sheets away, baring her body, drawing her lover down upon her. Opening her legs, she lifted her hips, calling her lover to her. When a taut thigh pressed against the center of her arousal, she arched her back as a wild cry flew from her throat. The moan drifted off on the tide of her desire, a mixture of ecstasy and mourning.

Desperate lest she be left alone on the sharp pinnacle of her need, she claimed her lover's lips, her tongue demanding entrance even as she drowned in the flood of their passion. Her clitoris throbbed in time to the rhythm of the thigh thrusting between hers; the muscles in her stomach jumped as pleasure slashed through her. Gasping, shivering on the edge of orgasm, she dug her fingers into the tight, straining back above her, bowing upward until every inch of her flesh met fevered flesh.

She felt teeth on her neck, hot urgent breath thirsting against her own damp skin, and the slick sheen of arousal varnishing her thigh.

"Come with me," she panted, the spiral of release breaking deep within.

The answer was a helpless shudder and a low, tortured groan.

Hearing her lover's need, feeling the consuming desire, drove her over, and she fell into orgasm with a frantic cry. Even as the scream tore from her body and every nerve burned, she felt her lover tremble in her embrace, and, together, they surrendered to the power of their love. As she came, breathless and exultant, she gloried in the wonder of their union.

❖

When Honor opened her eyes, the sun was shining, the room was Sunday-morning-in-summer warm, and she was alone. She lay still for long moments, watching wisps of clouds float slowly by her window in a sky too blue to be real. But the beauty outside was real, achingly real, just as the still-lingering ripples of pleasure deep in her belly were real.

Sighing, she turned onto her back and closed her eyes. She could feel the dampness between her thighs and the faint echo of the pulse that had beat hard there as she had orgasmed. She had not awakened at the peak of climax but had lingered in the aftermath of passion, luxuriating in the comfort of a lover's embrace.

Explanations abounded, from the scientific to the psychological. None of them mattered to her, because she knew the simple truth. She had gone to sleep wanting a woman. She had closed her eyes with the image of a woman ablaze in her mind. While she had slept, a woman had come to her, had answered her need, and had pleasured her. And Honor could not deny that she had welcomed it, reveled in it, rejoiced in the joining.

She covered her left hand with her right and gently turned her wedding band. There had never been anyone other than Terry, but it had not been Terry who had come to her in the night. It had not been her lover whom she had longed for as she lay down alone. It had not been her lover whom she had envisioned behind restless lids as her body burned. It had not been her lover who had touched her in passion and incited her to lose herself in desire.

She was saddened by that. Saddened that a time had come in her life when it had not been the only woman she had ever loved who had moved her and claimed her so completely.

It was only a dream.

But she knew it was much more than that, and in the part of her heart that lived on past sorrow and loss, she felt something she had not felt for many years. She sensed the whisper of joy.

CHAPTER FOURTEEN

It was not yet six when Honor made her way to the kitchen to start coffee. She'd need to leave for work in an hour, and Phyllis would be over in half an hour to be on hand when Arly awakened. Ten minutes later, she stood at the kitchen window with a mug of steaming Hawaiian Blue Voodoo and looked out into the backyard. Quinn lounged in a lawn chair beneath a large willow tree, head back and eyes closed. Just seeing her gave Honor a jolt. A most pleasant jolt. After a moment's hesitation, she filled another mug and slipped quietly outside.

"Where's your sling?" Honor asked as she sat down in the chair next to Quinn.

Quinn rolled her head to the side, opened her eyes, and grinned sheepishly. "I lost it."

"Uh-huh. That's convenient." Despite herself, Honor smiled as she extended the coffee. "Can I tempt you with this?"

"Tempt me? You can have my soul for that, even if it's only *half* as good as it smells." She lifted the coffee and drank, then closed her eyes and sighed with pleasure. "God, this is fabulous."

"Mmm." Honor liked having been the cause of Quinn's undisguised satisfaction. A lot. Probably too much. But at that moment, relaxing in the warm, still, peaceful morning, she didn't care.

Smiling, Quinn said lazily, "So what do I owe you?"

"Well, your *soul* is probably safe for the time being." Pretending to consider, Honor finally grinned. "I'll have to get back to you when I've thought of something suitable."

"Okay," Quinn replied slowly. "You just let me know what, when, and where."

The husky timbre in Quinn's voice was not lost on Honor, although she refused to acknowledge the pleasant warmth that suffused her in response. Instead, she sipped her coffee and studied Quinn's face. There were faint shadows beneath her eyes but her gaze was clear, pain free. "Did you get *any* sleep?"

"Some." Actually, she'd tossed and turned and found it no easier to sleep *after* the shower than before. All she could think about was standing with Honor in the half-light of the hushed hallway and praying that Honor would touch her. The seething arousal that had accompanied the memories hadn't made for a restful night. "I woke up early, and when I looked outside, I had to come down here. You don't see mornings like this in Manhattan."

"No, probably not." Honor set her cup down and stretched out her legs, noting that Quinn held her left arm motionless across her stomach. "How's the shoulder?"

"Better. Stiff—about what I expected."

"You didn't ask me to help you with the immobilizer last night."

"I started to," Quinn said in self-defense, feeling partly embarrassed and partly guilty. "But when I peeked into your room, you looked like you were already asleep."

Yes, and dreaming of you. Honor blushed. "Sorry. You could have awakened me."

Quinn lifted her good shoulder. "I could have. But I didn't think it was necessary."

"Oh, really?"

"Well, I *am* a doctor, too, you know."

"And you're also a jock, and I know how jocks deal with injuries. Ignore them and pretend they never happened."

Quinn laughed. "Guilty." Contemplatively, she sipped her coffee. "How about you? You strike me as being the jock type yourself."

"Not so much, really. I was usually too busy with school. Terry was the jock."

As soon as the words were spoken, Honor stiffened. She didn't usually talk about Terry, at least not with anyone other than Linda and Robin or Phyllis. She couldn't imagine why she had mentioned her to Quinn, of all people.

"Was soccer her game, too?" Quinn asked casually, aware of Honor's sudden discomfort. But it seemed important to keep going. Honor had said they were friends, and if that's truly what they were to be, even if that was *all* they were to be, Terry could not be a secret.

"Soccer, softball, football—you name it, she played it." Honor's voice faltered, then she smiled, a tiny fond lift of her lips. "She was always getting banged up."

"Ah, now I understand Phyllis's comment about tough girls and injuries."

Honor studied Quinn, thinking that she ought to be surprised that Quinn even *knew* about Terry, but she wasn't. Quinn was one of the most instinctively insightful people she had ever met. "You don't miss much, do you?"

"I pay attention," Quinn said quietly. *Especially when it matters so much.*

"I know."

Quinn wanted to ask more, wanted to know about the woman Honor had loved, had married, had borne a child with. Not out of a sense of competition—at least, if she was honest, not so *much* because of that—but out of a deep desire to know Honor. But she also intuited that this was a subject that could not be rushed, and she prudently sought less volatile ground. "You're up pretty early for a Sunday."

"I'm working the day shift."

"Oh, yes." Quinn's eyes darkened, jolted abruptly from the companionable conversation back to the reality of their true relationship. Honor was her boss, and about to make a decision that would affect the rest of Quinn's life. Her voice was tinged with faint frustration and a hint of temper. "I *was* scheduled to work, too. But then, you know that."

Hearing the anger, Honor looked away, then forced herself to meet Quinn's eyes. "Since it's Sunday, I won't be able to reach anyone today about the...situation."

"I didn't expect anything to be resolved until next week," Quinn replied quietly, forcing calm when she felt anything but. Still, she didn't want to fight with Honor, and in her rational mind, she appreciated Honor's sense of responsibility.

"First thing Monday morning, I'll talk to the chief of medicine and the attorneys."

"Thanks. If you need my cardiologist's contact info, I can give you that." She hesitated. "I'll sign a release for you to get copies of my records, too, if you want."

"I don't think that will be necessary, but thank you for offering." Appreciating what an invasion of privacy this was for Quinn, and grateful for her cooperation, Honor sighed and rubbed her forehead. "I'm sorry to put you through this, Quinn. But I'm the head of the department, and I have to be certain that all contingencies have been considered and that we're free from liability."

A muscle bunched along the edge of Quinn's jaw, but she merely nodded.

Speaking almost to herself, Honor muttered, "This could have been avoided if Mary Ann hadn't hired you before I could interview you."

"What do you mean?" Quinn leaned forward, her expression piercingly intent.

Honor regarded Quinn steadily. "What would you have said if I had asked you why you weren't planning on practicing surgery? And I *would* have asked."

"I would have said that I had a medical condition that presently prevented me from doing that."

"And when I asked for details?"

"I would have told you," Quinn said immediately.

"Precisely." Honor ran a hand through her hair. "Mary Ann Jones is an excellent administrator, and I'm very happy to have her as my chief when it's time to negotiate for salary lines and to keep surgery from swallowing up my department." At Quinn's raised eyebrow, Honor laughed. "It's true and you know it. You're all a bunch of territorial bandits."

"She didn't ask me, Honor." She blew out a breath. "I needed this job. I *wanted* this job. I wasn't about to make an announcement that would endanger my chance of getting it."

"I can understand that," Honor replied. And she could. "But I'm responsible for the ER, Quinn, and at some point, I *should* have been involved in the decision."

"I guess I can see why you weren't real happy to see me show up." Quinn reached over and touched her shoulder. "Sorry."

Honor flushed, surprised by the contact, because Quinn rarely initiated it, and embarrassed by her behavior when Quinn first arrived. "I was irritated...actually, I was mightily pissed off...that Mary Ann had gone over my head in hiring you. That wasn't your fault. I apologize for the cool welcome—you didn't deserve that."

"No matter." Quinn turned the empty mug on her knee, staring out over the expanse of green lawn enclosed by a wood privacy fence. Honor's yard was smaller than Linda and Robin's, but still ample and more private. At the moment, it felt as if they were the only two people in the world. Softly, she asked the one thing that really did matter. "Would you have hired me?"

For a long moment, Honor didn't answer. She'd heard the uncertain note in Quinn's voice and seen the faint tremor in the fingers that cradled the ceramic mug. For the first time, she truly appreciated how difficult it must be for Quinn—a woman who was used to being the best, who had achieved far more than most people her age or even older—to suddenly find herself in a position where her value and worth were brought into question. "It would have been hard to turn you down."

Quinn turned her head in Honor's direction and smiled wryly. "Spoken like a true administrator."

"No, I'm completely serious." Honor reached out and rested her hand on Quinn's arm. "You're quite a catch, Quinn Maguire."

It was Quinn's turn to blush. "Is that your professional assessment?"

"Partially."

"And the other part?" Quinn found herself holding her breath as she watched the rich color swirl in Honor's eyes, heavy and drowningly deep.

"Personal...observation." Honor's voice was honey thick. "You're sensitive, and kind, and tender. All good qualities in an... ER physician."

"And you base that on what?" Quinn was embarrassed, but pleased. "My stellar bedside manner?"

"No." Honor's fingers drifted down Quinn's arm until they rested on the top of her hand. "On the way you treat my child." *And me.*

Quinn leaned forward, drawn to the tenderness in Honor's gaze. "She brings out my best side."

"Just wait," Honor murmured, watching Quinn's lips move as she spoke, mesmerized by their moist promise, "until you see what she can bring out in you on one of her *bad* days."

"I look forward to it." Quinn found it hard to take a full breath because she feared that the tiniest movement would fracture their fragile connection. "She must be like you, that way. You bring out... things...in me, too."

"Good things?" Honor's voice had dropped so low that the words were barely a hum in her throat.

"Wonderful things."

They were inches apart, their bodies nearly touching, their fingers lightly entwined. The air was still, warm, and somewhere a carillon sent its melody into the clear morning sky.

"Quinn."

"Yes?"

Honor blinked, and her eyes focused as if awakening from a dream. "I have to go to work."

"I know. And I should go home." Quinn eased back in the chair, oddly content even as Honor moved away and their hands separated. They had broached a few of the things that stood between them. Her illness. Terry. It was a start.

"I want to put your immobilizer on you first," Honor stated.

Quinn groaned.

"Yes." Honor's tone brooked no argument. "You need your meds, too, don't you?"

"Tylenol will do—I'm done with the narcotics. They make me too sluggish."

Honor hesitated. "I meant your heart meds."

"Oh." Quinn grimaced, hating that Honor would even think of it. "Yeah."

"Phyllis will be here any minute, and she'll be making breakfast. At least stay for that, all right?" It seemed like a natural request, and Honor saw no reason for Quinn to know that she just wanted her to stay a little while longer. Secretly, though, she found it harder and harder to deny that she enjoyed the way Quinn stirred her. Just when she thought she had everything under control, Quinn would say something or do something to turn her carefully constructed existence upside down. And she liked the way that felt. Edgy and exciting and *alive*.

"I don't have anything wrong with my head," Quinn said adamantly, rising and stretching. "If Phyllis is making breakfast, then I'm staying."

"Ah, I can see that you're a woman whose stomach calls the shots."

Quinn grinned. "Now and then." *With you, though, it's my heart.*

Seeing the echo of the sentiment in Quinn's eyes, Honor flushed. "Then come along, Dr. Maguire. Let's find your missing immobilizer, and *then* breakfast."

Knowing when she was beaten, Quinn just sighed. But as she followed Honor into the house, she was smiling.

❖

Thirteen and a half hours later, Honor pulled into the driveway, shut off the engine, and leaned her head back. Closing her eyes, she sighed and gathered herself to greet her family. After a long day at work, she was tired and talked out. But Arly would be waiting, excited to see her after the hours apart and eager to share the day's events. It wasn't that Honor wasn't interested, or didn't enjoy every moment with her daughter, but sometimes she simply felt drained. After a minute, she gathered her briefcase and headed for the house.

When she walked through the back door, the first thing she noticed was the unmistakable aroma of pizza. She groaned out loud in grateful anticipation. *No cooking, no cleanup. Thank God.*

The next thing she heard was Arly's excited chatter, and she frowned as she caught snippets of the conversation. It sounded very much as if her daughter was discussing livers and kidneys. *For dinner?*

Honor dropped her briefcase on the kitchen table and walked through the house to the living room, where she stopped in stunned surprise. Arly and Quinn sat on the floor with a newspaper spread out between them, covered with what appeared to be...body parts. Very tiny body parts.

"Hello?"

Arly looked up, her eyes shining. "Hi, Mom! Look. We're painting organs."

Eyes narrowing, Honor approached and squatted down between Quinn and her daughter. "I see that. A yellow liver and purple kidneys. Lovely."

"It's the Visible Woman," Arly informed her enthusiastically, pointing to the two halves of the plastic figure and its associated anatomically correct parts. "Quinn got it for me."

Honor glanced at Quinn, then did a double take when she saw that Quinn's cheek was streaked with blood. Blood that, upon closer inspection, revealed itself to be red paint. She reached out her thumb and brushed at the smudge. "Did she, now?"

Quinn's eyes widened at the soft touch that was almost a caress, but she kept her tone light. "It was a choice between unpacking boxes or going shopping. The choice was clear." She pointed to her left arm, dutifully restrained in the immobilizer. "Besides, I'm not supposed to do any heavy labor with my injured arm, so household chores were out."

"Oh, *now* you have an incapacitating injury," Honor said, laughing. "Where's Phyllis?"

"Right here, dear," Phyllis said, entering with a stack of paper plates and the pizza that she had just removed from the oven. "This morning, I made Quinn promise to come over for supper. Instead, she brought it. We were just keeping this warm until you got home."

Honor wanted to weep. The food smelled wonderful, and it didn't require any preparation. Arly was suitably occupied and loving it. And Quinn, whom she hadn't expected to see for at least a few days, and then under potentially difficult circumstances, was sprawled on her living-room floor, looking relaxed in jeans and a fresh white T-shirt, and appearing astonishingly at home. That very fact should have frightened her, but it didn't. For the first time in a very long time, everything felt precisely right.

Honor helped Phyllis pass out the plates with pizza and the napkins and then settled back on the floor next to Arly to simply enjoy the moment.

"Quinn," Arly said seriously, "what color should we do the heart?"

"Well," Quinn said thoughtfully, touching the miniature lifelike replica, "what color do you imagine when you think about it?"

Arly frowned in concentration. "Red, 'cause I have pajamas with hearts that color."

"I think red is a very good color for the heart."

Honor watched as Arly opened the red paint bottle and selected a brush to color the small plastic heart. Her movements were careful, and she appeared very serious as she worked. Smiling, Honor looked up to find Quinn watching *her* watch Arly. What she saw in Quinn's eyes made her heart turn over. She had said earlier that Quinn was kind and tender and sensitive, and she was. But that wasn't what simmered in those blue eyes now, or what made her own heart pound wildly. Now there was undisguised wanting so intense that Honor shivered with the heat of it.

"Is it okay?" Quinn whispered.

Quinn might've been speaking of her present to Arly, but Honor didn't think so.

"Oh, it's much more than okay."

Chapter Fifteen

Quinn gathered up the paper plates and pizza box and whispered to Honor, "I should go." She nodded in the direction of the sofa, where Arly had fallen asleep. Honor looked ready to join her.

Honor *had* been drifting, her feet curled under her on the sofa, a baseball game on television. Quinn sat on the floor, her back against the front of the couch, where she'd been since they'd finished the pizza an hour earlier. It had been an unexpectedly pleasant evening.

Voice still heavy with lassitude, Honor said, "I still have to take Pooch for his nightly neighborhood reconnaissance. If you wait until I get Arly upstairs, we'll walk you home."

"Okay." Quinn glanced down in the direction of her left arm, which was still restrained against her side. "I'd help carry her, but—"

"It's no problem. I'm used to it." Honor smiled and got to her feet. "But thanks. If you could give Phyllis a hand taking that stuff into the kitchen, that would be great."

"Sure." Quinn continued with the cleanup detail and watched as Honor easily lifted Arly, who curled up into her mother's arms without waking. It was obvious that the maneuver was second nature to them both. When Honor headed upstairs, Quinn went into the kitchen.

"Where should I put the trash?" she asked Phyllis.

"The bin is underneath that cabinet there to your right, but you don't have to do that, Quinn. Just leave it on the counter."

Quinn shook her head. "It's no problem. I've got it."

"It was nice of you to have dinner delivered. And especially to bring the model for Arly." Phyllis smiled fondly. "She loved it."

Faintly embarrassed, Quinn shrugged. "It was the least I could do after all of your hospitality last night and this morning." *And I wanted to see Honor again.*

"Well, you are very welcome, any time." Phyllis leaned against the counter and observed Quinn with interest. "How old are you, Quinn?"

"Twenty-eight." Quinn waited, curious.

"You seem older than that."

"Really? Why?"

"Well, let's see—you just moved here, you just started a new job, and you suddenly find yourself temporarily incapacitated." Phyllis nodded toward Quinn's shoulder. "Nevertheless, you seem to be taking it all in stride. That's pretty impressive."

"Not really." Quinn laughed. "I'm still living out of cartons, I'm worried about missing work because of my shoulder, and even without that, Honor might end up firing—" She broke off, blushing uncomfortably. "Uh..."

"As I said," Phyllis stated evenly, allowing the reference to Honor and Quinn's professional business to pass, "you're remarkably calm."

Settling on the stool beside the table, Quinn contemplated Phyllis's words. "I'm not sure I'm actually *calm*. I just seem to have this place inside me where things stop moving for a while. I go there, I guess, when everything *outside* of me is moving too fast."

Phyllis smiled softly at the simple way Quinn described something so essential. "I think there are a lot of people who would pay a lot of money to find a way to do something like that. That must be helpful when you're performing surgery."

"Yes," Quinn replied pensively. "In the operating room, even in the middle of a trauma, I can feel myself go there...everything becomes very clear and very sharp and very, very focused."

"A truly important skill, I imagine." Phyllis was captivated by Quinn's expression, a look both amazed and sad at the same time.

"I don't know if it's a skill." Quinn sighed softly, giving Phyllis a weary smile. "It just seems to be the way I'm made."

Honor leaned against the door from the hall, listening to the tail end of the conversation between her mother-in-law and a woman whose appeal she was finding very hard to resist. From where she stood, she could see Quinn's face in profile, and, listening to Quinn speak of surgery, she recalled their first meeting over the body of the gunshot victim. That day, her very first impression of Quinn had been one of intensity and competence along with a healthy dose of surgical arrogance. Now when she looked at her, she could still sense those things, but it was Quinn's exquisite tenderness and innate sensitivity that pulled at Honor's heart. Seeing the melancholy darken the handsome features, Honor wanted nothing more in that moment than to cross the room and put her arms around Quinn. *You're hurting, I can feel it. God, how I hate to be the one to hurt you more.*

Feigning a mood far lighter than she felt, Honor crossed the kitchen and announced, "She's out for the count." Glancing at Phyllis, she added, "I'll just take Pooch for a short run around the block."

"No need to hurry. I'll just watch television until you get back. I don't have anything else planned." Nodding to Quinn, she said, "You get some rest now. I'm sure everything will be fine."

Everyone keeps saying that. But I still don't see how. Quinn got to her feet. "Good night, Phyllis. It was good to see you again."

Having heard his name a moment before, Pooch had rushed to the back door and now sat expectantly, tail wagging, head cocked at an angle and bright black eyes fixed on Honor's face. A low-pitched whine reverberated in his throat.

"Just a *second*," Honor grumped in the dog's direction as she fished his lead out of the closet. "God, you'd never think that a walk around the block, smelling every little bit of odious detritus, could be so exciting."

Quinn laughed out loud. "My life should be so simple."

As Honor clipped the lead to the dog's collar, she laughed along with Quinn. Together, they walked down the back steps with the dog forging happily ahead.

It was just after nine, and it was not yet completely dark. Here and there the faint echoes of neighborhood children still at play drifted in the air. The aroma of a late-night supper on a backyard grill floated on a faint breeze. Quinn took a slow deep breath, and amazingly, felt some of her tension ebb as she looked at the woman beside her. Honor had changed into another pair of shorts and a baggy PMC T-shirt. She looked like the medical student that Quinn had mistaken her for on first sight. She looked beautiful.

As if feeling Quinn's gaze upon her, Honor turned her head and looked into Quinn's eyes, smiling. "What?"

Quinn considered not answering, or not acknowledging the truth. But there wasn't room inside her to keep one more secret—not from herself, and not from Honor. "With everything that's going on in my life right now, I can't figure out why I should feel so happy, but I do. I think it has something to do with being with you."

For a few seconds, Honor was speechless. From anyone else, it would have sounded like a come-on line, but Quinn had delivered it with such quiet sincerity that Honor knew that it wasn't. And because of that, she did not dismiss the sentiment with her usual quick brush-off.

There had been a few women over the years who had expressed interest in getting to know her socially. Some had been acquaintances of hers and Terry's, and they had waited what probably seemed to them like an appropriate length of time before calling to ask her out to dinner or a party. Others were women she met at the hospital or at neighborhood social functions who knew nothing of her past, at least not from her. Honor was certain that if anyone had asked around, they would have been able to hear some version of what had happened to her lover. It was not a story that she shared easily. She had said no to all of them, and eventually, the invitations, at least for dates, had stopped.

"Sorry," Quinn said quietly as the silence grew. "I didn't mean to offend—"

"No," Honor said swiftly. "No, you didn't. I...enjoy your company, too."

Honor knew that she could leave it at that, and sensed that Quinn would not press her for anything more. But that somehow seemed unfair, and Quinn had had so much unfairness to deal with lately that Honor could not add to it. "I *do* enjoy your company, Quinn. More than I have anyone's in a very long time. But—"

"Honor, you don't need to explain—"

"I know that." Honor reached over and brushed her fingers down Quinn's arm. "I just want to."

Having said that, Honor didn't know how to go on. It wasn't as if Quinn had even once intimated that she was interested in anything beyond friendship. But it was impossible to deny that some kind of attraction existed between them. It went beyond mutual respect or friendship. There was an emotional and, yes, a physical pull that had her doing things she wouldn't have conceived of a few weeks before. *For God's sake, I almost kissed her yesterday afternoon in the ER!*

Taking a deep breath, Honor squared her shoulders and plunged ahead. "I haven't been...involved with anyone...any woman...since Terry died. I haven't wanted to be. It never even occurred to me."

Quinn's stomach dropped and her pulse rate soared. She was pretty certain that she didn't want to hear what Honor was about to say, but she kept quiet, knowing that she had to. While the dog stopped to inspect each board in a picket fence, she and Honor slowed until they were barely moving.

"Terry and I were together from our junior year in high school." Honor laughed softly. "Phyllis came home unexpectedly one afternoon and found us *in the act* in a hammock on the back porch. I was never so scared in my life."

"I can imagine," Quinn replied. "Or, actually, I can't. Jesus."

"While we were scrambling for our clothes, she informed us that if I was staying for dinner, it would be ready in an hour." Honor pushed her hair behind her ear with her fingers, watching Pooch try to pull a candy wrapper out from underneath a bush on the other side of the fence. "We weren't exactly sure if she meant I *should* stay or what. Finally, we just decided to tough it out."

"I can't see Phyllis giving you a hard time."

"I could almost see her coming to a decision when she discovered us. She loved Terry like crazy, and that's what mattered the most to her." Honor gave a tug on Pooch's leash, and they all started walking again. "She told us to be careful, because not everyone would be accepting of us being together." She laughed again. "*And* she told us if we planned on sleeping together, we should do it *indoors,* preferably in Terry's room."

"Whoa. You got lucky."

Honor nodded thoughtfully. "Yes, I really did. On all counts."

Quinn couldn't miss the love in Honor's voice, for Phyllis and for Terry. It was strange, because it didn't hurt the way she'd thought it would. It was hard to begrudge Honor happiness, with anyone. Quinn cleared her throat. "I'm really sorry, about Terry."

"Did anyone tell you?" Honor stopped at the corner of the intersection of her street and Quinn's and leaned a shoulder against a large tree. Her face was partially in shadow, but Quinn's was highlighted by the glow from a nearby streetlight. Honor was glad for the cover of darkness, because she wasn't certain what Quinn would see in her face.

"No." Quinn wanted to step forward, to touch Honor in some way, if only to offer a small comfort. But she stood still, letting Honor control the moment. Some part of her wanted to tell Honor that it wasn't necessary to explain, but she also knew that Honor would only tell her as much as she wanted her to know.

"We were together almost nine years. For the first few years after high school, we lived with Phyllis. My parents weren't crazy about my relationship with Terry, but they also knew they couldn't change it. I went to college and medical school right here in the city."

As she spoke, Pooch must have heard the change in her voice because he came to sit by her side, pressing close against her thigh. She dropped her fingers onto the top of his head and slowly stroked him.

"For a long time, I couldn't decide if I wanted to be a doctor or an architect, but Terry only ever wanted to *build* things. She was so good at it, and she'd been helping guys in the neighborhood work on their houses since she was a kid. Right after high school, she started in with a construction crew, got her union card, and before long, she was running the crew." Honor laughed. "I don't think they even realized she was taking over until one day, she was just the boss."

Quinn had a feeling that Honor and Terry were very much alike, but she kept her own counsel.

"One day..." Honor's throat suddenly tightened, and she struggled for the words. "Ah God, I'm sorry."

"Honor," Quinn said quietly.

"I'm okay. Really."

It was killing Quinn to hear the pain in her voice and to be helpless to assuage it. "My house is right up the street. What do you say we go sit on the porch for a few minutes?"

"Yes. Okay." Honor gave Pooch's lead a tug and fell into step beside Quinn. A moment later, she followed Quinn down the narrow alley between Quinn's building and the neighboring one to the rear of the house.

"You'd better take my hand," Quinn said when they reached the stairs that led up to the deck off her kitchen. "It's dark back here. Will Pooch be okay?"

"He'll be fine. He'd climb trees if I'd let him." Honor slid her hand into Quinn's as they made their way up to the second-floor landing.

Once there, she released Quinn's hand and sat shoulder to shoulder with her on the top step, while Pooch stretched out behind them, pressing close. It was fully dark now, and the sky overhead was clear. The moon was out, the stars were bright, and the night was as gorgeous as any summer night could be.

Honor took a breath and tried to see past the memories of that morning when they had brought Terry into the emergency room. "She was in the basement of the house her crew was rehabbing, inspecting the joists. Something happened, no one knows what for sure, but a supporting beam came down while she was under it."

Quinn felt the fine tremors that coursed through Honor where their shoulders touched, and she gently placed just the tips of her fingers against Honor's knee.

"It was a freak accident." When she continued, Honor's voice was firm, but hollow, completely devoid of emotion. "The beam hit her in the back of the neck. Just like that. From one second to the next—she was here, and then—she wasn't."

"I'm so sorry."

"They brought her to the ER, but there was nothing I could do."

The ache in Quinn's chest intensified, and without realizing it, she reached for Honor's hand. Honor's fingers when they closed around Quinn's were cold, and Quinn drew Honor's hand against her middle and held it there, as if warming her hand would somehow ease her pain. She couldn't bear to think about Honor having suffered Terry's loss, let alone feeling responsible in some way.

Honor shuddered as if shaking off a dream and gave a small tremulous laugh. "I'm sorry. I didn't mean to tell you all of that. I never have before."

"That's okay," Quinn said gently. "Are you all right?"

"A little embarrassed."

"God, why?"

"You certainly didn't ask for my life story." Carefully, Honor withdrew her fingers from Quinn's grip, instantly feeling the chill return, even though the air was warm.

"You said we were friends, right?"

"Yes. I did." Honor shook her head, feeling slightly disoriented. "And what I started out *wanting* to say was that I value your friendship, but that's all I want. All I can offer."

"I understand." Quinn kept her voice steady and even, imagining that Honor must be vulnerable, emotionally raw, after revisiting Terry's death. She didn't want to do or say anything to add to her discomfort. "I'm so sorry about Terry, Honor. I feel privileged that you would trust me enough to tell me about her."

"You made it easy." Honor turned in the small space until she could face Quinn. Their knees touched, and although she wanted to reach out and take Quinn's hand again, she did not. "You're a remarkable woman, Quinn Maguire."

"I'm not so sure of that, but thank you."

Honor did touch her then, just a brush of fingers against Quinn's cheek. "I'm sorry, sorrier than I can say, about the situation at work. I'll do my best to clear it up quickly, I promise."

"I know you will." Quinn stood, because she needed the distance to say goodbye. "Will you call me as soon as you know anything?"

Standing as well, Honor nodded. "Of course. It might take a day or two until I can meet with the appropriate people."

"I'll be here." Quinn tipped her head toward the house.

"Good night then." Honor started down the stairs, Pooch scrambling after her. Several steps down, she turned and looked back up to where Quinn stood silhouetted against the night. "It helped, telling you about Terry. Thank you for that, Quinn."

"You're welcome. Be careful going home."

Then Quinn turned and disappeared into the house.

❖

Honor let herself in the back door, hung up Pooch's leash, and walked through the house into the living room. Phyllis sat on the couch watching one of the pseudoforensic cop dramas with the volume turned down low. Honor leaned over and kissed the top of her head, then sat down with her. "Everything quiet?"

"Not a peep."

"She could sleep through anything."

"That she could." The final credits rolled and Phyllis clicked the remote to shut off the television, then turned to regard Honor. "Did you have a nice walk?"

"Yes, it's a beautiful night."

Phyllis waited, wondering at the brooding expression on Honor's face. The explanation wasn't long in coming.

"I told Quinn about Terry. About what happened to her."

"Did she ask?" Phyllis kept her surprise to herself. Honor rarely discussed Terry's death with anyone.

"No, she didn't. I just...wanted to tell her."

"How do you feel?" Phyllis asked gently, sliding closer until she could thread her arm around Honor.

"Sad." Honor rested her cheek against Phyllis's shoulder and sighed. "I miss her."

"Me, too." Phyllis gave a little squeeze. "You okay?"

"Yes, I am." Surprisingly, Honor realized that she was. Terry's loss hurt to the depths of her soul, and probably always would. But the sharp edges of her pain, the ones that made her bleed, were tempered now in a way they never had been before. She wasn't certain when that had happened, but it had taken telling Quinn to make her realize it was so.

"How was Quinn with it all?"

"She was wonderful."

❖

Quinn tried to get comfortable, but it was impossible. She'd taken off the shoulder immobilizer in an attempt to find a position in which she could hope to fall asleep. After three Tylenols, her shoulder still throbbed insistently, but that wasn't what kept her awake. She couldn't stop thinking about Honor. Honor and Terry. Childhood sweethearts—fairy-tale lovers. It made sense, now, that Honor still wore Terry's ring.

The love in Honor's voice had been unmistakable, and the pain that rippled beneath every memory obviously unmitigated by time. Quinn reminded herself of her own words the very first time she had seen Honor Blake. *Never get involved with a married woman.*

Now, when her career was in the balance and she already felt more than she should for the woman who controlled her future, it was definitely time to heed her own advice.

CHAPTER SIXTEEN

"Linda, would you give the guy in seven a tetanus shot and call the lab for the results of the chem panel and coag profile?"

"Sure." Linda leaned both forearms on the counter and studied Honor, who sat writing notes in a chart. Honor had been oddly quiet all morning and almost seemed as if she was avoiding everyone, particularly Linda. "Something wrong?"

"Brown recluse bite."

Linda bit back a retort. "*Besides* the fact that you've got someone with a spider bite."

"Nope," Honor said shortly, keeping her attention focused on the discharge summary for the college student who had decided it would be fun to sleep out in the park with his buddies the night before. Now all he had to show for his adventure was a hangover and an area of inflammation the size of a palm print on his thigh. With any luck, the spider bite would heal without permanent tissue damage.

"Where's Quinn today?" Linda persisted. "Isn't she slated to work this shift?"

Honor looked up, her eyes flashing with annoyance. "Is there some reason you think *I* should know where she is?"

"Uh...maybe because you're the ER chief, and you make up the schedules?"

"She'll be off for a few days." Honor snapped the metal bifold chart closed and dropped it into a nearby rack marked Completed. "Who's next?"

Linda raised an eyebrow and said nothing.

"What?" Honor said in exasperation, unable to ignore her friend's appraising gaze.

Silence.

"In case you haven't noticed," Honor pointed out in an exaggerated tone of false patience, "we're up to our asses in patients around here. So maybe we could just concentrate on business for a while, okay?"

"Oh, absolutely. And if we had a surgeon to help us, we could probably get the boy in ten with the chin laceration taken care of and maybe even the little old lady in twelve who fell and most likely broke her hip."

Honor gritted her teeth and mentally counted to ten. "I'll see the possible hip fracture right now. Have the senior resident take care of the laceration."

"Yes, Dr. Blake," Linda said sweetly.

"Thank you." Honor slid the chart for twelve out of the rack and walked away.

She'd slept poorly, awoken tired, and now was agitated and out of sorts. As soon as she'd been able to get someone to answer the phone in the administrative offices, she'd set up an appointment to see the hospital malpractice attorney. Of course, the earliest opening she could get was the next morning. Which meant that the earliest she could even hope to have an answer for Quinn would be the next afternoon.

Two days. Two days isn't very long. Hardly any time at all.

Despite the fact that Quinn had only been working in the ER a short time, Honor couldn't help feeling as if something vital was missing after only a few hours without her. That sense of absence was a low-level ache that kept Honor edgy and distracted—and annoyed.

Stop making more out of it than it is. It's just a typical crazy Monday morning. No one wants to spend time in the ER on the weekend, but now *all of a sudden every little ache and pain is an emergency. It has nothing to do with the fact that Quinn isn't here. I certainly don't miss her. I mean, I miss her* expertise. *But I don't miss* her.

Satisfied that nothing was truly amiss, Honor pushed aside the curtain and stepped into the small cubicle with a smile. She glanced at the chart and then at the elderly woman in the bed. "Ms.

Richards? I'm Dr. Blake. Can you tell me what happened this morning?"

An hour later, Fiona Richards had been x-rayed, medicated with analgesics, and transferred to a bed on the orthopedic floor for treatment of her broken hip. Fortunately, the fracture was nondisplaced, and it was possible that she might be able to avoid surgery. Honor completed the paperwork and glanced at the clock. She was dismayed to see that it was only noon. The day was dragging and, at this rate, promised to be endless.

"Hey, Dr. Blake," Tom Finley called. "Is Dr. Maguire coming in? There's a fellow in three with a cold foot. I think he might have an arterial occlusion, and I thought if she—"

"No, she won't be in today, Tom. What's the history?" Honor stepped out of the path of the refrigerator-sized portable x-ray machine that an x-ray tech maneuvered through the hall with reckless abandon. Honor put her back against the wall to avoid being crushed, and Tom sidestepped as well and joined her.

"The usual. Heavy smoker, long history of calf pain with ambulation. And now he says he woke up this morning and couldn't feel his foot."

"Sounds like you're right about an acute arterial blockage," Honor muttered. "I'll take a quick look, and if he's got no pulses, we'll have to get him down for a flow study. Just give me a minute."

"Sure."

On her way back to the nurses' station to check the labs on the patient with the possible vascular occlusion, the second-year ER resident hailed her.

"Oh, Dr. Blake! I've got a fifteen-year-old with a metacarpal fracture. Is Dr. Maguire—"

"No," Honor snapped. "Page whoever's on hand call."

All of a sudden, the ER can't run without her? Honor forged on, leaving the resident staring after her, a perplexed expression on his face.

And the next few hours only brought more of the same—a steady flow of patients that kept Honor busy and her mind occupied. But during every lull, no matter how brief, she thought about Quinn. She thought of how easy it had been to talk to her, even about something as painful and private as Terry's death. Honor had only ever allowed herself to rely on a very few people, and *those* people she would have trusted with her life. Terry, Phyllis, and in recent years, Linda. And yet, with a few words and the gentlest of touches, Quinn had made her feel safe and comforted.

It's hard to believe that just a few days ago, I told Phyllis I didn't trust her. How could I have been so wrong?

Honor was startled from her reverie when Linda asked, "How about taking a break for lunch?"

"Thanks," Honor said, smiling briefly. "I'm not really hungry."

"I could be persuaded to get street dogs from one of the vendors out front," Linda said in a voice that suggested the chili-slathered hot dogs were the next best thing to caviar.

Honor laughed. "Thanks anyway. Listen, I'm sorry I was a bear earli—"

"Hey, Linda!" the ward clerk called. "Dr. Maguire is on the phone for you."

Linda raised a surprised brow. "Me?"

"Uh-huh. Line three."

Casting a questioning look at Honor, Linda picked up a nearby phone and punched in the extension. "Quinn? Hey, it's Linda."

Honor crowded close. "Everything okay?"

"What's that?" Linda asked, waving Honor away. "Oh, sure."

"Linda, is she all right?"

When Linda stepped back a pace, it was all Honor could do not to follow her in an attempt to hear the conversation. With a start, she realized that she desperately wanted to hear Quinn's voice. She wanted to ask her how her shoulder was, and how she'd slept, and if she was having a problem with her heart rhythm. She wanted to tell her how much it had meant to her that they'd talked the night before.

"...372. Uh-huh. Uh-huh. Great. Sure, no problem. See you later, maybe."

When Linda replaced the receiver and turned, Honor was an inch away. Linda jumped in surprise. "God, what is *with* you today?"

"Nothing." Honor flushed and backed up a step. With effort, she managed to quell the anxiety that had skyrocketed the moment that she realized Quinn was on the line. Trying to sound casual, she asked, "Everything okay?"

Linda cocked her head and studied her friend. "You first."

"What?" Honor asked impatiently.

"You tell me what's going on with you first, and *maybe* I'll tell you why Quinn called." Linda folded her arms across her chest and leaned back against the counter, looking resolute and unswayable.

Exasperated, Honor ran a hand through her hair, feeling her temper rise again. "I don't know. Just one of those days, I guess."

"You don't usually have days when you snap at everyone, don't feel like eating, and act like you're about to crawl out of your skin."

"I'm sorry. I've just got a lot on my mind." Honor sighed and gave Linda a rueful grin. "Honest. Forgive me?"

"Oh, okay." Linda put her arm around Honor's shoulders and gave her a hug. "I'm not sure I believe you, but I still love you."

"Thanks. So," Honor said intently, "what's happening with Quinn?"

"I was about to ask *you* that." Linda's expression was completely serious. "It's not her shoulder that's keeping her from working, is it."

Caught off guard, Honor looked away. "There are few administrative issues that need to be ironed out. Hopefully, this is just temporary."

"*Hopefully?*" Linda caught her breath in surprise. "Are you kidding? You can't seriously be thinking of letting her go."

"Do you think I'd *want* to?" The words were out before Honor could stop them, and she could tell by the expression on Linda's face that her distress was apparent. Instantly feeling exposed, she withdrew. "I need to get back to work. Just tell me, is she all right?"

"Sounds like it. She wants our home phone number to ask Robin where soccer practice is going to be this afternoon."

"Damn it. She can't coach with that shoulder."

"You might be able to keep her out of the ER, Honor," Linda said quietly. "But I don't think your authority extends as far as the soccer field."

The criticism in her friend's tone hurt, but Honor could hardly blame her since she wasn't explaining anything. And she *couldn't* give Linda the details of Quinn's absence because it would compromise Quinn's privacy even further. And even more importantly, she couldn't explain her own behavior since she didn't fully understand herself what she was feeling. Wordlessly, she picked up another chart and went back to work.

❖

"So what's the deal?" Robin asked as she and Quinn walked across the grass at Green Street Friends School to the far end of the soccer field. Kim, Dennis, and Arly had raced on ahead as soon as they'd piled out of Robin's minivan. "Is your shoulder keeping you from working?"

"No, it's coming along okay." Quinn had decided that morning that she'd had enough of the immobilizer. It'd been almost forty-eight hours, and it was time to start moving the joint again. "I just have a couple of days off, and I figured I might as well get my feet wet."

"Yeah, well, your feet are about the only part of you that's gonna get any exercise. You take it easy with that shoulder today."

"Yes, Coach." Quinn grinned. "Got it."

Laughing, Robin said, "Linda would have my hide if I let you get hurt. I imagine Honor would be standing in line to help her."

At the mention of Honor's name, Quinn's smile faltered. She'd been honest with Robin when she'd said that she wanted to help out at practice. What she *hadn't* said was that she'd been going crazy sitting around her apartment, wondering what was happening at work. Not just whether Honor had met with the hospital attorneys or Mary Ann Jones, but what Honor was doing, what she was thinking. Whether she was thinking of Quinn at all.

But why would she be? She's already made it perfectly clear what her feelings are. Or aren't.

Quinn shrugged, then bit back a wince at the sudden tension on her shoulder joint. "I'll just help run the drills and whatever else you need me to do."

If Robin heard the strained edge in Quinn's voice, she made no comment. Instead, she introduced Quinn to Dave Clark, the other coach, and within a few minutes, Quinn was caught up in the bubbling enthusiasm of the young soccer players. The hour and a half sped by, and before she knew it, she was supervising the kids as they packed up the team's gear.

"Quinn!" Arly called, breaking away from a group of teammates and racing over. "Are you going to have supper with us at Linda and Robin's?"

"I don't think so, kiddo. Not tonight."

Robin grabbed the gear bag and hefted it to her shoulder. "That's a great idea, Quinn. I'm cooking tonight, so you can just hang out while I get things ready. What do you say?"

Quinn was torn. She had nothing waiting for her at home. She enjoyed Robin and Linda's company, and the kids', too. But staying for dinner almost certainly meant running into Honor, if not actually sharing the meal with her. After the clear boundaries Honor had set the evening before, Quinn wasn't certain it was a good idea to see her socially, at least not so soon. It was time to get their relationship back on a purely professional basis.

"I appreciate the offer, Robin, but I'm a little bit tired. I'll take a rain check, if you don't mind."

"Sure. No problem. Next time, then."

Arly made a disappointed face and grumbled. "Why can't you come, Quinn? You wouldn't have to help make dinner or anything. I could do that."

Quinn bent down until she was eye level with the little girl. "That's really nice of you. You remember I hurt my arm, right?"

Arly nodded.

"Well, it's *almost* better, but I think I need to take a nap so it can get better faster. Okay?"

"Okay," Arly agreed seriously. "But maybe next time, right?"

"Yes," Quinn said softly. "Maybe next time."

❖

Honor didn't make it in time for supper, arriving to collect Arly at a little before eight.

"I packed up some leftovers for you," Linda said when Honor came into the kitchen.

"Thanks." Honor dropped into one of the chairs at the kitchen table and sighed. Linda stood at the counter packing Tupperware containers into a plastic shopping bag, and the sight reminded Honor of just how precious Linda's friendship was to her. "I'm sorry about being such an ass at work today."

Linda turned and gave her a long look. "You want to tell me now what's going on?"

"I can't." Honor pushed the salt shaker back and forth on the table restlessly. "It would be a breach in confidentiality."

"Okay," Linda said thoughtfully as she sat down next to Honor. "Since I already know it has to do with Quinn, just tell me this. Is there something serious going on with her heart?"

"I can't play twenty questions, Linda. It's not right."

"I haven't seen you this out of sorts in a long time." Linda rested her hand on Honor's, squeezing gently. "I just want to help."

"I know you do. And if I could tell you, believe me, I would." Honor blew out an exasperated breath. "Did you see Quinn tonight?"

"She stopped in for a second to say hi after practice. She's *so* cute."

Completely involuntarily, Honor's heart tripped. "Did she seem...okay?"

"Quiet. Her shoulder seems better." Linda narrowed her eyes, watching Honor's gaze grow distant. "Why?"

"No reason. Did she...mention me at all?"

Linda hesitated. "No. She didn't."

"Well," Honor said, rising quickly. "I need to get home. I'll see you in the morning."

"I'll pick you up at the usual time." Linda stood as well. "Get some rest, okay? You look worn out."

"I'm fine." Honor forced a smile. "Just fine."

CHAPTER SEVENTEEN

A ttorneys, Honor thought. *Why is it impossible for them to say anything using simple words and sentences of less than two paragraphs? God.*

Her head ached and her stomach roiled queasily. The meeting with Administration had been more difficult than she'd anticipated. Discussing Quinn in her absence, dissecting her medical condition and quantifying her liability risk as if she were no more than a hypothetical problem to be analyzed, had left Honor feeling disloyal and self-serving. Quinn was so much more than just a "new hire" who presented a thorny dilemma for risk-management. She was a talented surgeon with the noblest of intentions who was doing her best under difficult circumstances, and she didn't deserve to have her career threatened because everyone in medicine was running scared of the word *lawsuit.*

And I'm one of them. What's happened to me? When did I become so afraid of doing the right thing?

Disgusted with herself, Honor walked back to the emergency room, fighting the overwhelming urge to see Quinn. She'd thought of little else for two days. In between dealing with the responsibilities of work and family, her mind had been consumed with Quinn. It had become practically impossible for her to distinguish between what she ought to do as an administrator and what she wanted to do as a friend.

Friends. That's what I told her we were. I certainly haven't acted like much of one. And she never once complained or tried to use our...relationship to her advantage.

Honor glanced at her watch.

5:45. They're probably still at the soccer field.

She hunted down Brian Vaughn, one of the ER attendings. "I need to take off early, Brian. Is everything under control here?"

The sandy-haired, freckle-faced man gave an unconcerned shrug. "Is it ever?"

"Sorry." Honor grinned. "Wrong choice of words. Can you handle things?"

"Sure. It's dinnertime." He pointed to the To Be Seen rack, which held only three new charts. "You know we won't see the heavy nighttime action until after eight. By then the swing shift will be in, and we'll have plenty of people. Go ahead. We're good here."

"Thanks." Honor's spirits lifted immediately. As she turned and headed for the exit, she promised, "I'll owe you a couple of hours for this."

"Don't worry," he called after her. "I'll collect the next time my wife wants me to show up for some after-school kids' thing."

❖

Since it was Linda's day off, Honor had driven her own car to work, and she was on the road in five minutes and pulling into a parking space adjacent to the playing fields in ten. Robin's sturdy form, running along the sideline, gesticulating to the young players, was easily discernible. Quinn, recognizable even from a distance in gym shorts and a T-shirt, worked with a small group of children who were lined up in two facing rows doing drills. Honor sat behind the wheel, observing Quinn demonstrate a passing technique, running agilely as she manipulated the ball with her feet. Watching her, Honor got the same impression of confidence, skill, and natural ability that she'd seen Quinn display during surgery.

The children, one of whom was Arly, mimicked Quinn's every move like a line of baby ducks. Honor smiled, unable to look anywhere but at the charismatic woman who seemed to have no idea of her own allure.

Quinn Maguire. Do you do everything so naturally, as if you were born knowing how? The Pied Piper, indeed.

Five minutes passed while Honor debated the wisdom of her decision to come. Now that she really thought about it, it hardly seemed suitable to track Quinn down personally during non–work hours to discuss business. It would probably be more appropriate—not to mention more professional—to telephone Quinn either that evening or the next morning to set up an appointment. Honor gripped the key that was still in the ignition but stopped before starting the engine.

On the other hand, Quinn is *coaching my daughter's soccer team, and it* is *perfectly natural for me, as a parent, to stop by to observe.*

Before she could admit the transparency of her rationalizations, Honor got out of the car and started across the field.

"Mom!" Arly shouted excitedly as she broke away from the group of children and ran in Honor's direction.

Quinn trapped the ball beneath her foot and turned to look across the green, her mouth going suddenly dry when she saw the woman approaching. To glance up and unexpectedly see Honor brought a swift rush of pleasure that was momentarily paralyzing. All she could do was stare, marveling at the way Honor's hair glinted gold in the sunlight, mesmerized by the way she moved, all long limbed and graceful and sure. Honor's mere presence had a way of making everything else in Quinn's world—every worry, every care, every fear—disappear, and that was an exhilarating, terrifying experience. Even though she knew that it was folly, the sensation was too good to wish away.

"Hi," Honor said as she stopped a few feet from Quinn, one arm going out automatically to hug Arly close to her side. She leaned down and kissed the top of her daughter's head. "Hi, sweetheart."

"Quinn taught us a new passing drill today, Mom. I was really good at it."

"I bet you were great." Honor unconsciously stroked Arly's shoulder as she kept her eyes on Quinn, trying to determine her welcome. She had anticipated that Quinn would at the very least be angry with her, if not outright adversarial. With sweet relief, she realized that anger wasn't what she saw in the depths of those blue eyes slowly searching her face. There were questions, to be sure, but much more crucial than that, there was welcome. For the first time in two days, Honor felt some of the tension slowly ebb from her body.

"Hello." Quinn smiled, juggled the ball several times with her foot, causing it to bounce higher and higher, until she hooked her instep beneath it and then popped it up into her waiting arm.

"Slick move," Honor deadpanned.

A grin quirked the corner of Quinn's mouth. "It impresses the girls."

"Can you teach me to do that?" Arly asked intently.

Coloring instantly, Quinn's eyes dropped to Arly and then back to Honor in apology. "I...uh..."

"I'll bet she can. But not right now." Honor ruffled her daughter's hair. "Aren't you supposed to be practicing those drills?"

"Are you coming to dinner *tonight*, Quinn?" Arly made no move to leave.

"Well..."

"Quinn and I need to talk," Honor interjected seriously. "And *you* need to get back to your practice. Go on, go finish."

Arly hesitated for another second, then ran off.

"I'm sorry about that remark," Quinn said abjectly. "It just slipped out."

"It's fine." Honor laughed and clasped Quinn's hand briefly. "It wasn't anything serious enough to worry about. It's not like she doesn't know that some girls like girls and some girls like boys, but I don't even think she noticed."

Quinn glanced over to where the children were practicing. Parents stood around in small groups, conversing and occasionally calling out encouragement and praise to their children. There were a fair number of same-sex couples present. "Does she know about... I don't know, you know...the difference between being straight and not?"

"Not exactly in those terms. She knows that some kids have a mom and dad, and some kids have just a mom or just a dad, and that some kids have two moms or two dads."

Shaking her head, Quinn chuckled. "I'm not sure *I* could keep all that straight."

"The reason that she goes to the school she does is that there are a lot of other kids from alternative families, too, so she's not different." Honor smiled. "And having Robin and Linda and Kim and Dennis as part of the family really helps."

Quinn wanted to ask if Arly knew about Terry, but it didn't seem to be the time or place. She wasn't even sure why she wanted to know, except that everything about Honor *and* Arly interested her. She cleared her throat.

"So, did you just come to watch practice?"

Honor shook her head. "No, I came to find you."

"Oh?"

"How much longer until practice is over?"

Quinn glanced at the Timex watch, the one that her father had given her when she'd left for college. "Another fifteen minutes or so. But I have to make sure all the kids get home all right, so I might have to wait a few minutes until their rides show up."

"How about I wait, and then we grab a bite to eat somewhere. I'd like to talk to you."

"I'd need to change first," Quinn said, indicating her sweat-stained T-shirt and shorts.

"Robin can take Arly back with her kids, and I can take you to your place. Will that work?"

"It's a bit of a mess." Quinn considered that a blatant understatement, but at least the sofa was accessible, and she had orange juice in the refrigerator that she could offer as refreshment.

"I think I can handle that."

Before Quinn could reply, she heard her name being called. An instant later, warm fingers wrapped around her wrist and then slipped down to her hand.

"Quinn! How's your shoulder?" Mandy smiled a brilliant smile as she entwined her fingers with Quinn's and swung her right arm lightly. "We just finished an officials' meeting to finalize the game schedule, and I saw you over here. That was a nasty fall you took on Saturday." She pouted prettily. "You were gone before I could even see how you were doing."

"It's fine. Much better." Quinn tried to extract her hand as she glanced quickly at Honor, whose brown eyes had darkened to a dangerous simmer.

Following Quinn's gaze, Mandy spared a brief look in Honor's direction. "Oh, hi."

"Hello, Mandy," Honor said steadily as she contemplated dismembering her.

Mandy turned back to Quinn. "You know, my *other* day job is working as a massage therapist. I'm a *very* good Swedish masseuse." Her voice dropped low as she placed her other palm lightly in the center of Quinn's chest and rubbed gently. "I schedule sessions at the gym. It would be great for your shoulder."

"Actually," Honor interjected conversationally, "it wouldn't. Right now, too much direct muscle stimulation is only going to produce more swelling. So I think you should probably desist from the laying on of hands."

"Oh Honor, still as serious as ever, I see. You never *did* have a very good sense of humor." Eyes locked on Quinn, Mandy moved her hand from Quinn's chest and brushed it slowly down the injured arm in question. "We could start off with something nice and easy. Maybe in the hot tub. Call me."

"Thanks," Quinn said, finally managing to extricate her hand and stepping back out of reach.

"Any time." Mandy smiled a little too sweetly at Honor and sauntered away.

"I'm going to kill her someday."

"Why?"

Honor turned bright red, not realizing she had spoken out loud. "Could you pretend you didn't hear that?"

"Absolutely not," Quinn said with a laugh. "What's her crime?"

"Let's just say that she has an annoying habit of putting her hands, and other body parts, where they aren't necessarily welcome."

Quinn's eyes narrowed, no longer laughing. "Has she been after you?"

"No," Honor murmured thoughtfully, watching Mandy smile and wave to almost every lesbian on the field. "Terry."

"Ah. Well, I can't imagine that Terry would have bothered to look at her when she had you."

Honor met Quinn's gaze, and she wasn't thinking about Terry. She was thinking about the soft rumble of Quinn's voice and the way it made her heart race. She smiled and when she spoke, her voice was throaty. "Very smooth, Maguire."

"I meant it."

What about you? Do you feel that way, too? Flushing with pleasure now, Honor said softly, "I think practice is breaking up."

"I should go help."

"I'll wait."

"Thanks. I won't be long."

After walking Arly to Robin's car, Honor contented herself with observing Quinn. She moved easily among the children, answering their questions patiently and seriously while urging them to stow their gear, and then chaperoning them individually or in small groups to waiting vehicles. Finally, Honor and Quinn were alone on the field.

There was still an hour until sunset, and as Honor stood in the golden glow of the waning light slanting across the lush green, she experienced the pure and simple pleasure of a particular woman's smile. Quinn came toward her, her easy gait and confident carriage striking in itself, but it was the look in her eyes and the lift of her lips that caused Honor's legs to weaken.

"All set?" Honor asked softly.

Quinn nodded, thinking that in that moment there wasn't a single thing she could imagine wanting other than Honor's company. "Yep."

"My car is right over here." Honor started walking, resisting the urge to take Quinn's hand. She had to remind herself that she had come with a specific purpose in mind, and that issue wasn't personal. It was business, and business that might very well turn this pleasant interlude into a difficult evening. But despite her resolve, being around Quinn made it easy to forget everything except her.

Once settled in the car, Honor started the engine and headed toward their neighborhood. "How's your shoulder really?"

"Not bad. It's stiff, and I probably *could* use a massage."

Honor cut her a look, and Quinn laughed.

"A *shoulder* massage."

"Well," Honor commented acerbically, "unless you want to spend the time fighting off not-so-subtle advances *or* getting a whole lot more than your shoulder tended to, I'd suggest you make an appointment with someone other than Mandy."

Quinn angled her head and studied Honor's profile. Her teeth appeared clenched and a muscle bunched at the angle of her elegant jaw. "You *really* don't like her, do you?"

Honor turned her head and met Quinn's eyes for long seconds before glancing back at the road. "She put her hands on what was mine. I don't tolerate that from anyone."

The lethal conviction in Honor's voice made Quinn's stomach tighten. There'd never been anyone who had claimed her, or even anyone who had *wanted* to. It wasn't anything she'd ever considered needing or desiring. The intensity in Honor's voice changed her mind. There was something incredibly erotic about imagining a woman possessing her that way. *Not just* a *woman. Honor.*

"Sorry. I didn't intend to bring up old business." Honor tried to lighten her tone. Talking about Terry with Quinn was becoming so easy that she hadn't even considered that Quinn might not want to hear about her past.

"That's okay," Quinn said quietly. "I'm surprised you let her live."

Honor flashed her a grin. "If there's ever a next time, I won't."

Quinn's heart flipped, but she told herself that Honor was just joking—not really paying attention to what she was saying. That had to be the case, since Honor had made it very clear just a few days before that another serious relationship was not in her future.

"I'm right over here," Quinn said, pointing to a cream-colored house with ornate Victorian cornices and maroon detailing.

"I remember." Honor pulled to the curb, cut the ignition, and turned in her seat. "It meant a lot to me to talk to you the other night, Quinn. I just want you to know that."

"You never need to worry about discussing Terry with me. Or anything else." Fleetingly, Quinn touched Honor's thigh, then drew her hand away. She unclipped her seat belt, opened her door, and slid one leg onto the sidewalk. As she eased out, she turned and looked back inside, meeting Honor's eyes. "You coming in?"

Through a throat tight with emotions that she didn't dare examine too closely, Honor whispered, "Yes."

Chapter Eighteen

Once inside her apartment, Quinn hastily cleared a spot on the sofa and gestured to Honor to sit. "Can I get you something to drink? Soda or orange juice?"

Smiling, Honor shook her head. "No, I'm fine."

"Okay." Quinn backed up a few steps, barely able to believe that Honor was sitting in her living room. *Such as it is.* She grinned foolishly. "So...uh...what should I wear?"

Honor frowned. "Wear?"

"You know. Clothes? Where are we going for dinner?"

For the first time, Honor realized that this was coming very close to a date. It hadn't been what she'd intended. But she couldn't deny that the prospect of spending a few hours alone with Quinn, away from work, out of the house, without friends or family in attendance, was exciting. Immediately, she thought of the small neighborhood restaurant that was actually one of the best-kept secrets in the area. There were only eight tables, very elegant in an understated way, with excellent food and friendly service. And the best thing about it was that despite the intimate decor and a fine menu, the atmosphere was still casual. She was wearing the slacks and silk tee that she'd worked in. "Whatever the next step up from jeans is for you."

"I won't be long. There's a newspaper on the coffee table... uh...which is under those three boxes, if you need something to do."

Honor just grinned. "I thought I'd use the time to explore your apartment."

Quinn paled.

"I'm kidding," Honor murmured, taking pity on her. "Get going. I'm starving."

Quinn backed up another step, her eyes on Honor. She was almost afraid if she went into the other room to shower, that when she came out, Honor would be gone. "Just one minute. Okay?"

Something of Quinn's uncertainty showed in her voice, and that small vulnerability tugged at Honor's heart. Softly, she said, "I'm not going anywhere."

"All right. Okay." Nodding briskly, Quinn disappeared around the corner.

Honor walked into the kitchen and stood at the back door, looking pensively out at the deck. Only two nights before, she had sat on those steps outside telling Quinn about a precious piece of her heart. Standing on the inside now, listening to the shower run in the room next to her, she thought of how effortlessly Quinn had come into the very center of her consciousness. Quinn hadn't pushed, she hadn't pried, she hadn't pressured Honor in any way. She'd simply listened, and in the process, had awakened long-forgotten pleasures. The anticipation of an evening spent sharing secrets, the thrill of a certain voice speaking your name, the rush of heat beneath a particular touch. Simple pleasures made profound because of the presence of a singular woman.

Honor jumped at the sound of a husky voice behind her.

"All set."

Hoping to seem casual, Honor turned and knew instantly that she had failed. She felt the heat rise to her cheeks and knew that her reaction must be obvious, even in the waning light. Quinn wore dark chinos, so blue they were almost black, with a thin silver-buckled belt at her waist and a plain white shirt with the top two buttons open. Casual loafers, the flat, plain watch that she always seemed to wear, and wet hair nonchalantly combed. She was six feet away, and Honor could smell a hint of her cologne, dark and sharp.

At the first look, a wave of pleasure broke through Honor's depths. As the seconds passed, an avalanche of sensation followed close behind—lust and longing and shocked surprise all rolled together.

"Something wrong?" Quinn questioned quietly. She wasn't sure whether to stay or disappear. Honor had the strangest look on her face, as if Quinn were a stranger. "Honor?"

Honor gave a small start and an embarrassed laugh. "No! Nothing's wrong. You look great. Let's go."

Still uncertain, Quinn stepped aside so that Honor could pass. The kitchen was small enough that Honor's shoulder brushed Quinn's arm, and the brief contact sent goose bumps dancing along her skin.

"Where are we going?" Quinn followed Honor through the apartment, grabbing her keys from the small side table inside the door on the way out.

"A little place a few blocks from here." Honor stopped on the porch and turned to Quinn. "We can walk...if you don't mind."

"No," Quinn replied instantly. "I'd like to walk. I'm still getting a feel for the neighborhood."

Honor laughed. "Then let me be your tour guide."

❖

By the time they arrived, it was nearly eight. Since it was a weeknight, they were able to get a table right away and were seated in a nook near one of the front windows, where they could see passersby outside but still be separated from the other diners. It was cozy and intimate.

Quinn looked around the small, tidy restaurant, appreciating the local artists' watercolors on the wall and the muted light cast by the glass wall sconces. "This is nice."

"I'm glad you like it." Honor wondered how a situation that should have been awkward—dinner with someone she barely knew and with whom she'd had anything but a smooth start—could be so incredibly easy. But she knew the answer. It was Quinn.

"You know, you're a very unusual surgeon," Honor said musingly.

Quinn looked up questioningly from the menu she'd been perusing. "Oh?"

"You don't rush. You let things happen."

It wasn't what Honor said, but the way she looked at Quinn when she said it—intently, with just a touch of wonder—that made Quinn forget all about dinner. In an instant, it was all about Honor. "The things that really matter can't be hurried."

"Don't you ever get tired of waiting?"

Quinn nodded solemnly. "Yes, sometimes. It can get very lonely, waiting."

Honor's lips parted in surprise. "Are you...lonely?"

"Not right now." The corner of Quinn's mouth lifted. "Right now, I'm almost as happy as I could be."

"Almost?"

Suddenly serious, Quinn sighed. "Since I got sick, I've had a lot of time to consider what I wanted in my life. Up until then, the only thing I'd ever thought about was surgery."

"And now?" The answer, Honor found, seemed critical.

Quinn shrugged. "I want a life, not just a career." She blushed and looked away for an instant, then back to Honor. "I'd like to have some of the things that you have."

Honor's eyes widened in surprise. "What I have?"

"Yes," Quinn said softly. "Friends, family, children. The things that matter at the end of the day."

"And a lover?" Honor's voice was pitched low, heavy with feeling. *Were you just being kind, not mentioning that?*

"Yes. Most of all."

Honor looked at the woman across from her, so handsome and exciting, so charming, so exquisitely sensitive. "You'll have all of that someday."

"I'm patient. I don't mind waiting."

"Like I said," Honor forced a smile, uncertain of the conversation and frightened by the wild racing of her blood. "You're a most unusual surgeon."

Quinn laughed without rancor. "I'm not a surgeon anymore."

"I'm sorry."

"No, it's okay. That's not your fault." Quinn let out a long breath. "Are you going to tell me what you wanted to talk to me about?"

"Yes," Honor said definitely. She reached across the table and brushed her fingers across the top of Quinn's hand. "But after dinner, all right? Let's enjoy this place together first."

"I'd like that very much."

❖

Two hours later, they walked toward home, strolling slowly along a different route than the one they had taken to reach the restaurant. Honor pointed out some of the historic landmarks on the way. When they reached a small triangular park that jutted off the winding road that led from the river into their neighborhood, they sat on a bench beneath a tree, the sounds of the traffic behind them. It was fully dark, but the streetlights provided enough illumination for them to see each other.

As Honor sat facing her, Quinn stretched her arm out along the back of the park bench, her hand behind but not quite touching Honor's shoulder. "That was a great restaurant. Thank you."

"I enjoyed being there with you. No thanks are needed."

It took every ounce of Quinn's willpower not to rest her fingers against the back of Honor's neck and slip her fingers into the soft strands of hair that fell gently over Honor's collar. They were close enough that if she just leaned forward, she could take Honor into her arms. And she wanted to. She'd wanted to for the last few hours, the last few days, and, she realized now, even longer. For months she'd been wanting a woman who could make her feel what Honor did—hot and urgent, steady and cool, tall as a mountain, and as insignificant as a grain of sand. Everything, everywhere, right down to her bones.

"You're quiet," Honor said gently. "Is everything all right?"

Quinn ran a hand over her face. "God, Honor, I don't know." She blew out a breath. "Say what you need to say to me."

"All right." Honor straightened, her voice strong. "I met with the hospital attorneys today regarding the issue of your malpractice coverage and the kinds of cases we do in the emergency room."

"And my...condition." Quinn couldn't keep the bitterness out of her voice as she said the last word.

Gently, Honor said, "Yes. In relationship to your cardiac condition."

"And?"

"After much roundabout debate, the consensus was that you should be allowed to work in the ER."

Quinn studied Honor's face. Her expression was closed, guarded. "But?"

"But that there would be restrictions on the kinds of cases you can treat."

Quinn bolted to her feet so quickly that Honor jumped in surprise, giving a startled gasp. Quinn raked her fingers through her hair, then fisted her hand. "*Jesus Christ,* Honor! You're going to tell me that I can't operate, aren't you? That I'll have to work up only medical patients and let the trauma patients—"

"No!" Honor scrambled to her feet and put both hands on Quinn's shoulders, shaking her lightly. "That's *not* what I was going to say." The tension beneath her hands was frightening. Quinn's body was rigid. "Quinn, it's all right. Come sit down and listen."

For a moment, Honor thought Quinn was simply going to walk away.

"Please."

Eventually, Quinn relented and sat down, but this time the distance between them stretched wide.

As calmly as possible, Honor explained. "You can't do any open procedures—"

Quinn cursed.

"Any open procedures," Honor repeated succinctly, "*without* the immediate availability of a senior ER attending who is able to accept medical responsibility."

"What the hell does *that* mean?" Quinn's tone was suspicious, dark with frustration.

"It means me."

A minute passed, and then another. Quinn got up, paced a few steps away, turned, walked back, and sat again. "You're going to baby-sit me."

"No. I'm going to supervise you." Before Quinn could begin another protest, Honor slid closer on the bench and rested her hand just above Quinn's knee. "Quinn, it isn't unlike situations where board-eligible surgeons are required to do an additional year of training before they can sit for their exams."

"Those people need *remedial* training. I don't." It was adding insult to injury, and Quinn's head pounded with the injustice of it.

"Of course you don't. I know that. But this way, the hospital is covered should...anything happen." Honor could only imagine how humiliating this must be for someone of Quinn's caliber. "No one needs to know. I don't need to be in the room with you when you're doing a procedure—you just need to give me a heads up, which would happen anyhow. It's a formality."

"For how long?" Quinn asked dully. She couldn't fight it. Didn't *want* to fight Honor.

"Six months. That should be enough time to determine that there won't be any problems." Honor risked a quick stroke down Quinn's arm. "And I don't think that there will be."

Quinn nodded. "Fine."

Honor squeezed Quinn's hand. "Quinn—"

"It's fine. Whatever you say." Quinn stood and looked around, realizing for the first time that they were alone. Cars moved by on the street behind them, but the park, although small, was secluded. "We should get back."

"All right." Honor wanted to say she was sorry, but it would have been a platitude. It had been *her* judgment call to investigate the issue, and despite the fact that Quinn was unhappy, Honor thought the decision reasonable. But she ached for the pain she heard in Quinn's voice.

They walked a block in silence before Quinn said, "Does this mean I'm going to take call with you *every* shift?"

"Yes."

"Well, I guess that's the silver lining."

Honor cut Quinn a look, and Quinn grinned back. In another minute, they were both laughing quietly.

"Do you know that I hate this almost as much as you do?" Honor asked.

"Which part? The supervising or—"

"No." Honor's tone was vehement. "I hate that you lost something so critical to you, Quinn. Through no fault of your own, and after you'd already suffered so much. It's not fair that you should lose more."

Quinn stopped abruptly in the middle of the sidewalk and caught Honor's hand, spinning her around until they faced one another. She leaned forward, her body nearly touching Honor's. "I'm *glad* that I'm here. I'm glad that I met you. It's going to be all right."

Honor gave a shaky laugh, captured by the intensity in Quinn's face. There were moments like this when she glimpsed a different woman simmering beneath the calm exterior. There was fire there; Honor could feel the heat. She wanted to immerse herself in the flames of Quinn's passion and blaze with her. Her body wanted it. And she feared that her heart might want it, too. "So am I. Very glad."

"Good. That's good then." Quinn forced her fingers open and released Honor's hand. They walked silently the last half-block to Quinn's house and climbed the stairs to the front porch together. Under the shadows outside the small circle of light cast by the bulb above the door, Quinn said, "Am I going to work tomorrow, then?"

"Seven a.m."

"I'll be there."

"You know, you shouldn't be riding your bike for a few more days, not with that shoulder injury."

"You're probably right," Quinn agreed. "It's not that far. I'll walk."

Honor shook her head. "Of course you won't. Come over to the house around six fifteen. You can have a cup of coffee with me, and we'll ride in with Linda. She and I take turns driving depending on what the kids and Robin need to do in the evening."

Hesitating only a second, Quinn said, "All right. Thanks."

"Good. That's settled then."

Quinn didn't want to say good night, but she knew she needed to go inside. Being with Honor was the sweetest torture she'd ever known, but there was only so much restraint left in her. She was tired and disappointed, and she wanted so very much to lose herself in Honor's arms. Leaning forward, she brushed her lips against Honor's cheek. "Thanks for everything, Honor."

Before Honor could think, before she could reason or rationalize or regret, she stepped near, threaded her arms around Quinn's neck, and kissed her. She felt Quinn stiffen in surprise and then the lips against her mouth parted with a soft gasp. A heartbeat later, Quinn's hands were at her waist, drawing her gently closer. When she felt her breasts and her belly and her thighs press into Quinn's, a shiver played through her. Wavering on shaking legs, she slid her fingers into Quinn's hair, stroking her neck as her tongue leisurely traced the surface of Quinn's lips.

Quinn's thumbs pressed unhurriedly up and down Honor's sides as their tongues met—first exploring, then caressing. Honor moaned quietly, astounded by the fierceness of a simple kiss. Quinn's mouth was hot; her palms were scorching as they massaged the muscles of Honor's abdomen. Honor's blood seethed with long-forgotten yearnings.

"Honor," Quinn pulled her head back, her breath escaping her on a low, mournful groan, "we can't do this."

"I know." Honor trembled against Quinn's body, not certain she could stand alone. "I don't know...I'm sorry...I can't think why—"

"I *want* to make love to you," Quinn murmured, her lips against Honor's ear. "Every time I looked at you tonight, I wanted to touch you."

"Oh, Quinn," Honor moaned, pressing her forehead to Quinn's right shoulder, struggling desperately to think through the fog of lust and desire.

"I want more than that." Quinn cupped Honor's chin and tilted her head, finding her eyes and holding them fiercely. "I want to make love with you until you scream, until *I* scream. But I want what comes before and after that, too."

Dimly, Quinn's words came back to Honor.

"Friends, family, children. The things that matter at the end of the day."

"And a lover?"

"Yes. Most of all."

"Quinn," Honor confessed, her voice breaking. "I don't know if I can, again."

"I know." Quinn very gently backed away, lifting her fingers to Honor's cheek and caressing her lightly. "And that's why we can't do this."

Honor was silent as she willed her body to quiet. "Thank you. I hope I didn't...embarrass you."

Quinn gave an incredulous laugh. "You did a lot of things to me just now. Embarrassment wasn't one of them."

"I'll see you in the morning?" Honor's voice was wistful, sad. *Please say yes.*

"I'll be there."

"Thank you."

Quinn watched as Honor turned, walked down the sidewalk, and got into her car. She waited on the porch until the taillights of the Subaru disappeared around the corner, and then she sat down heavily on the front steps. She rested her head in her hands, her fingers clenched in her hair.

The only thing that had kept her from taking Honor to her bed was the certain knowledge that if she had, she would have lost Honor's heart. And that was the one thing she wanted most of all. The fist of arousal was so tight in her chest, she thought she'd choke on it. Need, desire, and desperate longing flooded through her. She groaned softly.

Finally, she rose and slowly climbed the stairs to her apartment. She didn't turn on the lights, but made her way by memory to her bedroom where the mattress now resided. Fully clothed, she lay down on her back and draped her forearm across her eyes. She could still feel Honor everywhere against her skin, taste her on her lips, smell her.

She feared that one fleeting kiss might be all she'd ever have. The agony was bittersweet, because as much as the memories taunted her, she wanted them. It was a long time before she fell into a fitful slumber, Honor's image playing through her mind.

Chapter Nineteen

Honor turned her head at the sound of tapping on the driver's side window. Linda stood there in the dark peering into the car, making a winding motion with her fingers. Hesitating, uncertain whether she *wanted* to talk, Honor eventually opened the window.

"Hi," she said distractedly.

Linda leaned her forearms on the car door and said conversationally, "You've been out here with the engine running for fifteen minutes." She held up a sweating bottle of Red Dog. "Want a drink?"

"Yes," Honor replied as she reached through the window for the beer. She took a swallow and sighed gratefully. "Want to come in and sit down?"

"Sure."

As Linda walked around the front of the car, Honor turned off the engine and leaned her head back, then closed her eyes and pressed the cold bottle to her forehead. She heard the passenger door open and felt the vehicle sway slightly as Linda slid in, followed by the thud of the door closing. She turned her head and opened her eyes. "Thanks for the beer."

"I had a feeling you might need one, since you're sitting in the dark at eleven thirty at night." Linda took a swallow from her own bottle and worked the lever by her side to slide the seat back far enough to stretch her legs out beneath the dashboard. "When Robbie brought Arly over this evening, she told me that you were going out with Quinn. Arly's asleep upstairs with Kim, by the way."

"Thanks. I would have called when it started getting late, but I knew you'd keep her here if Phyllis was tied up."

Linda shrugged. "Of course. Phyl called to check in with us about seven. She had an impromptu dinner with, and I quote—the studly new art teacher—unquote."

"Good for her," Honor murmured. "She's spent the last six years taking care of Arly and me. It's about time she started getting on with her own life."

"I can't imagine that anything Phyllis might do with her life would change the way she loves you two." Linda cocked her head and stared at her friend. She'd seen Honor devastated after Terry's death, and she'd seen her climb out of that agony of loss and depression to carry on. She'd never heard her sound quite this way—a mixture of angry, frustrated, and sad. "What's going on, Honor? Did something happen with Quinn?"

Honor laughed, a short hard sound entirely devoid of humor. "You could say that."

"What?"

"That's what I've been driving around for the last hour trying to figure out."

"Did you two have a fight?"

"No." Honor sipped her beer and curled the fingers of her left hand around the steering wheel, slowly turning it as she contemplated what she still couldn't quite comprehend. Finally, she looked at her best friend, her expression one of uncertainty and confusion. "I kissed her."

"A little kiss or an honest-to-God-for-real kiss?"

Honor's voice was pitched low, her throat still tight with the memory of Quinn's touch. "I wanted to go to bed with her...and I wanted her to make love to me until I forgot everything except her hands on me."

Linda's lips parted in surprise, and she exhaled sharply. "Well. That about does it for me. I need a cold shower now."

Honor leaned her head back against the seat again and laughed, blindly reaching out her right hand and feeling the comfort of Linda's fingers grasping hers. "I don't know what I'd do without you."

"No use wasting brain power thinking about it, because it's not going to happen." Linda squeezed Honor's hand. "So what happened? What's got you in such a spin?"

"She said no," Honor said on a sigh. "I *think* I'm glad that she did." She turned her head and regarded Linda seriously. "I can't stop thinking about her, but I'm not sure if that's just because she's the first woman who has made me *feel* anything since Terry."

"That's saying quite a lot, don't you think?" Linda struggled not to scream, *Don't run from her. She's the best thing that could happen to you!*

Honor nodded. "It is amazing. But I still don't know what it means."

"Do you have to *know*?" At Honor's look of confusion, Linda continued, "Why can't it be enough just to have the feelings, and see where they go?"

"It *was* like that with Terry, but we were so young. Now the idea of getting involved with someone, even just physically, seems huge." Honor looked out through the windshield, but she wasn't seeing the quiet residential street. She was seeing Quinn's expression as she'd stepped back from their kiss, regret and longing in her eyes. "And I'm pretty sure that Quinn wants more than just a roll in the hay."

Honor, sweetheart, so do you. Linda recalled the way that Quinn had looked at Honor at the barbecue, as if Honor were the only woman present. She considered, too, the tremendous intensity and focus with which Quinn did everything. It made sense that Quinn would want more than a brief affair. "So how did you leave it?"

Honor lifted both hands and let them fall onto the steering wheel, shaking her head as she did so. "She said she wanted more than just sex, and I said I wasn't certain that I was capable of anything more."

"And then she pushed?"

"Quinn?" Honor smiled, a fond sad smile. "She would never do that. She said she understood, and that she'd see me tomorrow at work."

Linda made a sound verging on a groan. "God, it's a damn good thing that Robin is so fabulous in bed, or else I'd have to arm-wrestle you for Quinn."

"Yeah, right. Like you'd ever look at anyone else."

"*Look,* maybe." Linda laughed. "At the risk of sounding sexist, even if she *weren't* the mother of my children, I'd never want anyone but her."

Honor met Linda's gaze. "I never thought I'd want anyone but Terry, either."

"And now you do?"

"I think so." Honor glanced down at her left hand, her wedding ring just a dull gleam in the glow from the streetlights. "I never imagined that I would."

"You never imagined you'd be at this place without her, either, sweetheart." Gently, Linda reached across the space between the seats and put her arm around Honor's shoulder. "But you are, and it's all right to keep on living."

Honor leaned her head against Linda's shoulder and sighed. "My head knows that, but I'm not sure that the rest of me is convinced."

"It sounds like your *body* already knows." Linda hugged her. "Give yourself a little time to get used to the idea, and if you still want to, go for it. I think Quinn is terrific."

"I'm not sure I'd even know what to do. I never really dated anyone but Terry, and we were just horny teenagers who were lucky enough to fall in love with the right person." Honor grinned wryly. "Besides, Quinn might not believe I'm really interested in her after my brush-off tonight."

"Romance her, sweetheart." Linda laughed. "She'll get the idea."

Romance her. Could I? Honor closed her eyes and sighed, then straightened. "I think I'm too tired to make any sense of this tonight. Should I get my munchkin?"

"Nah. She's out, and you know how she sleeps. Let her stay." Linda opened the car door. "Robbie can handle one extra." She hesitated before getting out. "In fact, she's talking about one more of our own."

"Oh my God. That would be great!" Honor studied Linda's face. "Wouldn't it?"

"Her last pregnancy was no cakewalk, and she's thirty-six now." Linda smiled fleetingly. "But yeah, I'm ready for the two a.m. feedings and the weeks of sexual deprivation again."

Honor laughed, truly laughed. "Keep me posted. I'll see you in the morning. Oh, Quinn is riding in with us."

"Yummy."

Satisfied, Linda slipped out and closed the car door to the sounds of Honor laughing once more.

❖

Honor called Phyllis to tell her she didn't need to come over because Arly was at Robin and Linda's, then she set the coffeemaker to autobrew, showered, and was dressed and ready for work forty-five minutes ahead of schedule. She fidgeted in the kitchen, choosing first one set of coffee mugs and then another, and then decided it would be better to use travel mugs. Once that was settled, she stared at the clock. At 6:10, there was a knock at the back door, and her pulse kicked into hyperdrive.

"Hi," Honor said as she opened the door to Quinn, who stood on the porch in jeans and a cotton shirt with the sleeves rolled halfway up her forearms, her leather backpack dangling from her right hand. There were uneasy questions in her eyes and shadows beneath them. Those traces of unhappiness were Honor's undoing. "I thought about you all night."

"Same here." Quinn's voice was raspy with stress. She'd slept badly and had awakened agitated and disturbingly aroused. Sometime in the night, she'd stripped off her clothes to lie naked beneath the sheets, surrendering to half-formed visions of pale skin and warm hands and urgent coupling. Barely asleep, she'd twitched and thrashed and shivered, riding the crest of desperate yearnings, her body throbbing on the brink of explosion. When she'd finally opened her eyes to a gray dawn, arousal beat like a fist deep inside. She brushed trembling fingers over her chest and down her belly, knowing relief, if merely physical, was seconds away. When the muscles in her thighs tightened and her breath caught in her chest, she bolted upright and headed for the shower on slightly unsteady legs. She wanted to come, *would* have come easily, but it was Honor's hands on her flesh that she craved. And for that, she'd wait if she could. "That was quite a kiss."

"I'm not sure what I'm doing." Honor leaned against the door frame, holding the screen open with her left hand.

Quinn stood on the other side of the threshold, inches away, but made no move to touch her. She wouldn't, not until invited, no matter how desperately she needed to. "It's complicated."

"Yes." Honor gave a tiny laugh. "Oh yes, that would be true."

"Any suggestions?"

"I think I'd like to ask you out for a date."

Quinn took a long breath and when she let it out, the light had returned to her eyes. Cautiously, she suggested, "Maybe we could take Arly to the zoo? I read that it's supposed to be a really good one...they have that hot air balloon that you can ride in and see the whole city."

"She would love that, and so would I." Honor reached out and took Quinn's left hand, drawing her slowly into the kitchen. She couldn't look away from Quinn's mouth, remembering how soft her lips, how hot her taste. She swallowed the desire beating in her throat, stealing her voice. "But I'd like our first real date to be just us."

"Honor?" Quinn murmured as the door closed behind her and she dropped her backpack on the floor. Honor's hand was still in hers, and they were mere inches apart.

"Yes?" Honor breathed, captivated by the sudden darkening of Quinn's eyes.

"Would it be all right to kiss again *before* the first date?"

Honor moved until their bodies merged, her hand coming into Quinn's hair, pulling her head down. Against Quinn's mouth, she whispered, "I don't see why not."

Quinn had been so hungry for her through all the long hours of the night that the feel of Honor now, warm and supple and yielding in her embrace, turned every cell in her body to pure desire. Groaning faintly, she pulled Honor more tightly to her, her hands spread on either side of Honor's spine, just above her hips. Her tongue found its way into Honor's mouth, thirsting for her. Her hips pressed tightly into the curve of Honor's pelvis, calling for passion to meet passion. Distantly, she heard a soft whimper. The fingers in her hair clenched, and the woman in her arms trembled.

Quinn lifted her mouth away enough to whisper raggedly, "Tell me to stop. Tell me, because I can't stop myself."

"You...ask...a lot," Honor panted unevenly. She pressed both palms flat against Quinn's chest, the fingers of her right hand brushing over the hard shape of the device beneath Quinn's skin. Gently, she pushed Quinn away until a breath of space appeared between them. "Last night you asked for more, and now today... for less."

"See what you do to me?" Quinn rested her forehead against Honor's, her chest heaving and her stomach so tight with urgency she ached. "I'm a mess."

"I think you're wonderful." Honor moved her fingers to Quinn's cheek. "Tell me why you wanted to stop?"

Quinn laughed shakily, her hands lightly clasping Honor's waist. "Besides the fact that Linda will be here any minute and we have to go to work?"

"Besides those small details," Honor said softly, steadfastly ignoring the swell of arousal that pulsed tormentingly between her thighs with every heartbeat. She wanted Quinn so much that she could barely think, but just beyond the edge of that consuming desire was the compulsion to know her. To understand this woman who had swept away barriers that Honor had believed unassailable, who had exposed needs that she had believed buried along with Terry. *Who are you, Quinn, that you can do this to me?*

"I meant what I said last night," Quinn whispered, her voice deep and husky with lingering excitement. "The things that matter shouldn't be hurried."

"Are you always so controlled?"

"Is that what you think?" Quinn shook her head, shuddering as yet another wave of need lifted from her depths and raced along her spine. "I am so close to coming apart right now, I can't even tell you."

Honor's legs weakened as the words struck at her core. She moaned softly. "God, I have to get away from you or we're going to end up rolling around naked right here on the floor."

"Good idea," Quinn agreed shakily.

"Which one?" Honor gasped.

"Both of them."

With effort, they backed away until just their fingertips touched, their eyes locked.

"About that date," Quinn said.

Honors brow lifted. "Yes?"

"When did you have in mind?"

"Friday night?" Honor felt suddenly shy, despite the fact that a minute before she had been ready to tear off her clothes and beg Quinn to ravish her. "There's a demonstration of Japanese drummers at the Annenberg. I think I can still get tickets."

"Mmm. That would be great, only..."

Honor's heart plunged. "No good?"

"It'll have to be an early night, because our first soccer game is Saturday morning. I have to be at my best for that."

"Really." Honor narrowed her eyes. "I certainly wouldn't want to interfere with your priorities."

"Absolutely not." Grinning, Quinn leaned forward, gently kissed Honor's mouth, and murmured, "I don't know how I'm going to make it until Friday night."

Honor drew a long relieved breath. "You're going to be so busy working your ass off in the ER, you won't even notice the time passing." Exerting every ounce of willpower she possessed, she let go of Quinn's hands, moved around her, and headed for the coffee. *Linda will be here any second. I've got to get myself together.*

"I'm looking forward to it."

Coffeepot in hand, Honor looked over her shoulder. "Which part? The part where I work your ass off, or the part where I take you out on the town?"

Quinn's heart did a fast roll, the kind that ordinarily had her bracing for a jolt. This time, though, it was pure pleasure. "Both, Dr. Blake."

Smiling, heart lighter than it had been in years, Honor turned away, afraid that Quinn would see more in her eyes than she was ready to reveal. "Smooth as always, Dr. Maguire."

CHAPTER TWENTY

Linda dropped into a chair at the nurses' station next to Honor and heaved a sigh. "God, what a day."

"Mmph," Honor grunted without looking up from the EKG she was studying. A minute later, she pushed back in her chair and ran a distracted hand through her hair. "It's been nonstop since we walked in this morning."

"Oh, how I love summer in the city," Linda moaned. "More sports-related accidents, more vehicular trauma, more fistfights. Ain't we got fun."

"Only a few more weeks until school starts, thank God." Honor glanced around the ER restlessly. The hallways were nearly impassable with stretchers, x-ray machines, and instrument carts parked haphazardly outside patient cubicles. She saw several residents, nurses, and attendings, but not the one person she was seeking. "Have you seen Quinn?"

Linda smiled. By her count, that was the tenth time that Honor had asked the same question since the three of them had arrived for work eight hours before. She doubted that Honor realized that she became agitated and outright grumpy whenever Quinn wasn't in eyeshot. "I think she's casting that navicular fracture in seven. The painter who fell off the ladder and landed on his wrist?"

"Oh, right."

"It's a damn good thing she came back to work today," Linda observed casually. "Half the patients in here have surgical problems."

"She's earning her salary, that's for sure." Turning on the swivel stool, Honor glanced behind her at the large intake board with columns of patient names, in and out times, and chief complaints. The flow *did* seem faster, and part of it had to be the fact that fewer patients were waiting for surgical consults because Quinn was dealing with their problems herself. "I just don't want her to burn out."

"I don't think you have to worry about that," Linda said with a snort. "She's incredibly fast, and I don't get the sense she's tired."

"I'm sure you're right." Honor tried to sound casual, but Linda knew her too well.

"What are you worried about?" Linda studied the shadows swirling in Honor's eyes, then asked gently, "Are you concerned about her health?"

"No, of course not."

"You *are*. Why? Is she having problems?" When Linda saw Honor's jaw set in the way it did when she was being stubborn, she added impatiently, "I already *know* what's wrong, remember? You're not giving away any secrets."

Honor's shoulders sagged slightly, and she shook her head. "I don't know what's bothering me. She seems perfectly fine. I've seen her running with the kids on the soccer field, and believe me, she's totally functional."

"You wouldn't be half this worried if you weren't falling for her."

"I'm not *falling* for her." Honor stood and gathered her paperwork. "I'm going to discharge the man in one with the chest pain. His EKG is fine, and his chest x-ray is clear. He's got esophageal spasm, and he needs an upper endoscopy. Can you give him the phone number for the GI department so he can schedule a follow-up appointment?"

"Sure." Linda stood as well and angled her body so that she was blocking the exit path. In an insistent whisper, she said, "And I saw the way the two of you were looking at each other this morning. I thought I was going to have to hose you both down before you got in the car."

Honor couldn't help smiling. "She's gorgeous, isn't she?"

"She most certainly is." Linda gave Honor a quick hug. "And so are you. I am *so* happy for you."

"There's nothing to get all excited about. We're just going on a simple date."

"A date!"

"Shh! God, will you be *quiet.*" Honor glanced around surreptitiously, relieved to see that no one was nearby. "I hate hospital gossip, and I'd rather not be the subject of it."

"When?"

"Friday."

"Who asked who?" Linda could barely contain her excitement. She was naturally curious and loved the details of other people's lives, but this was beyond exciting. *Honor on a date!*

"I did." Honor colored and looked away. "I have to go now. I've got patients waiting." As she turned to head down the hall, she nearly bumped into Quinn. Stepping back quickly, she mumbled, "Hi. Everything okay?"

"Perfect," Quinn replied with a grin. One of the best parts of the day had been looking up to see Honor nearby, concentrating on an x-ray or explaining a teaching point to a resident or bent over a chart, writing a note. Every time Quinn saw her, pleasure fluttered in the pit of her stomach. "You?"

"Good. Fine," Honor said abruptly, trying desperately to avoid Quinn's eyes. Because every time she looked into them, she forgot what she was doing. As the heat of Quinn's gaze washed over her, all she could think of was how it would feel were that touch made real. She was certain that she had never been so constantly aroused in her life. "I..." She lifted the chart in her hand. "Patient...have a patient."

"Yeah. Me, too. See you later?"

Honor sidled around her, careful that their bodies didn't touch. "Soccer. Maybe."

Quinn turned and watched Honor hurry away down the hall, a quizzical look in her eyes. From beside her, she heard Linda laugh softly.

"There used to be a time when she could speak in sentences of more than one word," Linda observed dryly. "Funny about that."

"She's incredible," Quinn whispered.

Linda rolled her eyes.

"So, what's next?" Quinn asked briskly, her expression becoming intent as her attention refocused.

"How do you feel about checking out a softball player who got hit in the cheek with a line drive?"

"Visual problems?"

"Too swollen to tell. He can't get his eyelids open, so I didn't force it."

"Do we have a facial CT yet?"

"Just say the word, Dr. Maguire." Linda reached behind her for an x-ray request form.

"Considerate it said. While you're getting that," Quinn glanced at the intake board, "I'll start on the woman with the upper abdominal pain."

"You've got a deal."

Quinn was in the process of performing an ultrasound examination of the fifty-year-old woman's gallbladder, looking for stones, when Linda stuck her head into the room. "Dr. Blake asked me to tell you that we have two level ones coming in, Dr. Maguire."

"I'll be right there," Quinn said calmly as she set the ultrasound probe aside. She smiled at Mrs. Lamont. "I'm sorry. I'm going to have to leave for a while, but I'll be back."

The woman merely sighed and closed her eyes.

When Quinn stepped out of the cubicle, she saw Honor hurrying toward the admission area and sprinted to catch up to her. "What's going on?"

"Rescue One is bringing in a drowning victim. A kayaker they pulled out of the Schuylkill. He's in full arrest."

"Crap."

Honor nodded grimly. "And Northstar's on the roof with a woman with chemical burns to both arms. I don't have a level on that."

"What do you want me to take?"

"Take the burn," Honor said immediately.

"I may need to do escharotomies," Quinn said quietly, referring to the incisions made through the thick burns to improve circulation. *I may need to operate. Just what everyone's so worried about.*

Honor, her eyes steady and calm, met Quinn's. "No matter what anyone says, you're a surgeon, Quinn. Just take care of it. I'll be around."

Before Quinn could do anything more than nod, a horde of EMTs pushing two stretchers, one after the other, came barreling through the door. Honor pointed to her left to the first group; the drowning victim appeared pale and unresponsive as he was whizzed past.

"Down here," Quinn directed the second stretcher to the larger procedure room.

For the next hour, Quinn was totally absorbed in the resuscitation of the twenty-five-year-old woman who had tripped and fallen and, in the process of catching herself, had immersed both arms in a caustic disinfectant solution. After the initial administration of fluid hydration and pain medication, Quinn had turned her attention to the circulation in the woman's hands. The blood flow was significantly impaired by the deep circumferential tissue damage in her forearms, and the fingers were white and cold.

As Quinn had anticipated, immediate surgery was necessary to release the constricting burn tissue and restore the normal circulation. Although the patient would be transferred to an area burn center for definitive care, it was imperative to re-establish blood flow to her fingers before permanent damage could result. It was precision surgery due to the many nerves and blood vessels in close proximity to tendons and other essential structures in the wrist. Quinn made confident, efficient incisions through the eschars on both wrists, relieving the tense pressure beneath. Immediately, the nail beds, which had been dead white, turned pink.

When Quinn was satisfied that the woman would not lose her fingers, she pushed the instrument tray aside and stood, stretching her back to ease the cramps in her shoulders.

"Dress the wounds with Silvadene and sterile gauze," she instructed the resident who had assisted her. "She's ready to transport."

"Thanks," the resident said with a hint of awe in her voice.

"And don't forget to finish the chart work."

"No problem," the resident called after Quinn as she walked away.

Quinn didn't see Linda at the nurses' station, so she continued down the hall to the treatment room where she had seen Honor direct the EMTs earlier. At the open door, she stopped abruptly. Honor knelt astride the stretcher, performing closed cardiac compression while verbally directing the resident and Linda to administer a cocktail of cardiac drugs. From where she stood, Quinn could see the strain in Honor's face and the sweat beaded on her face and neck.

Moving to Linda's side, Quinn asked quietly, "How long has she been at it?"

Linda took a quick glance at the clock. "Fifty-eight minutes."

"What's his status?"

"He came in flatline. No change."

Quinn knew that in near-drowning victims the absence of a pulse upon arrival in the emergency room almost always indicated a very poor chance for survival. However, most drowning victims were young, and while it was always difficult to stop resuscitative efforts, it was the most difficult in the young. She moved to Honor's side.

"How about I take over for a while? I'm fresh."

Honor looked up briefly, her vision blurred by the sweat running into her eyes. She'd been going on automatic for the last half-hour and could barely feel her hands. "Okay, yes. Thanks."

Quinn put her hands over Honor's and began compression as soon as Honor withdrew hers. Rhythmically, she pumped her arms to the count of five compressions to each breath delivered by the respiratory therapist, who had attached a breathing bag to the endotracheal tube that ran down the young man's throat. In the background, she could hear Honor instructing Linda to administer another round of drugs.

"Let's shock him again," Honor said a minute later. "Charge the defibrillator to 300." As she put the paddles down on the pale chest, she met Quinn's eyes. "Stand far clear of the bed, Quinn."

Quinn nodded and, when Honor called clear, stepped several feet away, knowing that the slightest bleed of current from the patient's body or the metal stretcher or even along the surface of the floor would in all likelihood trigger her own arrhythmias. As soon as the charge had dispersed, she moved back in to continue compressions. They repeated the cycle twice more, without success.

"That's enough," Honor said quite clearly.

Slowly, everyone in the room stopped what they were doing.

Honor glanced at the clock. Flatly, she stated, "Time of death, 5:05 p.m."

Quinn watched Honor as she turned and left the room, then looked down at the lifeless body, colorless but still warm. Across the table, her eyes met Linda's. "You okay here?"

"Yeah, we'll take care of things," Linda replied with the muted sadness of someone for whom tragedy was not new but would never be routine. "Go ahead."

There was no one in the small staff lounge except Honor, who sat alone at one of the rickety round tables. Damp tendrils of hair streaked across one cheek, her scrub shirt clung to her chest with sweat, and her hands trembled where they rested on the plain gray surface.

Quinn walked to the soda machine, slid in a dollar bill, and punched the button for a Diet Coke. She repeated the process and carried both to the table, twisted off the tops, and put one bottle in front of Honor.

"You should drink that. You're probably dehydrated."

"Thanks." Mechanically, Honor picked up the soda and drank nearly a third of it.

Quinn took a long swallow of hers and set down the plastic bottle. Then she took the seat next to Honor's. "Anything I can do to help?"

Sighing, Honor shook her head. "No. The police are tracking down his family. If they call here, I'll talk to them."

"Are you okay?"

Honor raised an eyebrow, her nerves raw. "Why wouldn't I be?"

"I don't know," Quinn said quietly. "Something tells me that it hurts you when you lose one, *not* that you did. I guess I should say when you *can't save* them all."

"That's what we're supposed to be doing here, isn't it? Saving people?"

"Yes. All the ones we can." There was a hint of bitterness in Honor's voice that most people would have missed, but Quinn was listening for it. She covered Honor's hand with her own. "I'm sorry about this one." *And all the other ones whom no one could have saved, but for whom you feel responsible. All the way back to Terry.*

"I'm okay," Honor said softly, her fingers briefly entwining with Quinn's. She squeezed lightly, and then withdrew her hand. "Thanks for the help in there. Daniels was tied up with a child with epiglottitis. In fact, I should check on him now. How's your burn patient?"

"Already on her way to the burn center."

"I don't know how we managed without you." Honor forced a light note into her voice. It was so hard when she had to let one go. She knew the statistics, understood and intellectually accepted the realities of her work, but for just a few moments—every time—it was Terry all over again. She didn't know how, but she sensed that Quinn knew this, and she didn't feel quite so alone with the pain.

Quinn watched some of the shadows disappear from the dark depths of Honor's eyes and a bit of her own sadness lifted. "I just can't imagine."

Smiling now, Honor stood. "What do you say we hit those boards and clear this place out. Then you, Linda, Robin, and the kids are invited over to my place for Chinese."

Quinn rose as well, resisting the urge to take Honor's hand. "I can't think of anything better."

It amazed Honor to discover that she believed her.

❖

By ten p.m., all three children had fallen asleep wherever they'd happened to land, and the adults weren't far behind. Linda was curled up in Robin's arms at one end of the couch, her head on Robin's shoulder, her eyes nearly closed. At the opposite end, Honor sat on the floor in front of Quinn, who was gently kneading her shoulders. The local news droned on the television.

"Better?" Quinn asked softly, leaning forward, her mouth close to Honor's ear. Her fingers curved along Honor's neck, her thumbs playing up and down the tight muscles on either side of Honor's spine.

"Mmm." Pressing back into Quinn's hands, Honor shivered as the warm breath wafted over her ear. Quinn's thighs rested lightly against the outside of her arms, and the heat from Quinn's body seemed to surround her. Hot, heavy pleasure slowly rolled through her, leaving her feeling ripe and sensuous. "Heaven."

"It is," Quinn murmured. Honor's hair lay softly over the backs of her hands, a tease of golden silk. She imagined awakening with those silken strands scattered across her chest, with the exquisite softness of Honor's cheek against her breast. The ache of desire beat so hard she nearly groaned, and it was all she could do not to brush her lips over the tender skin of Honor's neck. "I recommend a warm shower and a good night's sleep."

Honor shifted around, letting her head rest against Quinn's inner thigh as she looked up into the deep blue eyes. The pleasure simmering in her belly flared at the undisguised wanting in Quinn's face. "Do you, now?"

Quinn nodded, drawing one finger slowly along the edge of Honor's jaw, then down her throat, stopping at the small hollow between her collarbones. "It's been a long day, and you're tired."

I don't feel tired. I'd be happy if you never stopped touching me. Honor glanced over at her friends. Robin's chin rested against the top of Linda's head, and both of them now appeared to be asleep. Fondly, she smiled. "Our numbers are dwindling."

Very slowly, Quinn leaned down and brushed her lips over Honor's mouth. It was far less than she wanted, but piercingly sweet nevertheless. "I should go."

"I don't want you to," Honor whispered.

Quinn's breath caught in her throat, and she closed her eyes for an instant. Her fingers trembled against the damp skin just above the swell of Honor's breasts before she drew her hand back. When she met Honor's gaze, the look of longing nearly broke her resolve. "You make it very hard for me to remember why we should wait."

Honor's lips curled into a satisfied smile. "Good."

Beside them, Linda grumbled and sat upright, blinking. "What a lively crowd."

The four friends laughed, and reluctantly, Honor rose. She extended her hand and tugged Quinn to her feet. While Robin and Linda roused their children, Honor walked Quinn to the back door.

Outside on the porch, in the shadows, she wrapped her arms around Quinn's neck and pressed close to her. Just before her lips found Quinn's, she whispered throatily, "I love the way you feel."

Quinn circled her arms about Honor's waist and lost herself in the swirling kiss—aware only of Honor's breasts against hers, Honor's hands stroking her neck and back, Honor's thigh edging firmly between hers.

"Uh...my advice would be to take this upstairs," Linda remarked dryly from a few feet away.

Honor leaned back in Quinn's arms and regarded her friend lazily. "Why, thank you *so* much. I never would have thought of that."

Grinning, Quinn slowly eased away from Honor. "Night, Linda." Then she kissed Honor gently. "I'll see you tomorrow."

"Be careful going home," Honor murmured, lightly stroking Quinn's cheek. She watched as Quinn descended the stairs and disappeared into the night, then turned back to Linda. "Great timing."

"You should thank me." Linda laughed and threaded her arm around Honor's waist as they walked back into the living room. "Think how embarrassed you would have been to find yourself stark naked on the floor of your back porch when you finally came to your senses."

Honor had the briefest flash of herself and Terry, nearly naked and in a similar position, when Phyllis had discovered them what seemed like a lifetime ago. She gave Linda an affectionate squeeze. "I'll let you know when I'm in need of rescuing."

As Linda hefted one of her children and Robin the other, Linda smirked. "I think it's too late for that."

Honor kissed both of her friends at the door, then carried her own sleeping child off to bed. She tucked Arly in, switched on the action hero night-light, and leaned in the doorway regarding her child. She thought of all the nights she had stood there wishing that Terry could share the incredible wonder of watching Arly grow up. Of all the nights that she had lain down to sleep alone wondering how she could face the rest of her life while feeling so empty inside.

As she walked back to her solitary bed, she realized that what she felt now, where there had once been only loneliness and pain, was excitement and, distantly, hope. She turned on the bedside lamp and crossed to the dresser that stood against one wall. The detritus of her ordinary days lay scattered across the top—keys, spare change, a fountain pen, a few scraps of paper with unrecognizable telephone numbers scrawled on them. There was also a jewelry box and a framed photo of Terry that had been taken at a softball game a few months before she had been killed. She looked incredibly young and vital in gym shorts and a sleeveless T-shirt, her glove tucked under one arm, a broad grin on her wildly attractive face.

Honor picked up the photo and held it in both hands, turning it in the light and watching the reflections in the glass sparkle from Terry's eyes. Briefly, she touched her fingertips to Terry's face. "I love you. You know that, right? Forever and always."

Tenderly, she placed the photo back in the center of her dresser. Then she very carefully removed her wedding ring and placed it in the jewelry box. She stared at it, a dusty gold against the black velvet, before she gently closed the lid.

CHAPTER TWENTY-ONE

Honor opened the refrigerator and removed a container of orange juice. She carried it to the counter by the sink, lifted a glass from the dish drainer, and filled it. Phyllis sat behind her at the kitchen table, her coffee and morning paper at hand.

"I asked Quinn to go to the Annenberg with me on Friday night," Honor said quietly, turning to face her mother-in-law. "Can you watch Arly?"

"I'm free," Phyllis said. "I'll take her to see that new animated movie she's been talking about."

"That would be great. Thanks." Honor hesitated, reaching unconsciously to the ring on her left hand. The shock of its absence was momentarily distracting.

Phyllis watched the familiar movement, saw what had caused the odd expression on Honor's face, and then slowly raised her eyes to the uncertain brown ones that waited as if for judgment. "I like Quinn."

"So do I." Honor's voice was husky. "It's...a date...Friday night."

"You know," Phyllis said, rising to cross to Honor's side, "I don't just love you because you loved my daughter. I love you because I think you're a wonderful, warm, loving woman. I have only ever wanted you to be happy."

Honor bit her lip, her eyes brimming. It had been a very long time since she'd sought comfort in anyone's arms, but it felt right to rest her head on Phyllis's shoulder and shed the last of the tears for a past she could not change.

"I don't know what Arly or I would ever do without you."

"Well, I never intend to get very far away, so you don't have to worry." Phyllis leaned back and brushed the moisture from Honor's cheeks. "There's something special about Quinn—I could see it right away. And I approve of the way she looks at you."

Honor blushed, hoping that Phyllis couldn't see *too* clearly what had been transpiring between her and Quinn. "We're not...I mean, we haven't..."

Phyllis laughed and patted Honor's cheek. "I'll see if Kim and Dennis want to go to the movies with us, and afterward the kids can have a sleepover at my place. I'll even bring Pooch over for the night. You'll have the house here to yourself."

"Thanks," Honor said, still coloring. She was trying not to think too much about what might happen *after* the show Friday evening. The only thing she knew for certain was that she couldn't spend too many more nights dreaming of Quinn in her bed. Rather than finding the increasingly erotic fantasies satisfying, even when physically they *ought* to have been, she awoke with a craving that verged on pain.

As unsettling as the idea of opening herself to Quinn—to anyone—after all this time might be, the thought of remaining alone was far worse.

❖

Friday evening, fresh from a shower and still in her favorite shapeless cotton robe, Honor knocked on Arly's partially open door and leaned her head into her daughter's room. "Do you need any help packing your overnight bag?"

"I can't find my pajamas." A scattering of toys, favorite books, and clothes lay over Arly's bed. Her Harry Potter duffel bag lay open on the floor.

"Which ones?"

Arly looked at Honor in amazement. "My *dinosaur* ones."

"Ah." Honor nodded seriously. "They're downstairs on top of the laundry basket."

"'Kay. I'll go get them."

"Are you excited about going to the movies tonight?"

"Yes! And Kim and Denny are coming, too, and then we're going to have ice cream at Grandmom's."

"Sounds like a lot of fun."

Arly nodded vigorously. "You and Quinn could come with us."

"Maybe some night, we will. Tonight, though, we're going to do something else. Just us."

Arly sat on the edge of her bed and regarded her mother. "Is it like...a date?"

Honor's brows rose, and she crossed the room to join her daughter. She cleared a space for herself on the bed and curled up on her side, her head propped on her elbow, her other hand resting lightly on Arly's leg. "Do you know what a date is?"

"Not really."

"A date is when two people who like each other spend time together. So yes, this is kind of like a date."

"Do you like Quinn a lot?"

"Yes, I do."

Arly bounced lightly on the bed. "So do I."

"That's good."

"Do you like Quinn the way you liked Terry?"

The question was so innocent, and so casually put, that Honor failed to feel the usual ache at the mention of Terry's name. When Arly had asked about the photo of Terry in Honor's room, Honor had explained that the three of them had once been a family, just like Robin and Linda and Denny and Kim. Arly'd seen pictures of herself as a baby with both Terry and Honor, but she had no specific memories of Terry.

"Everybody we care about is very special to us, right?" Honor asked with just a hint of unsteadiness in her voice.

"Uh-huh."

"But we care about each person a little bit differently, too. Does that make sense?"

Arly considered the idea seriously, then nodded. "Like I love you and Grandmom the same, only different."

"Exactly." Honor smiled. "So I can care about *both* of them a lot."

"Okay." Arly jumped down from the bed. "I'm going to go get my pajamas."

Alone, Honor lay on her back amidst her daughter's favorite objects, staring at the ceiling and contemplating her date with

Quinn in just a few hours. Mixed with the thrill of anticipation was a healthy dose of nerves and misgivings. She vacillated between the certainty that she wasn't ready for any kind of emotional involvement and the equally clear knowledge of her compelling attraction to Quinn Maguire. When she couldn't reason her way forward, she simply decided to follow her heart.

❖

At 6:30, the phone rang. Honor's heart sank. *She's canceling.*

She let the phone ring, reluctant to answer it. A second later, she snatched it up, berating herself for her cowardice. With a calmness she didn't feel, she said quietly, "Hello?"

"So what are you wearing?"

Honor's breath left her on a rush of exasperation and relief. "God, Linda! You scared me."

"Huh?"

"Never mind."

"So? Let's hear it."

Smiling despite her nerves, Honor leaned back against the corner of the sofa, keeping one eye on the front door. "We're going to the Annenberg, Linda. It's hardly a formal event."

"It's your first date. I want the details."

"Black brushed-silk slacks and a royal blue blouse."

"The one where the top button is just about at nipple level and shows a nice bit of your cleavage?"

Honor burst out laughing. "I never thought you noticed that sort of thing."

"You might be my best friend, but I still notice." Linda gave a hum of approval. "I don't suppose you'll tell me if you're wearing a bra?"

"Noo, I don't think so."

Linda's pout was nearly audible over the phone. "What a spoilsport." Her voice suddenly serious, she asked softly, "Are you nervous?"

"A little," Honor confessed. "I like Quinn, but I'm not totally certain this is a good idea. I have to work with her every day, and things could be awkward if this turns into a disaster."

"Quinn seems solid. I can't imagine her giving you a hard time, no matter what happens." Truly sympathetic and hoping to defuse her friend's nerves, Linda added, "I can tell that you like her, and I know that she likes you. Just try to have fun tonight."

At that moment, the front doorbell rang, and Honor jumped, her heart racing as she peered at the shadow-shape visible through the curtains. "I have to go. She's here."

"Have fun, sweetie. And call me in the morning prepared to tell all."

Another laugh eased some of the tension as Honor said goodbye and replaced the receiver. Then she hurried to the door and pulled it open. She hesitated before speaking just long enough to enjoy the sight of the woman at her door. Quinn wore a light gray linen blazer with matching trousers and a dark silk shirt that hugged her torso. Highly polished dress shoes and a thin black belt completed the urban-chic look. "Hello."

"Hi," Quinn said softly, extending an arrangement of freesia, baby's breath, and a single white rose. She smiled as her gaze traveled from Honor's face briefly over her body, and then back to Honor's eyes. "You look beautiful."

"Thank you," Honor said, reaching for the flowers to cover her charmed embarrassment. *Flowers. I can't believe she brought me flowers. Does anyone do that anymore?* Honor swallowed around a sudden surge of pleasure. "They're wonderful. Come inside so I can take care of them."

As she walked through the house, Honor was exquisitely sensitive to Quinn's presence just behind her. The air surrounding them felt heavy, like the electrified atmosphere just before a summer storm. Her skin tingled and the fine hairs on her arms stood up as she shivered lightly.

Once in the kitchen, she said casually, "I'll just put these in some water, and then we can go."

Quinn waited, watching Honor's quick, efficient movements. She enjoyed watching Honor do anything, but her anticipation of the evening had been building all week, and at that moment, all she really wanted to do was touch her. Afraid that she might, and afraid that it would be too much far too soon, Quinn slid her hands into the pockets of her trousers. "Arly get off to the movies okay?"

"Couldn't wait." Honor turned from the counter with the beginnings of a smile that faltered as she looked into Quinn's eyes. The deep blue she was used to had edged to purple, and the focus, always intense, was so sharp now that her body quickened instantly. She caught her lower lip between her teeth and willed herself not to reach out, certain that if she touched Quinn now, she wouldn't *stop* touching her until sunrise. Voice thick, she added, "She asked me tonight if we were going on a date."

Blinking, Quinn pulled herself back from the fantasy of sliding her palms under the rich silk of Honor's blouse and over the smooth expanse of her back. "Is that okay?"

"She thinks it's neat." Honor took a step closer, tilted her head, and brushed her lips over Quinn's. Before she succumbed to the temptation to slip her fingers into Quinn's hair and press even closer, she backed away, catching Quinn's hand in hers. "So do I. Come on, let's go."

Because she had no choice, and wouldn't have done otherwise even if she had, Quinn allowed Honor to lead her away. Away from everything she had known or even imagined, toward a place that she had scarcely dared dream of.

❖

In the darkened theater, a series of overlapping spotlights highlighted the nearly naked men and women who reclined on the stage floor, enormous drums clasped between their thighs, tautly muscled arms beating a rhythm that pounded through the air, through the floor, through the bodies of the spellbound audience. Sweat glistened on smooth skin, nostrils flared with the rush of hot breath, and blood boiled close to the surface in a flush of heat. The beat was so primitive, so primal, that the collective consciousness of performers and audience alike pulsed as one—hearts and loins and desires joined in an ancient rite.

At one point, when it seemed that the intensity, the furor, could climb no higher, with a tremendous show of passion and will, the drummers arched their backs and pounded the huge mallets even faster until their limbs were a blur. Quinn, riding the waves of exuberant abandon, glanced at Honor, whose eyes, shining with excitement, were riveted on the stage. Her slightly parted lips were full and sensuous, and Quinn was certain she had never seen a more glorious woman.

At that instant, Honor turned her head, thrilling to the ardor in Quinn's expression. When Quinn wordlessly turned her left hand palm up on the armrest between them, Honor laced her fingers through Quinn's. At the jolt of electricity, her eyes widened in concern, and she leaned close, her mouth against Quinn's ear. "Was that you?"

Swiftly, Quinn lifted their joined hands and kissed the back of Honor's, then shook her head. Raising her voice against the thunder that reverberated through the very walls, she shouted, "No. That was *us.*"

Wild with relief and the glory of the moment, Honor pulled Quinn's hand into her lap and held it there with both of hers as the drummers, along with her very soul, raged on.

❖

Honor maneuvered through the late Friday evening traffic, her eyes on the road but her mind on the woman next to her. She hadn't really thought about the nature of the performance when she'd invited Quinn. She'd seen the Japanese drummers before and loved the energy and passion of their art. Self-consciously, she wondered if Quinn had felt any of the arousal that she had experienced as the pulsating rhythm had inundated them. She couldn't remember it having been quite so sexual an experience before and hoped that Quinn did not think it had been intentional on her part to orchestrate such a suggestive first date. It concerned her that Quinn had been quiet since they left the theater.

"Everything okay?" Honor finally ventured to ask.

Quinn reached across the distance and slid her fingers into Honor's hair, lifting it away from her neck. Leaning over as far as her seat belt would allow, she ran her lips over the rim of Honor's ear. "Everything is perfect."

"Quinn," Honor breathed thickly, her stomach doing a slow roll, "you can't do that while I'm driving."

"Must be why I can't get car insurance," Quinn mused, moving her lips to a spot just below Honor's ear. "Judgment problems."

Honor gripped the wheel with both hands and ignored the tantalizing fluttering in her depths. "Get yourself back into your own seat."

Laughing softly, Quinn settled back, but she kept her hand on Honor's thigh. "That was the first date to end all first dates."

"I hope so," Honor said without thinking. Then she blushed and stammered, "I mean...hell... I just..."

"I had a great time," Quinn said genuinely. "They were unbelievable."

"I know." Breathing a bit easier as her blood pressure came down out of the stratosphere, Honor turned off Lincoln Drive, the torturous narrow road that led from Center City into their residential neighborhood, and onto her street. "I'm really glad you enjoyed it."

"Honor," Quinn said tenderly. "It's all right if you take me home."

Honor slowed and glanced at Quinn. "Is that what you want?"

Quinn shook her head. "No."

Nodding, Honor accelerated for half a block and then coasted into her driveway. She turned off the engine and shifted on the seat until she faced Quinn. In the semidarkness, she found Quinn's hands and clasped them tightly. "I thought about tonight for days. I can't tell you that I understand everything that I feel, or even that I'm totally comfortable with it, but I want you to come inside with me." Her voice was shaking, but she had to finish. In fairness to Quinn *and* herself. "*Tonight.* But tomorrow...I don't know."

Quinn could have walked away. She could have insisted on waiting until Honor could tell her everything that she wanted to hear. Instead, she ran her thumb over the surface of Honor's ring finger. "You're not wearing your wedding ring."

"No," Honor replied softly. "I'm not."

"How come?" Quinn's voice was low and heavy, a languorous caress.

"Because..." Honor swallowed, her heart beating furiously in her throat. "Because I wanted tonight to be just us."

"I promise," Quinn leaned forward, her mouth moving gently over Honor's as she whispered, "it will be."

CHAPTER TWENTY-TWO

Honor waited for Quinn in front of the car, then took her hand and together, they climbed the back stairs to the kitchen. Wordlessly, Honor led her down the hallway, dimly lit by a muted chandelier, to the stairs ascending to the second floor and her bedroom. At the foot of the stairs, she turned and met Quinn's gaze.

"We could have a drink in the living room and listen to some music, or—"

"You know," Quinn interrupted gently, "you've been taking all the risks lately. It's about time I took some."

At Honor's questioning gaze, Quinn smiled. "You asked me out tonight, remember? And you asked me to come in just now, too. I know neither of those things was easy for you." Skimming her fingertips through the hair at the base of Honor's neck, she framed Honor's face in both hands, palms lightly cupping her jaw. Carefully, she brought her mouth to Honor's and kissed her, a slow, thorough kiss that left them both slightly breathless. "Let me be the one to say that I want to make love with you now. Right now."

"Yes." Honor's voice rang with both certainty and longing. Her grip on Quinn's hand tightened as they climbed the stairs.

In the bedroom, Honor released Quinn's hand to cross the room and turn on a lamp in the far corner. It illuminated the room in a warm golden glow. Hesitantly, she turned to Quinn, who waited just inside the door. "Unless you'd rather not have the light?"

"It's perfect." The corner of Quinn's mouth lifted. "I want to look at you as much as I want to touch you."

Honor trembled even as heat suffused her. "I...believe it or not, this is new for me."

"Me, too." Quinn walked to within a foot of her and stopped. She looked into Honor's eyes as she said, "I've never been with a woman I've wanted so much in so many ways." She lifted her hand, rested her fingertips against the curve of Honor's cheek. "I want to see you, touch you—know you. All of you—everywhere."

"Quinn," Honor murmured thickly. She slipped her hands inside Quinn's blazer, careful not to touch Quinn's body as she lifted the jacket up and off, enjoying the waiting as much as the wanting. Then she wrapped her arms around Quinn's neck and melted into her.

Each time they embraced, it was as natural as breathing. With a groan, Quinn did what she'd been wanting to do for the last five hours. She slid her hands around Honor's waist, gently pulled the blouse from the waistband of the silk slacks, and spread her hands across Honor's naked lower back. The flesh beneath her fingers was hot, the muscles quivering. She spread her fingers lower, over Honor's buttocks, and guided Honor against the curve of her abdomen and thighs.

Rocking her hips indolently, Honor nuzzled Quinn's neck, then the undersurface of her jaw, then her earlobe, catching skin gently between her teeth before licking the tiny pinpoints of pain with the tip of her tongue. With a hand between their bodies, she deftly loosed the buttons on Quinn's shirt and slipped her hand inside, pressing her palm to Quinn's lower abdomen, fingertips barely grazing the upper edge of her briefs.

Quinn jerked at the touch and brought her lips to the hollow at the base of Honor's throat. "I've wanted this so much."

"Oh," Honor breathed as the muscles jumped beneath her hand, "I love the way you get so tight when I touch you." Slowly, she raked her nails up the center of Quinn's belly as she flicked her tongue along the edge of Quinn's ear. When Quinn shuddered and groaned again, she murmured, "You like?"

"You're killing me."

Honor tilted her head back and laughed, the sound throaty and deep. Delighted. "Not just yet I'm not."

Fighting to clear her head of the haze of desire, Quinn kissed Honor's neck, then moved her lips in a languorous trail down the center of Honor's chest. She worked the first button on the royal blue blouse free and parted the material with her fingers so that she could press her face between Honor's breasts. When she turned her head and kissed the swell of firm flesh, Honor's fingers came into her hair and drew her even closer.

"Your lips are so soft," Honor gasped as Quinn's tongue flicked teasingly against the edge of her nipple.

The catch of excitement in Honor's voice made Quinn's head swim. The rush of arousal was so swift it nearly brought her to her knees. She wanted to touch Honor everywhere, with her hands, with her mouth, to be deep inside her, surrounded by her. The need was so overpowering, it terrified her. Nearly choking on the urgency, she lifted her face from Honor's breasts and, with trembling hands, slowly released the remaining buttons on Honor's blouse. After lifting it off, she reverently cradled her palms beneath Honor's breasts, her thumbs stroking the hard nipples.

"Oh! I...think it's time to lie down." Honor's head was thrown back, her back arched as she unconsciously thrust her breasts harder into Quinn's hands.

"Let me undress you first." Quinn caught a taut nipple with her teeth and tugged sharply.

A startled cry of pleasure tore from Honor's throat, and she sagged against Quinn's body, her legs trembling. "Baby, please."

The endearment—so unexpected, so sweet—broke Quinn's control. She dropped to her knees, her deft surgeon's hands already working the zipper open on Honor's slacks while she rested her face against Honor's abdomen, sucking at the soft skin around her navel. With one hand she slid the fabric down to bare Honor's legs; with the other she stroked the satin-smooth skin high on her inner thighs.

Honor, the blood draining from her head to pool and pound between her thighs, put her hands on Quinn's shoulders to steady herself. She felt the heat of Quinn's mouth move down her abdomen and the clever fingers teasing her. She wanted Quinn's touch, had craved it for so long, but now the pleasure was so sharp she was close to exploding. Summoning all her willpower, she pulled Quinn's head back until Quinn's eyes, clouded with lust, rose to hers. "Not yet. I'll come too soon."

Quinn groaned, but she stilled her hand. "Tell me what you want."

Honor smoothed her fingers over Quinn's damp face, running a finger over her lips, then dipping the tip into her mouth. "I want you to make love to me until I scream, until *you* scream."

Closing her eyes, still on her knees, Quinn sucked Honor's finger, then bit the tip gently. As she did, she unbuckled the belt at her waist and slid down her fly. When she released Honor's finger, she rose and swiftly stripped bare. Holding Honor's gaze, she found Honor's hand and lifted it with trembling fingers to her lips. "Anything."

Honor let her gaze drift slowly over Quinn's naked form, glorying in the sleek muscles and sweat-sheened skin. She placed both palms on Quinn's abdomen, then slid her hands upward, massaging the dancing muscles and tracing the curve of ribs until her hands covered Quinn's breasts. When she squeezed gently, Quinn moaned, her lids nearly closed, and dropped her head to rest her forehead against Honor's. With a single finger, Honor tenderly traced the scar on Quinn's chest, outlining the hard shape beneath the velvet skin.

Quinn brought her hands up to cover Honor's. "It's all right."

"Oh, yes," Honor whispered, moving Quinn's hands aside and leaning to kiss the scar. "It's just fine."

"I don't think I can wait any longer," Quinn confessed, her lips against Honor's neck, shivering as their bare bodies touched. "I need to touch you."

"I want you to."

Together, they moved to the bed. Honor lay down, reached for Quinn, and pulled her into her arms as she spread her thighs and lifted her hips in welcome. When Quinn fit effortlessly against her, firm muscles pressing into her tender, swollen flesh, she moaned. "Oh, you feel so right."

Quinn braced herself with her arms on either side of Honor's shoulders and thrust gently, thrilling to the answering rise of Honor's hips. She'd come quickly if she wasn't careful, and careful was what she wanted to be this first time. Careful to ensure that Honor felt the depths of her desire and knew nothing but pleasure. She would have been fine if Honor hadn't arched up and captured a nipple in her mouth. The unexpected shaft of pleasure that shot through her nearly undid her.

"Oh God," Quinn cried. Her clitoris twitched dangerously, and she knew that orgasm was seconds away. She shifted to ease the ominous pressure between her thighs, but Honor moaned in protest at her withdrawal. Voice rasping in her throat, she pleaded, "Wait, Honor...oh please, wait."

Through the mists of nearly overwhelming need, Honor heard the desperate edge in Quinn's voice. Wrapping her arms around Quinn's back, she shifted until Quinn was beneath her and she was straddling Quinn's hips. Breathing hard, she swept the hair back from her face with one hand and rode Quinn rhythmically. "You are...so so sexy."

It was Quinn's turn to reach up and clasp the rose-tipped breasts that swayed above her. When she closed her fingers around the swollen flesh, Honor whimpered wildly.

"I'm going to come...on you," Honor gasped, fingers digging into Quinn's forearms.

"Yes, oh yes." Quinn thumbed Honor's nipples harder, pushing her closer to the edge with each stroke. Her own hips bucked and tossed, pumping involuntarily as she hovered close to climaxing. Honor was so beautiful, so fierce and strong, Quinn wanted to shout with the wonder of her. She would have, if she'd been able to draw a full breath, but Honor was wet against her stomach, pistoning her hips faster and faster as she rocketed toward orgasm, and all Quinn could do was marvel.

"Oh!" Honor shouted, half surprised and half ecstatic, as she stiffened and then shuddered. Head back, eyes closed, she gripped Quinn's hands and held them to her breasts, their fingers interlacing, an anchor in the storm of sensation.

Quinn stopped breathing as Honor climaxed, too stunned by the beauty of it to even notice the wild pounding of her own heart or the churning need deep inside. When at last Honor emitted a final small whimper and collapsed, Quinn caught her with an arm around her waist and a hand cradling her head, drawing her down into a soothing embrace.

"Honor," Quinn breathed reverently, her lips against Honor's damp cheek. "Oh, Honor."

Still shivering in the aftermath of her explosive release, Honor pressed her face to Quinn's neck and clutched her strong shoulders, needing her solid presence while inside a tempest raged. Nearly overcome with the unexpected intensity of her response, she couldn't think, couldn't speak. It had been more than physical, more than sex—Quinn had reached inside her and touched a place that had lain barren for so long that the awakening was like rebirth. She ached with the joy of it.

"Oh my God," Honor gasped.

Quinn stroked her back, her shoulders, her face, not with passion now, but with tenderness. She was more than a little frightened. Honor was still shaking, and she very much feared that there were tears falling on her neck. She whispered, "Honor? Are you all right?"

Honor shook her head and shifted until her cheek rested against Quinn's chest. "Uh-uh."

Quinn's stomach clenched with dread. "Then what is it?"

"I didn't expect to feel this way."

God, what way? Sorry? Regretful? Quinn swallowed around the lump of anxiety in her throat. "Tell me."

Honor smoothed her palm down the center of Quinn's chest to her abdomen and slowly circled over the firm muscles. Quinn twitched, making Honor smile. "I was hoping I would feel comfortable...being physical with you." She gave a self-conscious laugh. "I was mostly hoping I'd remember what to do."

"Believe me, you remember just fine." Quinn was trying hard to concentrate on what Honor was saying, but the teasing fingers, straying lower and lower, consumed all her attention. Her hips lifted in silent supplication, the blood racing once again into already oversensitive tissues, trumpeting her desire. She reached down and covered Honor's hand, stilling the agonizingly sweet touch. "Are you upset?"

"No," Honor said in amazement. "I feel...*wonderful.*"

Wonderful? The relief that followed so closely upon the fear sent Quinn's head spinning and her heart speeding again. "Oh... that's good. Very good."

Honor levered up on an elbow and rested her palm against Quinn's cheek, reveling in the darkly handsome face in the pale lamplight. "Just being close to you was enough to send me off. I can't...that's never happened to me before."

"I've never experienced anything as incredible as being with you," Quinn whispered, tracing trembling fingers over Honor's face. She made a small choking sound when Honor smoothed a hand between her thighs. "Oh God."

"Quinn, you're so beautiful." Honor's lids flickered, her pupils dilating with a sudden resurgence of arousal. Slowly, reverently, she stroked the length of Quinn's clitoris, squeezing very lightly, then dipping lower into the waiting warmth.

Quinn pressed her lips to Honor's palm, struggling to absorb the deluge of sensation—the heat of Honor's body, the scent of her excitement, the agonizingly slow torture of her sweet caresses. Her legs tightened, her stomach quivered, and she drew a sharp uneven breath. Desperately, she sought Honor's eyes. "I want to come. Can I come?"

Honor's lips curled into a tender smile while her eyes glowed with something more like triumph. She leaned over until her lips brushed Quinn's and murmured, "Yes. Now."

The first wave whipped through her, jerking her off the bed. The titanic contractions bent her nearly double and she curled into Honor's arms, clinging to her as the breath was ripped from her body on a strangled shout.

Never stopping her smooth, rhythmic strokes, Honor coaxed Quinn to yet another peak when she pressed inside and thrust deeply. She was lost in the velvet heat and would have continued forever if Quinn hadn't grasped her wrist and stilled her motion.

Gasping, Quinn croaked, "God, I'm done." She shuddered and laughed unsteadily. "Usually, I'm only good for one."

"Oh yeah?" Honor's voice wavered as she kissed the tip of Quinn's chin. "I don't think this is the *usual* situation."

"Neither do I."

Blindly, Honor reached down, found the crisp cotton sheet she had put on the bed earlier that afternoon, and pulled it up over them. She lay on her back and pulled Quinn close, wrapping her arms around her and insinuating one thigh between Quinn's. She couldn't bear for any part of them not to be touching. *Whatever this is, it's new to me.*

"Honor?" Quinn mumbled as she cupped Honor's breast in her palm, fighting the lassitude that suffused her in the aftermath of pleasure.

"Mmm?"

"Sure everything's all right?"

God, I have no idea. Honor brushed the hair back from Quinn's brow and traced her thumb along the arch of her cheekbone and over her jaw, cradling Quinn's face against her neck. "You feel so right here. That's all I know."

Quinn drifted off, knowing that it was more than right. It was everything.

CHAPTER TWENTY-THREE

Honor slowly stirred to the sensation of warm honey, thick and sweet, flowing through her limbs. Groaning with a combination of pleasure and utter contentment, she stretched, languid and graceful as a cat. Her left hand brushed a firmly muscled shoulder, and she stiffened, suddenly bewildered by the presence of another's presence where none had been for years. In the next instant, she remembered taking Quinn to her bed and the moments of wild abandon that had followed. Vaguely embarrassed, she felt her stomach tighten at the memory nonetheless.

Soft lips brushed her ear, and warm breath trickled over her neck as the familiar, deep voice murmured, "Sorry. I didn't mean to wake you." At the same time, deft fingers skimmed over her breasts, bringing her nipples to painfully pleasant erection. "Yet."

"Mmm." Honor gazed at Quinn through half-opened lids, aware of the tingling in her skin and the heavy urgency in the pit of her stomach. "Have you been awake long?"

Quinn leaned on one elbow, drawing strands of Honor's hair through her fingers as she smoothed the other hand over Honor's abdomen and thighs. "Five minutes or so."

"Have you been...touching me the whole time?" *Is that what has me so aroused, so ready right now?*

"Guilty." One corner of Quinn's mouth lifted in a satisfied grin. "Do you mind?"

Honor's legs tensed as Quinn traced a single finger slowly along the line between her abdomen and thigh. Her words came out on a gasp. "You have...oh God...an interesting way of saying good morning."

"Wait until you hear the rest of what I have to say," Quinn whispered, lowering her head to catch Honor's lower lip between her teeth. She sucked gently as she brushed her fingers between Honor's legs, her pulse racing crazily as Honor's hips lifted to press against her palm. As she slid her fingertips on either side of Honor's clitoris, caressing lightly, she echoed the movements with her tongue in Honor's mouth—long, teasing, relentless strokes. She didn't hurry, not even when Honor shuddered and moaned. Her own arousal was coiled tight in her belly, a wild thing demanding to be let loose, but she kept a firm hold on her desire. This time, the only thing she wanted was Honor's pleasure.

"I can't wait to find out." Honor breathed unevenly as Quinn drew back from the kiss and stilled the movement of her hand. "Oh, don't stop."

Quinn smiled lazily and twitched her fingers teasingly, watching Honor's pupils flicker in response. "Soon."

"Please, tell me now." Honor reached up and fisted her hand hard in Quinn's hair, pulling her head down to claim her mouth. At the same time, she arched her hips and closed around Quinn's hand, moaning as pleasure pulsed through her at the press of Quinn's fingers inside her. Distantly, she heard Quinn groan. This time, the kiss was fierce, hungry and urgent, echoing the ache in her depths.

Quinn's head reeled as velvet muscles closed around her, but she clung stubbornly to control, refusing to follow the call of Honor's thrusting hips. Deep within her now, she eased her lips away from Honor's mouth. "Not *yet*."

"Can you feel me?" Honor's fingers trembled against Quinn's neck as she caught her breath on a sob. "I'm so close."

"I know," Quinn murmured, thrilling to the minute contractions rippling around her fingers. She eased down on the bed until she could bring her mouth to join her hand in answering Honor's need. Still, she went slowly, bestowing soft kisses on the hard peak of Honor's desire, sucking gently to tease even more pleasure from the engorged tissues.

Moaning, Honor twisted on the bed, one hand thrust into Quinn's hair, the other clutching the sheets tightly. Her legs tightened as the pressure bore down, coalescing into a white-hot fist of arousal against Quinn's mouth. "Oh! I'm coming. Baby... I'm coming."

Scarcely breathing, Quinn waited until she felt the first wave undulating beneath her lips, and then she drew her fingers nearly free before beginning the deep, steady thrusts that drove Honor to orgasm.

Honor gave a hoarse cry and arched from the bed, holding Quinn's lips to her raging flesh as she climaxed. Heart thundering and belly convulsing, she triumphantly shouted her release before collapsing bonelessly back onto the pillows. In a faint, stunned voice she murmured, "Oh, Quinn. Quinn."

Quinn stayed inside her, stroking gently as she soothed her still-pulsating clitoris with her tongue. When at last Honor quieted, Quinn carefully withdrew and slid upward, gathering Honor into her arms. When Honor trembled against her, a small cry wrenching from her depths, Quinn pressed her lips to Honor's forehead and rocked her tenderly. "You okay, sweetheart?"

Unable to do anything but nod, Honor pressed her face to Quinn's neck, wrapping her arms around Quinn's shoulders. Her stomach still rolled with the aftermath of the cataclysmic orgasm, but even beyond the unexpected force of her physical response, she was staggered by the power that Quinn possessed to touch her in the far reaches of her soul. Places she had been certain were lost to her forever.

As Honor slowly returned to herself, she became aware that Quinn was trembling, too. Beneath her cheek, Quinn's heart pounded fiercely, and for the first time, Honor recognized the fragility of the moment, and the very real fragility of the woman. And she was afraid. Afraid of what she felt inside, afraid of what she felt beneath Quinn's breast, afraid of what she could lose again if she allowed herself to care. She brought her hand between them and pressed her palm to Quinn's rapidly beating heart. Leaning back to look into Quinn's eyes, she asked, "Are *you* all right?"

For a second, Quinn stared, puzzled, and then she laughed softly. Resting her forehead against Honor's, she answered quietly, "Never better. That is, if you don't count the fact that I'm crazy out of my mind over you."

To her amazement, Honor felt herself blush. Nothing that had transpired between them, not even the furor of their lovemaking, had touched her quite as much as that simple admission. *And considering what she just did to me...God.* Working to keep her voice light, Honor tapped a finger against Quinn's chin. "I was talking about your heart."

"So was I," Quinn said completely seriously, lightly kissing Honor's lips. But she could hear Honor's concern. "I feel fine." She hesitated, wondering if she should go on, but knowing, too, that anything less than total honesty would endanger Honor's faith in her. And that was something she could not risk. "This is the first time I've made love since I got sick."

Honor stiffened. "Oh, Quinn. You should have told me. God, I didn't even think—"

"That was the point," Quinn interrupted firmly. She smoothed her hand down Honor's back to the small hollow at the base of her spine, holding Honor closely against her with the slightest bit of pressure there. "I wanted you to lose yourself with me. I didn't want you to be thinking about anything—especially not my goddamned heart."

"I don't suppose you considered what *I* might want?" Honor drew her fingers along the edge of Quinn's jaw to soften her words.

Quinn turned her face and kissed Honor's fingertips. "I considered it, and then decided to do it my way."

Honor growled softly. "I hope that isn't going to be your usual modus operandi."

"I'm a surgeon." Now Quinn caught Honor's index finger and sucked it lightly. "It's not in my nature to seek consultation before making a decision."

"Really?" Honor brought both palms to Quinn's shoulders and pushed her flat on her back. Then she leaned over her for an instant to stare into her insolently handsome face before bending down to bite her lower lip. "I can see that we're going to have to work on that."

"Would that be like...homework?" Quinn ran her tongue softly over Honor's lips, then nipped back. "Because I could probably use some practice."

"Quinn," Honor said seriously, "was last night the first time..." She laughed and shook her head. "God, I can't believe after the way

I was with you last night that I could feel embarrassed now. Was last night the first time you've climaxed, since your surgery?"

With a sigh, Quinn nodded her head in the affirmative. When she saw Honor's eyes narrow, she hastily said, "I wasn't given any restrictions on sex. My cardiologist said it was fine. The opportunity just never arose."

Honor's eyebrow quirked. "Actually, I'm rather glad. I was getting a little worried about Mandy."

"Please." Quinn grinned and kissed Honor again. "I did have a few close moments thinking about you, though."

Remembering the vivid dreams she'd had of Quinn and the nocturnal pleasures associated with them, to her complete and utter consternation, Honor blushed once again. "I'd have to say we were on the same wavelength there."

"Really." Quinn grinned, pleased. "So you've been...thinking about me?"

"I don't usually have the urge to tear a woman's clothes off and climb all over her in a sexual frenzy after a simple evening out," Honor said dryly. "So considering what happened last night, I think it's safe to say that I've been...lusting after you."

Quinn shifted onto her side and ran her hand over Honor's hip and down her leg, murmuring in appreciation. "If you keep saying things like that, we're not going to get out of this bed today, and I have a big game."

"And I expect that my daughter and her grandmother will be arriving here in another hour or so," Honor said softly, glancing past Quinn to the clock on the bedside table.

"Jesus," Quinn said, sitting up quickly. "I need to get out of here."

Laughing, Honor drew her back down until they lay facing one another again. She brushed her fingers through Quinn's hair, realizing that she didn't want to let her up. She didn't want to let her go. She didn't want to spend the day away from her. The feelings were foreign and frightening and exhilarating all at the same time. "You have a few more minutes. It's Saturday morning. And considering that the kids were probably up half the night, I don't expect them to arrive early."

"I don't want to upset Arly," Quinn said quietly.

"Oh, you are so sweet," Honor murmured as she shifted on top of Quinn and kissed her, long and deep. As they moved together in the easy rhythm of seduction, she slipped her leg between Quinn's and groaned appreciatively when Quinn's thighs tightened around her. She pressed rhythmically into Quinn as she explored her mouth, enjoying her heat and her hunger. When she felt Quinn tense and heard her gasp sharply, she lifted her head to watch the passion take her. What she saw nearly swept her away.

Quinn's eyes were clouded with need, and the muscles in her neck stood out with the strain of the impending explosion. Honor found her at once vulnerable and incredibly beautiful, open and trusting and so powerfully honest in her giving and her taking. "Quinn," she breathed in wonder.

Quinn grasped Honor's hips as she came against her leg, jerking once with an astonished cry. What began as a ripple that trailed along her spine built rapidly into a fist that beat within her blood, until finally her nerves caught fire and her muscles melted in the flame. "Oh God."

For long moments, Quinn was unaware of anything except Honor's arms around her and the joyful ache of completion. She couldn't feel the tears upon her cheeks.

"It's all right, it's all right," Honor murmured as she held Quinn close. *I'm not going to let anything hurt you. I promise.*

"Honor, you're magic," Quinn whispered. "The things you make me feel...I never knew it could be this way."

Honor had no words. She had anticipated the physical passion, because the pull had been so strong from the beginning. She hadn't expected the tenderness or the longing or the terrible frightening need. She hadn't expected to want to keep Quinn safe, to want to have her near, to want to feel her in every part of her being.

"You scare me, Quinn Maguire."

Quinn placed trembling fingers against Honor's cheek. "Why?"

"The things you make *me* feel...I'm not sure I want to."

"But you might, someday?" Quinn's heart was in her throat waiting for the answer. *Just don't close the door. Just don't shut me out. Please.*

Honor took a long shaky breath. In a voice so soft, it was barely audible, she said, "I might."

"Like I said, I'm patient."

Although she wondered if Quinn really meant that, Honor knew she had nothing more to give her and no promises to make at that moment. As much as she didn't want to, she drew away. "I put the coffeemaker on the timer last night. It should be ready about now. You can shower here if you want to or just relax while I get us some."

Quinn felt the withdrawal sharply, but did not try to hold her back. "I'll just get cleaned up now and shower later at my place."

Honor kissed her swiftly then slid from the bed. "I'll be right back."

❖

When Honor returned to the bedroom a few minutes later with two mugs of coffee, Quinn was dressed and standing by the bureau, gazing at the photo in its center. Honor walked to her and extended one of the cups. "Here you go."

Quinn turned with a smile and accepted the coffee. "Thanks." She took a sip and made an appreciative murmur. Then she nodded toward the photo. "Terry?"

"Yes." Honor picked it up and studied it for a second, then looked up at Quinn, trying to imagine what she was thinking. *Do you know that I still love her? Will that keep us apart?*

Reaching out, Quinn asked gently, "May I?"

Wordlessly, Honor handed over the photograph and watched Quinn as she looked at Terry. When Quinn looked up, there was sadness in her eyes.

"She looks so young."

"She was." Honor sighed. "She was twenty-six in this photograph. She died later that year."

Carefully, Quinn replaced the photo in the center of the bureau, then turned and looked steadily into Honor's eyes. "If there were any way that I could go back in time and change that, I would. Even though it would mean not standing here today." She took a deep breath. "And I want to be here with you more than I've ever wanted anything in my life."

Honor's lips parted in stunned surprise, and her hands shook so badly that she had to put the cup down to prevent spilling its contents. When Quinn would have reached out to her, she held up a hand. "No. I'm all right."

"I'm sorry," Quinn said swiftly. She wanted to touch her so badly she ached, but she didn't move. "I didn't mean to upset you."

"No. You didn't. Just the opposite." Honor smiled tremulously. "Since the moment we met, you've constantly surprised me."

"Is that bad?"

"I'm not sure yet." Honor stepped closer and put her palms lightly on Quinn's chest, stroking her fingertips along her collarbones, then slipping one hand behind her neck, caressing her gently. "I loved her very much. I still do."

"I know." Quinn tilted her head slightly, and her smile was soft, her blue eyes deep as a summer sky. "Do you think I want that to change?"

"Do you?"

"No." Quinn placed both hands gently on Honor's waist, but she did not pull her any closer. "All I want is what you want to give me."

"What if it's not enough?"

Quinn leaned forward and kissed Honor gently. "What if it is?"

CHAPTER TWENTY-FOUR

"If you don't stop staring at her like that, she's going to burst into flames."

Honor jumped, then exclaimed in irritation, "Will you stop sneaking up on me? And I have no idea what you're talking about."

"I'm talking about the way you're watching the new coach," Linda remarked sweetly. "You know, kind of like all hungry and desperate."

"I'm *watching* my daughter," Honor said icily, pointedly ignoring Linda's smirk. She had intentionally chosen to stand a little apart from the enthusiastic throng of family and friends gathered to watch the soccer game. She didn't feel like casual conversation, not even with Linda. It had been all she could do to maintain a normal façade with Phyllis and Arly at breakfast that morning, because all she could think about, or *wanted* to think about, had been Quinn.

Not just the way she had felt touching Quinn, or when Quinn had touched her. Gloriously free and wildly alive. That in itself was close to a miracle. But it was the way that Quinn had held the image of Terry, so tenderly and with such honest sadness in her eyes, that had truly shaken her. It was hard for her to believe that Quinn could accept the fact that part of her heart would always be Terry's, but she could not deny the truth of it in Quinn's eyes. Nor could she refute that Quinn truly cared enough about her to want to change the past, an astonishing admission that stirred her still.

Now, though, all she wanted was to be left alone to look at Quinn, simply because it felt so good. "If you don't mind, I'm trying to enjoy the game here."

"Ooh, somebody's very cranky this morning." Linda linked her arm through Honor's and gave her shoulder a little nudge. "Sexual frustration getting to you, is it?"

When Honor failed to respond with the anticipated cutting repartee, Linda studied her curiously. There was a flush of color high on Honor's sculpted cheeks and a wash of heat in her eyes as she followed Quinn's movements on the opposite sideline. Linda blinked, then caught her breath, stunned to silence when she recognized the signs. She had almost given up hope of ever seeing that look on Honor's face again.

I can't believe it! They slept together. Quinn must be some kind of miracle worker to have gotten Honor to let her that close. And now Honor must be scared to death.

Wordlessly, Linda slid her fingers down Honor's arm and grasped her hand.

"We were together last night." Honor squeezed her friend's fingers gently, appreciative of the comfort and unspoken solidarity. She still couldn't quite believe it. Oh, she *knew* it, because her body reverberated with that peculiar combination of excitement and satiation that only good sex could instill. But she still couldn't absorb the fact that she'd allowed Quinn to touch her in a place, she feared, far beyond the reach of the physical. It had been so easy. *Too easy.* Now, as she watched the dark-haired woman sprinting effortlessly up and down the field, stopping now and then to brush off a dirt-skinned knee or to murmur encouragement to an uncertain player, Honor found herself amazed at the panoply of sensation she experienced. Admiration, respect, and aching desire. *God, what have I done? What have I started?*

Linda cleared her throat. "You can tell me all the details later. Are you okay?"

Honor kept her eyes straight ahead, hoping to sound less frightened than she felt. "I'm a little surprised. She's very attractive and very sweet, and I guess—" She shrugged. "I guess I got a little carried away."

"Carried away. Uh-huh." Linda turned the idea over in her mind. "Honor, my love, you never get carried away. It's just not your style."

"It certainly was last night." She couldn't deny that she'd been attracted to Quinn from the moment she'd seen her. It didn't make the slightest bit of sense, but she supposed that it was only natural that someone with Quinn's considerable charms should have sparked a physical response. Just because she hadn't felt that way about anyone since Terry didn't mean it wasn't possible. "She's attractive."

"Is she? I suppose—if you like your women hot blooded and drop-dead gorgeous."

Honor cast her another irritated glance. "So I decided to enjoy her. Is that a crime?"

"*I* have no problem with it being just a...sexual thing." Linda struggled not to roll her eyes. "Seems perfectly reasonable. Everyone needs a good turn on the sheets now and then."

Not entirely certain why, Honor objected to the impersonal sound of that, as if Quinn were just a nice body and a handsome face. "Well, of course, I *like* her. How could you not like her? She's intelligent and kind and gentle and..." Honor sighed in exasperation. "Well, you know."

"Yes," Linda replied gently, wondering how long it would take for Honor to admit the rest of it to herself. "I know."

Honor watched Arly execute an exceptionally flamboyant pass nearly perfectly and thought she could see some of Quinn's movements in her daughter. The idea warmed her even as she retreated from the evidence of how deeply Quinn was already part of her life.

"I was afraid," Honor said very softly, "that I would think of Terry when she touched me."

Linda caught her lower lip between her teeth, stilling the trembling as a wave of sympathy washed through her. There had been times over the last six years when she had wanted nothing more than to take Honor into her arms and rock her like one of her children, to take all of her pain into her own body, because carrying the pain herself would've been so much easier than watching Honor break from it. But she couldn't, of course, and Honor had not broken. She had bent, but she had refused to succumb. Perhaps if she had not had Arly, she would have. Whatever the reason, Linda was grateful for her friend's strength. She could not have borne losing them both.

"But you didn't?" Linda asked tenderly, barely able to imagine how difficult that first step must have been for Honor. Or how badly she must have wanted Quinn to risk taking it. "It was...good?"

Honor nodded. "I didn't *think* of anything. If I did, I can't remember." She turned confused, uncertain eyes to her best friend. "I can't remember anything except Quinn."

"I think that's exactly how it's supposed to work." Linda smiled at Honor's bewilderment before remembering that Honor and Terry had been barely more than children when they'd fallen in lust and then love. Quinn Maguire was no teenager, and Honor was a woman whose passions had lain buried in grief for a very long time. "So, you're basically okay with it?"

"I haven't quite figured it out yet." Honor's voice was calm. She could think her way through this. That was what she did, that was how she approached life. She gave a small start when Quinn caught her eye from across the field and grinned, sketching a brief wave in her direction. She waved back. "But Quinn isn't pushing for anything serious, which is good."

It took all of Linda's control not to gape in astonishment. Was she the only one who could see what was going on between those two? No, she had a feeling that Quinn Maguire knew exactly what was going on. And she wondered just how long Quinn would be willing to let Honor ignore it. "Uh-huh. Yes. That *is* good."

Honor raised an eyebrow at Linda's odd tone of voice. "What?"

"Nothing." Linda smiled sweetly. "So, why don't you and Quinn and Arly come over to the house this afternoon after the game? I'm sure that Quinn and Robin will want to rehash every play. The kids can swim."

When Honor didn't answer, Linda followed her gaze and discovered what had put the angry light in Honor's eyes. Mandy, in her referee's shirt and tight black jeans, was talking to Quinn on the opposite side of the field, and as Mandy was wont to do whenever she was near a woman between the ages of eighteen and eighty, she had her fingers wrapped around Quinn's forearm. Linda thought she heard something resembling a growl coming from her friend. "I'm sorry? What did you say?"

"I said," Honor hissed through her teeth, "if she doesn't keep her hands off Quinn, one of these days I'm going to tear her arm off and beat her to death with it."

Linda nearly choked holding back her triumphant laugh. *Yep. Just a little* un*serious roll in the hay.*

❖

Sighing with contentment, Quinn, in shorts and a T-shirt, stretched out on a lounge chair next to Robin and cradled a bottle of beer in one hand. "This reminds me of afternoons back home. Shade trees and beer."

"Where you from?"

"Pittsburgh, more or less." Quinn smiled faintly, thinking how unlike her existence in Manhattan this simple life was, and how happy she was to be a part of it. "So what do you think, Coach? How'd our team do today?"

Robin sipped her beer and said with feigned seriousness, "Well, we're not supposed to promote competition, you know."

"Of course not," Quinn answered just as gravely. "It's all in the spirit of cooperation and teamwork, I always say."

"Right—it's not the winning that counts..."

They looked at one another and grinned.

"But it's always nice to win," they said nearly simultaneously.

Thinking of how much she had enjoyed Honor's warm smile of welcome at the end of the game and Arly's excited chatter about all the "neat" passes she'd made, "just like Quinn showed us," Quinn sighed again. "Yeah, it's been a very good day."

"It doesn't get a whole lot better."

Nodding in agreement, Quinn idly watched Arly come down the slide head-first into the pool, skim beneath the water for another few yards, and surface like an otter, leaving barely a ripple. "Man, that kid can swim. She should go out for the swim team."

"She *ought* to be good. I think Terry had her in the water before she was two months old." Robin looked quickly at Quinn, unable to read anything in her still expression. "Uh—"

"I guess you knew her pretty well."

"Yeah." Acutely uncomfortable, Robin looked around the yard for her spouse, hoping for a rescue. Linda was the one who handled the emotional side of most relationships. Linda could talk to anyone about anything, and she always knew the right thing to say. That worked fine for Robin, because she wasn't much of a talker. But Quinn was her buddy, and anyone could see the way things were for her with Honor. Plus, not only was there no point in denying what anyone would tell her, she knew Quinn would want to hear it straight. "Everybody liked Terry. She was real solid, and she was nuts about Honor."

"I kind of got that idea. And it went both ways." Quinn turned the bottle, damp with condensation, on the arm of the chair, watching the wet circles left by the bottom overlap and eventually blur together. In a voice pensive and low, she said, "Those are pretty big shoes to fill."

"You're not thinking of trying to do that, are you?"

Quinn gave her a look, her eyebrow raised in question.

Robin looked back at her steadily. "You're not Terry, Quinn."

"No." Quinn thought about the happiness she felt every time Honor was near, and the longing when they were apart. She remembered the joy of waking beside her that morning. "But I'm falling for Terry's girl."

"Well," Robin finished her beer and set the bottle on the ground beside her chair. "I'm not very good at this sort of thing. Linda more or less informed me on our first date that I was the one for her, and I was smart enough not to argue. Next thing I knew, we were married, and I was pregnant."

Quinn laughed. "Somehow, I think I'll be safe from that."

"But," Robin continued, smiling as well, "I think you should work on showing Honor that she's *your* girl now."

My girl. Will she ever want that? Quinn glanced up at the house as the screen door slammed and Honor and Linda came toward them carrying trays of food and fresh drinks. Honor was the only woman who had ever been able to make Quinn's heart stand still just at the sight of her.

"Hi, gorgeous," Linda said, leaning down and kissing Robin soundly on the mouth. "Another victory for the home team, huh?"

Robin shrugged nonchalantly. "Yep, our kids really kicked some ass today."

"Shh!" Honor chided, nodding toward the children. "They'll hear you."

"Don't worry," Quinn assured her, trying not to laugh at the genuine concern in Honor's eyes. "We'll be sure not to contaminate them with our competitive vices."

"They'll discover competition all by themselves, and probably sooner than we think, too." Honor, her gaze following her daughter in the pool, sat on the end of Quinn's lounge chair, resting her hand casually on Quinn's bare thigh. "It'll be nice for them to be kids for a little while longer."

"Denny and Kim are talking about karate class," Linda announced, opening a bag of chips and passing it around. She pushed upward on the chair until she was between Robin's legs, nestled in the vee of her thighs, and shifted automatically so Robin could thread an arm around her waist. "I was worried they're too young, but the school over on Germantown Avenue has four-year-olds in the class."

"I took karate when I was a kid," Quinn said with effort. The heat from Honor's palm was distracting, but very pleasantly so. She wanted to be even closer. Her breasts felt heavy and full, her nipples tight, and she wanted to press against the curve of Honor's back, to feel the pleasure of that contact the way she'd felt it when she'd awakened that morning with Honor in her arms. She shivered. "It's good discipline and great physical training. It never hurts to be comfortable with self-defense, either, especially for girls."

Honor sighed. "Well, if your kids do it, then Arly's going to want to join, too." She turned to Quinn, leaning forward and extending one arm alongside Quinn's hip. "Is it safe?"

"With a good teacher, it is." Quinn tried desperately not to look down at Honor's breasts, but it wouldn't have mattered. Honor was so close now that Quinn could smell her scent, and it was making her a little dizzy.

"Well," Honor murmured, caught in the reflections of sunlight swirling in Quinn's eyes, "I guess we'll wait until they ask." She had begun circling her hand on Quinn's thigh without realizing it, enjoying the feel of the muscles tensing beneath her fingers. "Maybe you can help pick the school."

"Sure." Quinn shifted uncomfortably. She was hot. The blood pounded in her ears, and she had quickly grown hard and wet. Casually as possible, she slid her legs away from Honor and stood, certain that if she remained, she was going to have to touch her. "I'm just going to run into the house for a few minutes."

In the kitchen, Quinn pulled another beer from the refrigerator and leaned against the door, rolling the cold surface of the bottle over her forehead. *Jesus. Jesus, she's beautiful. I want her. Jesus, I want her.*

"Quinn?" Honor stepped inside and let the door close behind her. The sight of Quinn with one arm braced against the refrigerator, eyes closed and trembling faintly, sent a bolt of fear straight through her. She crossed to her quickly, putting a hand on her back. "Quinn? Are you all right?"

"No." Turning, Quinn opened her eyes and set the bottle blindly on the counter beside her. Then, she put her hands on Honor's waist and pulled her close. "No, I'm not all right at all."

Ignoring the question hovering on Honor's lips, she covered Honor's mouth with her own. Groaning low in her chest, she kissed her, not gentle now, not patient, but hard and fierce. She pressed her chest and thighs to Honor, bending Honor back with her arms around her waist, tight and possessive. It could've been a minute, it might have been an hour, but she didn't stop feasting on Honor's mouth until she felt Honor's hands tighten in her hair and yank her head back.

"Another second and I'll have you right up against that refrigerator," Honor gasped. *I'll take you where you stand, until you can't stand. Oh God, Quinn.*

Quinn found Honor's breast through the soft cotton of her T-shirt and the thin silk of her bra beneath. She squeezed the hard nipple, her voice low and raw. "Not before I had you."

Honor's eyes turned liquid, swirling like rich chocolate, sensuous and sweet. "I might argue that, but why bother." She rubbed her hand over Quinn's chest, then down her abdomen. "It's a win-win situation."

"Your friends are outside," Quinn panted, her stomach quivering beneath Honor's fingers. "And the kids."

"I know." She put her mouth to Quinn's neck and bit just shy of hard. "Are you busy later?"

"I hope so."

Honor's mouth curved into a slow, satisfied smile. "Count on it."

CHAPTER TWENTY-FIVE

Quinn tapped gently on the back door and waited, acutely aware of the swiftly approaching dark, the still, sultry heat of the late-summer night, and the rapid beat of her own heart. Every sensation seemed magnified, momentous, all because in a few seconds, Honor would appear. And that instant of breath-catching, stomach-twisting pleasure when she first saw her was all she'd been thinking about for hours.

All afternoon and evening, Quinn had tried unsuccessfully to occupy her mind by clearing the last of the boxes from her apartment. She'd unpacked, stowed away clothes and books, and carried cardboard boxes down to the recycling bins in the alley. At one point, she'd considered going to the gym, but finally decided she didn't want to have another conversation with Mandy. She wasn't particularly bothered by Mandy's not-so-subtle flirtations, but the only hands she wanted on her skin were Honor's.

She'd taken a long shower that, instead of relaxing her, had only brought her blood to the surface and added to the arousal that cried out for a touch. Honor's touch.

"Quinn?"

"Phyllis!" Quinn blushed, glad for the shadows because she was certain her desire must be evident. "I'm sorry. I thought Honor said 8:30. I'll just come ba—"

"Honor's upstairs." Laughing, Phyllis pushed the screen door open. "She put Arly to bed, and I think she's in the shower. Come on in."

Vaguely uncomfortable, Quinn followed until she was just inside the door. The kitchen was dimly illuminated by only a few lights beneath the cabinets over the kitchen counter, and the air still held the lingering aroma of dinner. Arly's Visible Woman lay amongst scattered body parts on the table. Pooch snored softly on a dog bed in the corner. Quinn was struck again by the sense of family that permeated the space, and the sharp knowledge that someone was missing. She looked across the room to Phyllis, who leaned against the sink, observing Quinn with a mixture of kindness and question.

"Would you like some coffee?" Phyllis asked. "I just made it."

"That would be great. Thanks." As Quinn took the offered mug a minute later, she added, "I'm sorry I missed you at soccer today. Arly was terrific."

"I had to run as soon as the game was over. I had a date for a matinée performance of *Rent* downtown." Phyllis picked up her own cup and gestured toward the porch. "Let's go outside. It's so beautiful this time of night."

Side by side, they leaned against the porch railing and breathed the rich warm scent of summer. Quinn sighed, wondering what, if anything, Honor had said to Phyllis about their relationship. She didn't want to broach the subject for fear of invading Honor's privacy, but she didn't deal well with secrets, either. And Phyllis was much too important to Honor and Arly for there to be unresolved issues between her and Quinn.

"Did you enjoy the drummers last night?" Phyllis asked conversationally.

"Very much. It was special." *All of it. So very special.*

Phyllis turned, edged a hip against the railing, and smiled at Quinn. "This is a very unusual situation, isn't it?"

"Yes." Rather than being uncomfortable, Quinn's uneasiness began to dissipate. It was her nature to confront issues head-on if she could. Still, it was Phyllis who had to lead this time, even as it was Honor who had to define what Quinn and she could share. If Honor had not been wounded so deeply, Quinn would have pursued her with the same intensity and focus that she did everything else in her life. But she had only to look at Honor to see her uncertainty and sense the fine edge of pain still so near the surface. Only when they touched did she know without question how right it was between them.

"If it helps," Quinn continued, "I think Honor is the most remarkable woman I've ever met and that Arly is a fantastic kid. I wouldn't do anything to hurt either one of them, ever." She held Phyllis's gaze steadily. "Or you, Phyllis, if I could possibly avoid it." *But I won't let Honor go unless she tells me to leave. Not even for you.*

"If Terry were alive," Phyllis said evenly, without the slightest hint of censure, "you wouldn't be here. Not like this."

"I wouldn't want to be." Quinn's voice was gentle, her expression calm.

"I know that." Phyllis smiled softly and patted Quinn's shoulder gently. "And that's exactly why I'm glad that you are."

Quinn released a long slow breath. "Thank you. That means a lot to me, but it will mean much more to Honor."

Phyllis tilted her head, regarding Quinn fondly. "You seem to understand her very well. Why is that, do you think?"

"I don't know. I felt something the minute I saw her, some... connection." She shrugged, frustrated for the first time. "I can't put words to it, but it doesn't seem like I need to. Not to me. It just feels...right."

"I think you put just exactly the right words to it, Quinn." Phyllis picked up her coffee cup. "I expect that Honor will be right down. I'm going to go home, take a long bath, and see if I can't talk a certain gentlemen into a late-night drive."

"Good luck," Quinn called after her as Phyllis descended the back porch steps and disappeared around the corner toward her own half of the house. Soft laughter and what sounded like *You, too* floated back to her on the breeze.

Smiling, Quinn returned to the kitchen, rinsed her coffee mug, and turned it upside down on the drain board. When she turned around, Honor was watching her from the doorway into the hall.

"I came downstairs to tell Phyllis I was running late." Honor's voice was husky and low.

The breath flew from Quinn's chest and her stomach dropped like an elevator cut free from its cable. Honor, her hair still wet from the shower, wore a pale green silk robe that came to midthigh, belted at the waist. She was barefoot, and faint drops of moisture had soaked through the material just beneath the swell of her breasts.

Quinn could imagine the dampness anointing the smooth skin and her own burst to life, tingling with a fine sheen of perspiration. Throat suddenly dry, she gestured toward the back door. "She just left."

"Good timing." Honor leaned her shoulder against the door frame, enjoying the stunned expression on Quinn's face. Quinn had changed into black jeans and a blue cotton shirt, and she looked lean and beautiful and coiled tight as a spring. Honor had an irresistible urge to make her snap. She pushed away from the door, saying, "Arly's asleep. Once she goes down, she never wakes up."

Quinn was rooted to the spot. She had just enough time to utter "You're sure?" before Honor fisted her hands in Quinn's shirt front and spun her against the refrigerator.

"I'm very sure." Honor pressed against the length of Quinn's body and with her lips brushing Quinn's, murmured, "I've been wanting to do this since Linda's."

Then Honor took Quinn's mouth with a fury that surprised them both. Quinn closed her eyes and let Honor claim her, opening herself, body and soul. She felt the force of Honor's tongue searching her mouth for connection and met the probing thrusts with equal fervor. When Honor drove a hand between them and cupped her palm between Quinn's thighs, squeezing steadily, Quinn swallowed a moan and lifted her hips, giving Honor whatever she demanded. Honor tore her lips away, and Quinn gasped, reeling and unsteady.

"We'll be...safer, though," Honor panted, her vision dimmed by a hunger that nearly consumed her rational mind, "behind... closed doors."

"God, yes." Trembling, Quinn nodded. "I can't think...I... Jesus, I need you to touch me."

"I know, baby," Honor crooned, rocking her hips once more into Quinn as she stroked her face and ran a fingertip over her parted lips. "I know."

Quinn whimpered as another surge of painfully sweet pleasure cut through her. Desperately, she cupped Honor's hips, needing the contact. "We have to go *now*. I don't trust myself down here."

With her eyes never leaving Quinn's face, Honor reached back and took firm hold of her hand. "Don't worry. I've got you."

Barely aware of walking, Quinn stumbled behind as Honor led her upstairs and into her bedroom. She stood still in the center of the room as Honor engaged the lock.

"Arly's room is at the other end of the hall," Honor said quietly as she reached for the button on Quinn's jeans. "Take your shirt off."

Quinn's hands shook so badly she could scarcely manage the simple task. The sound of her zipper sliding open made her clitoris jump and throb, and when Honor's fingers brushed against the bare skin of her stomach, she shuddered, groaning from deep in her chest. "You make me want to come when you do that."

"Mmm." Honor smiled, watching the muscles twitch in Quinn's abdomen as she continued to tease her with steady strokes of her nails on slick skin, edging lower each time until she heard Quinn stop breathing. "I could tell the first time I did it...when you got tight this way. I like doing this to you." She raised hazy eyes to Quinn's. "I like what touching you does to me."

"Open your robe," Quinn whispered.

Wordlessly, Honor reached for the tie at her waist and slowly slid the sliver of silk through her fingers but did not release the knot. "You do it."

Gaze locked on Honor's, Quinn reached for the belt and flicked the knot open with a deft turn of her wrist. Never breaking eye contact, she delicately slid a finger under each edge of the partially opened robe, starting at Honor's waist and traveling slowly upward, just skimming the flesh beneath. Honor quivered and moaned quietly at the feathery caresses. When Quinn reached Honor's breasts, she slipped her hands completely beneath the material and over the soft swell of flesh, rubbing the nipples into hard points beneath her palms.

"Oh." Honor jerked abruptly and put one hand on Quinn's shoulder for support, swaying slightly as the heat of arousal coalesced in the pit of her stomach. "I never knew...if you keep touching me there..."

Lifting the delicate fabric until just the peak of Honor's breast was exposed, Quinn slid one arm around Honor's waist and lowered her mouth to suck the rose-tipped nipple between her lips. When she closed her teeth gently around it and tugged, Honor made a soft mewling sound in the back of her throat that nearly caused Quinn's head to explode. Her own arousal was so razor edged that when Honor drew a hand up the inside of her thigh and stroked voluptuously through the heat between her legs, she felt the first ripples of orgasm. Her head snapped back, she fumbled for Honor's hand and rasped through gritted teeth, "Stop."

"Oh no. Let me." Honor pressed her forehead hard to Quinn's chest, loving the ache in her nipples, yearning for Quinn's hands on them again. "Let me make you come."

"Oh, I will." Quinn laughed shakily. "And a lot sooner than you think if you're not careful."

Honor leaned her head back, her lips swollen with desire, her lids nearly closed with the weight of her arousal. "I don't want to be careful. I don't want to wait. I want you now, and then again, and then again after that."

Later, Quinn would wonder how she managed it, but in that second, she didn't even consider her actions. She tightened her hold on Honor's waist and slid the other arm behind her knees, then lifted her in one motion and carried her in three long strides to the bed. She followed Honor onto the bed as she laid her on the pillows, covering Honor's body with her own, her lips already seeking Honor's mouth. She pushed her thigh between Honor's as Honor grasped her hips. Before they were even completely recumbent, their hips were driving in the desperate search for completion, hard muscles against hot, swollen flesh.

Neither led, neither followed. Their desires were evenly matched, their passion perfectly attuned, their hunger in harmony. Quinn threaded her fingers into Honor's hair, her mouth close to Honor's ear, and whispered hoarsely, "I'm going to come. Come with me."

"Yes. Oh yes." Honor dug her fingers into the hard pumping muscles and buried her face in the curve of Quinn's neck as the pleasure took her. When she felt the reins of her control snap with the exquisite rise of her orgasm, she cried out softly, muffling the sound against Quinn's skin.

Quinn stiffened, the sound and feel of Honor climaxing igniting her own release. Biting back a sharp cry, she came in Honor's arms, knowing in her heart that she had come home.

❖

Honor thought she must have drifted, because she had no idea of the hour when she opened her eyes. This time, the feel of Quinn beside her was not a surprise, but it was still a wonder. Sometime after they had both collapsed, Quinn had shifted onto her back and Honor now lay with her cheek against Quinn's shoulder and a thigh across Quinn's. Quinn's breathing was steady beneath her ear and the beat of her heart a quiet reassurance. Honor's limbs felt heavy and a ripple of arousal still pulsed inside. Totally satisfied, she was still aware of a persistent hunger. Not just for the physical pleasure, which pulsed in her depths like a distant drumbeat, but for the way Quinn filled the places within her that had been so empty for so long. She shivered, frightened by how quickly and how easily Quinn had come into her heart.

Softly, Quinn stroked Honor's hair. "Cold?"

"No," Honor said, her throat tight. She reached beside her for the crumpled sheet and drew it over them both. "I didn't think I could do that."

"What?" Quinn circled her palm down the center of Honor's back, hoping to soothe her. Despite the fact that Honor lay curled against her, warm and pliant in the aftermath of their lovemaking, there was an unmistakable edge of disquiet in Honor's voice.

"Come with anyone that way." *Let you in so deeply that your blood beat in my veins, that your passion filled my body, that your release was my pleasure.* "I've been close before...but I've never..." She pressed her face to Quinn's shoulder, closing her eyes tightly. "Oh God, Quinn. What's happening?"

"We're discovering us."

Us. The very concept seemed foreign and threatening. To want again, to need again. Honor trembled. "Quinn, I don't think I can."

"It's all right." Quinn tightened her hold but kept her voice calm and steady. "I won't hurt you. I promise."

"Don't. Don't make promises."

Gently, Quinn lifted Honor's face until their eyes met. "I won't, if you don't want me to. But saying the words or *not* saying them won't change what's in my heart."

"I don't know what I want," Honor whispered. "I don't know what I can give."

"That's all right. We'll find out together." Quinn raised her head enough to see the faint red glow of the bedside clock. She pressed her lips to Honor's forehead and sighed. "I should go home."

"No." Honor drew even closer, her grip suddenly fierce. "I know it's selfish, but I need you here with me a while longer. I can't...everything is open inside of me right now. If you go, I'm afraid I'll bleed."

"It's not selfish to need me, sweetheart. I need you—more than you can know." Quinn ached to ease the pain she heard in Honor's voice, felt in her trembling body. Knowing that she couldn't, she kissed her gently before easing Honor's head back down against her shoulder. "I'll stay. I *want* to be here for you, for just as long as you want me."

Honor closed her eyes, afraid to embrace the truth of Quinn's words, trying instead to believe that the present was all she wanted.

CHAPTER TWENTY-SIX

With a gasp, Quinn came sharply awake in the dark, her skin still tingling from the electrical discharge. She hadn't felt the cardiac irregularity that had triggered her defibrillator, but her body had registered the erratic heartbeat followed by the synchronizing current. Quinn was instantly thankful that Honor, still curled against her, had not been awakened by the shock. She did not want Honor to worry about what could not be changed.

The third time this week. Christ. It's supposed to be getting better, *not worse.*

Turning her head carefully, Quinn checked the clock once again and saw that it was after five. Now that her breathing had returned to normal and the writhing anxiety in the pit of her stomach had abated, she gently eased away from Honor and toward the edge of the bed.

Unconsciously sensing Quinn's withdrawal, Honor tightened her grip and then rose through the layers of sleep to open her eyes and inquire groggily, "What are you doing?"

"I have to go home," Quinn replied in a whisper. She stroked her fingers over Honor's cheek and then into her hair while leaning down to kiss her possessively. "I shouldn't be here when Phyllis arrives and Arly wakes up."

Fully awake now, Honor sat up in bed, the sheet falling away to expose her nakedness. "God, is it morning already?"

"Just about." Sitting on the edge of the bed and casting a glance around for her clothes, Quinn sighed. "Where the hell are my pants?"

Honor smiled, remembering her pleasure in stripping those jeans off Quinn's hips the night before. Still hungry for the touch of her, she leaned against Quinn's back, her cheek on Quinn's shoulder, and circled one arm around her waist. She fanned her hand over Quinn's stomach and began to rub slowly up and down, using her nails intermittently to coax the muscles to twitch.

"On the floor somewhere," Honor replied languidly.

Quinn groaned. "You *can't* do that. It makes me so hot I can't think."

"Really?" Honor's tone was completely ingenuous. "I never noticed that."

"Like hell." In defense, Quinn grabbed Honor's hand and stilled the torturously wonderful caresses. "We don't *have time.*"

Time. It echoed in Honor's mind. *Too little time. Lost time. Gone before it was time.* She curled her other arm around Quinn's waist and brought both palms up to cradle Quinn's breasts. She didn't caress her or tease her now, but merely cleaved as tightly to her as she could. As if holding Quinn within the circle of her body could make time stop.

Quinn raised her hands to cover Honor's, linking their fingers against her skin. "What is it?"

Wordlessly, eyes tightly closed, Honor merely shook her head and pressed her cheek harder to the back of Quinn's shoulder.

"Sweetheart, I can feel you hurting. Tell me."

Honor's voice was a whisper, the words so hard to admit. "I don't want you to go. I don't want this night to end."

Surprised not only at the sentiment but also by the admission, Quinn turned slightly until she could cup her fingers beneath Honor's chin. "Why? What do you think will happen?"

"I don't know," Honor replied, her eyes dark pools of anguish. "All I know is that you're here right now and that later...you might not be."

...hit her in the back of the neck. Just like that. From one second to the next...she was here, and then...she wasn't.

"Oh no," Quinn murmured, pain lancing through her. She framed Honor's face in gentle hands and kissed her forehead, then her closed lids, then her faintly trembling lips. "I'm going to go home and shower, and in a few hours, I'd like to come back so that you and Arly and I can go to the zoo together. *Tomorrow,* I'll see you at work and then in the evening at soccer practice. Some night later in the week, whenever Phyllis is free to watch Arly, I'd like it if you'd go to the movies with me. *Next weekend,* I'll coach at the game and then we can all rehash our victory at Robin and Linda's. *That's* what's going to happen after I leave here this morning."

"You make it sound so simple." Honor opened her eyes and searched Quinn's, finding the steady calm she was coming to rely upon.

The corner of Quinn's mouth lifted into a lazy grin. "Not simple. Not even routine. But certain."

"You forgot something," Honor whispered, trailing her fingers along the edge of Quinn's jaw and then down her throat until she pressed her palm against the center of Quinn's chest.

"What?" Quinn's voice's was husky, her blood rising as it always did when Honor touched her.

"The part when we're alone, here or at your apartment, and we're inside each other's body." *Inside each other's hopes and dreams.*

"Oh, no. I didn't forget." Quinn shuddered, arousal leaping into her stomach and threatening to erupt. "That's there, always there, right at the heart of us."

Us. That terrible, frightening, exhilarating word.

Honor shivered now. She leaned into Quinn and kissed her, a deep, slow, probing kiss that she continued until she was positive that she would carry the taste and feel of her all day. Then she drew back, trembling. "You should go now. Go *now,* because I'm aching for you."

Quinn had to grit her teeth to tear herself away. Even when she was beyond arm's reach, she could feel the pull of Honor's touch upon her skin. Hoarsely, she said, "I can feel you inside of me right now. I want to feel you that way all day, every day." *Every day for the rest of my life. Say yes, Honor. Tell me you want that, too.*

Honor couldn't tell her how much she wanted those feelings never to change; she wanted it so deeply that she couldn't speak at all. But she could feel Quinn reach past the barriers that shielded her heart and touch her where she so desperately needed to be touched. She felt the passion beneath the gentle caress and heard the unwavering certainty in Quinn's voice. She feared to answer, but she dared, for the first time in so very long, to hope.

"I'll see you later," Quinn said softly, turning away to gather the rest of her clothes from the floor.

"I'll miss you," Honor finally said.

Quinn shrugged into her shirt and walked to the door. Before she reached to unlock it, she looked back over her shoulder to where Honor sat naked amidst the aftermath of their passion. "Good. I want you to."

The door closed gently behind Quinn, and although Honor tried, she could not hear her footsteps on the stairs. *You can't possibly know how much I'll miss you.*

❖

It was almost nine when the back door opened and Phyllis walked into the kitchen.

"Hi, Grandmom." Arly was perched on her stool at the table spooning biscuit dough from a bowl with an ice-cream scoop and arranging the sticky mounds in carefully spaced rows on a baking sheet. The evidence of her culinary adventure was visible on the table, the floor, and portions of her person.

"Hello, darling mine." The joy shining in Arly's eyes made Phyllis's heart lift.

When Honor was not working Sunday, it was a ritual for the three of them to have breakfast together. Honor always awoke early whether she was working or not, and since Arly was an early riser as well, breakfast was usually well underway by 8:30.

"I was just about to call you," Honor said as she glanced up from the stove with a concerned expression. "I thought you were going to miss breakfast."

"I wouldn't think of it." Phyllis leaned down and kissed Arly's head. "Mmm, don't they look good."

Arly grinned proudly. "Mom measured, but I mixed everything together myself."

"Wonderful." Phyllis stepped over Pooch, who was sprawled at Arly's feet, and joined Honor. "Anything I can do to help?"

"Nope. We're having vegetable frittatas and homemade buttermilk biscuits." Honor poured the eggs into the frying pan, added the vegetables she'd prepared, and turned the flame down low. "Another few minutes and it'll be ready."

"We're going to the zoo today," Arly announced excitedly.

"That should be fun," Phyllis said as she efficiently set the table.

"We're going with Quinn. It's like a date."

Phyllis merely smiled at the small choking sound that came from Honor's direction. "I can't wait to hear all about it."

As soon as breakfast was over, Arly took Pooch into the backyard to play. Honor and Phyllis carried their coffee onto the porch to relax and keep an eye on them.

"Is something wrong?" Honor asked as soon as they were settled.

Phyllis propped her feet onto a low wicker footstool and watched Arly try to coax Pooch into chasing the soccer ball with her. "It's amazing how coordinated she is. I can't remember now if Terry was that good so young."

"Terry was good at everything," Honor said quietly.

"It seems that way now, doesn't it?" Phyllis sipped her coffee and watched her granddaughter. "And I'm fine. I just overslept."

Honor regarded Phyllis suspiciously. "You never oversleep. Are you sure you're feeling all right?" Now that she looked carefully, Honor noticed that Phyllis had an unusual amount of color in her face that morning. She appeared flushed. "Cough? Sore throat?"

"There's no need to worry, Dr. Blake," Phyllis said with a laugh. "I had a late evening and just forgot to set my alarm."

"Okay," Honor relented. "If you're certain that's all it is."

Phyllis reached across the space between them and fondly squeezed Honor's hand. "I saw Quinn arrive when I was leaving last night. Every time I see her, I like her more."

"So do I."

"Arly's already more than half in love with her."

I think I might be, too.

As if hearing the unspoken words, Phyllis turned to look into Honor's eyes. "You certainly don't need my permission, nor would I presume to give it. But that young woman has a great deal of feeling for you, and it's a pleasure to see."

Caught off guard, Honor stared at her hands, linking her fingers and resting them in her lap. "She spent the night here last night." She raised her head, met Phyllis's kind gaze. "I haven't wanted...to be with anyone since Terry."

"Then she must be as special as I imagined."

Honor colored, still shaken by the furor of emotions that Quinn stirred in her. "She's very special."

"When are you going to tell Arly?"

"Tell her what?" Honor's voice rose in surprise.

"That you and Quinn care for one another."

"Oh, it's far too soon for that." Honor's words came out in a rush. "We haven't known each other all that long and we've only had a few dates and Quinn could decide that she doesn't want a ready-made family and I'm not even certain that I want anything serio—"

"I wasn't suggesting you tell her that you and Quinn are getting married," Phyllis chided with a laugh. "But you *might* want to tell her that you and Quinn are special friends and that sometimes Quinn might stay for a sleepover."

Honor tried out the word. "A sleepover." She closed her eyes and rubbed the bridge of her nose. "God. I didn't expect this kind of complication."

"It seems that more often than not, we never do." Phyllis smiled a secret smile, recalling her own evening. "Do you want me to talk to her?"

"No, I will. I just thought I'd have more time to see...to see about Quinn."

"You know how bright that child is, and she sees everything. It will be easier for her to accept the changes in your life if you let her be a part of whatever happens with you and Quinn."

"I don't know that anything's *going* to change," Honor protested.

"Oh, Honor," Phyllis said tenderly, "it already has."

Before Honor could reply, Arly gave an excited shout. "Quinn!"

"Hey!" Quinn called back. When the child and dog came racing toward her, Quinn knelt down, caught the dog's collar in one hand to forestall a wet tongue in the face, and held out a small yellow rectangular object to Arly with the other. "This is for you for when we go to the zoo today."

"Wow! Thanks!" Arly took the present and then streaked across the yard and up the stairs to her mother. "Look, Mom. Quinn gave me a camera."

Dutifully, Honor made appreciative noises over the disposable automatic camera. "That's terrific, honey. Why don't you go get cleaned up, and we'll leave in a few minutes."

"Okay." After retrieving the gift from her mother, Arly ran into the house.

Honor's pulse raced alarmingly as she observed Quinn, who now leaned against the porch post, a happy grin on her face. She looked casually attractive in a navy blue T-shirt, new jeans, and old Nikes. It was hard for Honor to believe that they'd only been apart a few hours, because the only thing that she wanted to do was pull the shirt from Quinn's jeans and run her hands over the hot, smooth skin beneath. *God, I'm regressing. I don't think I was this bad when I first discovered sex.*

"Thank you," Honor said abruptly, struggling to keep her feelings from showing on her face.

"My pleasure. Hi, Phyllis." Quinn hooked her thumbs in her pockets, wondering if Honor really thought she hadn't noticed the way Honor's eyes had traveled over her body. She liked being looked at that way, as long as it was Honor who was doing the looking. It gave her a nice warm feeling, a trickle of arousal in her stomach that wasn't quite enough to make her crazy, but left her feeling unmistakably alive.

"Good morning." Phyllis rose, cup in hand. "It's nice to see you again so soon."

"Thanks. You, too." Quinn grinned. "Did you have a nice evening?"

"Very fine indeed," Phyllis said primly. She patted Quinn's cheek on her way into the house. "And I don't intend to ask how *yours* was."

Honor looked after her mother-in-law and then raised mildly accusing eyes to Quinn. "Don't tell me you two have been discussing our sex life."

Quinn took one quick glance into the kitchen to see that they were alone and then leaned down to kiss Honor on the mouth. "Nope. Just Phyllis's."

"Is *everyone* in my family falling in love with you?" The words were out before Honor realized it. Embarrassed, she hurried to take them back. "Quinn, I didn't mea—"

"No, don't say anything else." Quinn kissed her again. "It sounded nice just the way it was."

Honor didn't argue, because it *had* felt good to say it. She stood and brushed her fingers over Quinn's chest. "I'm going to collect my daughter. Then let's go play with the animals."

"Why don't you ask Phyllis to come with us?" Quinn called after her.

"I will," Honor answered from the kitchen, touched that Quinn would suggest it. *Falling in love. Is that what this feeling is? Of wanting to be with her, touch her, know her? How is it that I don't know? That I don't remember?*

When she found Phyllis and extended the invitation to join them, her mother-in-law thanked her, but said that she intended to do nothing but sit with her feet up all day and read. Then Arly came running downstairs, her new camera in her hand and an enormous smile on her face.

"I'm ready, Mom. Are we going now?"

The swift surge of love was nearly overpowering, and Honor could only nod and smile. Love, it seemed—that critical connection that defied logic or definition—came in so many forms, none less essential than the others, only different. She took her daughter's hand and walked out onto the porch, extending her other hand to Quinn. "We're ready for our adventure."

Quinn linked her fingers with Honor's. "So am I."

CHAPTER TWENTY-SEVEN

Honor jumped as the beeper on her waistband vibrated. She glanced at the readout and grimaced.

"Quinn, can you keep an eye on Arly while I find a phone to answer this page? It's the ER."

Quinn turned away from the spectacle of cavorting sea lions, taking in Honor's slight frown of irritation. "I thought you were off today. I don't even have my cell phone."

"I'm *supposed* to be off, so I left *my* cell in the car." Honor shrugged in resignation. "It's probably just some administrative issue and they need me to confirm the official party line. I'll only be a few minutes."

"No problem. We're headed to the monkey house next," Quinn replied. "We'll wait for you there."

Since arriving at the zoo, Quinn and Arly had been busy studying the pictorial map in the color brochure that came with the price of admission and plotting their course around the enclosure. Honor was amused to discover that her daughter and Quinn shared a very strong sense of order and a love for structure. Left to her own devices, Honor would have wandered in whatever direction her interest led. However, it had rapidly become clear that with Arly and Quinn in charge, this was to be a very systematic safari.

"Yeah, Mom," Arly announced excitedly. "We're going to take pictures of them when they're outside in their...natural habitat." She glanced at Quinn, who gave her a thumbs-up of approval for remembering the new term.

"That's great, honey. I'll be right back." Honor fixed them both with a mock-stern look. "And *don't* get into trouble."

The angelic blond child and the devilishly good-looking dark-haired, blue-eyed woman both grinned, and Honor's heart melted.

Unfortunately, she looked at Quinn for just a second too long, and a few other parts of her anatomy grew disturbingly warm. She left in search of a phone before she could become any more distracted.

It was closer to fifteen minutes before Honor made her way back through the heavy throngs of visitors toward the screened-in expanse of tall grass, trees, and man-made climbing devices that composed the outdoor extension of the monkey house. Her daughter and Quinn were nowhere in sight. With just the slightest sense of unease, she turned slowly, scanning the people lined up along the railing that separated the paved pathway from the animal habitat. Then she heard, above the cacophony of the crowd, the sound of one child laughing. Unerringly, she pivoted toward the voice, and her gaze fell directly on Arly and Quinn.

Arly stood on the bottom rung of the metal railing that edged the moat surrounding the monkey house. She leaned as far over the railing as she possibly could with her camera at eye level, a posture which, Honor was certain, was frowned upon by zoo officials. Ordinarily, she would have been too anxious to allow Arly to climb up on the barrier. However, Quinn stood immediately beside Arly with her fingers curled around the waistband at the back of the child's shorts. Honor had not the slightest doubt that Quinn would keep Arly safe.

As she watched, she saw Quinn point to two monkeys frolicking on a wooden scaffolding and caught a glimpse of Arly's thrilled expression as she aimed her new camera toward them. The sight of her daughter's pleasure and the easy, tender way that Quinn related to her brought Honor a surge of joy. Smiling, she joined them and rested her hand in the center of Quinn's back, stroking gently up and down.

"Hi," Honor said softly.

"Everything okay?"

"Mmm. Just an insurance snafu with an ER transfer." She kept her hand lightly resting on the small of Quinn's back. "You two look like you're having fun."

"We are." Quinn continued her hold on Arly and, while the child was occupied taking another picture, leaned over and kissed Honor quickly. "Missed you."

Honor's lips parted in surprise and pleasure. Her stomach did a quick roll and she suddenly felt far more than warm. Quinn's muscles tightened beneath Honor's fingers and she saw her blue eyes darken with desire. That was all it took. She wanted to jump her. "God."

Quinn raised an eyebrow, laughter and arousal warring in her expression. "Are you talking to me?"

"Definitely not." Laughing, Honor wrapped her arm around Quinn's waist and leaned into her. "What's next, Captain Quinn?"

Grinning, Quinn turned to Arly. "Where to, navigator?"

Arly finally looked away from the primate enclosure. "What's a navigator?"

"The person who's in charge of directions," Quinn explained.

"Where's the map?"

Quinn retrieved it from her back pocket and held it out. Arly climbed down from the railing and studied it, then looked around. With a frown that was a replica of her mother's, she held out the map to Honor.

"I can't tell where I am."

Honor knelt down and looked at the simplistic diagram of the zoo. She pointed to an image that was presumably the monkey house.

"This is where we are. See? There are the monkeys." She drew her finger to another image. "What about this?"

"It's a lion." Arly turned in a circle and gestured triumphantly toward the stone statue to their right. "There! Right?"

"Very good." Honor stood and handed the map back to Quinn. With a salute, she declared exuberantly, "To the lion house."

Quinn was about to reply when Arly slid a small hand into hers. She glanced down to see that the child had taken Honor's hand, too, linking the three of them. It seemed so completely natural and right that for an instant, Quinn had the sensation of always having been with them. Then, just as quickly, she realized that had fate and circumstance been less fickle, less cruel, someone else would have been standing there with the woman she loved and her child. She experienced a sudden surge of sadness, but it was quickly replaced by the certain knowledge that the past, with all its tragedy and heartbreak, was truly behind them. Fate, it appeared, was not fixed, but fluid, and Honor and Arly were her destiny. She knew it as certainly as she had ever known anything, to the depths of her soul.

"Lead on." Voice husky, Quinn smiled into Honor's eyes and was rewarded by a long sultry look that was both tender and hungry. "I'll follow."

"For a little while." Honor let her eyes drift down over Quinn's body and then slowly rise once again to meet her gaze. She was pleased to see the flicker of arousal in Quinn's eyes. "I like it— sometimes—when you're in charge."

Quinn's stomach clenched. *Sweet Jesus.*

Arly tugged their hands and forged ahead, dragging the adults behind her. "Come on. We don't want to miss anything."

Laughing, Honor and Quinn hurried to keep up.

❖

"Quinn?" Arly asked. "Can you stay and read with me after my bath?"

After the zoo, they'd had an impromptu barbecue in Honor's backyard, just the three of them and a happy Pooch, who had had his fill of dropped morsels. Now it was nearing nine, and Honor had just announced that it was time for Arly to get ready for bed. Quinn looked questioningly over Arly's head to Honor.

Smiling, Honor nodded.

"Sure," Quinn replied. "I'll pick up down here while you go with your mom."

When Quinn had covered the grill, carried in the dishes, and stowed away the condiments, she went upstairs to Arly's room. A pajama-clad Arly sat up in bed, the covers drawn up to her waist and an enormous book propped on her knees.

"Harry Potter, huh?" Quinn remarked as she crossed to the bed.

Honor stuck her head in the door. "Don't make her read the entire thing tonight, okay, honey?"

"Mom." Arly giggled. "It's hundreds and hundreds of pages."

"Well then, no more than half." Honor gave Quinn an amused look. "If you can handle the storytelling duties, I'm going to take care of a few things downstairs."

Quinn kicked off her Nikes, propped a pillow against the headboard, and settled onto the bed next to Arly. "You go ahead. We're fine."

Honor was ambushed by a sudden swell of affection and blinked away an unexpected wash of tears. The picture before her was not the one she had imagined night after night, standing alone in this doorway. It was not the picture she had longed for, ached for, wept for. To her astonishment and confusion, she felt nothing but happiness now. Unable to speak, she merely nodded and slipped away.

"Okay," Quinn said briskly. "What's the drill here?"

Arly gave her a perplexed look. "You're supposed to read the story to me."

"How come you're not going to read it to me?"

"Because *some* of it is too hard for me." Arly's tone suggested that Quinn should know that.

"Oh. Okay." Quinn leaned closer and held one side of the book open as Arly held the other and began to read.

"Quinn," Arly interrupted after a few minutes.

"Huh?" Quinn had quickly become engrossed in the story.

"Do you like my mom a lot?"

Uh-oh. Quinn stiffened. "Yes, I do."

"Do you like my mom like Linda and Robin like each other?"

Oh, man. Where's Honor? Quinn cleared her throat, cursing herself for not having seen this coming. "I don't know. How do you mean?"

Arly closed the book and shifted on the bed to regard Quinn seriously. "Linda and Robin like each other more than anybody else in the world, and that's why they live together."

"Well, I like your mom more than anybody else. And you, too." Honesty seemed the only course, and Quinn desperately hoped it was the correct one. She took a long breath. "But living together is very special, and it's something that you have to think about very hard before you do it."

"Are you thinking about it?"

God, she's single-minded. She's going to be a surgeon some day. Or president. Quinn forced herself not to fidget. "Well, right now, your mom and I are just finding out if we like each other the way Linda and Robin do."

"Oh," Arly replied, sounding sleepy. "When will you know?"

"Don't worry." Smiling, Quinn rescued the book from where it was about to fall onto the floor and eased to the side of the bed. She tucked the covers around Arly and leaned over to kiss her on the forehead. "We'll let you know first thing."

As Quinn moved quietly toward the door, Honor appeared outside in the hall.

"Everything okay?"

Quinn hurriedly took Honor's arm and led her further down the hall.

"She's asleep." Quinn leaned against the wall. "She asked me about *us*."

Honor struggled not to smile at the hint of panic in Quinn's voice. She'd rarely seen Quinn show nerves over anything. "What about us?"

"If we *liked* each other." Quinn's voice was a desperate whisper. "You know. *Like* liked."

"What did you tell her?" Honor bit her bottom lip, but the laugh was about to erupt despite her best attempts to contain it. Quinn looked adorably flummoxed.

Quinn ran a hand through her hair. She felt like pulling it out. "I told her I liked you a lot but that we're not ready to live together yet."

"Live together?" Honor's voice rose along with her eyebrows. "That's a leap."

"You had to have been there."

"I'm sure." Honor took Quinn's hand and drew her to the door of her bedroom. "So, you wanna have a sleepover?"

"I do, except..." Desire leapt like a living thing into Quinn's throat. "I'm not really tired yet."

Honor slid her fingers under the waistband of Quinn's jeans. "Good. Neither am I."

Then she tugged Quinn into her bedroom, reached around her to lock the door, and then laced her arms around Quinn's neck. Sighing at the first touch of their bodies, she nuzzled her face in the curve of Quinn's neck. "I had a wonderful time today. I wouldn't change a thing about it."

Quinn encircled Honor's waist and spread her hands over Honor's hips, snugging her closer still. With her lips against Honor's forehead, she murmured, "But?"

"But," Honor replied indolently, her mouth brushing over Quinn's lips, her hips rocking gently, "I thought I was going to die if I couldn't touch you soon."

"Mmm." Quinn moved her mouth along the edge of Honor's jaw in quick, feathery kisses, then caught an earlobe between her teeth and nipped, drawing a sharp gasp from the woman in her arms. "You can touch me now."

"I'm going to make you pay for that," Honor warned breathlessly, tugging the T-shirt from Quinn's jeans.

"Promise?"

In lieu of an answer, Honor kissed her, darting her tongue between Quinn's lips until Quinn groaned. With the kiss unbroken, they stumbled their way toward the bed and tumbled onto it. Then they drew apart, laughing quietly. Honor slid her hand under Quinn's T-shirt and over her breasts, teasing her nipples into hard points of desire. Breathing rapidly, Quinn worked the button loose on Honor's shorts with one hand and then dipped her fingers inside. Honor stiffened and caught her breath sharply.

"Quinn, darling...that's not exactly my idea of punishment." With a swift lift of her hips, she dislodged Quinn's hand and rolled over on top of her, straddling her hips. Laughing at the look of consternation on Quinn's face, she pulled her shirt and bra off over her head and dropped them behind her onto the floor. She arched her back and gave a low contented sigh, drawing both hands up her abdomen to stop with her fingers splayed over her breasts. When Quinn raised her shoulders to reach for her, Honor shook her head.

"No, I don't think so." She cupped her breasts, squeezed gently. "You can look, but not touch."

Quinn's eyes grew round with surprise at the same time as her pulse skyrocketed. Her throat went dry and arousal poured through her like quicksilver, hot and slick. She groaned. "Do you know what that will do to me?"

Honor cocked her head and smiled, a slow teasing smile. She flicked one of her hard nipples with a fingertip and barely managed to hold back a moan. Breathless, she said, "Let's find out."

The muscles in Quinn's legs were so tight she thought she'd cramp as she watched Honor push her shorts down over her hips, shifting quickly back and forth until she kicked free of the restraining material.

"Hands on the bed, now," Honor murmured as she unzipped Quinn's jeans and worked them off.

When Honor settled back down, a leg on either side of Quinn's body, she was nude, and Quinn was desperate with the scent and sight of her.

"I like the way you look at me," Honor whispered, trailing the fingers of her right hand between her breasts and then down over her belly. She fixed on Quinn's eyes as they followed the movement of her fingers, and it was almost as if it were Quinn touching her. Honor's excitement escalated and she pulled her lip between her teeth, biting down to hold her focus. She was wet, throbbing, and she wanted Quinn's hands on her. "You look a little wild. A little dangerous."

"I *am* dangerous. I want you." Quinn dared to touch her then, because she couldn't bear not to any longer. Still, she only rested her palms against the outside of Honor's thighs, needing to feel the heat of her skin. "All of you." She smoothed her hands up Honor's sides and then down to clasp her hips. "I want to be inside of you like you're inside of me."

Honor rested her fingertips on the insides of her spread legs and drew her hands upward until she framed the center of her desire, then brushed her fingers lightly over herself. Someone groaned. She thought it was Quinn. It might have been her. Her lids closed as the pleasure settled in the pit of her stomach, and she heard Quinn panting softly as her hips jerked between Honor's thighs. She held her fingers still then, afraid that her control would snap. "Do you know how ready I am for you?"

"Honor," Quinn pleaded, cupping Honor's hips and urging her upward. "Let me have you. Please."

Unable to hold back, Honor leaned forward and braced her arms on the headboard, letting Quinn guide her to her mouth. She cried out softly as warm lips enclosed her, her head dropping between her arms, her thighs trembling. "Oh," she moaned, "oh God, Quinn."

Quinn caressed Honor's back in long strokes that echoed the movement of her tongue, soothing even as she stoked the embers of Honor's passion to bright flame. When she felt the pulse beat wildly between her lips and sensed Honor gathering her strength for the climb to completion, she gripped Honor's waist and held her firmly. When Honor sobbed out her pleasure, Quinn drew her deeper, claiming her with relentless tenderness.

Even before the last gripping spasm had released her, Honor collapsed into Quinn's waiting arms. She shuddered with the still-powerful aftershocks, pressing her face to Quinn's neck. "Please don't let go."

Quinn tightened her hold, molding her body to Honor's and wrapping her arms around her. "No," she murmured, her lips pressed to Honor's damp hair. "No, sweetheart, I won't."

Eventually, Honor stilled and her breathing returned to normal. "When you touch me, I feel so exposed."

"I love the way you let me touch you." Quinn caressed Honor's cheek and kissed her softly. "You can trust me."

"I think I do."

Quinn closed her eyes, gratitude and desire filling her in equal measure. "By the way, you can punish me any time you please."

"I don't think...that plan worked very well." Honor laughed just a bit wildly, remembering how easily she had given herself to Quinn, how she had wanted so desperately for Quinn to take her. *God, how can she turn everything around and make it feel so right?*

Gently, Quinn took Honor's hand and drew it between her own thighs, gasping softly as warm fingers brushed her painfully swollen clitoris. *"I* think...it worked...just fine."

"Is that right?" Laughing with delight now, Honor leaned up on an elbow and watched Quinn's face as she worked her slowly but inexorably to orgasm. When Quinn's eyes, fixed on her face, lost focus and her stomach tightened on a groan, Honor moaned softly. She felt powerful and humbled and blessed by the exquisite connection she had never hoped to experience again.

"That's right, baby," she murmured as Quinn, shuddering violently, pressed her face to Honor's breasts. "That's right. Everything is fine, just fine."

"Oh," Quinn gasped after a time. "You make me feel so good." She leaned her head back, searching Honor's face, her expression still dazed. "So damn good—everywhere."

Smiling tenderly, Honor brushed her fingers through Quinn's hair, then eased Quinn's head back to her breast, loving the sensation of holding her in her arms. "Then we're even, because you make me feel so good, too."

"I'm happy," Quinn mumbled, floating on the edge of sleep. "Really happy."

"Yes," Honor whispered wonderingly, her voice just barely audible. "So am I."

CHAPTER TWENTY-EIGHT

Quinn awoke on her side, her breasts pressed to Honor's back, an arm around her waist, and Honor's hips nestled into the curve of her belly. She cradled the heavy warmth of Honor's breast and thrilled to the heartbeat beneath her palm. Honor was everywhere, everything. Quinn nestled her face in the curve of her lover's neck, nuzzling the soft skin just below her ear. She smiled to herself when Honor murmured her pleasure and rocked her hips against Quinn's pelvis. She couldn't think of a single thing that worried her and would be content never to move from that spot.

Close to drifting off to sleep once more in sated torpor, Quinn groaned in near-ecstasy as the faint but exquisite aroma of coffee reached her. *Oh God, yes. Coffee.*

Coffee!

Quinn's eyes flew open. "Holy Christ."

"What?" Honor questioned, drowsy and slightly grumpy.

"Coffee. Phyllis is downstairs—in the kitchen—making coffee."

Honor grasped Quinn's hand and held it tightly between her breasts, preventing Quinn from jumping up. "She always comes over in the morning around this time when I have to work."

"Yes," Quinn whispered urgently. "But *I'm* not usually upstairs in bed with you."

"Mmm." Honor worked her hips a little tighter into the bend of Quinn's body, eliciting a startled but appreciative gasp from Quinn. "Maybe we can work on that."

"And *maybe* I can make it down the maple tree outside your window, too."

"Well," Honor muttered, pressing Quinn's hand to her breast a second longer before releasing her hold, "I can see that you're immune to my charms this morning." Laughing, she turned onto her back and regarded Quinn with lazy, satisfied eyes. "Phyllis is *not* going to care that you're here."

"Yes, but she'll know what we've been doing."

Honor's lips curved into a full, ripe smile. "I very much doubt that she'll know *that*."

Quinn grinned and couldn't resist kissing the beautiful mouth. When she drew away, Honor's eyes were liquid and warm. "I *meant* in generic terms."

"Kiss me like that again, and she *will* have all the details."

"Oh no. Not on your life." Quinn dipped her head, stole another kiss, and then slid from the bed. "I'm going to get dressed and *try* not to look like I spent the entire night reveling in your body."

Honor sat up and pushed her hair back with both hands, her breasts lifting with the motion. "Did you?"

"What?" Quinn asked, losing her train of thought as she followed the rise and sway of Honor's breasts.

"Revel?"

"Oh yeah." Quinn brushed her palm down the center of her own chest and abdomen, unconsciously trying to contain the sudden surge of arousal. "I feasted."

"You *did*, didn't you?" Honor's voice was low, throaty. Her eyes followed the path of Quinn's hand over the gentle swell of breast and taut muscles, imagining her own in its place. "Either get dressed or get back into this bed."

"Work. We have to go to work." Quinn tore her eyes away from Honor's hungry gaze and found her jeans. She tugged them on and closed the fly with trembling hands. Her T-shirt lay by the side of the bed, and as she reached to get it, she felt Honor's fingers drift along her spine. She shivered and stepped out of touching range. "Do you have any idea how much I want you? Any idea at all?"

Through the mind-blurring mists of arousal, Honor heard the nearly agonized tone of Quinn's voice. Her vision cleared instantly, and she searched Quinn's face, startled to see a flicker of pain wash through her eyes. Without another thought, she slipped naked from the bed and quickly went to Quinn. She framed the handsome face gently in her palms. "Quinn." She tenderly kissed her mouth. "I never want to hurt you. Am I?"

Quinn closed her eyes and shook her head. She rested her hands on Honor's waist. "No. Sometimes, I feel...so much, it hurts. But I don't mind." She opened her eyes, smiled faintly. "I wouldn't want it any other way."

"As long as you're sure." Honor brushed the hair from Quinn's forehead, then softly stroked her cheek. *I want to give you more, I want to. I just...can't...yet.*

"I'm sure." Quinn grinned, stronger this time. "I have to go home and shower. I need to change for work."

"Yes, you do. You don't want to be late." Honor raised her brows. "I've heard your chief is a ballbuster."

"Yeah." Quinn shrugged into her T-shirt. "But I kinda like it."

Honor's voice was honey warm. "Oh, really?"

Quinn didn't answer, glancing around the room in consternation. "Shit, I left my sneakers in Arly's room." She glanced at Honor in concern. "She shouldn't know I spent the night, right?"

"She'd probably be fine with it, but I'd rather tell her ahead of time if you're going to be here when she gets up. Plus, she's going to want you to stay for breakfast." Honor gave Quinn an affectionate pat on the rear. "I'll get your sneakers and bring them down to the kitchen for you. She won't wake up just yet."

"Great," Quinn sighed.

While Honor went to retrieve her Nikes, Quinn pulled on her socks and headed downstairs. She hoped that Honor was right about Phyllis. There was a big difference between knowing something in theory and being confronted with it in fact. Regardless of anything that Phyllis might have said, she was still Terry's mother, and Quinn had taken Terry's place in Honor's bed, if not her heart.

❖

Phyllis , a cup of coffee in her hand and a smile on her face, turned at the sound of soft footsteps behind her. She blinked at the sight of Quinn, shoeless and uneasy, framed in the kitchen doorway. Her untucked T-shirt was rumpled, her hair was mussed, and her eyes were apologetic. *Quinn. Honor's new love.*

For just an instant, Terry's face flashed into Phyllis's mind. That heart-melting grin that could charm the spots off a leopard. *Oh, baby love. I miss you so much.*

"Hi, Phyllis." Quinn didn't move, watching Phyllis's face. "I'm sorry I took you by surprise."

"That's all right." Phyllis gestured to the coffeepot. "Do you want some?"

Quinn shook her head. "I need to get home. I was just—"

Honor appeared at Quinn's side, sneakers in hand. "Here you go." She ran a hand down Quinn's back, the gesture intimate but discreet, then stepped around her and into the kitchen. "Morning, Phyllis."

"Hi, sweetie."

While Quinn leaned against the wall and tugged on her Nikes, Honor poured coffee into a travel mug. She held out the mug to Quinn. "If you're only going to have one cup today, it should be Phyllis's. Are you going to bike in, or do you want a ride?"

"I think I'll bike." Quinn crossed the room and reached for the cup. Her eyes met Honor's and, uncertain, she lifted a shoulder. "I'll talk to you later."

Leaning forward, Honor kissed Quinn lightly on the mouth. "Be careful. See you soon."

Honor waited until Quinn had disappeared off the back porch. Then she turned to Phyllis and softly touched her arm. "Are you okay about Quinn?"

"Yes." Phyllis rested her hips against the counter, sipped her coffee, and regarded Honor thoughtfully. She'd seen Honor almost every morning for the last six years. This morning, Honor looked different. Phyllis hadn't realized until just now that she had grown used to the hollowness in Honor's eyes, the emptiness left in the wake of unrelenting pain. Now, something else had taken its place. Something that looked a great deal like happiness. "It wasn't as if I didn't expect it. In fact, I've rather been rooting for it."

"For Quinn to spend the night?" Honor's lips curled into a fond smile as she remembered the pleasure of waking in Quinn's arms. She didn't realize how much that simple smile revealed.

"More than that," Phyllis murmured. *I've been waiting for you to let someone into your heart.*

Honor blinked, caught in the memory. "What? I'm sorry..."

"Nothing." Phyllis laughed and handed Honor an empty coffee mug. "Here. Pour your coffee and get going, or you'll be late. I'm going to make Arly's lunch."

Dutifully, Honor did as she was told. She stopped in the doorway on her way out and turned back, regarding Phyllis tenderly. "I don't know how I would have managed without you. I don't think I could have. I hope my being with Quinn doesn't hurt you."

Phyllis stood in front of the kitchen table with a jar of peanut butter in her hand. She met Honor's gaze steadily. "Does she make you happy?"

For an instant, Honor closed her eyes, afraid of the feelings. Then she opened them and nodded. "Yes. She does."

"Then I'm happy, too."

❖

Linda frowned at the closed curtain in the last patient cubicle at the far end of the hall. She was certain that she hadn't put anyone in that one since it was too small to work in comfortably, and she usually reserved it for overflow or for boarders who were waiting for a bed to open up on a regular floor upstairs. Plus, there were no charts on the rack for that room. She reached for the curtain irritably. The last time she'd checked a supposedly unoccupied cubicle, she'd come upon one of the surgery residents bare-ass naked humping one of her nurses. At the last second, she decided not to fling the barrier open and risk giving the entire ER a show. Pulling the stiff blue material aside a few inches, she peeked into the room. What she saw had her stepping quickly all the way inside.

"Are you all right?"

Grimacing, Quinn looked up from the treatment table upon which she was stretched out, shirtless, trying unsuccessfully to position a series of EKG pads across her own torso. Honor was at an administrative meeting, and Quinn had thought she'd have enough time and privacy to run a twelve-lead EKG and rhythm strip.

"Yes. Fine." Another lead fell off. "Fuck." Casting Linda a desperate glance, she pleaded, "Look, can you help me with this?"

Linda folded her arms over her chest and regarded Quinn solemnly. "It depends."

"On what?"

"Are you going to tell Honor what's going on?"

"What makes you think anything is going on?" Quinn sat up and strapped a leg lead around her ankle. When she did, another of the six pads on her chest became disconnected. She groaned.

"I thought we were friends," Linda said quietly.

"I'm sorry." Quinn blushed. "I don't...want her to know."

"Know what?"

Quinn gestured to her chest and the scar over the implanted defibrillator. "Did she tell you?"

Linda shook her head. "No. But I saw your chest x-ray the day you injured your shoulder. It wasn't her fault. I just walked in on her."

"It doesn't matter. I don't mind that you know." Quinn ran a frustrated hand through her hair. "I need to send a rhythm strip to my cardiologist in Manhattan. Could you help me, please?"

"Are you having any symptoms? Palpitations, light-headedness, shortness of breath, chest pain?"

"No." Quinn saw Linda's look of disbelief. "The defibrillator's been discharging too frequently lately. But I feel fine."

"We can run a diagnostic on the unit and check the settings and voltage levels."

"I already did that. It seems to be working all right. So I thought I'd run a rhythm strip and see if I'm having a lot of irregular beats."

Absently, Linda lifted Quinn's wrist and felt her pulse. It was a maneuver so second-nature to her that she didn't even think about it. "Why don't you want Honor to know?"

Quinn hesitated. "She'll worry."

Linda's eyebrow lifted. "And that would be bad...why?"

"I want to make her happy. I want to put the light back in her eyes." Quinn's expression darkened. "Worrying about my cardiac condition is not going to do that."

As Quinn spoke, Linda lifted a stethoscope from around her neck and placed the auscultation diaphragm on Quinn's chest. "Quiet for a second." After listening for half a minute, she swung her stethoscope back into its usual position and fixed Quinn with an appraising glance. "If she finds out that you have a problem and that you kept it from her, she'll be hurt. That would make me very angry." She held up a hand when Quinn started to protest. "Worse, she'll feel betrayed because she cares for you, and you didn't trust her. That's something *you'll* regret for the rest of your life. Don't be an asshole."

Quinn opened her mouth, then clamped it shut. "I'm a little out of my mind over her. Sometimes, I don't think too clearly, especially when I'm afraid I could blow it. Thanks." She took a long breath, let it out. "I'll tell her."

"Good." Briskly, Linda set about applying the extremity and chest leads with practiced efficiency. Then she turned on the power and watched the trace as the paper scrolled out of the electrocardiogram machine. "Honor looks happy these days. I'd like to see her keep looking that way."

"So would I," Quinn said as Linda pushed the off button.

Linda met Quinn's eyes, and the expression in hers was tender. "Honor is a very brave and very stubborn woman. She won't let you go just because you have a problem. Is that what you're afraid of?"

"She's already lost the woman she loved." Quinn held Linda's gaze. "I wouldn't blame her for not wanting to risk something like that happening again."

"Honor lost *one* woman she loved. This isn't about Terry. It's about you." Linda gave Quinn an affectionate shake of her head. "Honor's with *you* now, Quinn."

"She hasn't said that," Quinn murmured.

"Does she really have to?"

Quinn thought of the myriad ways that Honor touched her every day, physically and emotionally, tenderly and exuberantly and demandingly. With a sigh not of frustration but of peace this time, she said softly, "No. She doesn't."

"Amazing," Linda commented as she removed the leads and handed Quinn her shirt. "A surgeon who is actually capable of listening to reason. We *have* to keep you."

❖

Honor leaned in the doorway of her office while Quinn used the phone to call her cardiologist. She held Quinn's EKG tracing, the one they'd just transmitted to New York, in her hand. It looked normal this time, just as it had the previous ten times she'd studied it.

The minute Quinn hung up, Honor asked, "What did he say?" She kept her voice steady, but her stomach was clenched into a painful knot.

"He doesn't see any problem."

"What about the defibrillator discharges?" She'd been upset when Quinn had told her about the most recent episodes, partly because Quinn had not told her right away, but primarily because it frightened her to realize that Quinn's cardiac condition was still not well stabilized.

"The same thing as he always does." Quinn shrugged. "Could be the threshold setting on the defibrillator is still too low. Could be that I'm having short runs of tachycardia that I'm not aware of."

"You need to go up there to be examined, or you need to get a cardiologist down here." Honor's tone was harsher than she'd intended, but she couldn't seem to maintain her usual professional equanimity.

"I have an appointment with him in three weeks."

Honor's jaw tensed. "Three weeks is a long—"

"He said he thought that would be fine."

"Oh, what the hell does he know? He can't even get your goddamned medication straightened out!"

Quinn heard the sharp edge of fear beneath the anger. Quickly, she crossed the room, took Honor's hand and drew her inside the office, and then closed the door. She gently clasped Honor's waist beneath the white lab coat she wore in the ER. "I'm not having any symptoms. I feel great. And in case you haven't noticed, my heart's been *stressed* quite a bit lately, and it's held up just fine."

Honor rested her palm over Quinn's heart. Her voice was thick when she answered. "I've noticed. I love the way your heart pounds when I make love to you." She raised her eyes to Quinn's. "I don't want to be afraid when I feel that. I don't want..." She looked away, swallowed hard. "I don't want to lose you."

"You *won't.*" Quinn pressed her lips to Honor's forehead. "People live normal lives with this condition. I will, too."

"I know." Honor took a deep breath, consciously stilling the dread that threatened to rise from the shadows of her darkest nightmares and choke her. She drew her fingers down Quinn's face, then kissed her lightly on the mouth. "I know."

"I'm sorry, I'd better get back to work," Quinn said with regret. "I'm waiting on labs for a patient."

"You go ahead. I'll be right out."

"You okay?" Quinn's blue eyes were dark with concern.

Honor forced a smile and nodded. "Fine. I just have to return a couple of calls."

"I'll see you later, then."

"Yes."

When Honor was alone, she leaned back against her office door and closed her eyes. She knew without doubt that she couldn't survive the loss of another lover. Given the choice, she might choose not to care for Quinn. The problem was, she wasn't certain any longer that she still had a choice.

Oh, Quinn. Baby. Do you know what you mean to me?

CHAPTER TWENTY-NINE

Late Friday afternoon, Quinn drew Honor aside in the hallway outside exam room seven, where Honor had just finished ordering a battery of tests and x-rays on a forty-year-old construction worker who had arrived at his job site and discovered that he couldn't remember his name.

"I think we might have a problem," Quinn said in a voice low enough that it wouldn't carry to the surrounding cubicles.

"What is it?"

"I have a twenty-five-year-old graduate student who presented with a two-day history of abdominal pain, nausea, and low-grade fever."

Honor gave Quinn a questioning look, because the symptoms were fairly common and could be almost anything. They probably saw ten cases of nonspecific belly pain every day. "Something unusual about it?"

Quinn nodded. "Her liver is huge and exquisitely tender on exam, so I ran a liver profile. Her enzymes and bilirubin are all elevated. She's got hepatitis."

"Damn."

"That's not all," Quinn said with concern. "If you remember, I saw a guy three days ago with acute hepatitis A. I asked the student where she'd been out to dinner in the last month or so, and then I called the first patient to see if they had some place in common."

"And they do?"

"Yep. The Mexican place over in East Falls." Quinn sighed. "It could be a coincidence; it's a popular restaurant. But I think we need to report this to the public health department and probably the CDC."

"I agree," Honor replied, thinking about the administrative nightmare to come and concluding that she might as well handle it all from the beginning. "I'll do it now. It *might* be absolutely nothing, but if we've got an epidemic in the making, we need to get the appropriate authorities on board as soon as possible."

"Yeah, that's what I thought, too."

Honor glanced at her watch. "Oh, *hell*. This is going to tie me up for God knows how long, and Phyllis has a date tonight. She was going to make dinner for Arly and then leave as soon as I got home." She rubbed the bridge of her nose, thinking fast. "I'll call Robin and Linda. They can watch Arly—"

"I'll be off shift soon. I'll do it."

Honor smiled. "Quinn, you don't need to baby-sit. I appreciate it—"

"I want to." Quinn's tone was even and firm, but her smile soft. "Please."

"If you're sure," Honor said, still uncertain. Even though Arly loved to spend time with Quinn, it seemed like such an imposition. She and Quinn were dating, that was true. But this—this simple act of shared responsibility spoke of something far more intimate. *Dating. This is nice, what we have now. It doesn't have to be more. But it already is, isn't it?*

Quinn watched the internal struggle that Honor thought she couldn't see. It seemed that each time something drew them closer, causing their lives to become more inextricably entwined, Honor resisted. Even though Quinn understood Honor's hesitation, each time she witnessed it, each time she felt Honor put distance between them, her frustration grew. "Honor, for God's sake, when are you going to let me in?"

"Don't you think I *have*?" Honor's words were out before she had time to censor them. She glanced over her shoulder, checking to see that they were still alone. In a low voice, she continued, "Do you know what it took for me to be with you? To touch you? To care about you?"

"*Yes,* I know." Quinn wanted to take her hand, but she couldn't, not only because of where they were, but because it wasn't comfort Honor needed. And it wasn't what Quinn needed to give. They both needed the truth. "I love you. Don't *you* know that by now?"

Honor's mouth opened, and she blinked wordlessly. Then she slowly smiled. "You certainly can pick your moments, Dr. Maguire."

"That wasn't how I intended to say it the first time." Quinn grinned and shrugged. "You have a way of upsetting my timing."

"Really?" Honor's voice grew throaty. "I never noticed that. I've always found your timing...exquisite."

As it never failed to do, the suggestion in Honor's tone brought a rush of heat into the pit of Quinn's stomach. She drew a shaky breath and laughed quietly. "You're trying to change the subject."

"Not exactly." Honor drifted her fingers fleetingly over the top of Quinn's hand. "What you said...I felt it inside." *In my heart, in my body.* She met Quinn's eyes. "I don't know what to say. I don't think I can say anything right now."

Quinn nodded, just happy for the moment that Honor had not tried to object to Quinn's feelings. "That's okay. That's not why I said it."

"Why did you?"

"Because it's true," Quinn said softly. "And because it feels so good to say."

"I wish we were alone right now, anywhere but here." Honor's eyes shimmered with tenderness and desire.

"Me, too." Quinn's voice was rough edged with the effort it took not to touch her.

"It would be wonderful if you could take care of Arly tonight. Thank you." Honor sighed regretfully and stepped back a pace. "I need to get started with these reports. I'll call you at the house later when I know where I am."

"I'm going to get the student admitted, and then I'll head over to your place."

"Thank you." When Quinn started to turn away, Honor caught her arm. She smiled into Quinn's eyes. "It matters. What you said."

"Yeah. It does," Quinn murmured. "See you at the house."

❖

"This is really very kind of you, Quinn," Phyllis said as she hastily gathered her things to leave.

"I don't mind," Quinn replied, leaning against the table in Honor's kitchen. "It'll be fun."

"I could stay and make dinner for the two of you—"

"No, you go ahead," Quinn insisted gently. "We'll be fine."

Arly rushed into the room, her face shining. She held out her hands. "I'm clean. Where are we going for dinner, Quinn?"

"Where would you like to go?"

"McDonald's."

Quinn gave Phyllis a questioning look. At Phyllis's nod of assent, Quinn replied, "Sure. There's one over on Chelten Avenue. We'll take a walk, okay?"

"And then you're going to stay here with me until my mom gets home, right?"

"Right. We'll stop and get a video and watch a movie."

"Are you going to stay overnight, like Grandmom does sometimes?"

"Uh..." Quinn wondered when she was going to remember that Arly was a contingency planner. She also revised her opinion of Arly's future career path. It was beginning to look more like she'd end up as the chair of the Joint Chiefs of Staff.

"Maybe if Mom is late getting home," Phyllis suggested mildly, "Quinn will stay for a sleepover."

Arly's eyes lit up. "Cool. And we can all have breakfast together." She looked at her grandmother. "Right?"

"Right." Phyllis laughed and tousled Arly's hair. "Now I have to go. You and Quinn have fun tonight."

Quinn gave Phyllis a grateful look, not just for handling the issue of her spending the night so painlessly, but for welcoming her into the family. "Thank you."

"No need for thanks," Phyllis said on her way out the door. "It's time."

I hope so. Quinn reached down for Arly's hand. "Come on, Arls, let's go find us some dinner."

❖

Tired beyond words, Honor quietly let herself into her house through the back door. The kitchen was dark and the hallway beyond blue-gray with reflected light from the living room television. She deposited her briefcase on the table, made her way to the refrigerator, and quietly foraged for a beer. She found a lone can of Heineken on the bottom shelf, popped the tab, and took a grateful swallow. Then she headed toward the sound of an oddly familiar voice that, as she drew closer, began to resemble Ellen DeGeneres talking underwater.

When she reached the door to the living room, she realized that it *was* Ellen DeGeneres. Or, rather, the animated fish version of her in *Finding Nemo*. Quinn was slumped in the corner of the couch, her head resting against the back, eyes closed. Arly, in her dinosaur pajama bottoms and a mismatched top covered with soccer balls, was curled against Quinn's side, fast asleep. Honor couldn't decide which of them was the more beautiful.

She braced her back against the door frame, sipped her beer, and idly watched the movie. As the tension drained from her body, she felt nothing but a pleasant sense of well-being. She glanced back at Quinn and smiled when she found the deep blue eyes on her. She walked to the couch, leaned over the back, and kissed Quinn softly on the mouth. "Hi."

"Hi," Quinn murmured. She glanced down at the sleeping child, then back up at Honor. "We can probably make some room for you down here with us."

"Mmm." Honor folded her arms on the top of the couch and rested her chin on them. "It sounds tempting, but I'd either fall asleep too, or else I'd get ideas."

"Ideas?" Quinn's eyebrows rose as her voice dropped a register.

Honor smiled slowly and nodded. "In fact, I'm getting *ideas* right now."

"Okaay." Quinn shifted Arly into her arms and stood, cradling the child against her shoulder. "That decision's made. I'll take her up to bed."

"Right behind you."

When Quinn deposited Arly in bed, the child woke for a second, smiled at her mother, then immediately turned over and went back to sleep. Honor took Quinn's hand and together they walked toward the bedroom.

"How are you doing?" Quinn asked gently. "You look beat."

"I am." Honor sighed. "You know the routine. Lots of forms, lots of phone calls, lots of repeating myself with everyone in the chain of command. It turns out that Temple has two cases as well. It looks like we're going to be seeing a lot more before the incubation period is over."

"That's not good news."

"No," Honor agreed as she settled onto the side of the bed. "But you did a good job of picking up on these early cases."

Quinn leaned down and lifted Honor's foot, slipped off her shoe, and then reached for the other foot. "Thanks." Then she opened Honor's slacks and slid down the zipper. Grasping the waistband, she said, "Lift up and let me get these off."

"You're spoiling me," Honor murmured, leaning to one side to set her beer can down on the bedside table.

"I'm trying to."

Honor rested back on her elbows and watched Quinn undress her. It was comforting and exciting at the same time. "Are pajamas next?"

With a crooked grin, Quinn looked up from her task of unbuttoning Honor's blouse. "I guess you noticed that Arly and I had a hard time finding matching tops and bottoms. Finally we decided that it was more interesting to mix them up." As she spoke, she slid the blouse off Honor's shoulders and down first one arm, then the other.

"Yes. Very cute, and I'm sure that will be her favorite look from now on." Honor reclined in only her bra and silk bikinis, and when Quinn reached around her to smooth a palm over her back, she closed her eyes. "God, this is nice."

"Yes, it is." Quinn's stomach tightened as her gaze followed the arch of Honor's neck. When Honor's head dropped back and a low groan escaped her, Quinn carefully released the clasp on Honor's bra and drew it off. Reverently, she whispered, "You're so beautiful."

Honor's lips parted slightly in a lazy smile as she observed Quinn through half-opened lids. "I don't think I've ever been so relaxed and so hot at the same time in my life."

Quinn knelt between Honor's thighs by the side of the bed and rested her cheek against Honor's stomach. With one hand, she cradled Honor's breast, running her fingertips over the small hard nipple. Honor's heart fluttered beneath her face and her own raced in time with it. "I love you."

Wordlessly, Honor stroked Quinn's face and neck, pressing Quinn more tightly to her body. The fingers on her breast stirred her flesh, but Quinn's tender attentions and gentle words fired her passion. For long moments, she luxuriated in the simple pleasure of Quinn's body against hers. "You make me feel so wonderful."

Nearly drunk on the sight and sound and scent of her, Quinn pushed upright and braced herself with one hand against the mattress. She glanced down to the damp silk between Honor's thighs, then brought her palm to cover the small triangle of fabric. Honor arched against her and sighed.

"I love you." Quinn drew the thin barrier aside and slid smoothly into Honor's depths, watching Honor's face as she filled her.

"Oh...you feel so good." Dazed, Honor kept her eyes on Quinn's as her hips slowly lifted and fell to the steady cadence of Quinn's strokes. Before long, she felt the orgasm unfurl along her spine, hot and feathery. "Oh, yes. Like that, Quinn. Like that."

Quinn gripped the sheets in her fist, concentrating fiercely to contain her own wild need to go faster, deeper, harder. Distantly, she was aware of her own excitement, a hard ache rising on the crest of Honor's pleasure. Her breath came in shallow gasps, echoing Honor's rasping pants. Her muscles trembled as Honor's closed around her fingers.

"Baby, I'm coming. I'm coming." Honor arched her back and pushed down hard against Quinn's hand. The added pressure triggered the climax that had hovered teasingly, just beyond her reach. With a cry, she reared up, wrapping her arms around Quinn's shoulders. She buried her face in the curve of Quinn's neck, wracked with tremors.

"Oh yeah," Quinn moaned, pressing her face to Honor's shoulder, holding her close with one arm as the other gentled between her thighs. As Honor quieted in her embrace, moaning softly with contentment, Quinn let out a long shaky sigh. "Sometimes when I'm that close to you, I feel like my heart will burst. It's a good feeling."

Honor brought trembling hands to Quinn's face and lifted her head until she could look into her eyes. "You touch me. You touch me in ways I've never been touched."

"That's all I want."

Honor closed her eyes and rested her forehead on Quinn's. "That's everything."

❖

The ringing phone awakened them at just after five.

"Blake," Honor grumbled into the receiver. Quinn stirred beside her, and Honor drew her close. "Uh-huh. Uh-huh. Okay. Right." She fumbled the phone back onto the base and groaned. "The team from the CDC just arrived at the airport from Atlanta and will be in the ER in forty-five minutes."

Quinn opened her eyes and stared at the ceiling. "I guess there's not enough time to hire a band."

"No, probably not." Honor laughed. "I guess *I'll* have to do as the reception committee."

"I'll come in with you." Quinn sat up and pushed the covers back. She was tired, but it was only from lack of sleep. The weariness that had plagued her soul for so long had lifted.

"You don't have to, baby." Honor ran her fingers down Quinn's back. "I'm sorry I fell asleep last night."

"No need to be." Grinning an altogether satisfied grin, Quinn glanced over her shoulder at her lover. "It made me feel like a superstar."

"Oh, you are," Honor purred as she wrapped both arms around Quinn from behind and lay her cheek against Quinn's back. "Still, I want to please you the way you please me."

"As fabulous as you make me feel, if I could only have one thing, I'd rather touch you."

"Mmm." Honor moved her lips indolently over the edge of Quinn's shoulder blade as she caressed her palm over Quinn's stomach. "Me, too. That's something of a conundrum, isn't it?"

Quinn guided Honor's fingers down her belly and between her thighs. She stiffened at the first electric contact and heard Honor gasp in surprise. Quinn's voice was husky as she said, "Should be interesting solving that particular problem." She covered Honor's hand with her own and pressed hard, hard enough to make her body twitch and her vision dim. Then she shifted her hips and rose abruptly, breaking Honor's startled grip. "Guess it'll have to wait, though."

"You..." Honor sputtered indignantly. "I can't believe you did that!"

Quinn grinned. "Just wanted to give you something to think about today."

Honor came off the bed so quickly that it was Quinn's turn to jump. "I'm going to make you pay for that, Maguire."

"Promises, promises," Quinn laughed, making a quick dash for the adjoining bathroom.

"Later," Honor muttered, gathering their clothes from the floor. "You'll get yours later." Smiling, she followed Quinn. "And so will I."

CHAPTER THIRTY

Almost a week passed before Honor had even a moment to consider making good on her threat. During that time, she worked eighteen hours a day and admitted thirty-two more patients with acute hepatitis. Close to three hundred new cases were diagnosed in the greater Philadelphia area. Unfortunately, there were also two deaths.

At the height of the outbreak, the CDC epidemiology team interviewed patients, constructed demographic charts, and investigated dozens of potential sources of the contagion. Honor was constantly on call, interfacing with her own emergency room physicians as well as the out-of-town consultants. She and Quinn saw each other in passing at work, but by the time Honor got home, there was barely enough time to sleep before she needed to be back at work.

By Friday evening, the number of new cases had dwindled, and it appeared that the source of the infection—a contaminated delivery of scallions from Mexico—had been identified. With the crisis waning, Honor was able to leave the hospital by seven p.m., and the first thing she did when she walked out the ER doors was to punch in Quinn's number on her cell phone.

"Hello?" Quinn said.

Honor smiled just to hear the sound of her voice. "It's me. Are you free?"

"Well, not really."

"Oh." Honor worked to hide her disappointment as she fumbled her keys from her briefcase and leaned to open the door of her car. "Well, then..."

"Hold on a second."

A new voice came on the line.

"Mom? Are you on your way home now?"

"Honey? What's going on? Where are you two?" Honor slid into the front seat of her car and tossed her briefcase beside her. She hadn't seen Arly all week, because her daughter had been asleep by the time she'd gotten home. As far as she knew, Arly should have been with Phyllis.

"Home. Quinn and I are making pizza."

"You are?" Quickly, Honor dispelled the image of pizza sauce all over her kitchen. "Is there enough for me?"

Honor heard a giggle followed by mumbling, but she could not make out the words. She keyed the ignition and started to drive as Arly came back on the line.

"Quinn says it'll be ready in twenty-five minutes. But we're awfully hungry."

"Well, you tell Quinn that I'll be there in five, and I'm hungry, too."

Arly laughed. "'Kay, Mom. We'll share with you."

❖

Quinn waited on the back stairs. When Honor pulled into the driveway, she walked around to the driver's side door, opened it, and leaned in to kiss Honor. "Hi. Dinner will be ready soon."

"This is a nice surprise." Honor grasped her briefcase and slid out.

"You haven't seen the kitchen yet."

"No, but I can imagine." Honor smiled and wrapped an arm around Quinn's waist as they walked toward the house. "I'll just have to keep my eyes on you."

"The chef's upstairs getting ready for a bath," Quinn informed her. "I thought that would be smart before you saw *her*."

"Where's Phyllis?"

"Another hot date." Quinn brushed her lips over Honor's temple. "And don't even think about thanking me. I missed Arly this week. I missed you." *Every second.*

Honor dropped her briefcase at the bottom of the back stairs, turned to Quinn, and put both arms around her neck. She pressed against her and kissed her lingeringly. She kissed her until she could feel her in every cell. "I missed you, too."

"Oh, yeah." Quinn sighed contentedly, then reluctantly backed away. "I'd better get upstairs and give Arly a hand with her bath."

"Let me change, and I'll help."

They linked hands and climbed the stairs together.

❖

"Mom," Arly said over pancakes and bacon the next morning, "are you and Quinn going to live together soon?"

"That's a very important decision, sweetie, and Quinn and I haven't really talked about it yet." Honor glanced at Quinn across the table. This was the first time that Quinn had spent the night and been there the next morning when Arly got up. The three of them had made breakfast together, and Arly had seemed to take it all in stride. Phyllis, interestingly, had called to say she would be "detained." "How would *you* feel about that?"

"I think it would be cool. Then I'd have two moms like Kim and Denny, right?" Arly looked from Quinn to Honor expectantly.

Quinn cleared her throat. "Remember when I told you that we would tell you as soon as we could?"

"Uh-huh."

"Well, it really helps to know that it would be okay with you if we wanted to do that," Quinn said carefully, looking from Arly to Honor. "But your mom and I need some more time to think about it. So we need you to be patient, okay?"

"Okay." Arly finished the last of her orange juice. "How long do I have to be patient?'"

Quinn smiled. "Well, sometimes you have to wait until just the right time, like when you don't kick on goal until you see the perfect opening and you *know* it will go in."

Arly nodded seriously and then looked at her mother. "You're coming to the game today, right?"

"I'll be there." Honor smiled as her daughter ran from the room to gather her gear. She sighed and glanced at Quinn with a wry expression. "Sorry. I have a feeling we're going to hear these questions again."

"Do they bother you?" Quinn asked quietly. She was very aware of the fact that Honor had consistently avoided the discussion of any kind of commitment. She wanted to be part of Honor's life, and it took every ounce of willpower not to push.

"No," Honor said softly. "They don't bother me. What about you? My life is a bit complicated."

Quinn had to smile. "You mean because of Arly?"

"Among other things."

"She's terrific. I...I'd love to be a part of her life." Quinn met Honor's gaze. "And yours."

"God, you're better than a dream come true." Honor reached across the table and stroked Quinn's cheek. "I hope you know I care. Can *you* be patient a little longer?"

Quinn turned her head and kissed Honor's palm. "I've probably got just a *little* more willpower than a seven-year-old." When Honor laughed, Quinn added, "But not much."

"Mmm, I seem to remember you weren't all that patient last night."

"That was different," Quinn replied, leaning forward to kiss Honor on the lips. "I hadn't seen you all week. Of course I couldn't wait."

Honor's blood ran a little hotter just thinking about the relentless demands of Quinn's mouth and hands and... She shivered and pushed back from the table. "I have to get away from you. You do...things...to me. Scary, wonderful things."

Quinn laughed as Honor walked away. "You can run, but you can't hide."

Honor stopped in the doorway and regarded Quinn tenderly. "I think I'm done with both. Now, I'm going to shower and get ready for the game."

Heart pounding, Quinn watched her go. *I love you.*

❖

"I saw you, Quinn, and Arly leave the house together this morning," Linda said as she sidled up to Honor on the sideline.

"Uh-huh."

"The three of you looked cute together."

Honor turned and gave Linda a piercing glare. "Whatever it is you want to know, just ask so I can watch the game."

"Okay," Linda said accommodatingly. "How serious are the two of you? Is she wonderful in bed? Has she told you yet that she loves you?"

"I don't know. Definitely." Honor hesitated and glanced at Quinn, who stood only yards away, her attention riveted on her young players. "Yes, she's told me."

"It sounds like things are very serious, then." Linda's tone was serious as well. "Do you love her?"

"I—" Honor broke off as Quinn turned to her with a stunned expression on her face. She saw Quinn press her right hand to the center of her chest just before she collapsed abruptly to the ground. Even as she started to run, Honor snapped to Linda, "Call 911 and keep the kids away from here."

In less than five seconds, Honor was kneeling on the ground by Quinn's side. Quinn lay motionless on her back, eyes closed. When Honor pressed two fingers to the carotid artery on the right side of Quinn's neck, her stomach seized, and for an instant, her mind went completely blank. She couldn't feel a pulse. Then, with instinct born of years of training and motivated by a resolve that burned through her with white-hot fury, she brought her closed fist down sharply in the center of Quinn's chest. *You will not die. I will not lose you. God damn you, you will not do this to me.*

Just as Honor, preparing to start CPR, pressed both hands to the center of Quinn's sternum, Quinn's eyes fluttered open. The breath stopped in Honor's chest as unfocused blue eyes met hers.

"Honor?"

"It's all right, baby. You're all right." Honor, almost weak with fear and relief, fought desperately to keep her voice steady. "Just lie still."

"What happened?" Quinn tried to push up on her elbows but found that she was light-headed. "I'm a little dizzy."

"I know." Honor wrapped her fingers around Quinn's wrist, enormously comforted by the strong, steady pulse. "You fainted. We need to take you to the hospital so I can evaluate the situation."

She didn't see any point in telling Quinn that she'd had a cardiac arrest. It had been a brief episode that had responded immediately to the "cardiac thump," and in all likelihood, no heart muscle damage had been sustained. Still, the danger remained that she'd have another arrhythmia that Honor would not be able to convert so easily again. She needed to get Quinn into the EMS van where she would have a defibrillator at hand.

"I think I'm okay," Quinn said quietly, slowly realizing what must have transpired. Honor was white as a sheet and her eyes were huge, all pupil. *God, please, don't let me lose everything now. Not now.* "Sweetheart, I'm okay."

"You seem to be, but I still need to run some tests." Honor brushed her fingers over Quinn's forehead but kept one hand on her shoulder to prevent her from trying to rise again. "Baby, please don't argue."

"No," Quinn replied, catching Honor's hand and holding it firmly. "I won't. Can I see Arly before we go? Or do you think it would be better not to let her see me now?"

The sound of the siren grew nearer. Honor glanced around and saw that a ring of adults had enclosed them, keeping everyone else away. Linda stood nearby, her attention on Honor and Quinn.

"I'll get her if you promise not to move." When Quinn nodded her assent, Honor motioned to Linda. "Will you stay with her while I get Arly?"

"Sure." Linda took Honor's place and automatically grasped Quinn's wrist. "How you doing, honey?"

"I'm all right." Quinn turned her head and tried to follow Honor's movement through the crowd. "Listen, will you take care of Honor? Just in case I have another problem. She shouldn't be the one running a code if this goddamn defibrillator misfires again."

"She's not going to let anyone else take care of you," Linda said quietly. "You'll both be fine. Now here comes Arly, so look sharp."

"Quinn? Are you sick?" Arly hunkered down next to Quinn between her mother and Linda. Her expression was concerned, but she wasn't afraid, because her mother had told her not to be.

Quinn shook her head. "I didn't feel very good a few minutes ago, but I feel much better now. Your mom wants me to go to the hospital so she can check me out. So we're going to go for a ride in one of the medical vans, okay?"

Arly nodded intently and glanced at her mother. "Can I come?"

Honor rested her hand on her daughter's back. "I'm going to be busy for a while taking care of Quinn. Linda will bring you over later, I promise."

"Okay."

Quinn patted Arly's knee. "I think you should get back to the game now. I'll see you in a little while."

"Come on, honey," Linda said, taking the child's hand. "Robin is going to need you back on the field."

"Is she going to be okay?" Quinn asked as Arly disappeared.

Honor nodded, waving the EMTs over. "Yes. She understands that I'm a doctor, and she trusts that I'll take care of things. She'll be fine as long as she can see you later."

"Good," Quinn said with a sigh and closed her eyes. "I'm sorry about this."

"Don't ever say that to me again." The words were delivered gently, but when she stood and addressed the first EMT on the scene, her command tone was in evidence. "I'm Dr. Blake. We need transport to PMC. She has an unstable arrhythmia and needs to be monitored all the way."

"Yes, ma'am," the technician said as he and his partner started an IV in Quinn's arm and attached EKG leads to her chest.

While holding Quinn's hand, Honor observed everything the EMTs did, even though she knew they were well trained to handle that kind of emergency. She walked alongside the stretcher and climbed into the back of the van, and, despite her anxiety, she allowed them to do their job as they traveled the short distance to the hospital. Once in the ER, she directed members of her staff to get the equipment she needed as the EMTs wheeled Quinn through the hall to the procedure room.

As was so often the case after the event was over, by the time Quinn was settled onto the exam table, she felt close to normal. The IV that the EMTs had started was taped to her right arm. Her shirt was off and EKG leads were spread across her chest. The portable monitor by her bedside beeped with comforting regularity, and the tracing appeared normal. But just as Honor walked into the room, the EKG monitor gave a series of rapid beats, and Quinn felt a fluttering sensation in her chest. The same flutter that had preceded her collapse at the field. Both she and Honor stared at the monitor. Several misplaced beats skittered across the screen, and then the steady pattern returned.

"Something's wrong, Quinn," Honor said quietly, a rhythm strip from the electrocardiogram in her hand. "And I'm not so certain it's your heart. You *are* having irregular beats, but they look almost as if the defibrillator and not your cardiac muscle is triggering them. I think you're going to need the device replaced."

"It certainly malfunctioned this afternoon." Quinn took a deep breath and met Honor's troubled gaze. "I felt the run of V-tach, and I could tell the defibrillator didn't fire. I only had a few seconds before..." *Before I went out.* She shivered. "It didn't pace me."

"I know, baby." Honor reached for Quinn's hand and squeezed it gently. "But you're being monitored now, and we'll keep monitoring you until we get this fixed." Then she said what she knew Quinn wouldn't want to hear. "I want to admit you to a telemetry floor until I can get one of the cardiac surgeons in to see you."

"I'd rather go back to Manhattan and let my cardiologist there deal with it."

"I understand, but you're too unstable to travel." Just saying the words was enough to bring a surge of nausea roiling through Honor's stomach. Now that the immediate crisis was over, she couldn't prevent the enormity of what had nearly happened from penetrating her consciousness. *She almost died. I almost lost her out there.*

"I don't intend to lose you, Quinn," Honor said quietly. "I love you."

"You certainly can pick your moments, Dr. Blake." Quinn's voice was gentle, her eyes soft with longing.

Honor bit her lip, suddenly terribly afraid that she would cry. She swallowed and forced a smile. "You tend to disrupt my timing."

"Would you agree to me going to Manhattan if I went by ambulance?" Quinn took a deep breath, wishing she didn't have to explain. "If they need to reposition the leads, it's going to be tricky. They had problems with that the first time."

"What kind of problems?" Honor's voice was flat, her eyes betraying none of her apprehension.

"They triggered a run of V-fib and I...ah, Christ...I arrested during the procedure."

"I see." Refusing to allow the horror of that statement to penetrate her consciousness, Honor calculated the options. The period when Quinn might suffer a potentially fatal arrhythmia was the time up to and *including* the surgery. "All right. I'll call your cardiologist now and find out if he can line up the surgeons for you right away. *If* he can, we'll transport you this afternoon. But if he can't, and there's going to be any kind of delay, we're not waiting."

"Agreed." Before Honor could turn away, Quinn grasped her hand. "I love you, Honor. I love you, and I love Arly. It's going to be okay."

Honor leaned down and kissed Quinn tenderly on the mouth. When she drew away, she whispered, "I love you. And we're going to get through this."

CHAPTER THIRTY-ONE

"ETA—five minutes."

Leaning against the partition separating the driver's space from the treatment area in the EMS truck, Honor nodded wearily. "Thanks."

Quinn was beside her, lying on the narrow portable stretcher, EKG leads still attached. She'd slept through most of the ninety-minute ride.

"Honey?" Honor brushed a hand over Quinn's hair. "We're nearly there."

"Yeah, I heard him." Quinn turned to search her lover's face. "Once I get settled, you can go ho—"

"We've already had this conversation," Honor said gently. "I'm not leaving you. If they do the procedure this afternoon, *we'll* be able to go home tomorrow. Arly's fine with Phyllis for one night."

"I know that, I just thought..." *I just thought it would be easier on you if you didn't have to wait in the hospital. You've got to be thinking about Terry now.*

Honor leaned close so that the EMT, who was strapped into the small pull-down seat at the other end of the van, wouldn't hear them. Her voice was a whisper of steel. "What did you think, Quinn, when you made it impossible for me *not* to fall in love with you? Did you think that I would leave the first time we ran into a problem? Any kind of problem?"

Quinn opened her mouth to answer, but it was a full minute before she actually spoke. "I wanted you so much that I refused to think about what might happen if...this happened." She looked stricken. "That wasn't very fair, was it?"

"Oh, Quinn," Honor said with a sigh and an affectionate shake of her head. "*Fair* has nothing to do with it. Life isn't fair. Love isn't fair." She traced her fingers over Quinn's cheek. "But when love is good, it's everything. And I love you."

"I love you, too." Quinn reached for Honor's hand and held tightly. She was scared. Less scared of dying than she'd ever been, but more frightened than she'd imagined possible at the thought of not having the chance to live her life with Honor. "And I'm very glad you're here."

"Good. Then stop trying to get rid of me."

The ambulance slowed and had barely come to a halt before the rear double doors opened. Honor was surprised when a lean, dark-haired woman in navy blue scrubs climbed into the van, ignoring the EMT, and crouched down by Quinn's side.

"Christ, Maguire. What have you gotten yourself into now?"

Then the woman reached out to the portable EKG machine and pushed a button. After twenty seconds, she tore off the rhythm strip that had scrolled from the machine and glanced at it. "This doesn't look bad enough to call out the troops. Getting soft in that cushy new job of yours?"

"Excuse me," Honor said coldly. "But I think it might be prudent to move Dr. Maguire into the emergency room where she can be properly monitored."

The newcomer gave Honor an appraising stare and a raised eyebrow. Honor returned the stare while a muscle jumped along the edge of her jaw.

Before fireworks could erupt, Quinn made hasty introductions. "Dr. Saxon Sinclair, Dr. Honor Blake, the chief of emergency services at PMC. Honor is—"

"Her lover," Honor said succinctly. She leaned around Quinn's previous chief and said to the technician, "Let's move her, shall we."

"It's a pleasure, Dr. Blake." Sax gave Quinn an approving grin and got out of the way.

"Take her into the trauma bay, guys," Sax instructed as the group proceeded toward the hospital. She glanced at Quinn. "When Caroli called and said you were on your way up, I got Wisnicki on the phone. He's waiting upstairs in the OR in case it looks like that pacer has to be changed."

"Is that the cardiac surgeon?" Honor took rapid stock of Saxon Sinclair. In many ways, she resembled Quinn. They were both dark haired, blue eyed, and aggressively good looking, and both had that classic surgical air of competence bordering on arrogance. Sinclair was fundamentally different from Quinn, however. The first thing Honor remembered noticing about Quinn was the unusual core of tranquility beneath her assertive exterior. It was one of the things she loved about her, that calm, steady certainty. In contrast, Sinclair radiated so much electricity that Honor was surprised her skin wasn't tingling. The air around the surgeon seemed to vibrate with the force of her energy. "He's the best you have?"

"He's the best on the East Coast." Sax led the way into her trauma unit and supervised Quinn's transfer to the examining table. A blond man in scrubs appeared at her side. "Aaron, draw the routine bloods on her and let's get a chest x-ray stat. I had her old films brought down for comparison. Put those up on the view box for me as soon as you get a chance, will you?"

"Sure, Doc."

"I have her records from Philadelphia with me," Honor said, handing the oversized envelope to the trauma surgeon.

"Thanks." Sax favored her with a grin. "What's your assessment?"

"Anybody interested in my opinion?" Quinn asked, leaning up on her elbows on the stretcher.

Honor and Sax turned and spoke as one. "No. Just lie still."

The two women looked at each other and laughed.

"Perfect," Quinn grumbled. But, relieved to see that the woman she loved and the woman she respected unconditionally appeared to be getting along, she relaxed and settled back down.

"Let me show you the traces we have from this afternoon and a few weeks ago," Honor said, walking to the counter against the far wall that served as a desk.

While Honor and Sax talked, Dr. Caroli, Quinn's cardiologist, arrived. The three doctors reviewed the serial EKGs as well as the chest x-rays, and eventually, Honor returned to Quinn's side.

"Your cardiologist thinks that the leads are out of position," Honor said quietly. She took Quinn's hand and held it gently. "So do I. Probably from that fall you took the day you injured your shoulder. He wants to reposition the leads and change the battery unit, too, just to be safe."

Quinn closed her eyes for a second, then took a deep breath. When she met Honor's gaze, her expression was resolute. "Okay. Sounds like a plan. When?"

At that moment, Sax walked up to the bed. "Now. I thought I'd give Wisnicki a hand. Keep him honest."

"Probably not a bad idea," Quinn said, a rush of gratitude causing her to choke slightly on the words. She cleared her throat. "He's probably in a rush to get back to the golf course. With you watching, he's not as likely to forget to attach something important."

"Not to worry." Sax grinned and squeezed Quinn's shoulder. "Besides, if he's too slow, I'll do it myself so you won't miss dinner tonight."

Honor watched the trauma surgeon saunter out, then looked at Quinn with some concern. "She won't really take over the case, will she?"

Quinn hesitated.

"Oh, for God's sake," Honor muttered. "I don't know how you turned out so sane being trained by that maniac." Nevertheless, she felt strangely comforted by Saxon Sinclair's presence. She could feel the woman's love for Quinn, and that was all she needed to know. Quinn would be taken care of when Honor couldn't be there to do it herself.

"You ready to go, Quinn?" Aaron, the trauma nurse, asked.

Honor helped gather up Quinn's records and walked beside the stretcher with her hand on Quinn's shoulder as Aaron directed the moving bed unerringly through hallways resembling obstacle courses toward the elevator.

"Hey!" a lithe, strikingly attractive redhead called as she hurried down the hall toward them. Breathless, she skidded to a stop beside the stretcher, leaned down, and kissed Quinn soundly on the mouth. "God, I thought I'd missed you. How're you doing, sweetheart?"

"I'm fine." Quinn grinned. "It's not that serious. The medical people are just fussing."

Honor made a sound resembling a growl.

Quinn reached for Honor's hand and smiled. "Honor, this is Jude Castle, Sax's partner. Jude, Honor Blake."

Honor extended her hand as they all crowded into the elevator. "Pleased to meet you."

Jude took Honor's hand and tilted her head pensively. "You came up with Quinn from Philadelphia?"

"Yes." Honor smiled down at Quinn. "She seems to have stolen *my* heart."

"Wonderful," Jude exclaimed as the elevator doors opened. She turned at the sound of someone calling her name, and her eyes took on a warm, tender glow. "Hello, Dr. Sinclair."

Honor wouldn't have believed it if she hadn't witnessed it: a fleeting stillness came over the hyperdynamic Saxon Sinclair as she looked at Jude Castle, and an expression of deep peace eclipsed her features. Then Sinclair grinned, and the spell dissolved.

"I'm glad you made it," Sax said to Jude, brushing her fingers over Jude's shoulder and down her back. Then she turned her attention to her former trauma fellow. "We're all set, Quinn. Time to saddle up."

"Just a second," Quinn replied. She tugged Honor's hand and drew her close. "This isn't a big deal. I'll be fine. I love you."

Honor kissed Quinn firmly, then brought her mouth close to Quinn's ear. "You have to be fine, Quinn. Arly and I love you. And we need you." She straightened and brushed her fingers through Quinn's hair tenderly. "I'll see you in a little while, baby."

"Yeah," Quinn said through a throat tight with longing. "See you soon."

Then Saxon Sinclair took hold of the side of the stretcher and pulled it toward the automatic doors that opened into the operating room on the other side. Honor watched until the doors slowly swung closed and Quinn was gone.

"Can I get you anything? Something to eat or a cup of coffee?" Jude Castle offered.

Honor smiled wearily and shook her head. "No, thanks." She glanced at her watch and saw with amazement that it was after six p.m. She hadn't had anything to eat since breakfast, but she wasn't hungry. Quinn had been gone just over an hour.

"Wisnicki is apparently a fabulous surgeon, and Sax is with him. Believe me, she won't let anything happen to Quinn," Jude said softly.

"Dr. Sinclair does seem to inspire confidence," Honor remarked wryly. *When she isn't being completely aggravating.*

Jude smiled this time, a fond, indulgent smile. "She's actually as good as she thinks she is."

"Right now, that's very encouraging to hear, although you *might* be just a little bit prejudiced."

"I might be, if I hadn't spent a year watching her work. I'm crazy in love with her, but I'm not exaggerating about her skill."

"I saw some of the documentary that you filmed here. It was very good work." Honor found that the distraction of casual conversation helped her *almost* ignore the undercurrent of fear that rippled and swelled with each breath. She hated that Quinn was somewhere she couldn't see her. Couldn't take care of her. She knew it was irrational, but she couldn't bear to think that Quinn might slip away, and she might not be there to stop it. She shivered. *I couldn't bear to lose you. I just couldn't.*

"Thanks." Jude wanted to do something to comfort the other woman, because it was impossible not to see her pain and fear. "You're Quinn's boss, aren't you?"

"Technically, yes, but I'd say that we're more colleagues than anything else." Honor glanced toward the operating room doors as if Quinn might walk through them at any moment. Her voice was distant. "Other than lovers. God, I hate this."

"Is there anything I can do?"

Honor gave the redhead an appreciative glance. "It helps that you're here to keep me company. I could tell that Quinn was glad to see you, too."

"We're both very fond of her. Sax always has terrific fellows, but Quinn is special. I was very sorry that she couldn't stay..." Jude laughed softly. "But it seems that it's worked out for the best. I'm so happy that the two of you are together."

"Yes. So am I."

"I'm sure she's—" Jude looked up as the doors whooshed open and Sax strode out.

Honor got immediately to her feet and took two steps forward, her eyes riveted to Sax's face. There was nothing else in the world except Saxon Sinclair's eyes, steady and strong and sure.

"Is she—"

"Fine. She's fine." Sax's voice was as certain as her expression. She took Honor's arm, cupping her hand beneath Honor's elbow. "Come over here so I can fill you in."

Unexpectedly, Honor was light-headed. Her knees were weak, and she leaned slightly against the surgeon, grateful for the firm hand to support her. "She's awake? Her heart?"

"Sit down," Sax repeated gently, guiding Honor to one of the well-worn chairs in the waiting area. Once Honor was settled, Sax pulled over another chair so that they were eye to eye. "Wisnicki replaced the leads and the battery pack. No problems. But I've got even better news."

In that moment, Honor was no longer a doctor, merely a terrified loved one who needed reassurance and the belief that this doctor would somehow answer her prayers. She couldn't take her eyes from Sax's.

"Since Quinn was being monitored and we could handle any arrhythmias that might come up, the cardiologist did an electrical mapping. Her heart's much better than it was six months ago. The focus of irritability is very small."

Honor closed her eyes and lowered her head. "Oh, thank God."

Sax looked across the room toward Jude and motioned for something to drink. Jude signaled her understanding and rose quickly. Then Sax leaned forward and rested her fingertips lightly against Honor's knee. "She might not even need the defibrillator, but Caroli wanted to be careful, so we replaced it for now."

"All the problems she's been having..." Honor raised her head, her voice incredulous. "It's been a technical problem with the device, hasn't it?"

"Probably a lot of it. It happens."

"Oh, I know." Honor brushed at her cheeks, stunned to find tears. She hadn't felt them escape. She looked up gratefully as Jude handed her a cold soda. "Thank you."

Sax reached up for the other soda Jude held out and gave her a blazing smile. "Thanks, babe."

"Everything okay?" Jude rested one hand on Sax's shoulder and caressed her softly with the unmindful intimacy of longtime lovers.

"Yep. Quinn is going to be good as new." Sax took a long pull of her soda. "Before the year is out, she ought to be back operating, back where she belongs."

Back where she belongs? Honor's stomach rolled again, this time with a new kind of alarm. *Back here, in New York?*

CHAPTER THIRTY-TWO

"Hi," Honor said softly as she leaned down to kiss Quinn gently on the mouth. "How do you feel?"

"I'm fine." Quinn, the only patient in the recovery room, was propped up on the stretcher with several pillows behind her back. She smiled and reached for Honor's hand. "I more or less slept through the procedure, although I remember watching the fluoroscope when Wisnicki was placing the new leads."

"Are you having any pain?"

"No. He went through the old incision to change the battery pack, so there's very little discomfort. I should be out of here in fifteen minutes or so."

"Has anyone talked to you yet?"

"You mean about the current state of my heart?" Quinn squeezed Honor's fingers. She was still reeling from the impact of the news. "Yeah. Caroli was here just now and gave me a rundown. He said there's a good chance I won't need the defibrillator in another six months."

"I'm so happy for you, baby." Honor brushed her fingers through Quinn's hair. "That's the best news."

"I'm happy for *us*," Quinn said quietly, her eyes fixed on Honor's face. "I don't want you to worry about me all the time, and I don't want you to be cheated out of anything you deserve."

Honor frowned, her eyes darkening. "I didn't expect you to come along, Quinn. I didn't expect to love anyone the way I love you. And I certainly never dreamed of anyone making me feel the way you do."

"Honor—"

"No, let me finish," Honor chided gently. "*I love you.* You make me terribly happy. I could never feel cheated because of having you in my life. When I think of the future now, I see *you*. And it's wonderful."

"I love you so much." Quinn's voice was husky.

"Ditto, Dr. Maguire." Honor blinked away tears and smiled. "Sinclair says you'll be operating again soon, too. Did she tell you that?"

Quinn shrugged. "Yes, but for the time being, I have a job." Then she grinned, blue eyes sparkling. "And since I have a thing for my boss, I'm not in a big hurry to switch."

"Well," Honor murmured, "since your boss has a thing for you, too, that's good to hear." She took a breath to be sure her voice was steady. "When the time comes, maybe you'll consider a position at PMC in the surgery department."

"If not there, someplace in Philadelphia will need a trauma surgeon." Quinn regarded Honor intently. "Because I have no plans to leave."

Honor kissed her again. "Even better."

"Would you mind calling Arly on your cell phone so I can talk to her?" Quinn glanced toward the other side of the room where the recovery room nurse sat writing notes in her chart. "I'm the only patient in here, so I don't think we'll disrupt anything critical with it."

"Oh, no," Honor laughed. "Except if we happen to interfere with the telemetry to that monitor you're wearing, Saxon Sinclair will be in here pounding on your chest before I have a chance to explain."

Quinn grinned. "I trust you to handle her."

"Thank you," Honor said dryly. "Even so, I'll use the phone in the waiting area in a few minutes and tell Arly that you'll call her as soon as you can. Okay?"

"Okay." Quinn leaned her head back against the pillows. "Then how about checking the Amtrak schedule to see if we can get a train back to Philadelphia tonight."

"Jude invited us to stay here in Manhattan tonight with them," Honor replied. "I think we should. That way you can get a good night's sleep before we travel."

"I don't want to miss one of Phyllis's breakfasts." Quinn lifted Honor's hand and kissed her fingers gently. "And I want to see Arly."

"Most people would jump at the chance to spend a night in New York City without their children, you know," Honor pointed out with another laugh. It wasn't until she had said the words that she realized how easily she had begun to think of them as a family. She searched Quinn's face and found the calm certainty there that she loved so much.

"Give me a year or so, and maybe I'll feel that way, too. *Maybe*." Quinn locked eyes with Honor. "I was kind of hoping I could count on having the next fifty or sixty with you."

"Make it seventy, and you've got a deal."

Quinn reached up and brushed a single tear from Honor's cheek. "Done."

"Did you just propose?"

"Yes."

"Good, because I just accepted." Still holding Quinn's hand tightly, Honor unclipped the cell phone from her belt and flipped open the cover. After she punched in the number, she found Quinn's eyes again and said softly, "Let's hope this doesn't set off any alarms."

"I think we're safe," Quinn whispered.

"Phyllis?" Honor watched the steady rhythm of Quinn's heart as it traced across the monitor above the bed. "Tell Arly she can stay up late tonight. Quinn and I are coming home."

The End

About the Author

Radclyffe is the author of numerous lesbian romances (*Safe Harbor, Innocent Hearts, Love's Melody Lost, Love's Tender Warriors, Tomorrow's Promise, Passion's Bright Fury, Love's Masquerade, shadowland,* and *Fated Love*), as well as two romance/intrigue series: the Honor series *(Above All, Honor* revised edition, *Honor Bound, Love & Honor,* and *Honor Guards)* and the Justice series (*Shield of Justice,* the prequel *A Matter of Trust, In Pursuit of Justice,* and *Justice in the Shadows)*, selections in *Infinite Pleasures: An Anthology of Lesbian Erotica,* edited by Stacia Seaman and Nann Dunne (2004) and in *Milk of Human Kindness,* an anthology of lesbian authors writing about mothers and daughters, edited by Lori L. Lake (2004).

A 2003/2004 recipient of the Alice B. award for her body of work as well as a member of the Golden Crown Literary Society, Pink Ink, and the Romance Writers of America, she lives with her partner, Lee, in Philadelphia, PA where she both writes and practices surgery full-time. She states, "I began reading lesbian fiction at the age of twelve when I found a copy of Ann Bannon's *Beebo Brinker.* Not long after, I began collecting every book with lesbian content I could find. The new titles come much faster now than they did in the decades when a new book or two every year felt like a gift, but I still treasure every single one. These works are our history and our legacy, and I am proud to contribute in some small way to those archives."

Her upcoming works include the next in the Provincetown Tales, *Distant Shores, Silent Thunder* (2005); the next in the Justice series, *Justice Served* (2005); and the next in the Honor series, *Honor Reclaimed* (2005).

Look for information about these works at www.radfic.com and www.boldstrokesbooks.com.

Other Books Available From
Bold Strokes Books

Change Of Pace: *Erotic Interludes* (ISBN: 1-933110-07-4) Twenty-five hot-wired encounters guaranteed to spark more than just your imagination. Erotica as you've always dreamed of it.

Fated Love (ISBN: 1-933110-05-8) Amidst the chaos and drama of a busy emergency room, two women must contend not only with the fragile nature of life, but also with the mysteries of the heart and the irresistible forces of fate.

Justice in the Shadows (ISBN: 1-933110-03-1) In a shadow world of secrets, lies, and hidden agendas, Detective Sergeant Rebecca Frye and her lover, Dr. Catherine Rawlings, join forces once again in the elusive search for justice.

shadowland (ISBN: 1-933110-11-2) In a world on the far edge of desire, two women are drawn together by power, passion, and dark pleasures. An erotic romance.

Love's Masquerade (ISBN: 1-933110-14-7) Plunged into the often indistinguishable realms of fiction, fantasy, and hidden desires, Auden Frost discovers a shifting landscape that will force her to question everything she has believed to be true about herself and the nature of love.

Beyond the Breakwater ISBN: 1-933110-06-6) One Provincetown summer three women learn the true meaning of love, friendship, and family. Second in the Provincetown Tales.

Tomorrow's Promise (ISBN: 1-933110-12-0) One timeless summer, two very different women discover the power of passion to heal and the promise of hope that only love can bestow.

Love's Tender Warriors (ISBN: 1-933110-02-3) Two women who have accepted loneliness as a way of life learn that love is worth fighting for and a battle they cannot afford to lose.

Love's Melody Lost (ISBN: 1-933110-00-7) A secretive artist with a haunted past and a young woman escaping a life that proved to be a lie find their destinies entwined.

Safe Harbor (ISBN: 1-933110-13-9) A mysterious newcomer, a reclusive doctor, and a troubled gay teenager learn about love, friendship, and trust during one tumultuous summer in Provincetown. First in the Provincetown Tales.

Above All, Honor (ISBN: 1-933110-04-X) The first in the Honor series introduces single-minded Secret Service Agent Cameron Roberts and the woman she is sworn to protect—Blair Powell, the daughter of the president of the United States. First in the Honor series.

Love & Honor (ISBN: 1-933110-10-4) The president's daughter and her security chief are faced with difficult choices as they battle a tangled web of Washington intrigue for...love and honor. Third in the Honor series.

Honor Guards (ISBN: 1-933110-01-5) In a journey that begins on the streets of Paris's Left Bank and culminates in a wild flight for their lives, the president's daughter and those who are sworn to protect her wage a desperate struggle for survival. Fourth in the Honor series.